DEMON BLOOD

"Brook brings together two broken heroes in the high-stakes sixth Guardian paranormal romance . . . Fiery attraction and steamy love scenes . . . Fans won't be disappointed." —*Publishers Weekly*

"An excellent Guardian thriller that stars two delightful heroes . . . Set aside time to read this wonderful tale in one sitting, because Meljean Brook has her fans hooked from the Bedtime Story summary of the past to the powerful finish." —*The Best Reviews*

"Brook's characters leap from the page. Deacon is the perfect hero, tortured but worthy, and Rosalia is just the woman to save him." —*RT Book Reviews* (★★★★½)

DEMON FORGED

"Dark, rich, and sexy, every page makes me beg for more!"
—Gena Showalter,
New York Times bestselling author

"Another fantastic book in a beautifully written series. [It] has all the elements I love in Meljean's books—strong, gorgeously drawn characters, a world so real I totally believe it, and the punch of powerful emotion."
—Nalini Singh,
New York T

con

DEMON BOUND

"An excellent entry in a great series . . . Another winner as the multifaceted Guardian saga continues to expand in complexity while remaining entertaining . . . As complex and beautifully done as always." —*Book Binge*

"Be prepared for more surprises and more revelations . . . Brook continues to deliver surprising characters, relationships, paranormal elements, and plot twists—the only thing that won't surprise you is your *total* inability to put this book down." —*Alpha Heroes*

"Raises the bar on paranormal romance for sheer thrills, drama, and world-building, and hands down cements Brook's place at the top of her field." —*Romance Junkies*

DEMON NIGHT

"Meljean is now officially one of my favorite authors. And this book's hero? . . . I just went weak at the knees. And the love scenes—wow, just wow." —Nalini Singh

"This is the book for paranormal lovers. It is a phenomenal book by an author who knows how to give her readers exactly what they want. What Brook's readers want is a story that is dangerous, sexy, scary, and smart. *Demon Night* delivers all that and more! . . . [It] is the epitome of what a paranormal romance should be! I didn't want to put it down." —*Romance Reader at Heart*

"Poignant and compelling with lots of action, and it's very sensual. You'll fall in love with Charlie, and Ethan will cause your thermometer to blow its top. An excellent plot, wonderful dialogue . . . Don't miss reading it or any of Meljean Brook's other novels in this series."

—*Fresh Fiction*

"An intense romance that will leave you breathless . . . I was drawn in from the first page." —*Romance Junkies*

DEMON MOON

"The fourth book in Meljean Brook's Guardian series turns up the heat without losing any of the danger."

—*Entertainment Weekly*

"A read that goes down hot and sweet—utterly unique—and one hell of a ride." —Marjorie M. Liu, *New York Times* bestselling author

"Sensual and intriguing, *Demon Moon* is a simply wonderful book. I was enthralled from the first page!"

—Nalini Singh

"Fantastically drawn characters . . . and their passion for each other is palpable in each scene they share. It stews beneath the surface and when it finally reaches boiling point . . . OH WOW!" —*Vampire Romance Books*

continued . . .

DEMON ANGEL

"I've never read anything like this book. *Demon Angel* is brilliant, heartbreaking, genre-bending—even, I dare say, epic. Simply put, I love it." —Marjorie M. Liu

"Brook has crafted a complex, interesting world that goes far beyond your usual . . . paranormal romance. *Demon Angel* truly soars." —Jennifer Estep, author of *Tangled Threads*

"I can honestly say I haven't read many books lately that have kept me guessing and wondering 'what's next,' but this is one of them. [Brook has] created a unique and different world . . . Gritty and realistic . . . Incredibly inventive . . . This is a book which makes me think and think about it even days after finishing it." —*Dear Author*

"Enthralling . . . [A] delightful saga." —*The Best Reviews*

"Extremely engaging. . . . A fiendishly good book. *Demon Angel* is outstanding." —*The Romance Reader*

"A surefire winner. This book will captivate you and leave you yearning for more. Don't miss *Demon Angel*." —*Romance Reviews Today*

Titles by Meljean Brook

DEMON ANGEL
DEMON MOON
DEMON NIGHT
DEMON BOUND
DEMON FORGED
DEMON BLOOD
DEMON MARKED

THE IRON DUKE

Anthologies

HOT SPELL
(with Emma Holly, Lora Leigh, and Shiloh Walker)
WILD THING
(with Maggie Shayne, Marjorie M. Liu, and Alyssa Day)
FIRST BLOOD
(with Susan Sizemore, Erin McCarthy, and Chris Marie Green)
MUST LOVE HELLHOUNDS
(with Charlaine Harris, Nalini Singh, and Ilona Andrews)
BURNING UP
(with Angela Knight, Nalini Singh, and Virginia Kantra)

DEMON MARKED

MELJEAN BROOK

BERKLEY SENSATION, NEW YORK

THE BERKLEY PUBLISHING GROUP
Published by the Penguin Group
Penguin Group (USA) Inc.
375 Hudson Street, New York, New York 10014, USA
Penguin Group (Canada), 90 Eglinton Avenue East, Suite 700, Toronto, Ontario M4P 2Y3, Canada
(a division of Pearson Penguin Canada Inc.)
Penguin Books Ltd., 80 Strand, London WC2R 0RL, England
Penguin Group Ireland, 25 St. Stephen's Green, Dublin 2, Ireland (a division of Penguin Books Ltd.)
Penguin Group (Australia), 250 Camberwell Road, Camberwell, Victoria 3124, Australia
(a division of Pearson Australia Group Pty. Ltd.)
Penguin Books India Pvt. Ltd., 11 Community Centre, Panchsheel Park, New Delhi—110 017, India
Penguin Group (NZ), 67 Apollo Drive, Rosedale, Auckland 0632, New Zealand
(a division of Pearson New Zealand Ltd.)
Penguin Books (South Africa) (Pty.) Ltd., 24 Sturdee Avenue, Rosebank, Johannesburg 2196,
South Africa

Penguin Books Ltd., Registered Offices: 80 Strand, London WC2R 0RL, England

DEMON MARKED

A Berkley Sensation Book / published by arrangement with the author

PRINTING HISTORY
Berkley Sensation mass-market edition / September 2011

Cover art by Cliff Nielson.
Cover design by George Long.
Interior text design by Laura K. Corless.

For information, address: The Berkley Publishing Group,
a division of Penguin Group (USA) Inc.,
375 Hudson Street, New York, New York 10014.

ISBN: 978-0-425-24269-8

BERKLEY SENSATION®
Berkley Sensation Books are published by The Berkley Publishing Group,
a division of Penguin Group (USA) Inc.,
375 Hudson Street, New York, New York 10014.
BERKLEY SENSATION® is a registered trademark of Penguin Group (USA) Inc.
The "B" design is a trademark of Penguin Group (USA) Inc.

PRINTED IN THE UNITED STATES OF AMERICA

10 9 8 7 6 5 4 3 2 1

CHAPTER 1

Ash hadn't meant to frighten the girl. She hadn't even noticed the little blonde until after the subway train pulled away. The disembarking crowd quickly dispersed, leaving the underground platform empty but for Ash and a few other waiting passengers. In a blue princess's costume and a plastic tiara, the girl stood next to her mother, clutching a bag of party favors to her small chest. Though her face was turned away and Ash couldn't see the girl's smile, she could *taste* the happiness emanating from her, unsurprisingly sweet.

Had Ash ever felt that much joy as a girl? She couldn't remember. Emotions must have touched her deeply at some point in her life, because she recognized how little they touched her now—as if her ruined memory hid enough data to compare an *After* to a *Before* that she couldn't recall. And though she knew those emotions were missing, Ash didn't feel their loss like a hacked-off limb. Even her sense of emptiness remained on the surface, no different from noticing a bruise on her knee and idly wondering when she'd gotten it.

With the same idle interest, Ash observed the girl, who lifted the side of her hem and twirled around her mother as if circling a ballroom. The tiara's paste jewels flashed beneath the fluorescent lights, and a name leapt into Ash's mind—

Cinderella—but there was something else, an impression just beyond it, like lightning seen from the corner of her eye, like a word at the tip of her tongue.

Her name? No longer idly curious, Ash stared at the girl, mentally replaying that twirl and the flash of light, willing the impression to strengthen into a solid connection, so that she could trace the memory to its source. Was Ash's full name at the end of it?

Cinderella wasn't right. Reminded by the girl's dance, Ash could suddenly recall images from the animated movie, the gliding waltz around the ballroom with the prince, but the connection she sought wasn't there. Ash was looking for something a step aside from Cinderella. The girl in the cinders and *ashes . . .* ?

That wasn't right, either. Not quite.

Why couldn't she remember? Frustration skimmed over the surface of her mind like a blade over ice, leaving little evidence of its passing. *What had happened to separate Before from an After that contained memories, but was still so empty?*

Dimly, she became aware that the girl had dropped her bag of party favors to the train platform. Treats and noisemakers forgotten, she tugged insistently on her mother's hand, her widened eyes never leaving Ash's. Happiness had changed to sour fear, far stronger than the unease children usually projected when they glimpsed the vermillion symbols tattooed over the left side of Ash's face. The girl's distress intruded on Ash's focus, and the impression of the name she'd been seeking faded.

It disappeared altogether when the mother's gaze followed her daughter's. Unlike the girl's sour fear, the mother's tasted of bitter cold, like icy sweat against Ash's tongue.

Dread and terror.

From the tunnel came the clatter of an approaching train. The woman gathered up the girl and set off for the far end of the platform at a stiff-legged trot. The look she threw over her shoulder included bared teeth—the mother protecting her young.

Fear wasn't just an emotion. Sometimes, it was a survival instinct.

But why consider Ash a threat? Not just the tattoos, obviously. In this part of London, heavy ink sometimes provoked fascination or disgust, but was common enough that it didn't incite terror.

Ash glanced down, where more symbols marked her hands. Around the tattoos, the skin was tan, not the crimson it sometimes became. Her jeans and leather jacket hadn't disappeared—and when her clothes vanished, she knew very well that titters and gasps followed. Not fear.

Brakes screeched as the train stopped. Ash's image reflected faintly in the car windows. Beneath the sweep of blond hair across her forehead, Ash's eyes shone as brilliantly red as two small stoplights.

Ah. So that was the cause of their fear. Ash wasn't surprised; when she'd lived at Nightingale House, the same glow had come a few times, and she'd only noticed when the lights in her room were out—and because she'd once terrified a ward nurse making the night rounds.

The hysterical nurse had returned less than a minute later with an orderly in tow, but Ash's eyes had looked like any other person's eyes by then.

Glowing eyes, red skin—the changes always faded within moments of Ash noticing them. In the train window's reflection, her irises had already returned to a more human blue, her pupils were black, the whites white. She glanced toward the girl again, but the mother had hustled past the disembarking passengers and taken a seat. The woman held her daughter, staring at Ash through the window—likely praying that she wouldn't board the train with them. The girl huddled on her lap, her blue dress twisted around her legs, and Ash's earlier impression suddenly solidified into a word: *Aschenputtel.*

Ash's disappointment was a soft weight, barely felt. Though the first syllable of Ash's name sounded similar, Aschenputtel was Cinderella's name, not hers. So she would have to keep searching.

The train began to move. Not so frightened now, the little blonde peeked beneath her mother's arm and met Ash's gaze. Brave girl. Ash smiled faintly and lifted her hand in acknowledgment.

Hello, little princess. You've escaped a monster who can't remember her name, or even what sort of monster she is. But don't worry that I'll crawl under your bed . . . unless, of course, you have answers there.

The train clattered down the tunnel, taking the girl with it. To avoid further notice, Ash drew up the hood of the sweatshirt layered beneath her jacket, then settled in to wait for another ten minutes. That *had* been her train, but she didn't feel impatience any more than she did frustration or disappointment.

Curiosity wasn't an emotion, however, but a state of being—and so Ash *did* wonder why she hadn't boarded despite their fear. After all, frightening a little girl was the least of her sins. She'd also jumped the high gates at the subway entrance instead of paying her fare. Later that evening, she planned on breaking into a dead woman's home.

Disregarding the girl's terror hadn't felt *right*, however—and Ash spent the next ten minutes trying to decide whether "feeling right" was an emotion, or something else.

A month ago, shortly before had Ash escaped from Nightingale House, she'd slipped into Dr. Cawthorne's office after midnight and read through every file and notebook that referred to her. Cawthorne knew nothing of Before, not even her name. She'd been committed as a Jane Doe, and in the computers and on the file labels she was called "Mary Bloggs," a placeholder designation often followed by the date of her admission. That day, during one of Ash's therapy sessions, he'd written into his notebook: *Schizoid personality disorder?*

He'd underlined the question mark twice.

After almost three years in the care of his private mental hospital, the psychiatrist still hadn't known how to classify her. Not that Ash had helped him along. Two years had passed before she'd spoken aloud, and nine more months had gone by before she'd cared enough to wonder who she was and what had happened to her.

Though he'd speculated, Dr. Cawthorne hadn't figured that out, either.

In his earliest notes, he'd attributed her lack of verbal response to brain damage caused by her persistent febrile temperature—a fever hot enough that Ash should have been hospitalized. Cawthorne's records didn't indicate why she hadn't been given emergency care; he only indicated that her fever didn't respond to medications or external remedies. Finally, when it became apparent that neither weakness nor delirium accompanied the fever, Dr. Cawthorne had stopped trying to lower it.

Ash had clear memories from those days. She remembered nothing from before Nightingale House, and everything after. She could recall how she hadn't spoken, but had automatically obeyed every instruction given to her: to get up in the morning, to shower, to dress, to eat breakfast, to sit and watch television, to eat dinner, and then to lie in bed until she was told to get up again. At the end of the first year, Cawthorne had noted in his spidery scrawl:

> *Mary-052007 will not respond to any name, but displays clear comprehension of verbal and written instructions when they are spoken directly to or placed in front of her. She performs both menial tasks and more complex operations, such as solving mathematical equations, tending the garden, or typing and sending an e-mail (dictated).*

They'd instructed; she'd performed. When they asked her to accomplish tasks that were impossible to carry out, such as urinating into a cup, they never tried to force her. The nurses simply noted "Mary's" lack of response in her chart, and Dr. Cawthorne would write the name of another disorder in his notes, followed by another question mark.

The second year had passed in the same way. A few weeks into the third year, the doctor had been thumbing through the calendar on his desk and making his usual, halfhearted attempts to draw out a response—

How are you today? Pause. *The rain has let up. You'll be able to take your afternoon walk through the garden, though it will be too wet for planting. What sort of flowers should we add this year?* Pause. *Peonies would be lovely, wouldn't they?*

—when he'd cut his thumb on the edge of the calendar paper. Another pause had followed the peonies as he'd stuck his thumb into his mouth, and Ash had remembered that she'd once drunk her own blood, too. She'd remembered the blade carving symbols into her face, her torso and arms. She'd remembered the knife at her chest, and the dark figure pronouncing her name—but she'd only heard the first syllable before his terrible voice had torn everything apart.

Sitting in Dr. Cawthorne's office, that memory had quickly faded—or she'd stifled it, just as she stifled the tremors that shook her body when she thought of that dark figure. Just enough of the memory remained, however, to remind her that she had to tell Cawthorne something.

"My name isn't Mary," she'd said.

Dr. Cawthorne's hand dropped away from his mouth. He'd stared at her, his jaw agape. Whenever someone on the television wore that expression, a faceless crowd laughed on the soundtrack. No one in Cawthorne's office laughed in the background. The only reaction that Ash could detect was the sudden shift of Cawthorne's emotions: from frustration and resignation to surprise and excitement.

But though she could sense his exhilaration, he didn't show it. Evenly, he'd asked, "What *is* your name, then?"

"Ash . . . *something*. I don't know the rest."

"Ashley?"

"No." She was certain.

He'd nodded in that same slow, calm way, but to her ears, his heart pounded almost as loud as his voice. "Until we know, may we call you 'Ash'?"

"Yes."

Smiling, he leaned back in his chair and studied her. "And you're an American? Canadian?"

"I don't know."

"But your accent is . . ." He'd shaken his head. "No matter. You're here now, and it's wonderful to hear your voice after all this time. Is there something you'd like to tell me?"

"No." She'd already told him that her name wasn't Mary. That was all she'd had to say.

His excitement dimmed, followed by his relief when he'd continued talking and she'd continued answering him. But by the time he'd ended the session—an hour later than usual—unease threaded through his curiosity. He'd already been jotting notes when she rose from her chair to leave.

She'd stopped long enough to ask, "What does 'complete lack of affect' mean?"

His pencil lead snapped. He'd looked up from his notebook, his face carefully blank and his emotions an indistinguishable riot. "Why do you ask?"

"Because you've written it about me in your notes."

It was one of the few phrases he'd scribbled that hadn't been followed by a question mark. Another had been "source amnesia," but he'd explained that while they'd been talking: It meant her procedural memory and factual knowledge remained, though she'd no recollection of how or when she'd learned them.

"Ah." His gray eyebrows had lifted into an open expression. A friendly smile shaped his mouth. "A lack of affect simply means that someone doesn't display a marked emotional reaction . . . or empathy for others."

His conflicting feelings and facial expressions suggested that he assumed Ash would be disturbed by that explanation, and that he was trying to soften its delivery.

She wasn't disturbed. She'd already known that she didn't feel anything like the emotions she regularly sensed in other people. Nodding, she'd turned to go.

"Ash . . ." When she'd glanced back at Dr. Cawthorne, he wore a puzzled frown. "How did you know what I'd written? My notepad was angled away from you."

"Yes. But it reflected in the glass."

She'd pointed to the framed diplomas hanging on the wall behind him. He'd looked around; when he'd turned back to Ash, his smile had been bright. He'd said something about her cleverness, but she'd tasted his sour fear.

The reaction of the nurses and caregivers had echoed his: excitement followed by unease, and punctuated with spurts of fear. They began calling her Ash, but when they spoke together in other rooms and thought she couldn't hear them, they referred to her as "the American," as if trying to put distance between themselves and her. Ash paid closer attention to the actors on television after that, particularly the never-ending soap operas. Mimicking those accents upset the nurses more, however. Only after she'd overheard two of them discussing how unsettling they found her tendency to watch everyone without evincing any emotion, Ash had finally understood that her American origin had never been the issue. It was her lack of affect that disturbed them.

"Even psychopaths learn to fake it," one of them had said.

But Ash didn't care enough to fake her emotions, and by the time she'd decided to leave Nightingale House, the nurses didn't even refer to her as "the American" anymore. She'd become "that one."

That one, who'd caused an uproar of hilarity and shock when her clothes had vanished during a group therapy session—followed by greater shock and fear when, after Ash had noticed her nudity, jeans and a T-shirt that the nurses hadn't seen before simply appeared on her body. That one, whose blond hair—which the nurses had kept short for easy care—had grown to the middle of her back during a walk through the garden one August afternoon. That one, who'd pulled a prank with glowing eyes, and terrified one of the nurses so badly that she'd quit her position the next day. That one, whom the nurses had found crouching atop the roof of Nightingale House one morning, and who'd given no believable explanation of how she'd climbed the turrets. That one, who'd dropped from the roof to the ground as easily as another person stepped out of her bed, despite their pleas for her to stop.

They'd shrieked when she'd jumped—but Ash hadn't detected any relief from them when she'd landed on her feet, uninjured. There'd only been fear, followed by hot anger.

Another nurse had quit after that, screaming to her supervisor that she'd expected Nightingale House to treat only drug-addicted celebrities and depressed aristos, and that she'd left the government-run hospitals for a posh situation to *avoid* the psychos. Ash had decided to leave, too, albeit for a different reason. The answer to the one question that interested her—*Who am I?*—hadn't been at Nightingale House. No answers were there—except for one, and she'd asked Dr. Cawthorne for that information during her final therapy session.

"A posh hospital must be expensive," she'd said. "So who is paying for my treatment?"

He'd paled. In the months since she'd begun speaking, the wrinkles around Cawthorne's eyes and mouth had become more pronounced. His skin had loosened as if he'd dropped weight. But although she'd frightened him at times, he'd never lost color in his face or broken out with a sheen of sweat, as he had then.

His gaze had skidded away from hers. "The money comes from a numbered account. The donor wishes to remain anonymous."

"But you know who it is."

His hands trembled. "Yes."

"And she knows who I am."

"Probably," he'd answered, before looking at Ash with surprise. "How did you know it was a *she*?"

Because a woman had brought her to Nightingale House. Ash avoided the memory of her almost as fiercely as the memory of the dark figure, but she could recall the woman's face, surrounded by dark hair—and the eyes containing a madness that went deeper than anyone else's at that hospital. Yet despite her obvious insanity, the woman hadn't remained here; she'd left Ash behind instead.

Dr. Cawthorne leaned forward, his urgency and panic rushing his words. "I cannot tell you, do you understand? It was part of the deal. If you woke up, I wasn't to tell you anything. I wasn't to tell *anyone*. But no one thought you would wake up. She said the weak halflings rarely did."

"Halflings? What is that?" And was Ash one of them?

He only shook his head. "I made a bargain. So I can't tell you, *do you understand*?"

Ash *had* understood, though she couldn't remember how or why she did. She knew that bargains should be avoided, but if they had to be made, they should *never* be broken. At the very thought of it, ice seemed to form the length of her spine, similar to the cold fear she sensed from Cawthorne.

Similar to his, but so much stronger. *A survival instinct.*

With effort, she'd suppressed the tremors threatening to shake her body, her voice. "You can't tell me who I am or anything about her," Ash had said. "But what do you get out of this?"

"She knows that I once made an . . . error during the treatment of a patient. I keep you here in exchange for her silence." He'd brought a handkerchief to his brow and mopped away the sweat. "And eventually, I'll publish a series of papers about you. You're a fascinating study, Ash."

So he was saving his own ass, and using her for his professional advancement. Ash had watched enough television to know that the appropriate response to his confession was a sense of betrayal and outrage. She didn't feel either emotion, but she had no intention of letting him continue to use her—and if he couldn't give her answers, she'd find someone who would.

His relief had been palpable when she dropped the subject and they'd continued the session as usual. She'd waited until after he'd gone home for the evening before entering his office a final time, hoping to find a hint of information in that session's notes. There hadn't been anything useful, only a single, self-indulgent rumination that he probably intended to use for a journal article:

The name she's chosen for herself is appropriate—as if the fires have left nothing human, only a faint ash.

He truly knew nothing, Ash had realized. She hadn't chosen her own name. And whatever had happened between Before and After, Ash was certain she hadn't burned.

She'd frozen.

The temperature had dropped below freezing by the time she emerged from the subway station at Sloane Square. Ash tilted her face down to let her hood take the brunt of the wind and shoved her hands into her jacket pockets. The cold couldn't hurt her—a month of walking outside during London's wintry nights without so much as a shiver had taught her that—but she didn't like the feel of icy air against her skin.

Though Ash couldn't recall taking this route before, she didn't need to verify the directions during the six-minute walk to the St. Croix town house. A left turn into a garden square was taken without hesitation. Although the buildings in this exclusive neighborhood looked similar to one another, all constructed of red brick and accented by wrought iron, she found the correct home without consulting the house numbers.

So she'd been here before. Ash didn't recognize the place, but she knew that beyond the red front door lay a marble-tiled foyer and a staircase leading to the upper floors. To the right lay the entertaining salon, which opened into the dining room. Farther down the hall, a library overlooked the small garden. Upstairs, the second level had been divided between two bedroom suites, one of which had been renovated into a modern office.

An American woman with a face identical to Ash's had allegedly been murdered in that office.

After Ash had left Nightingale House, finding information had been easy. Access to that information had been her primary obstacle—but as soon as Ash had learned to memorize the numbers on the credit cards that people flashed so casually when they made their purchases, she used those numbers at Internet cafés. From there, it was a simple matter of searching for American women who'd disappeared in London. Her earliest parameters were too narrow—she'd set them to search for missing persons from three or four years ago—but when Ash had widened the search to ten years, she'd found Rachel Anne Boyle.

The blonde in Rachel's photo didn't have symbols tattooed down the side of her face, but their features had been the same. So Ash had looked deeper.

Six years ago, Rachel Boyle had worked as personal assistant to one of England's most successful independent financiers, Madelyn St. Croix. Both Rachel and her employer had disappeared not long after Madelyn's estranged son, Nicholas St. Croix, had returned from America and began a hostile takeover of Wells-Down Investments, Madelyn's company.

According to reports, Rachel had quickly become Nicholas St. Croix's lover. Probably for his wealth, Ash thought. Ash had few needs, but after a month on London's streets, even she recognized the appeal of a ready source of money . . . and she could see little else in him that might be appealing. Though undeniably handsome, with short dark hair and magazine-perfect features, neither warmth nor humor was apparent in his pictures—and after the women had vanished, she couldn't detect any emotion in those press photos, either.

Surely, when a man's lover died in his arms, he'd feel *something*. Wouldn't he?

Unless he'd lied.

The night they'd disappeared, Nicholas had told police that he and his mother had argued over business matters. During the fight, Madelyn had fired a gun at him—but Rachel Boyle had jumped into the bullet's path, and the slug had ripped through her chest. Nicholas had claimed he'd been holding Rachel when she'd died, but the police hadn't located her body or any blood at the site or on his clothing. Madelyn had vanished, too, and Nicholas became the primary suspect in their disappearances. But although the police were certain of foul play, they'd never been able to pin Rachel's and Madelyn's murders on him.

Ash didn't know if Nicholas St. Croix had killed Rachel or

if he'd told the truth about that night . . . but she knew that his mother had still been alive. Ash had recognized the woman from the photos in the news reports, and terror had scraped like ice in her chest.

Only three years ago, Madelyn St. Croix had left Ash in Dr. Cawthorne's care.

Ash *wasn't* Rachel Boyle; of that she was certain, just as she knew "Rachel" wasn't her name. But a connection between Ash and the American woman clearly existed, and Ash hoped to find answers in the house where Rachel Boyle had worked and—perhaps—died.

She watched the darkened windows for movement, listened for any sounds from within. All was quiet. Though six years had passed since Madelyn's disappearance, the property was still listed under her name. Most likely, she had an arrangement with a housekeeping service and an estate that handled such necessities in her absence. A security system probably protected the house, but if an alarm sounded, Ash would run before the police arrived.

And if Ash couldn't find answers here, she'd seek out Nicholas St. Croix . . . and hope that looking for him before trying to find Madelyn wouldn't be a horrible mistake. Perhaps Madelyn had a reason for what she'd done; perhaps she was hiding from her son, and she'd stowed Ash away at Nightingale House for her protection.

But although the man in Nicholas St. Croix's picture appeared capable of fewer emotions than Ash, his image didn't terrify her. So Ash hoped she wasn't wrong.

And she hoped that he knew her.

The security system activated when Ash broke the lock on the front door. No alarm sounded, but Ash knew where to look for the security panel, positioned discreetly behind a framed oval mirror that opened like a medicine cabinet. Inside, the status light blinked red. Ash couldn't have recited the numbers that she tapped into the pad; her fingers simply moved in a pattern, as if she were typing an oft-repeated word into a keyboard.

The status light changed to solid green.

Should she have been astonished that her code was correct?

Ash pondered her lack of surprise. Inputting the number hadn't seemed any different than walking the route here. Obviously, she'd done it many times before—and her procedural memory was still intact.

So she didn't feel surprised, but she did wonder why the code hadn't been changed in six years. After Madelyn St. Croix's disappearance, why hadn't the security company updated the entry codes?

Perhaps they'd been instructed not to. Perhaps they expected Madelyn to return—or perhaps someone else did. A dedicated employee?

Ash couldn't guess, but obviously someone had cared for the house in the past six years. No dust collected on the carved mirror frame or in the corners of the foyer. The wainscoting and staircase banisters gleamed. The faint scent of cleaning wax lingered, but the air itself smelled stale, as if the house had been shut up for a while. No live-in caretaker, then—or the housekeeper had taken off for the holidays and left it empty.

Good. Ash wouldn't have to be quiet when she searched the rooms.

She started in the parlor. The décor could have filled a checklist for *expensive* and *tasteful.* The requisite antique vase reigned over an ebony-inlaid table. A thick Oriental rug anchored a seating arrangement upholstered in cream silk. Two large, modern paintings featuring slashes of bold oranges and gold bookended the open entrance to the dining room.

Had Ash eaten at that table? She didn't know. Nothing familiar stood out to her—and she saw nothing unexpected, either. Ash wanted to spark a memory, or at least a sense of déjà vu, but she only had the vague feeling that fewer fresh flowers decorated the sideboard than should be.

Flowers didn't offer any answers. Perhaps the library would.

As she stepped into the hallway, a faint noise sounded from upstairs. Footsteps?

Ash paused with her head cocked, but didn't hear anything more—nothing that she could pinpoint, at least. When she listened closely, noises from every home in the square sounded as clear as from within this house. Usually, she ignored background noise, and perhaps this was just that: a sound from another home that had leaked through her mental filters.

Perhaps. She'd listen more carefully, in any case.

She stepped into the library—and forgot about listening. Terror coated her stomach like ice, threatening to crack.

Madelyn's portrait hung above the mantel. The artist had captured her beautiful, warm smile and the keen intelligence in her blue eyes. But those eyes had once been mad, and the smile a twisted grimace. She remembered Madelyn's hands—not folded demurely, as in the painting, but holding Ash's shoulders in an unbreakable, painful grip, shaking her, and Madelyn telling her—

Do everything they ask you to do. I'm not ready yet. I have to find the Gate, I have to prepare. So listen to them. But above all else, follow the Rules. Don't kill them, don't hurt them. Don't prevent them from exercising their free will. If you do, you're dead—and I'll be in that frozen waste. So don't break the Rules. Don't!

—telling her how to stay safe.

Ash's heart pounded. She closed her eyes, shutting out the image of the woman's face.

This was a memory. Not from Before, which she couldn't remember at all, but from almost three years ago, before Ash and Madelyn had arrived at Nightingale House . . . and after they'd left the dark figure behind. A memory ravaged by terror and buoyed by relief—and Ash recalled that she'd been so sorry.

Regretting the bargain already.

Ash shook her head. What bargain? What had she agreed to do? Though she tried to recall, that hole in her memory remained.

But she *had* felt regret. Ash remembered that clearly now. Regret and relief, which meant that terror wasn't the only strong emotion to hold her in its grip after . . . whatever had happened to her. Why hadn't she felt regret or relief since then?

A shiver raced over Ash's skin when she looked at the painting again. Madelyn didn't *appear* dangerous, yet Ash's instincts screamed at her to run. Perhaps she hadn't felt regret or relief after being admitted to Nightingale House because she'd had no reason to feel them—but Ash apparently had reason to fear this woman.

If only she could remember *why.*

A quick search of the library didn't tell her. Ash returned to the foyer and took the stairs. The snap of her boot heels echoed on each wooden step. That seemed odd. Shouldn't a stair runner muffle the sound? Perhaps one had, once. When she reached the second-floor landing, the door to Madelyn's office already stood ajar, as if inviting her in.

Unlike the timeless elegance of the first-floor décor, the office told the story of its owner's long absence. A heavy, outdated computer screen took up a fourth of the desktop. A fax transmission from the day of Madelyn's disappearance still sat beside the keyboard, listing the current values of several oil company stocks.

Six years ago, Nicholas St. Croix had succeeded in taking over his mother's company and tearing it down. But if Madelyn still owned those shares, she didn't need to worry about cash when—*if*—she returned.

A second, smaller room lay beyond a connecting door—Rachel Boyle's office. Unlike Madelyn's office, all of the tables and cabinet surfaces had been cleared of papers. Ash opened the drawers and looked through the shelves, hoping to find a personal item of Rachel's. *Anything.* A single object to touch, to hold—and to see if it felt familiar.

She finished the search and came up empty. Nothing of Rachel remained here, and Rachel's own apartment had been let to someone else shortly after her disappearance. She'd been survived by her parents in America; her belongings had probably been shipped to their home. Which meant Ash had nowhere left to look for answers—at least not in London.

So her next step would be finding Nicholas St. Croix.

Was it odd that no evidence of Madelyn's son existed in this house? Ash thought it must be. No pictures of Nicholas as a boy graced the tables; no family photos depicted happier times. Did Madelyn order them removed from her sight—out of spite or pain—or had they simply never been a part of the décor?

Curious, Ash followed the hallway to the master bedroom. Maybe Madelyn hadn't expunged Nicholas's presence from her house; perhaps she'd simply kept the evidence somewhere more private.

Or perhaps not. Ash opened the door to another expensively appointed room devoid of any personality other than "tasteful."

Aside from Madelyn's painting in the library, the entire house could have been anyone's home—except that anyone else would have left more of an impression on their surroundings.

Unless, of course, this house *did* reflect Madelyn's personality: sophisticated, disinterested . . . perfect.

But not everything was perfect. Something seemed wrong. Ash studied the room, trying to determine what didn't fit—and for the first time, not searching for something familiar, but just *looking*. Her gaze landed on the bed. The blankets stretched unevenly over the mattress. A pillow lay askew and dented at its center.

Someone had been sleeping in that bed. How long ago? A housekeeper wouldn't have left it like that. Breathing in through her nose, Ash detected a recent scent that she'd begun to associate with *male*—and a connection suddenly lurked at the back of her mind, that half-seen lightning, that forgotten word.

Like Cinderella, a memory—another story. *Who's been sleeping in my bed?*

Ash knew the answer to this one: Goldilocks, who'd broken into the bears' house. Although Ash had broken into this home, that wasn't the connection that teased her. She didn't sleep in anyone's bed, not even her own.

Every night, she'd lain motionless beneath her blankets when the nurses had ordered her to, but she hadn't actually *slept* in almost three years.

So what was her mind trying to tease out of this memory? Ash moved closer to the bed, attempting to follow the tenuous association formed between now and Before. She didn't care about the man who'd been sleeping here. He wasn't in this room now, but a connection to her past was . . . somewhere.

What was the rest of that story? *Who's been eating my porridge?* That wasn't her, either. Though she'd eaten whenever they placed a meal in front of her, Ash hadn't been hungry. Since her escape from Nightingale House, four weeks had gone by without food passing her lips.

Perhaps her mind wasn't trying to remember an association with the story itself; perhaps the connection lay in the circumstances in which she'd heard it. But she *couldn't* remember that. She couldn't remember who'd told the story to her—or even whether she'd read it, instead. She couldn't remember *where* she'd been, or *when*. She tried to, but came head up on the memory she didn't want, a memory of a memory, her first memory and it was of regret and terror—

Burning cold, her body gone, she'd heard screaming and she'd been screaming but she didn't have to return to the cold, that endless frozen agony, because she'd made a bargain and the dark figure said her name, Ash— and the rest of her ripped apart, was gone, gone

Her stomach heaved. Doubling over, Ash braced her hands against the edge of the bed. She sucked in air that her lungs didn't need, but the motion of her chest felt familiar. It felt right.

But why didn't she *need* air?

Someone had to know. Someone had to know who she was. *What* she was.

"Rachel?"

The man's voice came from behind her, full of shock and disbelief. Ash whipped around. Nicholas St. Croix stood at the doorway, holding a crossbow aimed at her heart.

Instinctively, Ash raised her hands to show him that she was unarmed. She didn't know if Nicholas had killed Rachel, but she wouldn't give him a reason to fire now. She doubted he would, anyway. Instead of aggression, she sensed faint hope in him, combined with ragged uncertainty.

He couldn't see her clearly in the dark, Ash realized, whereas she could see him perfectly. Shirtless, he wore only a pair of black trousers that hung low on his hips—zipped, but not buttoned. He must have yanked them on when she'd broken in. Had she woken him, or had he simply been lying in the bed?

Lying in wait.

As soon as Ash thought it, she couldn't shake that impression. Nicholas St. Croix's photos suggested he was a dangerous man, hard and emotionless—but the most recent picture had been taken more than three years ago. Instead of cold elegance, he appeared pared down and roughened. His dark hair had been cut brutally short. A few days' worth of scruff shadowed his jaw, and his body . . .

Ash's gaze fell to his chest. In the photos, he'd obviously been well acquainted with a gym. But the taut, wiry muscles on display hadn't come from a single hour's workout followed by a rich man's meal. His body reflected an obsession of some kind, one that ate away at him no matter how much he fed it—and Ash didn't think that obsession had anything to do with his looks.

Perhaps that obsession explained why he'd lain in wait at his mother's house *with a crossbow.*

Ash didn't lower her hands. "I'm not her. But if you look at me, can you tell me who I am?"

His aim didn't waver as he flipped a switch on the wall. Light flooded the room. Ash blinked rapidly, adjusting to the glare. His eyes narrowed. Their icy blue focus shifted to the symbols tattooed over the left side of her face.

The warm hope she'd sensed in him burst into a hot, swelling pressure. But even as she recognized the change, he began hiding it from her, somehow. The pressure didn't vanish, yet he closed his emotions away, as if shutting them behind a door.

Strange. No one had done that before. Everyone she'd met in London kept their emotions wide open, and had no clue Ash could sense them.

"You're Rachel Boyle," he said flatly.

"No." Disappointment touched her, swift and light, but it couldn't gain any traction and slid away. "I look like her, but that's not my name."

"Oh?"

Now his voice softened, and though he lowered his crossbow, Ash's wariness sharpened. He approached her on silent feet, and his movements reminded her of the predators she'd seen—not the agile cheetah or the majestic, powerful lion. Not any animal driven by hunger or a need to protect its territory, but the human variety driven by deadly intent. She'd seen many of them prowling the dark London streets, had sensed the malevolence they'd felt toward others. Often, they hid it behind bland pleasantries and smiles, but she'd recognized what they were.

Ash couldn't sense anything from Nicholas, but she recognized the same malevolence. A quick step back—*not fear, but survival instinct*—brought her up against the bed. Trapped. Escape would be easy, but now that she'd touched the bed, her mind began its desperate search again, reaching for the connection—

Someone's been sleeping in my bed.

Had her memory been searching for *him*? Obviously, he'd

been lying there—but on some level, had she known exactly *who* had been in that bed before he'd appeared with his crossbow? Had she been reminded of something from Before—something about Nicholas St. Croix?

If she had a connection to him, then he must know *her*. Not Rachel, but Ash. That realization kept her in place, despite the urge to flee.

Nicholas stalked close, halting less than an arm's length away. He stood several inches taller than Ash; she had to tilt her face up to watch his eyes. Slowly, he examined her every feature. Did she look *any* different from Rachel? Ash waited, listening to the steady beat of his heart. Her own heart hammered, constructing unfamiliar emotions in her chest. Hope, trepidation? She couldn't distinguish them amid the racket of her pulse. Ash wished she knew what he felt, but his expression gave nothing away.

She had to try again. "Who am I?"

"Who else could you be but Rachel?" With a sudden, thin smile, he tugged a pale lock of hair forward over her shoulder, rubbing the long strands between his fingers as if considering their texture. "Who else but the woman I love?"

Love? No, that wasn't what she'd tasted in that swelling burst of emotion before he'd closed himself away from her. Disappointment, grief, and rage—she'd sensed all of those. But not love.

His head lowered, his gaze holding hers on the way down. Would he kiss her? Curious, Ash let him. Firm and cool, his lips settled against hers.

Emotion burst from him, blasting through the door he'd shut—a feeling that wasn't hot but bitter *withering* cold, and Ash recognized the hate behind it before he hid that from her, too. She should have moved then. The hate felt like a warning, and she disliked the cold, but when he opened his lips over hers, his taste was fascinating—mint, because he'd readied for bed, and there was something else that was familiar, *so* familiar here. She *knew* the touch of his mouth, the heat that slipped through her like a warm drink when his tongue sought hers. So she remained still, searching for the connection sparked by the kiss and lurking in her ruined memory.

She didn't find it before Nicholas lifted his head. Ash wanted to follow him up to prolong the contact, but she remembered—

don't break the Rules, respect their free will—and waited, panting, not needing the oxygen but relishing the sweep of air over her lips, wet from his kiss.

She'd felt all of this before. She'd felt—

A cold prod against her throat. Ash's eyes widened—*this was surprise!*—and she heard a click. Pain stabbed her neck. White-hot, it yanked her muscles taut and raced up behind her eyes.

Then, for the first time in three years, darkness fell over her mind, and she felt absolutely nothing at all.

CHAPTER 2

The moment Nicholas had spotted the woman's pale hair, hope had shot through him. *Rachel had become a Guardian.*

Even though the Guardians had told him that Rachel hadn't been transformed into an angelic warrior, no one could explain to him why she wasn't one now. After sacrificing her life to save Nicholas's, she *should* have been transformed into one of their kind. So despite the demonic symbols tattooed over the woman's face and her claim that she wasn't Rachel, he'd hoped her sudden appearance meant the Guardians had lied to him.

He'd hoped . . . until the feverish heat of her mouth instantly revealed that she wasn't a Guardian or human. Neither of those beings had such high temperatures.

Goddammit. The woman was a demon.

Fortunately, he'd been expecting one—and kissing her had brought him close enough to the tall mattress that he could reach the modified Taser beneath the pillow.

He shocked her with enough juice to kill a human. The demon only seized once and shape-shifted. Her clothes vanished, revealing suddenly crimson skin. Gleaming black horns curled from her forehead around toward her ears; leathery wings snapped wide, the sharp talon at the left tip scoring a long vertical line on the wall. Nicholas released the trigger, cutting off the electric current.

The demon crumpled to the floor in a pile of loose, naked limbs. Her wings folded over her body like a blanket. She hadn't fully transformed: She wore skin instead of reptilian scales, her knees weren't jointed backward like a goat's hind legs . . . and her slack face still resembled Rachel's.

It didn't matter. He knew who this must be.

Madelyn.

He'd spent years trying to find the demon who'd replaced his mother, destroyed his family, and murdered Rachel. At the beginning, Nicholas hadn't known how impossible it might be to find her. Hell, at the beginning he hadn't even known *what* she was—or that Madelyn could shape-shift to resemble any person she chose. But after he'd learned how unlikely his chances of finding her were, Nicholas hadn't stopped looking.

Though he hadn't found Madelyn, Nicholas had found a few answers—and enough information about demons that he learned *how* to look for her.

He'd learned that demons were creatures of habit who followed familiar patterns, particularly if those patterns had been successful in the past. So instead of searching for a woman who resembled Madelyn, he'd searched for a family who'd been ripped apart as his had been.

That search might have taken him forever, he knew—but he'd also learned that demons were vindictive and possessive. That suited Nicholas. He was vindictive and possessive, too, and his gut told him that if a new identity didn't satisfy her, Madelyn would eventually come for him and try to reclaim everything he'd taken from her.

So he'd prepared. He'd kept watch over the properties that she'd once called hers. That diligence had paid off three weeks ago, when someone had entered the house using Madelyn's old security code. He'd known it had to be her—probably returning to look at the items that she wanted to possess again. He'd been waiting for her to come back . . . and she had.

Finally, after almost six years of searching, Nicholas had her—and soon, he'd send her back to the burning pit in Hell where she belonged.

Except he didn't feel the elation he should have. He was

only sorry the demon crumpled on the floor wasn't the woman she'd appeared to be.

Stupid, that he'd almost fallen for her trick. By taking Rachel's face, the demon had known exactly how to shove him off-balance. He should have known, dammit. He should have been prepared.

No doubt she'd try to get to him again as soon as she woke up. He should kill her now—chop off her head, cut through her heart.

He couldn't slay her yet, though. He had to make certain this truly was Madelyn, not some demon lackey running an errand for her. Even if it was Madelyn, Nicholas wouldn't kill her until he had answers. Unlike in the movies, a demon's spirit didn't take possession of a human's; a demon shape-shifted its corporeal form and physically took the human's place. When Nicholas had been eight, Madelyn had transformed herself into a duplicate of his mother—which meant that his mother must be out there, somewhere. He didn't have any hope that his mother was still alive, but he needed to know what had happened to her.

And he needed to know what had happened to Rachel's body after her lifeless form had vanished from his arms. At the very least, she deserved that for saving his life. For loving him.

Nicholas only wished he'd loved her back. She'd deserved that, too.

He'd continue to let this demon think he had loved Rachel, though. Growing up with Madelyn for a mother had taught him that emotion could—and would—be used against him. He'd pretend to have once loved Rachel and let the demon try to manipulate an emotion he'd never felt, rather than let her rip him open with the guilt he *did* feel.

He'd lock away that guilt, just as he locked away almost every emotion. If he thanked Madelyn for anything, it was that she'd given him the ability to conceal his feelings and to think like she did. Now he'd use that against her.

He tossed the crossbow to the foot of the bed. The weapon would be useful later, but first he had to make certain she didn't try to run—and a demon could run fast enough that he wouldn't have time to blink before she'd gone. He bent to haul her onto the mattress. Beneath his hands, her wings felt like old leather left out in the hot sun. Roughly, he pushed them aside and gripped her shoulders, dragging her up. Her head rocked forward, as if weighted by the horns.

No need to worry about waking her; she couldn't hurt him without breaking the Rules. When he held her, she couldn't even try to loosen his grasp.

He let her flop back onto the bed and shoved her legs up. She didn't stir, but he couldn't have much time left. With one hand locked around her left wrist, he opened the nightstand's top drawer, scanning the weapons there.

She wouldn't give him a chance to shock her with the Taser again. His pistol was useless against a demon. She could easily break the handcuffs. The darts filled with hellhound venom would paralyze her, but he needed her to talk. And though he could prevent her escape by holding on to her wrist, Nicholas preferred not to touch her.

The collar, then. A quarter-inch thick and constructed of steel, she wouldn't be able to rip it from her neck. Its heavy battery pack could be activated by remote to deliver another electric shock, briefly incapacitating her.

With the crossbow backing him up, "briefly" was all that he needed. He snapped the collar around her neck. Snagging his shirt from the bench at the end of the bed, he slipped his arms into the sleeves and waited, the remote in hand. Not long now—she was coming around. The crimson had faded from her skin; her wings had vanished. For the first time since he'd electrocuted her, she took a breath.

God, she looked so much like Rachel. Her gestures had been Rachel's, too. When he'd come into the room and she'd turned to face him, the way she'd swept her long blond bangs away from her forehead as if to get a better look at him had been *so* familiar.

Those red symbols weren't. He realized now that the tattoos didn't just cover the side of her face, but continued down her neck and arms. Hundreds more of the inch-high symbols were tattooed over her torso and halfway down her legs, and an elaborate, palm-sized glyph decorated the skin between her breasts.

Why was this demon wearing those markings if she'd meant to impersonate Rachel? Nicholas couldn't understand the purpose of it, not when a demon could imitate a person's appearance so precisely. He couldn't believe the tattoos were a mistake, not when she'd made certain to get the other details exactly right. Hell, the demon had even worn Rachel's favorite clothing: the black leather jacket she loved, the knee-high boots with their three-inch heels, the snug jeans.

Would Madelyn have known about that jacket, those boots? Rachel had never dressed like that around her. It hadn't been professional. Rachel had worn those clothes only away from work, and on the few weekends she and Nicholas had taken . . .

God. Nicholas shook his head. He couldn't let himself do that. He couldn't go back to those few months when he'd cared for her, as much as he could care for anyone. It hadn't been love, but when this demon woke up, it would twist any available emotion, and those memories brought his guilt and his grief too close to the surface. So he couldn't think about Rachel.

And he had to remember that every word coming from a demon's mouth was a lie designed to mislead him—or a truth designed to fulfill some other destructive goal. He couldn't risk listening to her, or believe anything she said.

He only needed to know if this demon was Madelyn. If she wasn't, he'd slay her.

Or he'd use her to find Madelyn . . . then slay them both.

Three minutes later, the demon opened her eyes. Her gaze immediately found him standing at the end of the bed, his crossbow aimed at her chest. Without a word, Nicholas showed her the remote in his left hand, his thumb resting on the red activator button.

Her brow furrowed, but she caught on quickly. Her fingers flew to the heavy rectangular battery at her neck.

"It's an explosive collar," Nicholas said. "If you move, your head is gone."

Lies. It would only stun her and give him time to capture her again. He didn't mention that the broadheads of his crossbow bolts would detonate on impact. She'd discover that for herself if he had to use one.

She nodded and looked down at her naked form. No shock or embarrassment registered on her features. Rachel had always been a bit nervous when they'd undressed. This demon's lips tilted, but he wasn't certain if that faint smile indicated amusement. It didn't seem to indicate much of anything.

Of course, Nicholas's reaction to the beautiful woman lying naked on the bed wasn't his typical response, either. No thoughts of sex intruded—only a sharp awareness that this demon might have killed his mother and driven his father to suicide.

Unexpectedly, she didn't seem interested in trying to arouse him. She didn't adopt a seductive posture; he couldn't detect a hint of suggestion in her movements or her expression. Her clothes simply reappeared. She began to rise from the bed, but froze when he followed her up with the crossbow.

"I knew handguns were hard to come by in England," she said, sitting at the edge of the mattress. "I didn't realize crossbows were easier to find."

"A gun won't kill you."

"It wouldn't?" She glanced down at her chest, as if imagining a bullet slamming into it.

Nicholas imagined it, too—all too clearly. This demon would bleed. It would feel pain. Then it would heal. Rachel hadn't. She'd thrashed and choked on her own blood, and *nothing* that Nicholas did to help had—

No. Determinedly, Nicholas forced that memory away. Within seconds of this demon waking, he was already thinking of Rachel. This had to be what she'd wanted.

He wouldn't play her games. "You know a gun can't kill you."

"No. I didn't know." She tilted her head as if taking his measure. *Just like Rachel.* "If you know I can't be killed by a gun, then you know who I am?"

"You're not Rachel."

"No, I'm not," she agreed. "I don't know why I look like her. Or why I feel as if I *should* remember something. Perhaps this is her body, and there is an imprint of her memories in my brain? I don't know. I hoped that you would."

Playing dumb. Six months ago, Nicholas might not have known what the demon was doing. Then he'd met Rosalia, a Guardian who could have given a demon lessons in extracting the information she wanted without offering any of her own. Thanks to Rosalia, he recognized this tactic: The demon pretended ignorance to discover how much he knew. She couldn't physically fight him, and so her only power came from possessing more knowledge than he did. So she was trying to figure out what lies to tell.

Nicholas was just as interested in seeing what lies she tried to spin when he didn't give her anything first. "What *do* you know?"

She answered more easily than he'd anticipated. "That almost three years ago, Madelyn St. Croix brought me to a private psychiatric hospital and left me. I don't remember where I was before that. I don't remember *anything* from before that." If that frustrated her, she gave no sign of it. "And until a few months ago, I didn't care. Now I do. I want to know who I am, what I am. And I think you might have the answers."

Weren't demons better liars than this? She'd barely gotten into her story, and already he saw holes in it.

"You have no memory, but you recalled Madelyn's name?"

"Not until a month ago. I looked up pictures of Rachel Boyle's associates online, and recognized Madelyn as the woman who brought me to Nightingale House."

Nightingale House. Jesus. No question that this demon either was Madelyn or connected to her.

When Nicholas had been a boy, she'd had his father committed to Nightingale House—and it had destroyed his business, his reputation, his life. It had been Madelyn's first step in driving him toward suicide.

Fucking demons. His finger tightened on the crossbow trigger. As if she heard the movement, her gaze fell to his hand.

"I'd be grateful if you wouldn't," she said. "I'd rather not die."

Bullshit. She didn't sound grateful *or* concerned.

"What happens if you die?" He let curiosity lighten his tone, as if he was considering pulling the trigger just to find out. Let her sweat. "Do you return to Hell?"

"I don't know." She watched him steadily. No sweating. Dammit. "Nicholas, I need your help. Somehow, I'm connected to Madelyn St. Croix, just as Rachel was. And your mother—"

"She's not my mother," he stated flatly. The idea sent fury through his veins, but he wouldn't let her see that.

Her brows rose. "Then who is she?"

"A demon."

"A demon," she echoed. Something sparked in her eyes. Excitement? Whatever it was, the emotion quickly vanished. "Is that what I am?"

"Yes."

"And you are, too? You seem to suffer the same lack of affect that I do."

The demon probably intended that observation to hurt him, to make him question his humanity, but to Nicholas, it only showed that she couldn't read his emotions. *Good.* Rosalia's tutelage had paid off there, too. She'd taught him to guard his mind—and obviously she'd done it well enough, as this demon couldn't sense anything that he didn't want to give her.

"I'm human," he said.

"How can you tell?" Her gaze searched his face, as if looking for the differences. When he didn't answer, she asked, "Was Rachel a demon, too?"

Oh, that was clever. Introduce doubt about Rachel, throw him off-kilter. Too bad Nicholas had already considered the possibility that Rachel had been Madelyn's lackey all along.

Considered the possibility and discarded it. He'd been skin-to-skin with her too many times. She'd been human—and the only reason the idea had *ever* occurred to him was because it could assuage his guilt. If she'd been a demon and her death had been a setup designed by Madelyn, then Nicholas had nothing to be sorry for. An attractive thought, but not true. He preferred to live with his regret rather than blame Rachel.

"Try again," he said.

She didn't. Almost dismissively, she looked away from Nicholas and scanned the room. "Are any of Rachel's things still here?"

"No." He had a few items, including the overnight bag she'd packed for the weekend they'd intended to spend together—Madelyn had shot her before they'd left town. The rest of Rachel's belongings had been returned to her family. "Her parents took them back to the States. Why?"

"If you can't help me, perhaps they can." She touched the steel collar. "So let me go, and I'll leave you alone."

Not a fucking chance, especially if she truly meant to see Rachel's parents. Goddamned demons. If this was a threat, she'd chosen the perfect one.

Unlike the police and the press, Rachel's parents had believed Nicholas. When he'd told them that Rachel had thrown herself in front of him, they hadn't asked what Nicholas had done to deserve such a sacrifice; they'd only said Rachel's selfless act was exactly what they'd have expected from her. And though they hadn't understood how her body had disappeared any better than Nicholas had, they'd believed that, too.

And they were still looking for her. If this demon showed up at their home, no doubt they'd welcome her with open arms and call it a miracle.

The Boyles didn't deserve that. They'd suffered enough. No way in hell would Nicholas let a demon arrive at their house wearing their dead daughter's face. But he couldn't let her know that he felt the need to protect Rachel's family from her, because she'd use it against him.

Nicholas focused on how he intended to use the demon, instead. "So you want me to just let you walk away?" He shook his head. "The way I see it, you're the last person to have contact with Madelyn. That means you're my best chance of finding her. Where is she?"

"I don't know."

And he wouldn't get anywhere as long as she kept lying. All right, then. He'd call her bluff. She wanted to know who she really was? He'd discover how much she'd risk to find out.

"Okay." He lowered the crossbow. "Then I propose a bargain: You help me track Madelyn down, and I'll help you discover who you are."

She hesitated. Damn right she did. A bargain was the most dangerous agreement a demon could make. Any party to a bargain that didn't follow through on the terms would find their soul trapped in Hell's frozen field when they died, tortured for eternity. A human who didn't fulfill the terms would be trapped, too, but Nicholas was willing to take that risk to find Madelyn.

An emotion that might have been wariness entered her voice. "What would the bargain entail, exactly?"

"As I said. You use the knowledge you have to help me find the demon who impersonated my mother. And no lying to me for as long as we're bound together—that's part of this bargain. You can't conceal information about the demon who pretended to be Madelyn, or anything that might lead me to her. Every relevant bit of info, no matter how trivial, you give to me the moment you think of it. In return, I'll help you discover who you are."

"I won't be of use to you. I don't know where Madelyn is," she said.

Hedging, delaying. Nicholas hadn't expected anything different. He raised the crossbow again. "So that's a *no*."

"No, I didn't say that." She pressed her fingertips to her

forehead, as if forcing herself to think. Rachel used to do the same, but her eyes had never begun turning crimson as this demon's eyes were. "I just . . . I've entered into a bargain before. I don't know *what.* But I know that it's not something I should do quickly. So I'm telling you now that you'll be disappointed, because I don't have answers for you."

No. She was telling him now because if she entered into the bargain, she couldn't lie.

"I don't care," Nicholas said. "If you don't know where she is now, you can still agree to help. And I'll help you in return."

"What if we don't find Madelyn or discover who I am?"

"It only matters that we help each other, not that we succeed. It only matters that you don't conceal information or lie."

She nodded. God, what a terrible bargainer she was. She hadn't asked the same from him—probably because finding out who she was didn't really matter.

It mattered to him. If she was telling the truth and didn't know who Madelyn was, then tracing this demon's history might lead him to Madelyn, anyway. They were obviously connected.

The glow receded from her eyes, leaving them clear and blue. "And if we fail, are we stuck together for the rest of our lives?"

"If we exhaust every possibility, we'll agree to release each other from the bargain," he said. Even if they never did, her life would be much longer than his. Surely her immortality was a detail that every demon couldn't forget. "So, you help me, and I'll help you. Are we agreed? You have to say it."

She took a deep breath before slowly nodding. "Yes. We have a bargain."

She'd actually agreed? Nicholas stared at her, replaying each step, making certain he hadn't missed anything. He hadn't expected that she'd go through with it. But she'd said it clearly: *Yes.*

Surprise shifted to triumph. He *had* her.

"Are you Madelyn?" But no, that was the wrong question. She might not be able to lie, but technically, the demon he sought had never been Madelyn St. Croix; she'd just stolen a human woman's identity. He clarified, "Are you the demon who impersonated my mother?"

"What do you mean, am I your moth—" She broke off. "Can't you tell by looking?"

"I know demons can shape-shift." How ignorant did she think he was?

She blinked. "We can?"

Jesus, even a bargain didn't stop her from playing stupid. A direct question, then. She couldn't evade that.

"Are you that demon?"

"I don't know. I don't think so." Her lips pursed briefly. "I don't know who I am, so if I can shape-shift, I suppose that means I could be anyone. But I *saw* Madelyn St. Croix, or someone who could have been her twin, and she wasn't me."

Whoever she saw could have been any demon shape-shifted—but most likely, the other demon had been Madelyn. So Nicholas had to accept that *this* wasn't Madelyn . . . and that she truly didn't know who she was.

He fought his disappointment. Even if this demon didn't remember who she was, that didn't mean she had no other useful knowledge.

"Where is Madelyn now?"

"I don't know."

For God's sake. With effort, Nicholas concealed his frustration. "Who gave you the code to the house?"

"I don't know. The pattern was familiar, and I just . . . entered it." She demonstrated in the air, as if inputting a number into a keypad, then spread her hands. "But I don't remember where I learned the code."

Nicholas frowned. The bargain bound her to the truth. But how could she have no memory, yet know something as specific as a numerical code? "Did you come to this house in the past month?"

"No."

Then Madelyn had. "When was the last time you were in contact with her?"

"Almost three years ago, when she left me at Nightingale House."

Exactly as she'd claimed earlier. Nothing she'd said contradicted anything from before the bargain. Nicholas hadn't expected that. Either she was manipulating him in some brilliant way that he couldn't comprehend . . . or she had been telling the truth all along.

He didn't know what to think of that. So he could only press on, and try to figure out her game after he found Madelyn.

"How did Madelyn escape from Hell?"

After breaking the Rules and killing a human, Madelyn should have been punished by Lucifer, and either tortured or slain. Six years wouldn't have been long enough of a punishment—let alone three years, if this demon spoke the truth about when Madelyn had left her at Nightingale House.

She should have been punished in Hell . . . and even if she had escaped the Pit, Madelyn shouldn't have been able to leave the realm. Almost three years ago, Lucifer had lost a wager with a Guardian, and every portal between Earth and Hell had been closed. They wouldn't reopen for another five hundred years, and every demon who'd been in Hell would remain in that realm until the Gates opened again.

Almost three years . . .

Shit. The timing was exactly right. Somehow, Madelyn had escaped from Hell just before the Gates closed.

Had she brought this demon with her?

The demon shook her head. "I don't know how she escaped Hell. I didn't even know that Hell is a real place."

How could *that* be true? "Then where were you before Nightingale House?"

Demons were creatures of habit. If Madelyn had hidden in a specific location between the time she escaped from Hell and left this demon at the psychiatric hospital, she might return there to conceal herself again.

"I don't remember. Before Nightingale House, I don't remember anything clearly. Only that Madelyn and I were . . . somewhere. I don't know where. There was someone else with us. He cut these marks into me. His voice was so big—more painful than the knife." She closed her eyes. "And I was frightened."

For the first time, strong emotion came through in the tremble of her voice, in the clenching of her hands. But by the time she looked at him again, he couldn't see any fear. Only expectation. Perhaps a faint hope.

And for an instant, he *believed* it was hope. As if she wasn't acting, but truly thought he had answers for her.

God, he was in over his head. He didn't even know if this memory loss she claimed was possible. Maybe none of this was true. Maybe she'd already broken a bargain with someone else and had nothing to lose by lying to him now. Before he went any further, he had to find out.

He set the crossbow on the mattress and retrieved his mobile phone. "Don't move," he said. "Don't talk."

She only lifted her eyebrows as if to ask where she would go, and watched from the edge of the bed as he found Rosalia's number in his list of contacts.

The Guardian didn't like him, but she'd answer any questions he had—and she was one of the few people he trusted to be honest with him. Three hundred years ago, her father had also been replaced by a demon; she understood his quest for vengeance better than anyone else could. She'd taught him how to search for Madelyn, to distinguish demons from humans, and which weapons would be most effective against one of their kind. Most demons and Guardians fought with swords, but in a physical match, pitting a demon against a human was no contest at all. Nicholas wasn't fast or strong enough to pose a threat. Knowing the Rules—that a demon *couldn't* fight him or hurt him—evened the odds. So did knowing their susceptibility to electric shock, and how to kill or slow them down.

Rosalia answered on the third ring, her rich Italian accent rolling over his name. "Nicholas."

No need to ask why he was calling. He only contacted her when she was useful to him—when he had a question for her.

"Have you ever heard of a demon with amnesia?"

"Amnesia? No."

That's all he wanted to know. "All right—"

"But I've heard of those with their memories stripped away."

He frowned. On the bed, the demon had straightened, her gaze locked on the phone. She could hear everything they both said, and there was probably no point speaking in Italian rather than English. He'd never heard of a demon who hadn't lived on Earth long enough to pick up almost every human language.

But then, he'd never heard of a demon with her memories stripped, either.

"Why would that happen?" He switched to Italian and watched the demon's brow furrow with confusion. Maybe an act . . . but he didn't think so.

"As punishment, if they'd upset Lucifer—or just because he didn't want the demon to know something."

Perhaps that was what had happened to this demon. It didn't explain how or why she resembled Rachel, but he found punishment easier to believe than a demon breaking a bargain.

"Just tell me, Rosalia: Even if the demon had no memory, would you still slay them?"

"Of course, unless it was more useful at the time to keep them alive. But I'd slay them eventually—and I'd be wary all the while it was alive. A demon's nature doesn't change, even if its memories do. The rebel angels who followed Lucifer were physically transformed into demons, but their new forms only revealed what they were inside. So never forget that they are *evil,* Nicholas. Every single one of them."

He eyed the demon. "I suppose a former nun doesn't call someone 'evil' lightly."

To his surprise, Rosalia laughed. "No, I don't."

"What are you saying?" The demon got to her feet and started toward him. She froze when Nicholas showed her the remote device again. Her fingers curled at her thighs. Frustration? If so, good. She ought to feel a little of what Nicholas had, talking to her and receiving no answers at all.

She looked to the phone. "This woman knows more about demons than you? Who is she? Can I speak with her?"

Rosalia's voice sounded sharply in his ear, her laughter gone. "Who is that, Nicholas? If a demon is there, don't trust—"

Nicholas hung up, cutting her off. No, he couldn't trust the demon. But she might be his only way to find Madelyn, so he'd take the risk.

If they were going to risk anything, though, they had to do it quickly. Rosalia wouldn't wait around for him to call her back. She was probably heading to London right now—either flying with her wings or using her Guardian power to gather the darkness around her and speed through the night. If she found them, this demon would be dead within seconds.

Knowing Rosalia's skill with a sword, perhaps she'd be dead in *less* than a second.

He tossed the remote to the bed. "We need to go. Now, before the Guardians catch up to us."

She stood still as he reached for her neck. "Who are the Guardians?"

Whether she played stupid or just didn't know, he didn't

have time to explain it. The heat of her body had warmed the steel collar. He unlocked it, tossed it aside.

"All you need to know right now is that the Guardians will kill you. So let's head out."

She nodded and started for the door. "Where to?"

The demon didn't know how to find Madelyn, so they'd try to find Madelyn through her connection to Rachel . . . and get as far from London as they could.

"The States," he said. "We'll fly there tonight."

"I can't. I don't have any ID."

"And I wasn't thinking of a plane." When she looked at him blankly, Nicholas clenched his teeth and counted to three. "I know you can fly."

Her eyes widened and she looked down at her hands. "I can shape-shift into a bird? How?"

Jesus H. Christ. The next time he made a bargain, Nicholas would damn well make certain the demon knew more than a bag of bricks.

"You can't turn into a bird. You can only form wings—" Oh, fuck it. He turned for the door. "I have Rachel's passport. I'll charter a jet."

"That's good. It's probably less likely to crash into the Atlantic than I am." She hurried into the hallway after him. "Why do you have Rachel's passport? Did you kill her?"

Even if this demon truly didn't know that Madelyn had done it, why would she care? Perhaps she was just testing him to see if he'd break down into some guilt-induced confession. To see if Nicholas secretly felt that he was to blame, that his actions had killed her, boohoo.

Thanks to Madelyn, he'd stopped boohooing as a kid. Nicholas *did* feel guilt—that he'd used Rachel, that she'd fallen in love with him, that he couldn't save her when she was dying in his arms—but he wasn't responsible for her death. Madelyn had killed Rachel. Full stop.

He didn't know this demon's reasons for asking, and he didn't have to speak the truth. But in the end, *truth* was just simpler.

"No," he said, and started down the stairs. "I didn't shoot her. Madelyn did."

He glanced over his shoulder to catch her response. Her eyes had narrowed, and he easily read the suspicion in them.

She thought he was lying.

Now, wasn't that just fucking hilarious? Shaking his head, he pulled out his phone again. He'd take time to be amused when they were on American soil, and a Guardian wasn't hot on their asses . . . a Guardian who could come for them even *after* they were in the air.

It was going to be a damn long flight.

CHAPTER 3

Michael was gone, and the walls of his temple were cracking.

Taylor stared at the thin lines twisting through the pale marble. If there was one place a Guardian should have felt safe, it was here—in the center of Caelum, the Guardian realm, standing within Michael's great hall. The first and strongest of all the Guardians, he'd been entrusted with great powers by the angels themselves after killing a dragon and ending the second war between Heaven and Hell. He'd built the massive temple simply through the power of his voice and will. And for the past six months, almost without realizing the adoption taking place, Taylor had come to consider this temple her home. She *should* have felt safe.

But she was terrified, because Michael was gone. At least, part of him was—the part she could usually feel in the back of her mind, after he'd linked his psyche to her through blood and a kiss. The part of him that sometimes protected her, guided her. The part she often fought against. The part that was probably responsible for her coming to accept his temple as her home. But that was only part of him, and a tenuous connection, at best.

The rest of him was in Hell, tortured in the icy field surrounding Lucifer's throne. Buried, with only his face showing, his eyes frozen open and fixed on Lucifer's tower; his body eaten by dragons in the Chaos realm before it regenerated to be ravaged again.

Surrounded by the screams of the damned, he'd been in that field for a year now, and for the past six months, Taylor had visited him as often as she dared—using his power of teleportation, which was also a part of her, and which Taylor had begun thinking of as her own Gift. They'd come to an agreement of sorts: He wouldn't teleport her without her knowledge or against her will, but if she needed protection, he could take over her body and fight for her.

Obviously, that agreement had changed. Because whatever of Michael was left in Taylor's mind, he still allowed her to teleport . . . he just didn't allow her to teleport to Hell anymore.

That scared her more than the cracks in the walls, scared her more than the sense of shattering and pain that she felt when her hand flattened against the marble—because it meant that whatever was happening to him in Hell, Michael was protecting her from it. Through their link, Taylor had become used to the echo of the pain and horror he experienced, though she knew Michael shielded her from most of it. Now, whatever was happening, he shielded her from *all* of it.

Could it truly be that bad? *Worse* than what she'd already seen?

She was afraid of that answer. A former detective, she'd seen every evil that a human could visit upon another being. That evil didn't even scratch the surface of Hell.

Michael had sacrificed his life and broken a bargain to save Earth and Caelum, and in the faith and hope that, eventually, his friends and fellow warriors would find the right spell to release him. Six months ago, Taylor had sworn that she'd find a way to free him. But she was no closer to finding a solution . . . and she couldn't feel him anymore.

And she knew that was what scared her most of all: that she wouldn't be able to save him.

Outside the temple, Caelum's sun shone brightly in a cloudless blue sky—as it always did. The shining marble city was nearly empty of any other Guardians—as it always was.

At least, for as long as Taylor had known it. Through Michael, she had the faintest memory of the city filled with thousands of Guardians, mentors and novices, warriors and scholars. Less than a hundred Guardians remained now, and they didn't pass their time here. There were simply too many demons and too much to do on Earth.

A few were passing through, however, visiting the archives or taking a short rest between assignments. Taylor could hear their heartbeats and voices, and at times, it seemed as if she felt their footsteps vibrating through the marble streets and courtyards. She hadn't yet decided whether she truly felt those vibrations, or if it was another echo from Michael: his connection to the realm, channeled to her.

She doubted that her singing would reshape the arches and spires as Michael's singing did, however.

Across the courtyard facing Michael's temple, Rosalia emerged from beneath one of those arches, which doubled as a Gate between Caelum and the human realm. Used by the Guardians who didn't possess a teleportation Gift—which was most of them—each Gate led to a different location; Rosalia was coming in from France.

Dark-haired, stunningly beautiful, and so nice that it was impossible to hate her for it, Rosalia smiled when she spotted Taylor on the steps of Michael's temple. Her yellow sundress flirted with her knees as she crossed the courtyard, and she looked so sunny and cheerful that it was easy to forget that this woman could manipulate shadows like a weapon, and that behind those warm eyes lay a mind that had formulated a plan that tricked hundreds of demons into destroying each other.

And her warm eyes also saw too much. Her smile dimmed when she drew in close, and Taylor wondered if the cracks were showing inside her, too.

"Are you feeling well, Taylor?"

"Fine." No need to worry her about Michael or the temple yet. For all of Rosalia's brilliance, for all that she could manipulate people and form devastatingly successful plans, she knew no more than Taylor about spells or how to free Michael from Hell. "Just one of those days."

Rosalia nodded as if accepting that explanation, but Taylor wasn't certain that the other woman wasn't on the verge of feeling her forehead for a fever, even though Guardians couldn't become sick. Rosalia had that way about her.

But she didn't pull out a thermometer. She only sighed and said, "I see."

She probably did see, and understood that Michael was at the root of it, even if she didn't know the specifics. Rosalia had witnessed the worst of Taylor's battle with Michael for control of her own body. Hell, Rosalia had *healed* from the worst of it, when Taylor, possessed by Michael, had stabbed the other Guardian through the chest.

Strange how that incident had resulted in a bond of friendship between them. But then, since becoming a Guardian, a whole lot of Taylor's life had become strange.

Strange was her new normal.

Though now that she thought about it, Rosalia being in Caelum wasn't normal, either. The Guardian didn't visit the realm very often, and usually only when meeting her friends. Neither Radha nor Mariko was here now, so that meant she'd probably come looking for Taylor. If so, now Rosalia was probably wondering if she'd come at a bad time.

"Did you need me for anything? It's not *that* bad of a day, if you are."

Smiling faintly, Rosalia stepped close enough to adjust Taylor's white shirt collar, then smooth her hands over Taylor's shoulders. Though she might have punched anyone else, Taylor allowed Rosalia this, too. The poor woman couldn't stand seeing someone that she cared about looking untidy—and in any case, Rosalia wasn't really paying attention to what her hands were doing. She'd gotten that look in her eyes that said: *A demon would be dying soon.*

"Do you remember Nicholas St. Croix?"

Taylor frowned. Did she? The name was familiar, but she couldn't recall a face.

Rosalia helped her out. "The dungeon in Rome."

Ah, yes. No wonder Taylor couldn't immediately remember. She'd spent half of her time in the dungeon watching a few hundred demons being slaughtered, and waiting for Michael to take over her body and save the humans stuck in the center of the massacre.

St. Croix had watched the massacre, too. He'd made being present for it a condition before allowing Rosalia use of the dungeon.

"Let me see if I remember," Taylor said. "Caucasian. Six-two, one-seventy, black-brown hair, and blue eyes that remind me of ice chips from the frozen field in Hell. A handsome devil of the *GQ* variety, and if I'm not mistaken, you thought he actually was a demon for a while."

"You're not mistaken. He's a straight-up bastard."

"Who you helped anyway."

"Yes, well. He was useful." Rosalia stepped back, and seemed satisfied with the straight line she'd made of Taylor's button-up front. "I think he's found his mother."

"Oh." Yes, Taylor recalled part of that, too. He'd bought the dungeon because he'd been searching for a demon who'd posed as his mother. Maybe after he'd had his revenge, he'd be less of a bastard. Taylor doubted it, though. "So is he headed to Rome, intending to lock her up and slay her?"

"I don't know. I lost him in London."

"Ah." Now the reason for Rosalia's journey to Caelum became clear. The Guardians' base of operations on Earth, Special Investigations, could help her locate St. Croix. "So you were looking for me, or you were headed to San Francisco?"

"I was headed to SI, but you might be able to make it all easier. Can you teleport to him?"

Taylor should have been able to. In the dungeon six months ago, his mind hadn't been well shielded, and she'd been able to sense his emotions. That made his psyche familiar to her, and she could teleport directly to anyone with a familiar, unshielded mind.

But apparently not St. Croix.

Rosalia grimaced. "I taught him how to block."

"And you taught him very well, apparently, because I can't go to him. I'll save you the trip to SI, though." Not much of a save, since "the trip" was only a single step through a Gate. "I'm headed there now. I'll let them know to start looking for him."

"I'm grateful, thank you. That will allow me to return to Rome. Hopefully he'll show up there."

"Do you think he will?"

"No. Partially because he trusts no one, but also because he knows that I'll look there for him." Rosalia smiled. "But he also knows that I know that he probably wouldn't use the dungeon, so he might go anyway."

It took Taylor a second to sort that out. "So twisty."

"He thinks like a demon at times. So I will, too." Rosalia

turned to go, then paused, her gaze sweeping over the courtyard. "It's so empty. I forget. I turn around, expecting to see everyone . . . but they are all gone."

"Not empty. I think Khavi's hellhound is running around somewhere." A pet as big as a Hummer, straight out of Hell and Taylor's nightmares. She avoided the three-headed puppy as much as possible. "And hopefully, I'll be called to make more of us soon. Well, maybe not 'hopefully,' considering that means someone has to die. But you know."

Rosalia gave her another of those long, seeing-too-much looks. "You are not feeling inadequate in that way, I hope? Because it is beyond your control, Taylor."

Yes, it was. That didn't mean Taylor didn't feel responsible. Along with the psychic connection, Michael had also passed to her the powers of the Doyen. She'd become the Guardian who transformed the humans who sacrificed themselves while saving someone else from a supernatural threat.

But Taylor hadn't been called, not in the year she'd been Doyen. Everyone told her that there had been times when a decade had passed before a new Guardian had been transformed . . . but those had also been the times when there had been thousands of Guardians to take up the slack. In five hundred years, the Gates to Hell would open, and the Guardian corps needed to be thousands strong again. They couldn't afford to have one month go by without adding a new warrior to their ranks, let alone twelve months.

There wouldn't have been any more transformed if Michael had still been Doyen, either. She knew that. The Guardians couldn't go out on a recruitment drive; everything depended on a human's sacrifice. Still, she did feel added pressure, because Michael was gone and the corps wasn't as strong without him. She *needed* to be transforming more Guardians. Their survival—every human's survival—might eventually depend on it.

"Let's just say that I know exactly how one of those old-time queens felt, when everyone was expecting her to produce an heir to the throne, and years go by without one. Pretty soon, you know she's going to get beheaded and he's going to find another woman to make the babies."

Amusement shone in Rosalia's eyes, a warm golden light. "I

remember a few queens like that. The clever ones solved the problem by inviting another man to their bed."

Oh, this metaphor was suddenly heading somewhere that Taylor definitely didn't want to go. Having Michael in her head was enough to become accustomed to, and she'd carefully *not* thought much about sex while he was in there. Mostly so that he wouldn't know that he figured prominently in those thoughts, but letting him see her imagining another man seemed just as bad.

"I don't think there's a good 'another man' that works as a comparison." The problem didn't come from Michael or any other Guardian. "The humans just need to stop shooting blanks."

Rosalia's soft laugh didn't echo in the courtyard. Strange, but Taylor's did.

And even more strange, when her laughter faded and Rosalia had gone, she glanced back at Michael's temple again . . . and the hairline cracks in the marble had vanished.

She just hoped to God that if her laugh had sealed them, that it had helped Michael a little, too.

On the plane, Ash waited until Nicholas occupied himself with his computer before looking through the few items he'd had of Rachel's. When they'd stopped outside his hotel, she'd waited in the car while he'd retrieved Rachel's passport and his luggage—and he'd brought down another small packet with them. He'd claimed the things had been in Rachel's overnight case along with her identification, but Ash could have deduced that for herself. The packet contained a flat hairbrush, a toothbrush, a red silk dress, and strappy sandals. Tucked beneath the clothing lay a set of lacy lingerie, red and revealing . . . exactly the kind a woman might take on a special weekend away with a lover.

They meant nothing special to Ash. The items weren't even familiar. Rachel had obviously loved the shoes; the soles were scuffed, as if she'd worn them often. But although Ash liked the style, she had no urge to wear them or the dress. Had Rachel been nervous while she'd been packing for her weekend, or had she been excited? Had she wavered over what to wear, how many outfits to take? Ash didn't know. She'd hoped to sense some connection to Rachel's things, but she felt nothing, even though Rachel had surely chosen these items for a reason.

Whatever her reasons, they'd been lost when she'd died six years ago.

Six years. Ash examined the items again, no longer looking for a connection but simply *looking.* Only a few wrinkles marred the smooth silk. No dust had collected on the hairbrush or the sandal straps. Instead of musty, the dress smelled faintly of dry cleaning.

These things hadn't been sitting in an overnight bag for six years. Nicholas had kept them *and* cared for them. Why?

She let the dress fall into her lap and looked up. Nicholas sat in the seat across from her, booking a hotel near Rachel's parents' home, finalizing their travel arrangements, or simply working—she wasn't certain. Ash hadn't paid much attention to him since he'd lowered his crossbow. He might be able to help her, but right now he had no idea who Ash was, so she had little use for him.

Little use for him *except* for his bank account. Now that she had identification, Ash could have eventually made her way to America, but his ability to place one phone call and charter a flight made the process much simpler. She appreciated that.

Ash also appreciated that he'd given her Rachel's things. He hadn't liked giving them up, however. He'd tossed the packet to her with an abrupt order to "see if these improve your memory."

She knew he traveled often. What were the chances that he just happened to keep Rachel's clothes in a hotel room in London? No, he must bring them along wherever he went.

Had he cared for Rachel so much that he couldn't let these items go? Were they simply a daily reminder of his reasons to pursue Madelyn, or a statement of his guilt?

Guilt, Ash guessed. *Kept alive by a dress and underwear—and a weekend getaway that Rachel never got to have.*

She supposed some people were driven by less.

Did it bother him that a demon touched Rachel's things now? Trying to determine his mood by studying his features proved a futile exercise. Was he aware of her scrutiny, or did he simply sit stone-faced all the time?

Ash waited for a crack in his expression, but it didn't come. And she'd never *tried* to sense someone's emotions before, but that proved futile, too. The door he'd erected still blocked Nicholas's emotions from her. The flight attendants' and the pilots' feelings filled her senses with their various and ever-changing flavors, but she couldn't taste Nicholas's at all.

Without looking up at her, he said, "Did you learn anything from those?"

Ash glanced at the dress and shoes. "Not about Rachel."

She'd only learned more about him. And though she had little use for Nicholas St. Croix aside from the money and information he might offer, that didn't mean she didn't find him . . . interesting.

Unlike her emotions, Ash's curiosity remained strong. Right now, Nicholas had piqued that curiosity. She wanted to know more—especially if learning about him told her more about Rachel.

"You seem to be a cold, vengeful, unfriendly sort of man, Nicholas."

"You noticed." His tone suggested boredom and his attention remained on his computer screen, but Ash suspected that he'd focused completely on her. "Will you tell me now that I shouldn't be obsessed with revenge?"

"Why would I care about that?" How strange. Whether he pursued revenge or not wasn't any business of hers, except that now she was bound to help him. Other than that, it didn't matter if he did. "I want to know more about Rachel. So I wondered if she liked you, even though you're not very likable."

He glanced up then, his gaze assessing—as if calculating his response, Ash realized. What would he come up with?

To her surprise, he came up with an answer. "No. She didn't like me, not at the beginning. Madelyn told her too much about me."

"Madelyn told her lies?"

"No, the truth. Madelyn told Rachel that I intended to destroy Wells-Down—and destroy *her*—in any way that I could."

"So you were just as bent on revenge before Rachel died as you are now," Ash observed. "And just as unlikable. But you changed Rachel's feelings toward you."

Icy amusement touched his mouth. "I can be charming."

Ash didn't doubt it. Though he was cold now, she thought Nicholas St. Croix could probably pretend to feel something when it was convenient. He'd know how to flatter a woman, to make her feel special. He'd calculate her every reaction, and add her response to a reservoir of data that he could use to further his agenda.

"She loved you."

Though the icy amusement didn't leave his expression, Ash sensed a hardening within him, as if he'd put another lock on the door separating her from his emotions. *That*, she thought, was his true response. He showed her one reaction, and although the hardness didn't feel any warmer than his amusement and she had no idea what lay beyond that barrier he'd erected, the very act of strengthening that barrier told her enough. Some deep emotion lay within him, and he felt a need to hide it from her.

"Yes," he said easily. "She did love me."

"I suppose she must have. The police report said she threw herself in front of you." That sounded like love—a rather dramatic, soap-opera sort of love, at least. Ash had her doubts. "What really happened? Who really fired the gun? You said that Rachel blocked Madelyn's shot—but I can't believe Madelyn tried to shoot you. It would break the Rules."

His eyes narrowed. "You think I lied about not killing Rachel?"

"Yes." Ash could almost feel Madelyn's strong fingers digging into her arms, shaking her. *Don't break the Rules. Don't!* "Madelyn warned me not to kill anyone. It's one of the few things I remember from before Nightingale House. So I can't believe that she'd be foolish enough to shoot you."

"I see." He gave her that assessing stare again before abruptly continuing, "Madelyn didn't break the Rules when she fired the gun. I gave her permission to shoot me."

What? Ash hadn't expected that. Astonishment leapt through her, new and intriguing. But as much as she wanted to concentrate on the feeling, his admission proved more fascinating.

"You *told* Madelyn to kill you? Why would you do that?"

"When I swung by Madelyn's house that evening to pick her up after work, Rachel invited me in. Madelyn was still in the office upstairs."

"Did you know Madelyn was there, too?"

His thin smile could have been a yes or a no, and Ash couldn't decide which was more likely: She believed that Nicholas would have relished the confrontation with Madelyn, and she believed that Nicholas hated his mother enough that he wouldn't have entered the house if he'd known she was there.

In the end, she supposed it didn't matter. He'd gone in.

"Madelyn and I argued, of course." He said it casually, setting aside his computer and sitting back, as if settling in for a comfortable chat. "Madelyn drew a gun from her desk, and I told her: *Shoot me, then. You've wanted to get rid of me for twenty years. So do it.* She did, but Rachel got in between. Then they disappeared."

So he *had* given permission. But why? He'd been determined to destroy Madelyn, not himself.

"You didn't think she'd really do it," Ash guessed.

"No, I didn't. Pulling out that gun seemed like a rash, hysterical move, but Madelyn isn't impulsive—everything she does is calculated. She'd lose her company if she murdered me, and Madelyn wouldn't risk that. So I assumed she only meant to frighten me."

"So you egged her on."

"Yes. *Now* I know that a demon wouldn't resist a free pass to kill a human. Getting rid of the evidence would be easy—and it would have been her word against Rachel's."

But Rachel had thrown herself between them, instead. Sacrificing herself wouldn't have been the same as giving Madelyn permission to kill her—and so Madelyn had still broken the Rules, Ash realized. Was that why they'd disappeared?

"What are the consequences if a demon kills a human?"

"The consequences before the portals to Hell were closed, or the consequences now?"

"What portals to Hell?"

As if her question frustrated him, his jaw clenched. "The Gates between Earth and Hell," he said. "They closed three years ago."

After Madelyn had shot Rachel and broken the Rules. "So what should have happened to Madelyn six years ago?"

"She'd have been either punished in Hell or killed."

"And now? What if *I* deny a human's free will?"

"Are you planning on doing that?" He must have thought she wouldn't; he didn't wait for her answer. "With the Gates shut, you can't be taken back to Hell, so Rosalia and her partner would hunt you down. They'd have a psychic lock on you as soon as you broke the Rules, and they wouldn't stop until you were dead."

Punished or dead. With those as her only options, it was best just to heed Madelyn's warning, and not break the Rules.

Not that Ash felt a particular urge to break them, anyway. Strange, wasn't that? As a demon, shouldn't she be plotting how to kill or maim him?

At the very least, shouldn't she be trying to make him cry?

What would a demon do? Ash couldn't answer that. Nicholas didn't seem to subscribe to the "demons are rebels with a cause" interpretation that she remembered from several books and movies, so she must be the "utterly evil and corrupt" variety. But if that were so, shouldn't every step she took and word she spoke all be designed to bring about Nicholas's eventual destruction? Shouldn't it be instinctive?

Or was Nicholas completely wrong about demons?

She frowned at him. "If I'm a demon, why aren't I plotting your downfall?"

"Because we have a bargain," he said. "If you don't help me, you're screwed."

"But why aren't I already making plans for *after* we fulfill our parts of the bargain?" If Ash could have been disappointed in herself, she would have been. She obviously suffered from a severe lack of initiative. "I must be a shortsighted demon."

"Good." A spark of genuine humor seemed to flash across his expression before he added, "But I'll assume that you're only saying that to mislead me."

"To lure you into complacency?"

No doubt of his amusement now. He smiled, just a tilt at the corners of his lips, but it didn't seem cold at all.

"Yes," he said.

So, a demon misled men to make them feel safe. She'd have to use that tactic after she recalled *how* to be a demon.

How did her amnesia fit, anyway? "Do you suppose my memory loss is part of an elaborate demonic scheme?"

"Yes," he said—still smiling, but Ash could see that he meant it. "I'd have to be an idiot to believe that everything a demon said and did wasn't designed to fulfill some other motive."

"I must be an idiot demon, not to have some other motive."

Nicholas arched a brow, as if in silent agreement that she

might be an idiot. Ash arched hers in response, and felt her mouth curve. Smiling, if only a little.

Oh. She knew this emotion: amusement. A pleasant feeling, really, even when it seemed so thin and light.

Nicholas's gaze fell to her lips, then to the dress on her lap. His expression cooled again, leaving a smile that wasn't pleasant at all.

"Leave those things on the plane. The dress, the shoes. I'll arrange for their return to the hotel in London."

"Why?" Didn't he travel with them?

"They aren't Rachel's." He met her eyes, and she saw the satisfaction in his gaze, as if he'd just proven something. Whether he was proving it to her or to himself, she couldn't guess. "I took them from a rack of luggage in the elevator."

He'd stolen someone's clothes? How fascinating. What made Nicholas St. Croix break a basic human law?

And did the theft mean everything Ash thought she'd learned about him was wrong? *Guilt, driven by a dress and underwear.* But that didn't fit now, did it? Did he even have anything of Rachel's aside from the passport, or had he tossed it all six years ago?

"Why?" she asked.

"Do you truly think I'd give a demon anything of hers?"

"I obviously shouldn't have," Ash said. The passport had seemed to legitimize the other items. He hadn't faked or stolen that. "Why give me the identification?"

"You needed the passport to board the flight. It was necessary. I'd never have given you anything of Rachel's for any other reason."

That didn't surprise her. She wondered, "So you do have more of her things?"

"Yes." He lifted his computer again and focused on the screen, effectively dismissing her. "But they're not for you to ever touch."

Because he'd cared for Rachel and hated demons, Nicholas would apparently break human laws while seeking his revenge . . . or just to play a game on a demon who'd lost her memory.

Well, now. Ash's smile widened. That was *so* much more interesting than guilt.

CHAPTER 4

Nicholas ignored her for the remainder of the flight, but Ash didn't mind. She passed the time watching the attendants; one of them hated the other two, yet spent hours pretending that she didn't. Why the hatred? Ash didn't care enough to ask. Simply observing the attendant proved to be an intriguing study: The woman concealed her feelings, yet so desperately wanted the others to know how she felt.

The others weren't completely blind to it. Unease and uncertainty coated Ash's tongue in their vinegary flavors when a smile became too brittle, a laugh sounded too shrill, or a gesture appeared too abrupt.

Yet each time, the other attendants shrugged their unease away. Why? Didn't they trust their perception? Or was it just simpler to pretend they didn't notice?

Whatever their reasons, people were endlessly fascinating, Ash decided. And the man across her probably only seemed all the more fascinating because she couldn't read him as easily. Perhaps, unlike humans, demons didn't like everything to be simple.

Perhaps it was only Ash who didn't.

She turned her attention to Nicholas again, trying to sense beyond his emotional barriers. Did he have to consciously maintain those after erecting them? She waited, but they held strong—only cracking once, when the plane shook through a spat of turbulence.

Even then, she barely sensed anything from him other than mild surprise, followed by expectation. No fear. No dread. He only met her eyes and said, "If it's Rosalia, I hope that you'll catch me."

Rosalia, the woman he'd spoken to on the phone earlier—the one he'd called a Guardian. Did he truly think she'd attack a plane, or was he playing with the amnesiac demon again?

Ash decided that he was jerking her chain when he told her, "Or it could be a dragon."

Sure. Ash gave him a disbelieving look. He smiled that unpleasant little smile and resumed his work. By the time one of the flight attendants came over to assure them that the turbulence would pass soon, the cracks in his emotional barriers had closed again.

But the cracks *had* been there. His expectation had been real. And he *had* said something about demons having wings. Guardians might, too.

Did Ash have wings? She hoped so.

Ash didn't know if she'd bother to catch Nicholas St. Croix, though.

Fortunately for him, he never needed her to. The plane landed without incident in New York shortly afterward. Ash pretended to be Rachel through customs, where, despite the story she'd prepared in anticipation of questions about Rachel's disappearance, the officer spent more time reminding Ash to update her passport photo to include her tattoos than asking about the years she'd spent in England. After they verified her status as a U.S. citizen, she followed Nicholas to their waiting rental, a black luxury SUV.

Outside the terminal, the air hit Ash with an icy blast to her face, far colder than London had been. She gritted her teeth and shoved her hands into her pockets, only to yank them out again when Nicholas tossed the SUV's key fob at her. She caught it and stared at him over the hood of the vehicle.

He moved to the passenger door. "You know how to drive?"

"Yes," she responded automatically. But did she know how to?

She supposed they'd soon find out. He got in, and after she

climbed into the driver's side—yes, all the controls and pedals felt familiar—he reclined his seat and closed his eyes.

"You don't need sleep. I do. So you drive."

So he knew Ash didn't need sleep. How much more did he know but hadn't yet told her? Maybe she'd catch him, after all.

And she had to admit, he did look tired. Nicholas St. Croix couldn't conceal *everything* he felt. Shadows darkened his eyes and stubble roughened his jaw. Though it was only just past midnight in New York, given the time change, he'd essentially remained awake until dawn.

"All right." Ash turned the key. With a few beeps and chimes, the dashboard computer started up.

The screen had a map. She *didn't* know how to use that.

"Where do I go?"

"West on Interstate 80, then north to Minnesota. We'll stop in Duluth before we head up to her parents' house."

It would take a full day to drive that distance. "Why not just fly there?"

Nicholas opened his eyes and scanned her expression, as if to determine whether she was serious. He must have realized she was. Tiredly, he scrubbed his hand over his face and closed his eyes again.

"Why not just e-mail our destination to the Guardians and save them the trouble of *trying* to find us?"

Ah, yes. The Guardians. He hadn't had time to tell her about them before, but they had twelve hundred miles to kill now—and a tired man could still talk.

She checked traffic and pulled out into the lane. "So who are the Guardians?"

"Warriors with angelic powers. They were all human once, but they were transformed after sacrificing themselves to save someone else. I don't know the full story—I just know what matters: Guardians kill demons."

Oh, fun. They sounded almost as likable as Nicholas. "I can't wait to meet one," Ash said dryly.

A low, rough sound made her glance over. Was that a laugh? She hoped he hadn't hurt himself.

He caught her look. The laugh receded into a wry nod of acknowledgment. "I'm tired."

"I'll remember that exhaustion makes you more vulnerable." Just like a good demon would, surely. "So, Guardians kill demons. Why?"

"Because you're determined to destroy everything human."

Ash shook her head. "But I'm *not.* I don't recognize anything of myself in that description."

"Your memory—"

"That doesn't mean anything. I don't remember learning to drive, either. But some things *feel* familiar—and destroying humanity doesn't."

He rubbed his face again. "Look. This is what I know: Demons are evil. You *were* angels, but you rebelled, went to war in Heaven, and got your heads smashed in by the good angels. After that, you were transformed into demons and thrown into Hell. Now you all fuck with human souls, trying to damn us to the Pit, and follow Lucifer."

Lucifer.

Memory surfaced, hot and sharp as a blade. A dark figure. Raging pain. *I name you Ash—*

Then he'd ripped her apart. *Lucifer* had ripped her apart.

Terror closed her throat. She *remembered* that. His horrible voice. Ah, God, she could almost hear it now. Shredding everything she was, everything she'd been.

A scream clawed inside her chest. She bit it back, suppressing the tremors, her hands clenching on the steering wheel.

"Does it sound more familiar now?"

Nicholas's voice dragged her out of the memory. She glanced over and found him watching her, his eyes tired, but just as sharp.

Ash struggled for breath to reply. It took several tries. Finally, she admitted, "A little."

The Special Investigations warehouse in San Francisco housed their official law enforcement offices and less-official novice training quarters. Though Guardians *could* travel directly from Caelum using a Gate that led into the hall near the gymnasium, most of them avoided it—which was probably why Rosalia hadn't used it, either. The Gate had been created after a Guardian had sacrificed herself to save one of the novices a year ago; her death was too fresh for most of the Guardians here, and using the Gate seemed to trample on her memory.

Fortunately, Michael still allowed Taylor to teleport to Special Investigations—and if not for Michael, she'd have likely been living at the warehouse full-time, along with the other novices. Taylor could fight, she could shoot, but her skills were nothing against the abilities and speed of a demon . . . until Michael took over.

As frustrating as that was, Taylor had to be grateful for it, too. She'd have gone mad, cooped up in the warehouse instead of working in the field. Most Guardians had trained for a hundred years before they'd been allowed to fight a demon. Now, because they were so strapped for manpower, a Guardian might start working after only four or five decades of training, but that was still too long to wait.

So Taylor trained herself in the basic Guardian stuff like flying, shape-shifting, and weapons—she didn't always want to rely on Michael—but she worked, too. Her job tracking down demons wasn't much different than the one she'd had as an inspector in the San Francisco Police Department. She just lied a lot more, had a worldwide jurisdiction, covered up evidence instead of unearthing it, and when she located a demon, she tossed away anything resembling a fair trial and went straight to capital punishment.

All of that had gone against the grain when she'd begun, but the more demons she met, the more she saw the necessity of it. Demons didn't play by manmade rules; they played *with* them. So Guardians did the same. The difference was, Guardians tried not to hurt anyone while they did it.

Which, when it came down to it, was really the same as the spirit of human laws: Try not to fuck other people over or hurt anyone. If you do, you pay for it.

Simple, really.

Taylor mentally swept the building as soon as she teleported into the large hub at the heart of the warehouse—a habit she'd picked up from Michael, but now, apparently, she did on her own. Since the sun was up, no vampires were working, though she sensed a few sleeping upstairs. Most of the Guardians' minds were shielded, but a few sent a little mental probe in return; since they couldn't actually send thoughts, only project emotions and images, that psychic touch was the equivalent of a *Hello*.

A little disappointed that she couldn't sense Joe Preston, her former partner on the force and now a human working for SI in almost the same capacity that she did, Taylor headed for the director's offices, instead. She missed Joe, though she understood why they weren't paired up on assignments; Michael or not, it would be like putting two novices together. Maybe when she had a few more years under her belt . . .

Of course, in a few more years, Joe would hit retiring age. God, that was crazy to think about. Something that she didn't *want* to think about. Taylor knew she was lucky—a hundred years of training meant that most Guardian novices never saw their family and friends again—but she didn't know how well she'd take immortality when she saw her mother, her partner, and her brother aging themselves to death.

Maybe Michael could help her deal with that, too. He'd seen hundreds of human generations grow old and die.

Aaaaaand, no. That thought didn't help at all.

Shaking away the morbidity of it, Taylor rapped on the director's office door.

Her hope that a male voice would answer was dashed when Lilith called for her to enter. Crap. Taylor got along a little better with Hugh Castleford, a former Guardian who now shared the office with Lilith and served as a codirector when he wasn't training the novices. This obviously wasn't one of those times.

Lilith sat behind her big desk, and didn't glance up from her computer when Taylor came in. She must have had an outside meeting today. Instead of the leather pants and corset that Lilith usually wore, she appeared as she had the first time Taylor had met her: in a severely cut pantsuit, with her long black hair in a tight roll at her nape, and the bulge of her weapon just visible beneath her jacket.

Lilith had been an FBI agent then, and she'd deliberately fucked one of Taylor and Joe's murder investigations into a humping, unrecognizable mess.

Taylor still couldn't bring herself to like the woman, though she'd grudgingly come to respect her. Two thousand years old, Lilith had once been a demon halfling—a human who'd been given a demon's powers through a sick ritual of symbols carved into flesh, bloodletting, and a vow to serve Lucifer. Almost every halfling disappointed him, however, and so they'd all ended up in the frozen field . . . all of them except for Lilith. A master of lies and self-preservation, she'd outlasted the others—and eventually lied well enough that she'd tricked Lucifer into releasing her from her vow to obey him, and won a wager that led to the Gates of Hell closing for five hundred years.

She'd paid for it, though. Her demon powers had been stripped away and she'd become human again. Though the two thousand years had left its mark on Lilith, leaving her as strong and as fast as a vampire, she wasn't immortal anymore. She couldn't fly; she couldn't shape-shift.

She could still lie like the devil, though.

Despite that, Michael had trusted her enough to put her in charge of Special Investigations' operations—and Taylor couldn't fault his decision. Those two thousand years as a demon meant that Lilith knew their methods better than anyone else on Earth. When an assignment popped up and Lilith gave her opinion about the demon Taylor would be looking for and the places she'd probably find him, Taylor shut up and listened.

"Perfect timing," Lilith said. "I just got a ping from the novices trolling local police reports. A double murder. Apparently, the guy already confessed."

"But?" There was always a but.

"He said that the ghost of a dead girlfriend visited him, encouraging him to seek vengeance."

Probably not a ghost. Either the guy was delusional, or he'd been visited by a very solid, shape-shifted demon having a bit of fun with someone who'd been easy to take advantage of.

"I'll take a look," Taylor said. "Who am I taking with me?"

Lilith's mouth twisted a bit. "It's Marc Revoire's territory."

The Midwest, which wasn't exactly a thrill, but the expression on Lilith's face made it a little better. Though a Guardian, Revoire didn't take his assignments through SI, but he might know exactly who the demon was, and be in the process of hunting him down. Everyone understood that barreling into another Guardian's investigation might bungle the whole thing and let a demon slip away. So although Lilith would have probably liked to flip Revoire the bird and send a team from SI to handle the double murder, she was forced to play nice, Guardian-style.

Taylor didn't mind working with Revoire, anyway. She'd met him before in Caelum, shortly after she'd come out of the three-month coma following Michael's kiss, her transformation, and the link that had formed between them. Brooding and dark, with a hint of France in his voice, Revoire struck her as a solitary, silent type. He'd asked Taylor whether there was anything he could do for her and to let him know if there ever was, and then left to talk to Irena, who'd taken over as Guardian leader in Michael's absence.

Taylor hadn't seen him since, but she heard mention of him now and again—though the other Guardians referred to him as *Icarus* rather than his name. Why, Taylor didn't know, but after watching a few novices in their disastrous early flight attempts, she assumed that something similar had happened to him in his early years, and the nickname had stuck . . . for more than a hundred and fifty years.

Considering that it had taken ten years on the force and a promotion to inspector before the other rookies in her year stopped calling her *Red*, Taylor had sympathy for him.

"I'll contact him now," she said. "I also ran into Rosalia. She thinks that Nicholas St. Croix picked up a demon, but he's gone under."

"St. Croix?" Lilith's brows arched, her earlier irritation smoothing away. She turned back to her computer. "We're already keeping tabs. We have been since he consulted for Legion Labs. Handsome, rich, and working with a demon-run corporation? It was too easy. Now we know he was just searching for his mother, but at the time, he looked good for being a demon himself."

"Rosalia thinks he still looks good for it."

"We can't kill every asshole. Who would raise all of the asshole children?" Lilith narrowed her eyes at the computer. "And look at this. The asshole just landed in New York. No reservations or rentals yet, but if something pops, I'll send it through to you."

That surprised her. "Me?"

"You brought this to me. It's yours unless you want to pass it on."

"I don't," Taylor said. She really didn't.

"All right. If you're still with Revoire when the info comes, take him with you. Otherwise, I'll send someone to meet you in New York."

Suddenly rocking back in her chair, Lilith fixed a stare on Taylor's face, looking deep, and nothing like Rosalia's warm perusal. Lilith's gaze flayed—not skin and flesh, but the shields Taylor wore.

God damn her. Lilith didn't have psychic powers anymore, but she didn't need them. Two thousand years had told her how to read a woman's face, to pick out every uncertainty and fear—and right now, Taylor carried too many of them.

But the former demon only said, "Do you want Sir Pup to come with you?"

Lilith's hellhound. The mere sight of the three-headed beast could terrify a demon and there was little on Earth that could hurt it. If Michael's absence from her mind meant that he couldn't protect her, Sir Pup was more than an adequate replacement for the job.

Except the hellhound terrified Taylor, too.

"I'll have Revoire with me," she said.

Lilith's gaze sharpened. "And Michael?"

Of course she'd zero in on what Taylor hadn't said. Sooner or later, demons always found a weak spot.

"If we find this guy's ghost, I guess we'll find out," Taylor said.

CHAPTER 5

A steady vibration in Nicholas's pocket woke him. A text message. Not the kind of buzz a man hoped to wake up to, but it'd been a while since anything more exciting had been in his pants.

Vaguely aware of the wipers swooping across the windshield and the faint, static-filled country-western music coming from the speakers, he dug out his mobile and angled the screen away from the demon in the driver's seat. Nicholas kept several private investigators in his employ; his London PI, Reginald Cooper, had begun verifying the demon's story that morning. Nicholas had been expecting the investigator's initial report, but unless the man confirmed that the demon had been lying or Cooper ran into something unexpected while digging around, the report should have come via e-mail.

A text meant that Cooper must have unearthed a lie. *Goddammit.* Had the demon already broken the bargain? If so, that made her useless to him, and relieved Nicholas of his part in their agreement. He ought to just slay her now.

But he couldn't kill her while she drove on the highway, not without risking a wreck. And God knew how he'd explain a demon's decapitated body to the authorities. He'd have to wait until he could paralyze her with hellhound venom, and either leave her behind—alive—or make certain her body was never found. His plan already forming, Nicholas skimmed Cooper's message, picking up the words that anyone who'd ever met a demon might have expected: suicide, unusual circumstances, no warning, Cawthorne— Wait. *What the hell?*

Thoughts of slaying the demon vanished. Nicholas reread the message and let the meaning sink in. This *wasn't* what he'd expected. Cooper hadn't uncovered a demon's lie, but damn *good* news.

Three weeks ago, Dr. Ian Cawthorne had hanged himself in his office.

Bemused, Nicholas read the text again. So the crooked old bastard had finally done himself in. Nicholas couldn't be sorry. Given the chance, he'd have tied Cawthorne's noose himself. Twenty-five years ago, at Madelyn's urging, Nicholas's father had sought help from Cawthorne. After "treating" Nicholas's father for symptoms of delusional paranoia—all the result of Madelyn's shape-shifting tricks and lying tongue—the shrink had testified against his character, had taken away his pride, had ruined his business and his life.

Had Cawthorne been treating this demon at Nightingale House? Nicholas wouldn't ask her. He wouldn't ask until he knew more—until he knew whether her answers were lies.

Cooper hadn't been able to confirm the demon's story yet. Although his investigator had spoken to several nurses and administrators, they'd blocked him by citing patient confidentiality. Two nurses had recently quit their positions at Nightingale House, however, and the investigator planned to track them down.

Good enough. With enough money greasing palms, someone would talk—and Nicholas would have more answers.

He texted a reply and slid the phone back into his pocket, considering this new information. Cawthorne had killed himself three weeks ago. The same amount of time had passed since someone had first entered Madelyn's house, using her code and tipping Nicholas off to her presence. Considering the timing, he couldn't believe Cawthorne's suicide was a coincidence.

With demons involved, Nicholas couldn't be certain of anything—but two distinct possibilities seemed likelier than any other.

The first was that the demon had lied about her amnesia and

about escaping Nightingale House. That she'd lied about everything so far, despite the bargain.

That was the simplest possibility. Given any other circumstance, Nicholas would have calculated it as the likeliest. But *simplest* didn't fit any demon's scheme or methods, and didn't account for the lengths every demon would go to avoid breaking a bargain.

So the second, more probable scenario was that Madelyn had somehow escaped punishment in Hell. Then, for some unknown reason, this demon's memories had been stripped and Madelyn had left her in Cawthorne's care. God knew how long the man had been in Madelyn's pocket—twenty-five years, at least. Compared to destroying a good man's life and reputation, caring for a demon with amnesia amounted to little trouble . . . until the demon had escaped. Then Madelyn had returned to London and exacted payment for Cawthorne's failure.

Was Madelyn looking for this demon now?

If so, that suited Nicholas perfectly. When Madelyn caught up to the demon, she'd also find Nicholas—and he had a payment to exact from her, too.

He couldn't fucking wait.

Fully awake now, Nicholas levered the seat up and faced a wall of white. Sometime between the last stop for gas and the PI's message vibrating in his pants, they'd driven into a snowstorm. Fat flakes whipped past the windows, piling in a thick blanket on the windshield almost as quickly as the wipers shoved them away. He couldn't see a damn thing.

"Where are we?"

"Smack dab in the middle of BFE." Without taking her eyes off the road, the demon jabbed the "seek" button on the radio console. "We just passed into Indiana."

He checked the clock. A few past nine. He'd slept longer than planned, but they were also making good time despite the snow. A glance at the speedometer showed him why—and sent his stomach into a dive.

Christ. A demon's vision rivaled a hawk's, but a whiteout was a goddamn whiteout. "Can you see anything through this shit?"

"Not really. I can hear other engines, though, and can tell how far away they are and the direction they're in. Once I got used to that, it's almost like seeing." She flicked the blinker and angled smoothly into the left lane. A few seconds later, they passed a small hatchback crawling along like a bug. "The road isn't bad yet, but we'll need chains if this keeps up."

"I'll buy some when we stop for gas," Nicholas said.

"That'll need to be soon." The scanning radio stopped on another static-filled country station. Maybe the same one. The demon pressed "seek" again. "The two times we stopped for gas, you paid in cash. There's really no reason for that except you don't want the Guardian finding us. But if someone wanted to, they could track you through your phone."

Not so easily. He'd also used cash to buy a prepaid mobile, and only Cooper had the number. The Guardians *would* find him, eventually. No doubt of that. He just had to stay ahead of them, and so he'd taken steps to slow them down: renting the SUV under a false identification, and using yet another name to reserve a hotel suite in Duluth.

He wouldn't tell the demon that. "So you have no memory, you've only been out of Nightingale for a month, yet you know about tracking phones?"

"I watched a lot of television there. Cop shows."

"Violent television in a mental hospital. Brilliant."

"It's what I wanted to watch. The nurses let me alone to do it."

Yeah, Nicholas bet they'd let her alone. A demon was low maintenance. No need to sleep, eat, bathe—or piss. Jesus, he hoped they came across a gas station soon.

As for the phone . . . *Hell.* Nicholas wanted Madelyn to find them. He didn't want the Guardians getting there first—and there was nothing that Cooper could tell him now that couldn't wait. He pulled out his mobile, powered it down.

"Thank you," she said, surprising him. "I don't look forward to being killed on sight."

By the Guardians. Would Madelyn kill her, too? Nicholas didn't think so. Madelyn wouldn't have left the demon at Nightingale House unless she had some use for her. Considering the demon's resemblance to Rachel, that use probably involved some scheme to tear Nicholas's heart out.

If this demon didn't slay him through song first. She jabbed the radio button again, and the dial scanned through the frequencies before coming back to the same station. It must have been pissing her off. Her gaze actually left the road long enough for her to cast a deadly stare at the console.

Hell, any more force in those jabs, and she might stab her finger through it. "You don't like country?"

Rachel had. She'd often joked that she was the only woman in England who had Martina McBride sitting next to Marilyn Manson in her music collection.

"Like? That doesn't matter. Only 'familiar' does—and I don't know this song."

"You knew the others that have been playing?"

"Yes. Most of them. And when I didn't, I could find another station playing something else that I knew." Her eyes began to glow faintly red. "I can't find anything now."

"But you *remember* the music."

"As soon as I hear it, yes. I didn't know it before that—or didn't know that I knew it. But as soon as the song starts, I remember the lyrics, the singer. And I don't forget again." She pressed "seek" again, this time with less force. "But sometimes, it's more than just knowing the words. Some songs, it's like there's *more* there, some other memory attached, and I can almost . . . touch it."

All right. Nicholas understood that. He couldn't hear the Rolling Stones without remembering his mother dancing in the kitchen. Not Madelyn, but his mother. After the demon had wormed her way into their family, it had been all classical, all the time—to soothe his father's nerves, she'd said. Now, Nicholas recognized a thousand changes that she'd wrought when she'd taken his mother's place, claiming that everything she'd done had been to *help* his father. The demon bitch.

The Stones sure as hell couldn't tell him where his mother's body lay now. "You've spent the whole night listening for familiar songs?"

The crimson faded from her eyes. "Yes."

Strange. He didn't know what to make of that—or of her. Her every response seemed wiped of any emotion, yet she was actively searching for those connections?

"I should have spent the night plotting against you, I know," she added.

He laughed, damn it.

The demon didn't even crack a smile. Peering ahead through

the snow, she said, "The road sign says gas and food at the next exit. I know you're hungry."

Had she been listening to his stomach? "Not hungry enough to eat the shit they pass through a drive-up window."

He'd spent the past few years training—learning to fight, making himself strong, preparing himself to face Madelyn. Now wasn't the time to start shoving crap into his body.

"Maybe we can find a grocery. Or if you can hang on a few hours, there's an all-organic diner at a truck stop north of Chicago that serves—" She cut herself off. Her mouth remained open, as if in surprise. When she continued, her voice barely rose above a whisper. "Great omelets. They serve great omelets. And before you ask, I don't know how I know that."

Nicholas hadn't been going to ask. He was too damn unsettled. This demon *wasn't* Rachel . . . but he'd heard about that diner before.

The demon stared ahead. "This part of the highway isn't familiar, but I can almost picture the road from Chicago to Duluth, the same way I can remember a scene from a book or a movie after I think about it. But I don't remember *being* there. And no, I can't explain it."

Nicholas couldn't, either—at least, he couldn't explain why this demon would know that stretch of highway. He knew why Rachel would, though.

"Rachel finished her masters' degree at The Kellogg School," he said. "She drove back to her parents' house during breaks, on some weekends."

"Oh." That was all she said for several seconds. Then, "Kellogg has a good program. One of the best in the country."

Frustration exploded through him. That was her response? About a fucking business school? And how the hell did she know *that*?

"You remember the school's goddamn ranking?"

She didn't seem to feel the blast of his anger. "Some facts are easy to recall. Other things are familiar, but I don't realize they are until I think about them . . . and now I'm finding out that Rachel was familiar with them, too."

"You're *not* Rachel."

"I know. Oh—and *this* one is familiar. 'Friends in Low Places.'" Her gaze flicked to the radio. Unable to hear the music over the wipers and the static, Nicholas took her word for it. "I only mentioned Kellogg's rankings because it meant that Rachel had to be good enough to qualify for the graduate program. Was she?"

More than good enough. She'd had a killer instinct for the market, choosing when and where to invest. At the beginning of her senior year of high school, her parents had given her a gift of five hundred dollars. Four years later, Rachel had paid off their new mortgage with it, and, after local papers had run with the story, gained the attention of several financial schools—and Madelyn's interest.

"She was good," he only said.

The demon glanced at him, as if trying to gauge his expression. "Do you mean that, or are you damning her with faint praise?"

He sure as hell wasn't going to damn Rachel with anything. "She was brilliant."

"Coming from Stone Cold St. Croix, that's a powerful endorsement."

Stone Cold St. Croix. He'd earned that name buying up businesses, tearing them apart, and selling the pieces—all so that he could eventually get to Madelyn. No one would have used the nickname outside of financial circles, however. She wouldn't have found it in a news article.

"Is that nickname a fact you conveniently remember, too?"

"No. I found it on an old blog entry through Google about a week ago. I also took a look at Reticle. It's been faltering without you at the head. It's not nearly as strong as it was six years ago."

Not true. His company's profits weren't increasing as quickly as they once had been, but he'd left Reticle in capable hands that were guiding it along in a steady climb. And as far as Nicholas was concerned, if he had money to pursue his revenge, it was strong enough. "You read that, too? 'Not nearly as strong'?"

"I didn't need to read it. I saw the numbers. They were easy to interpret."

She glanced over again—but not at him. After checking the lane, she eased into the exit. Her gaze never touched his face, as if his reaction to her declaration didn't matter.

But this was exactly what a demon did. Sow doubts. Quietly

undermine. Perhaps plant the seeds that would lead him to abandon revenge and return to business. Not a fucking chance. He enjoyed working, but that didn't matter. His business enabled his revenge. Until he destroyed Madelyn, he had no use for his company except the money it provided him.

She didn't wait for him to say so. "If Rachel was that good, why was she only Madelyn's personal assistant?"

Because Madelyn had tricked her, too. "Maybe because she traveled often and made a six-figure salary."

"That's nothing compared to what she could have made on Wall Street."

"Few on Wall Street make as much as Madelyn's protégée eventually would."

"She was being groomed as Madelyn's replacement?"

"That's what she let Rachel think." Hell, that was what Nicholas had believed, too. Now, he thought differently. "But I'd bet it was the opposite: Madelyn intended to take Rachel's place."

"By shape-shifting and pretending to be her? Why?"

"Someone would eventually notice that Madelyn didn't look her age—and she's too vain to appear as old as she should. But Rachel was gorgeous, young."

As his mother had once been. How many women's lives had Madelyn stolen in the same way? Waiting for her opportunity, then stepping into their shoes.

"You obviously thought the same," the demon said. "Rachel was gorgeous, young—and so you got close to her. To find out Madelyn's secrets, or just to steal her protégée away?"

He hadn't needed Rachel to know how to destroy Wells-Down, but luring her away from Madelyn would have been a bonus. Rachel had been loyal, however.

"Maybe I intended to do both," he lied easily.

"But you fell in love with her, instead."

This lie twisted like a knife in his gut. "Yes."

"I don't think so." The SUV skidded at the end of the exit. The demon tapped the brakes until they came to a stop at the sign. "That wasn't what I sensed from you when we met in the town house."

"And a demon knows what love feels like?"

"I spent a month walking through London. I've *felt* love. Strong, weak. Between friends, between children and parents, between lovers of all stages—even those who were grieving. You *did* feel grief, though. So you must have cared for her. It just wasn't love."

She was right. But it pissed him off, knowing that she'd looked into him. "You don't know what the fuck you're talking about."

With a shrug, she drove forward again. The snow had let up a bit, enough for Nicholas to make out the gas station signs rising along each side of the road.

"Kissing you felt familiar, too," she said.

Goddammit. He'd kissed this demon *once,* less than fifteen hours ago, and only so that he could get close enough to electrocute her. There had been nothing for her to be familiar with or remember. So what was she trying to say now? "You're not Rachel."

"As I've told you. Several times."

"And you've also said you don't know who the hell you are. Yet here you are, so bloody *familiar* with Rachel's life. Are you trying to convince yourself or me?"

"I'm convincing no one." She pulled into a full-service bay and stopped beside the gas pumps. "*You* are supposed to be helping me figure out who I am. *I* am trying to give you as much information as possible, so that you can hold up your side of the bargain. Remember?"

She snapped off the last word between teeth that had sharpened to points. So he'd gotten to her, pissed her off, too. Knowing that soothed some of his own anger.

"I remember. And you've got fangs now. "

Her gaze snapped to the rearview mirror. She bared her teeth at her reflection. Her eyes widened.

Surprised? Not as much as the guy who pumped their gas would be. "You'd probably better get rid of those before the station attendant posts on Twitter about it. I'm sure the Guardians watch for that kind of thing."

"Oh." Her hand flew up to cover her mouth. "Thanks."

God. Why did she have to do that? He'd always found it difficult to be a bastard when someone was polite in return. Even, apparently, if that someone was a demon.

A demon. He hadn't thought of her in any other way. But she hadn't gone three years in a hospital without being given a name.

"So you don't know who you are," he said. "But I can't call you 'demon' in public—and I *won't* call you Rachel. What should it be?"

"Ash." She lowered her hand and tested the shape of her teeth with the tip of her tongue. Human again. No fangs. "My name begins with 'Ash.' I don't know the rest of it."

"Ashley?"

She looked heavenward, as if searching for patience—or guidance. An odd place for a demon to look. "Why do people assume that I'm too stupid to search through a baby name book?"

"A *demon* baby name book?"

She narrowed her eyes at him, but he sensed the anger that had forged her teeth into points had already passed. Unlike his anger, however, the emotion hadn't turned to amusement. It had simply faded to nothing.

"I'll look for one," she said, and turned to speak to the attendant when he appeared at her window.

Nicholas reached into the backseat for his coat. But although nature called, he waited before opening the door, studying her. *Ash.* Strangely, it didn't feel odd to think of her that way. Though she looked exactly like a tattooed version of Rachel, Ash acted nothing like her—and aside from those few gestures that had thrown him when he'd first seen her, Nicholas hadn't experienced a single moment of confusion between the demon and the woman. Did the tattoos make such a difference? Or was it the whole package?

He waited until the attendant moved off. "What about the symbols? What do they say?"

"What symbols?"

"Your tattoos."

"I don't know." Almost absently, she lifted her hand to rub her chest. The largest glyph had marked her there, he remembered. An intricate design between perfect breasts. "Should I be able to read them? Because I can't."

He didn't know. And they likely wouldn't have a chance to ask another demon. "A few Guardians can. If we don't discover any information in Duluth, we'll e-mail pictures of the symbols to Rosalia and ask what they mean."

"Oh." That faint hope brightened her face again. "That would be very helpful. Thank you."

Shit. With a sharp nod, he shoved against the door, escaping the SUV's warmth and plunging into the icy air. So polite again. He wished she'd stop doing that.

Or better yet—*he* needed to stop giving her reasons to be grateful.

CHAPTER 6

The omelets *were* good, and pulling off the highway a few hours later gave Nicholas a chance to stretch his legs, gave him some breathing space. The demon must not have agreed about the food, however, or *like* and *dislike* didn't matter. After only a few bites, she'd set down her fork, scraped her chair back, and stood.

"The taste isn't familiar."

She'd stalked away from the table after that announcement, leaving Nicholas to finish his meal alone. Since he was accustomed to eating by himself, her sudden absence suited him. So did knowing that her politeness had gone out the door.

She had, too. From his seat by the window, Nicholas watched her trudge through the foot of snow that hadn't yet been plowed from the edge of the parking lot. Hood up, hands in pockets, she did an excellent job of acting just like a human bracing herself against the cold. She reached their SUV, then must have remembered that Nicholas had the key fob.

Even from this distance, he could have unlocked it for her by remote. He signaled the waitress for another coffee, instead, and waited to see what the demon would do.

He wasn't surprised when she simply leaned back against the driver's side door, and began watching everyone else. She'd done that on the plane, he remembered. In this diner, too, before they'd been served—and she'd managed to unsettle half the people eating here. Some of that effect came from the tattoos; the reaction to the symbols had been visible as they'd come in. Many of the diners turned to look, and others flinched or recoiled. He'd heard more than one mutter about "ruining such a pretty face."

But most of that uneasiness stemmed from the unwavering, unreadable stare leveled at the person she observed, and that she didn't glance away when they caught her looking. A few had tried to stare her down in return. Not one of them had succeeded.

If Nicholas hadn't already been convinced that Ash wasn't Rachel, the way the demon unsettled everyone would have persuaded him. Rachel had been friendly, outgoing, and eager to strike up a conversation with any stranger just to learn about them. Ash didn't speak to or approach anyone. Rachel had killer instincts when she invested, but she'd been a negotiator at heart—always trying to find common ground. She began by putting the person at ease. Ash didn't bother. Rachel pointed out injustices and tried to fix them. She'd have made everyone who'd recoiled from Ash's tattoos aware of their reaction . . . and she'd have done it gently. Ash didn't seem to notice, though she must have sensed those same reactions. Apparently, however, she just didn't care that they'd judged her.

Yet still, she watched them all—and Nicholas didn't think she stared anyone down for the same reasons he might have. As a tool of intimidation, it had been a useful technique in his business negotiations. After an opponent backed down once, even over something as trivial as eye contact, that person would begin to concede in other ways, too.

He didn't think Ash looked for concession. He didn't think she stared to win. She simply watched.

Searching for something familiar? Perhaps. Her lack of emotional response made it difficult to guess exactly what she wanted to gain when she observed someone.

Shit. Difficult to guess? Not at all. She was a *demon.* And he needed to remind himself that she was probably just looking for their weaknesses.

Fucking stupid, that he needed to remind himself at all. By now, that knowledge should be ingrained.

Maybe Cooper had found something to drive that knowledge home. It was night in England; his investigator should have been able to speak with the nurses and sent his long report by now. How to check his e-mail, yet throw the Guardians off the scent if they were looking for him?

His gaze fell on a sullen-looking teenager in a nearby booth, slouching in his seat and holding a phone between his hands—scrolling through an online social site. Beside him, a harried-looking woman pored over a map, her finger tracing a southbound route.

Too easy.

He paid the kid fifty dollars for five minutes and the chance to check his e-mail, then quietly covered their lunch bill when he was through.

The demon had been telling the truth. At least, she'd been telling the truth about Nightingale House. The nurses had confirmed that a strange blond woman had lived at the hospital for almost three years—first under the name *Mary*, because she hadn't talked at all, then using the name *Ash* when she'd begun coming round.

Cooper reported that she'd creeped the nurses out, had been the reason they'd both left Nightingale House. Even though Nicholas didn't get the same impression, that sounded right for a demon—ruining lives, jobs. What *didn't* sound right was the patient's complete lack of emotion and empathy, which both nurses spoke about at length. Demons faked that shit.

Why hadn't Ash?

He finished his coffee, left money on the table. Outside, the sky had cleared. The bright sun glared over the snow. Ash watched *him* now, he saw. From within the shadows of her hood, her gaze had fixed on his. He wouldn't look away first.

She didn't call out to him as he crossed the parking lot. Madelyn would have, smiling and cheerful—and loud enough to make certain she was heard. *Nicky! There you are, love. I thought you'd become lost on the way to the loo!* Anything to make a boy blush and squirm, especially if they'd had an audience. Alone, she'd still have been cheerful. *So you've finally finished eating, have you? Oh, that's all right, love. Mummy didn't mind waiting. I don't have anything more important to do, such as running your father's business, do I? You obviously know that nothing can be as important as your little stomach, Nicky, because you certainly took your time, ha ha!*

God. That had just been the beginning of it, and she hadn't always been so cheery. As it was, fifteen years had passed before he'd exorcised the sound of her laugh echoing in his mind—a far longer time than he'd actually lived with her. Emotionally and mentally, Nicholas supposed he was still well and truly fucked up. Exorcising her from the face of the Earth wouldn't change that.

He'd sure as hell feel better after she'd been slain, though. And if this demon—Ash—screwed up any opportunity to destroy Madelyn, he'd take her down, too.

Though he let *that* determination shine through his emotional shields like a beacon, Ash didn't look away from him. She didn't even blink. Christ. Didn't a demon's eyes get dry?

Apparently not. She held his gaze until he was practically on top of her, and when she did glance away, he didn't think it had a thing to do with intimidation, with winning or losing. She simply decided to observe someone else.

He didn't look around to see who. And though he'd intended to drive the remainder of the distance to Duluth, he couldn't tolerate the thought of her watching him all that way—maybe learning too much about him. Better that she focused on the road. Taking her hand, he pressed the keys into her palm.

Her fingers twitched, her gaze snapping back to meet his. Startled? So was Nicholas. But she didn't pull away, and he didn't let go. He *should* have let go—and a demon's touch should have been repulsive, but the warmth of her skin seemed to soak into his. He held on, letting the heat sink into him. Enjoying the feel of it.

Until her eyes began to glow. *Jesus.* He dropped her hand, pulled away. The cold air must have left him more chilled than he'd realized if the heat of a demon's skin felt that good. Time to invest in a pair of gloves.

"Your eyes," he warned her, and within a blink they were blue again. Shaking his head, he started around the vehicle to the passenger side. At this rate, she'd have the Guardians on them by nightfall. Or with Rachel's face, a few humans.

He waited until she was in her seat. "You need to shapeshift."

"All right. How?"

Oh, for fuck's sake. "No lying. Just answer me directly: Can you shape-shift?"

"I don't know if I can. But even if I can, I don't know *how*."

Shit. They'd reach Duluth a little before midnight, and she might go unrecognized in the sleeping city. Not so the next morning, when they drove to the Boyles's house. He could make the trip by himself, leave her at the hotel, but he didn't trust her that far. Not alone, not where he couldn't keep an eye on her.

"Rachel lived in a small town," he said. "You'd be recognized."

Her eyes seemed to light. Not with crimson, but with anticipation. "Someone might know me."

"They'd know *Rachel*, not you. And word would reach her parents that someone had seen her." Fucked up he might be, but Nicholas wouldn't do that to them. "They'd try to find you."

"I want to meet them," she said slowly, as if just realizing it—and as if she were surprised by the realization. "I *want* to."

"Don't even think it. You can't. Not looking like that."

The anticipation in her eyes faded. Anyone else, Nicholas might have felt like he'd kicked a kitten. With this demon, he thought the emotion would have quickly vanished, anyway. No disappointment replaced it.

She studied his face, then looked away to stick the key into the ignition. Over the quiet start of the engine, she said, "They wouldn't believe I'm not their daughter, is that right?"

"Yes."

Her amnesia would only make it more difficult to convince them, especially since she couldn't shape-shift at will—and he'd end up staring down the barrels of Frank Boyle's shotgun if he electrocuted her in front of them. Seeing the wings and horns might not matter, regardless. If they wanted to believe this was Rachel badly enough, nothing would stop them from doing so.

So why hadn't this demon taken advantage of that before now? For someone who claimed to be searching for answers, she'd been slow to seek information from the likeliest source.

"Why didn't you contact Rachel's parents?"

"What purpose would it serve? They don't know anything about *me*."

"You're certain of that."

"If they had any idea that someone who looked like Rachel was alive, they'd have come for me. Nothing would have stopped them. But they didn't come, so obviously they don't even know I exist, let alone know who I am."

She was right. But it didn't explain *how* she'd learned that about the Boyles. "You read that on the Internet, too?"

"No. I just know it. It's like . . . remembering a fact. I don't realize the knowledge is there until I think about it, but when I do, I'm certain that it's true."

So her screwed-up memory treated the Boyles' love for their daughter as a fact. Knowing the Boyles, Nicholas couldn't argue that it wasn't. And since neither Nicholas nor the demon had any idea about *how* she knew that fact, he dropped the issue.

So did Ash. She sat, looking into the rearview mirror—as she had been for some time, he realized. She'd moved the transmission into reverse, but held her foot on the brake.

"Why are we waiting here?"

She lifted her brows at the image in the mirror. Nicholas turned, looked through the back window. Not much to see. Big rigs idling. Empty vehicles in the parking lot, and others at the station fueling up.

"There's a dog lying on the seat of that car," she said. "I've noticed that a lot more people in America keep one as a pet. If I got one, I'd seem more normal."

A dog? Rage blasted through him, so hot and viscous it felt like vomit. This demon thought he'd get her a *dog*? He'd cut off his legs before putting an animal in her care. Stomach roiling at the thought, he faced forward, jaw clenched. He wouldn't let her see how her comment affected him. *Fuck*. Maybe she already knew. Maybe Madelyn had told her.

And she wouldn't shut up about it. Wouldn't stop looking at the mirror. "Do you think the family will mind if we take it? They left it in a cold car while they eat. They can't care too much."

Nicholas forced himself to speak, and kept his voice even. He *wouldn't* give the demon this part of him. "A cold car isn't going to hurt the dog."

"Not physically. It's lonely, though. I can hear it whimpering."

And he could still hear the pained yip after his mother had

cuddled the terrier that had scampered at Nicholas's heels since he'd learned to walk. He could still see the surprise and horror in her expression when she'd called to him.

Nicky, love, come quickly! Something's happened to Ringo!

Even as a boy, part of him had understood what she'd done. He simply hadn't believed it, not for years. Now he knew that even though a demon couldn't hurt a human, animals didn't have the same protection—and if a demon could hurt a human by hurting something that he loved, she would.

"Get the idea out of your head and start driving, demon, or I'll contact the Guardians and have them come for you now." Their bargain and his soul be damned.

Ash didn't respond. Nicholas thought she was still looking at the mirror, but no. She was watching him. Probably assessing everything he'd said, cataloguing his weaknesses. Fuck this.

"Drive," he repeated. "Now."

With a shrug, she reversed out of their spot. "Did your dog know what she was?"

"What?"

"Did he sense that Madelyn was a demon? Is that why she killed him?" She flicked on the radio and adjusted the heat, turning the temperature all the way to high. "She did, didn't she?"

Goddammit. It was his fault, though. He had to do a better job of guarding his responses. "Yes."

"She killed more than one?"

"No."

Not that he knew of. One had been enough—and she'd milked it for years. *I don't think it's a good idea to buy another pet, love, until I'm certain you've learned to care for your furry friends a little better. You don't want him to end up like poor Ringo, do you?*

"Was she afraid it would reveal her true nature? Did he bark at her, like in *Terminator*?" Ash frowned. "They don't bark at me."

"That's because you're a demon, not a killer robot." Though Nicholas had to admit he'd once wondered the same thing. He wouldn't have ever used a dog to help him find Madelyn, not after what she'd done—but he'd wondered *why* animals didn't know. He'd only learned the answer after Rosalia had told him.

"What is a dog supposed to sense? They don't have psychic abilities. And you don't even have an odor, nothing to warn them."

So they'd come up to her, lick her, and look for love until she broke their necks. Humans didn't fare much better when they trusted demons, but at least their bones remained intact. Nicholas assumed that the only reason demons didn't go around killing animals for the fun of it was because they needed to do the same thing Ash wanted to do: appear normal. Too many dead animals would raise suspicions.

That point apparently swept right past the demon. She looked down at herself, as if in confusion. "I don't have an odor?"

"No."

She didn't take his word for it. Tugging out the front of her hooded sweatshirt, she dipped her nose beneath the neckline and sniffed. Jesus Christ. Suddenly, Nicholas didn't know whether to laugh or to go for some pansy-ass, horrified reaction. What the hell was that? If she wanted to appear normal, sniffing herself in public wouldn't help her cause.

She didn't seem to notice his struggle any more than she'd been aware of her gaffe. "I *do* have an odor," she said. "But I can barely smell it. It's nothing like yours."

His odor? God. He wouldn't ask. She didn't give him a chance to, anyway.

"Are all demons that obvious, then?"

He didn't follow. "What?"

"Killing dogs. It seems cliché."

"Tell that to an eight-year-old boy, and see how much a cliché matters. They do what works—and they do it again and again."

And he'd said "they," as if Ash wasn't included in their number. Maybe *that* was her game: making him believe that she was different, putting him off guard.

It wouldn't happen.

"I didn't say it wouldn't be effective. It's just not original. And if *I* think it's cliché, when my only experience with demons is what seems familiar from books and movies, then the whole 'killing a boy's dog' thing must be *really* tired."

An odd way to come around to it, but she wasn't wrong. "So it is," he agreed.

"I'd rather be a clever demon. Perhaps that's why it is taking me so long to come up with a plot against you. My standards are too high."

Nicholas bit back his laugh. *Damn it.* How did she turn his anger and suspicion around so easily? In all probability, she *was* plotting to destroy him. He ought to be preparing for it, not finding humor in it.

"Have you been trying to think up many plots?"

"Not really." She gave him a sideways glance. "It ought to be simpler now, knowing that I should think of something cliché. And you never answered me: Are demons all so obvious?"

"It's not so obvious," he said. "Not when there are so many humans doing the same things that you demons do."

"Oh. So what's one more bit of evil here and there?"

"Yes. They hide in plain sight."

"Then how will we find Madelyn? How can you tell demons from humans unless they give themselves away?" She paused. "How did you realize she was a demon in the first place? You didn't know it when she killed Rachel, and you haven't seen her since that night."

No, he hadn't. "I spent a lot of money."

"Oh, really? How did that help? Is there a code printed on the back of a thousand-dollar bill, like something out of a Dan Brown novel?"

Was she irritated? He couldn't be certain. She didn't show enough emotion to categorize her response as snippy, but with just a little more heat he might have. A little drier, and it might have been sarcasm. Either way, she obviously didn't appreciate indirect answers—or attempts to evade an answer.

Interesting. Demons were all about wordplay and obfuscation. They loved to twist words or give them double meanings. Ash didn't. At least, not in any way that Nicholas recognized. Every word from Madelyn's tongue had dripped with sweet poison, killing his father before she'd turned it on Nicholas. Yet even now, when he thought Ash *might* be irritated, she didn't attack him. Had she forgotten how to do that, too?

He could easily find out. "She and Rachel vanished. *Poof!* Gone. For a while, I'd wondered if I'd snapped. Even my therapist thought I might have had a psychotic break—"

"You have a therapist?"

And she'd jumped right on it. What would come next? Telling him that he possessed a weak mind and spirit? That he wasn't a real man?

He hoped she'd try. He'd better know how to deal with her if she began responding like every other demon.

"Yes," he confirmed. "With a mother like Madelyn, I needed one."

"For how long?"

"Since I came to the States at fifteen."

Thanks to his father, he'd had dual citizenship and enough money to escape Madelyn's influence. He wouldn't take the same way out his father had, however—and from the moment he'd stepped off the plane, he'd been planning how to return and destroy her. But Nicholas had also known that Madelyn had already managed to poison him with her words and her neglect, and that if he didn't seek help digging out the rot, he'd end up like his father, anyway.

Madelyn would have called his reliance on a therapist *weak*; he saw it as defiance and another form of vengeance. Despite everything she'd done, Madelyn *wouldn't* break him.

"You've had the same therapist for twenty years?"

"Yes."

"And he— Or is it *she*?"

"She."

Only by mistake. At fifteen, he hadn't wanted a thing to do with women, especially not someone the same age as his mother. So he'd picked Leslie Sinclair out of a directory, but when the appointment came, had discovered a woman with a man's name. Good manners had kept him on the couch, but by the end of the session, she hadn't had to twist his arm to return.

Now, Nicholas believed that Leslie hadn't just saved his life—she'd probably nipped some nascent misogyny in the bud. Just as well. According to many people he'd worked with or whose companies he'd ripped apart, Nicholas was already enough of a dick. No need to add woman hating to his list of sins.

"Does she know you're obsessed with revenge?"

"Of course."

Although the reason behind that revenge had changed over time. As a fifteen-year-old boy, it had been born from a sense of betrayal. *His mother had forsaken him.* Madelyn hadn't even attempted to stop him from leaving England, and he'd wanted her to regret that, and to regret every careless or razor-edged remark she'd ever made.

After months of talking to Leslie, he'd recognized exactly why he'd wanted revenge so badly: He'd wanted Madelyn to feel sorry, dammit. He'd wanted her to notice her son, to acknowledge the pain she'd caused him.

Within a year, he no longer cared whether Madelyn regretted anything, but he hadn't lost the desire to ruin her. Recounting every detail of his childhood to Leslie had shown him that his mother wasn't just thoughtless and neglectful—he'd realized that she was a sadistic, evil bitch who'd destroyed his father and tried to do the same to him. He'd been determined to destroy her in return by taking away the only thing she'd ever nurtured: her business. Nicholas had formed Reticle with that single goal in mind, putting Wells-Down and his mother in the crosshairs, and he hadn't let anyone stand in his way.

Then he'd discovered that Madelyn was a demon, that she'd likely killed his true mother and murdered Rachel, and everything had changed. He'd been driven by revenge before, but that was *nothing* compared to the need to destroy Madelyn now.

"And in twenty years, your therapist hasn't tried to redirect your hostility?"

"She tried. It didn't take. Now she just keeps me honest about what I'm doing, and why I'm doing it."

"You don't lie to her, then? You don't avoid her questions?"

At Ash's narrowed look, Nicholas couldn't stop his laugh. So that *did* irritate her. But as much as the demon wanted answers from him, she was also easily distracted by new information. "I tell her everything."

"Then I want to be your therapist." She huffed out a breath. "You even told her that Madelyn is a demon?"

"Yes."

"And she believed you?"

"No. But I don't pay her to believe me. I pay her to treat me, to force me to acknowledge my motivations and to challenge my assumptions. So far, I've met every challenge to my satisfaction—and although she might think I'm delusional, I know I'm not."

Ash didn't respond, but her brows lifted and a smile quickly touched her mouth.

"Why is that funny?" Nothing else had amused her, but *that* did?

"Not funny. It just finally makes sense. I wondered if you were lying about the therapist because you're too arrogant and certain of yourself to have one. But now that I hear 'I met every challenge' and 'I know I'm not crazy,' it finally fits what I already knew of you."

Nicholas wished that something about her would fit. Her assessment of his personality was spot on, but he couldn't hear any judgment in it. A man as driven as he was required a certain level of self-confidence, but usually people who called him "arrogant" used the word like a curse . . . and followed it up with "son of a bitch." Ash didn't, and it threw him off.

"I focus on what I want," he said. "And I don't allow anything to get in my way."

"I noticed. And in any case, you didn't have a psychotic break. Rachel and Madelyn *did* disappear. How?"

Back around to that, then? So she allowed distractions, but was tenacious about following through. He'd remember that. She could be diverted from her course for only a short time.

"A demon can make some things vanish—I think that's what happened to Rachel's body. Madelyn took it, and then ran off so quickly that it appeared as if she'd vanished, too."

"I can make things vanish?"

Distracted again, but not unfocused. She chased after stray bits of information like . . . like *he* did. But Nicholas was trying to discover everything, just in case the knowledge was useful later. He was trying to form an impression of her that he could understand and anticipate. Ash wouldn't have the same reasons.

Was she just that curious about everything?

"Everything goes into a psychic storage of some kind." Nicholas didn't know much more than that. "Demons and Guardians both have one. They call it a cache."

"A cache . . . like a pocket universe? Something small on the outside, big on the inside—and we put stuff in there, somehow?" She glanced at him, as if searching for the answer in his face. Nicholas didn't have one for her. "Like a TARDIS?"

Her references for understanding a demon's abilities were based on *Doctor Who* and Schwarzenegger movies? God. "I don't know if it's science or magic. You can't put living things in there, though."

"Why?" When Nicholas couldn't answer that, she wondered, "Is that where my clothes go?"

"When I gave you the electric shock? Probably."

"And the other times?"

Other times? Nicholas fought not to grin. "Do they disappear often?"

"Somewhat often. Then people start laughing, and the clothes come back. Ah, and see? You're laughing now, too."

So he was. He could almost picture it . . . Ah, hell. He *could* picture it. All too easily. When her clothes had disappeared earlier and he'd still believed she might be Madelyn, he hadn't really looked at her. Now his memory filled in the little he'd seen in delicious detail: the changing shadows beneath her knees as her skin had faded from crimson to tanned; the shallow depression of her navel, which demons didn't possess in their true forms; the silken fall of blond hair across soft breasts. Glimpses, impressions, because he hadn't been looking at her sexually . . . and made him wish now that he'd looked a little harder.

He wouldn't have been averse to her clothes disappearing. And if they did, Nicholas didn't think he'd be laughing. No, he'd be enjoying the view.

How screwed up was that? He'd ask Leslie when he saw her next. Did sexual attraction to a gorgeous demon suggest that he was even more fucked up than he'd thought, or was it healthier than planning to slay one?

He tried to imagine Leslie's reaction and couldn't help being amused. One of these days, she was going to have him institutionalized.

"No living things," Ash said softly, cutting into his amusement. "But Madelyn vanished the body—so that means Rachel *had* to be dead. Did Madelyn vanish the evidence, too?"

God. The memory of Rachel's bloodied chest replaced Ash's perfect breasts. The memory of his shock and utter helplessness as she died.

And it was exactly the slap that Nicholas had needed. Gorgeous demon or not, he couldn't cultivate that physical attraction. Sex complicated everything. Allowing anyone that close meant he lowered his emotional shields and exposed more of himself than he wanted to. Taking that risk with a demon . . . Hell, he might as well put a gun to his head and pull the trigger now.

A dead man couldn't pursue revenge. That was all that mattered. This demon didn't matter, and neither did his screwed-up attraction.

"Madelyn took everything with her," he said. "The gun, the bullets, the blood. And so, like I said, I spent money. I hired investigators to look for murders where the body and evidence had gone missing despite witnesses, to track down anyone with a similar story to mine. After a while, they found commonalities, but no answers. Not until about four years ago, when one investigator ran across Sally Barrows."

"Another demon?"

"No. A vampire."

"A vampire," she echoed flatly. "Is that like a dragon?"

Nicholas couldn't see her eyeteeth behind her compressed lips, but he guessed she had fangs again. "Yes," he said. "Because I'm not lying about vampires *or* dragons."

She didn't respond. Either struggling to believe him, he realized, or flat-out refusing to. *Fuck.* Never did he imagine trying to prove to a demon that vampires existed.

He damn well wasn't going to start now. Let her believe what she wanted. "That's when I began spending a lot more money. For the right price, Sally and her husband agreed to help me find Madelyn, and told me what they knew about demons."

"I notice they aren't helping you now."

"Because they're dead."

That grief must have slipped through his emotional shields, or Ash heard something in his voice. She looked away from the road, studied his face. "What happened?"

"A demon ripped them apart."

Sally and Gerald had known some information about demons, but they hadn't known a lot. Like many vampires, they were mostly ignorant of their origins, having heard only bits and pieces of the truth about Guardians and demons, but not the whole story. So they'd known enough to capture a demon, to take it down alive, but hadn't known enough to *keep* it down.

"How long did you work with them?"

"Three years, off and on. Sometimes they went into other vampire communities and gathered information." And other times, they'd worked together with him—Nicholas making certain their sleeping forms were secure when the sun rose, and then training with and learning from them by night. "I met Rosalia after that."

When she'd slain the demon who'd butchered Gerald and Sally. Still, that demon's death hadn't been enough of a punishment. Not after Nicholas had seen what it had done to his friends.

Nicholas had been going it alone since then. He wouldn't ask any other humans or vampires to risk their lives in pursuit of his revenge, and he sought help from Rosalia only because she could take care of herself—as she'd aptly demonstrated by beheading a demon several times stronger and faster than she was. One moment Nicholas had seen Rosalia and her partner facing the demon, and the next moment she'd been bleeding from her gut and the demon's head had been rolling across the floor.

"Rosalia is the Guardian?" Ash asked.

"Yes. And because that's what Guardians do—hunt demons—she had more information about how to find them."

"And how do you?"

"The most obvious sign is the temperature of their skin."

Ash rubbed the tips of her fingers together, as if feeling the heat of her own skin and considering that. Finally, she said, "It's obvious, but difficult to use for identification, I'd think. You'd have to touch a demon to know."

Not necessarily. Modern infrared sensors could detect higher temperatures from a distance, and the differences were noticeable, especially if the demon stood near a human. No reason to mention that, though.

"It's a problem," he agreed. "I can't walk down the street shaking everyone's hand."

"Or kissing them, like you did to me."

So she'd figured that out? "If I'd shaken your hand, you'd have noticed me grabbing the Taser."

"So? You could have just not let go of me. You know I can't pull free without breaking the Rules."

No, he couldn't have just held on. He'd needed payback, however small. "You showed up with Rachel's face, and I thought you were Madelyn. I *wanted* to electrocute you. So I got close enough to do it."

She nodded, as if in understanding. "All right. The kissing makes more sense, then."

No judgment? No pointing out that he was a sadistic bastard? Who the hell *was* this demon? He'd given her freebies all over the place, practically invited her to tear into his character, and she sat and nodded her head because it made sense.

"Is the hot skin the only difference?"

Her question made Nicholas realize that she'd been waiting for him to continue. He shook his head. "Demons count on people to explain away the unexplainable. A man disappears, and people tell themselves they must have been mistaken—that they just didn't see him turn a corner. Someone moves too fast, looks inhuman for just a second, and they come up with excuses: They're tired, their eyes are playing tricks, they—"

"Are going crazy," Ash said.

"That, too. Most of the time, they shake their heads and laugh it off." Others couldn't, and some, like his father, landed in the care of doctors like Cawthorne—and then took a dive from the tallest bank tower in London. "But if you know what it might *really* have been, you look a little harder."

"And then make sure you're right by touching them?" When he nodded, she said, "So it's all luck—a matter of seeing something at the right time? You'll be looking for Madelyn forever, then."

"*We* will be looking," Nicholas reminded her. Though he'd be stupid not to get out of this bargain as quickly as possible. The more time he spent with the demon, the less he could figure her out. He hadn't counted on that. When he'd made the bargain, he'd been certain of his ability to predict her reactions.

He *should* have been able to, goddammit. He should have been dodging her slings and arrows, not reminding himself that he shouldn't be attracted to her, that he shouldn't be amused by her. He'd expected subtle insults, not . . . whatever she was doing.

"We," she echoed. "And based on what you're saying, it really will be forever. Or until we die of old age."

She wouldn't grow old. Nicholas didn't correct her, though.

"It's not just luck," he said. "You called their methods unoriginal, and you aren't wrong. And that's how you look for them."

"A trail of dead dogs?"

Jesus. And people thought Nicholas lacked sensitivity. He wasn't bothered by her question, but he definitely wouldn't be letting her talk to the Boyles, even if she did learn to shape-shift.

"Not dogs. Dead people, sometimes. If someone says that a loved one came back to talk to them, there's a good chance it was really a demon. If someone undergoes a complete personality change, a demon might have taken their place. If members of a vampire community start disappearing, they are probably being killed by a demon. If vampires start killing humans, there's probably a demon in the background, prodding them into it. They use humans and vampires to do what they can't: break the Rules."

"I see." She was quiet for a moment. "That's still a lot to look for."

"A lot of shit to wade through, and a lot of dead ends," he agreed. Except for when it involved vampires, humans did everything he'd just mentioned without demon influence, too. "But I'm just looking for one demon, and I already know how she works. So I've been searching for something similar."

He'd searched for a mother whose personality had undergone a sudden transformation. He'd searched for a husband who'd been committed to a psychiatric institution. He'd searched for a wife who'd taken over her husband's business—probably in the financial sector—and who'd begun working all hours of the day and night, transforming the business into a burgeoning success.

He'd also searched for a kid battered by every recent change in his life. The ones marked by razor scars across their wrists or who'd spent nights in the hospital having their stomachs pumped. That had been the worst part of the search. He'd found far too many of those kids, and not a single one of them had ended up there because of a demon.

Did Ash know that part of his history? He hadn't been wearing a shirt in Madelyn's bedroom. If Ash had spotted the scars on the insides of his wrists, she could guess their origin, just as she'd guessed what Madelyn had done to Ringo. Not that it would matter if Ash *had* guessed; he was no longer self-destructive. All of the rage and pain he'd felt as a kid had cooled and hardened, and he'd channeled it into revenge.

"You searched for her and found me, instead," Ash said.

He'd find Madelyn, too. "Yes."

"And I resemble the assistant she killed—a woman you once dated." Her brow furrowed in a way that told him she'd been distracted by some detail again. "But I can't figure out why Rachel would date you, no matter how charming you were. As Madelyn's assistant, her association with you created an enormous conflict of interest and was completely unethical."

That had never been a problem for Nicholas, not where Madelyn was concerned. "Why is a demon bothered by something unethical?"

"I'm not bothered." She frowned, as if trying to decide whether she should be or not. Finally, she shook her head. "What *I* don't feel is beside the point. I'm trying to figure *her* out—and everything I've learned about Rachel says that she wouldn't behave unethically. Do you think Madelyn told her to date you, to undermine your takeover bid?"

"Probably." He'd used Rachel for the same reason: to undermine Madelyn. He had to assume the demon would have done the same thing. "If so, Rachel didn't follow her directions well. She tried to make us reconcile instead of destroy each other."

And Rachel had never understood that there'd never be a chance in hell of that happening. But then, Madelyn had been a different woman with her—a ruthless businesswoman, but not a cruel one. Rachel had been convinced that Nicholas's hatred was just born out of ancient misunderstandings and a teenager's rebellion.

"Did that amuse you?" Ash looked away from the road to study his face. "Or did it irritate you?"

Both, depending on how hard Rachel pushed him. He wouldn't tell the demon that, though. She was here to learn about herself, not about him.

Her eyes narrowed. Ah, now *she* was irritated by his refusal to answer. "At least Rachel's relationship with you makes sense now. I knew it couldn't be your charm."

Maybe she was right. "What did you think it was?"

"You said she was smart. So I assumed she dated you for your money."

"Rachel had more than enough of her own."

"As much as you do?"

No, but enough to live well for the rest of her life. Now, her assets hung in limbo. Only six years had passed since Rachel had gone missing, and she'd never been officially ruled dead.

A demon with her face and identification could access them . . . which was why he'd taken the passport back as soon as they'd passed through customs.

When he didn't respond, Ash bared her teeth, just a little—and there were those fangs. "I suppose money isn't incentive enough to put up with you, anyway."

He grinned. "Probably not."

She was still watching his face rather than the road. If her driving hadn't been so smooth, he might have been worried. As it was, he just wondered what she was looking for.

Her gaze dropped to his lap. "Maybe she wanted you for sex, then. Is your penis big?"

Was she serious or just winding him up? "I haven't had any complaints."

"If you haven't had any complaints, it must not be *too* big."

She slanted a look up at his face, and he realized that she wasn't serious at all. And fucked up as it was, Nicholas was getting a kick out of this, too.

"It's not monstrous." He'd never heard anyone compare his cock to an ogre's, at least. "Are you enjoying yourself?"

"Yes." She sounded slightly mystified by that fact. "And I want to be your girlfriend."

Now that seemed serious again. "What?"

"So that I'll have access to your money. And since your penis won't rip me apart, I'll even have sex with you." Her gaze turned inward, and though she spoke out loud, her question seemed directed at herself rather than at Nicholas. "I wonder if I'd enjoy *that*?"

She wouldn't. Demons *couldn't*. They could fake a sexual response, but they didn't actually feel desire or arousal. Did she truly not know that?

If so, that ignorance didn't give him an advantage that he could see. She knew so little, had no memory, and yet wasn't a bit naïve. Her cynicism rivaled his—perhaps the result of being able to sense everyone's true emotions. She might not know what someone was trying to sell her, but she didn't buy any bullshit.

"You have access to my accounts without that," he reminded her. "I'm bound to help you find out who you are. That includes giving you money when you need it."

"Oh." She focused on him. Her lips slowly curved before she faced forward again. "Good."

Jesus Christ. What the fuck was she doing to him? Rachel's smile had never kicked him in the gut, but here he sat, feeling like he needed to catch his breath after a single satisfied look from a *demon*. How in the hell could she have the same face as Rachel, the same *mouth*, and possess such a different smile? Rachel had always been weighing, judging, estimating the effect of her response on him, making certain he was at ease and comfortable. She'd cared for him, loved him. Yet it was Ash, who didn't seem to give a shit about his response and had no interest in judging him—or caring what he thought of her in return—who got to him with a little twist of her lips. And how the hell was he supposed to hang on to his cynicism when she beat him to it with her unabashed greed?

And why the hell did he like it? Like *her*? God help him, now he was wondering if he'd enjoy sex with her, too, despite knowing that *she* wouldn't feel a thing, and that it would fuck him up even more than he already was.

Any other woman, he'd manipulate her emotions and charm her until she wanted him in return, until he had the upper hand—just as he had with Rachel. But he didn't even know if Ash had any real emotions.

Goddammit. He had to take control of himself, and take the upper hand again . . . before she ground him under her heel.

CHAPTER 7

Since strange was normal now, Taylor didn't think anything of teleporting into a graveyard in Illinois after the sun had set. Revoire had asked her to meet him at that location, and as graveyards went, this one seemed kind of pleasant. No spooky broken fences, no precariously tilted headstones. Just Marc Revoire, standing in front of a grave marker, looking a bit like a farmer in a worn brown jacket and tan trousers. He had that lanky, wide-shouldered look to him, as if he rose with the sun and spent the day behind a plow. In the Midwest, what could be more normal than that?

Popping a coffin up out of the soil like it was a jack-in-the-box was still a little weird, though.

Revoire simply looked at the ground and pushed with his Gift. Taylor felt the psychic thrust of it, a shot of energy that tasted like dirt and smelled of freshly turned earth, and suddenly the casket that had been *in* the ground sat above it, instead.

Frozen grass crunched beneath Taylor's boots as she made her way around a headstone to his side. "Jason Matthew Ward," she read off the grave marker. "Twenty-three years old. Died two months ago."

"Local vampire community contacted me." Revoire broke the seal on the casket, lifted the lid. Taylor deliberately stopped breathing. "Ward was actually turned three years ago. He was living in the community, had a bloodsharing partner, was doing everything right."

"Who killed him, then?"

"I don't know. Ward's family found him—they're still human, and still don't know what he was. He made it into the morgue without the sun touching him. The teeth were written off as a cosmetic augmentation."

They always were. And shit, she had to take a breath to speak. The rotting stench hit hard, made her eyes water. "Cause of death?"

"Stake through the heart."

"You're kidding." That had to be the hardest and least effective way to do it. A sword through the heart or cutting off the head—quick and easy.

"No. The coroner found splinters." Revoire let the casket lid fall shut again. "His report matches what's left of the body in there."

And this was all exactly the kind of thing that Special Investigations looked for. "So why weren't you contacted earlier?"

"The local vampires covered it up. They've been taking care of their own in this area for a hundred years. They pay the county coroner to look the other way when something odd comes in."

Handy. "But now?"

"They've got a few more dead—but by the time they were found, the bodies were ashed, and it was impossible to determine what killed them. So the community leader is concerned they have a demon on their hands."

Taylor studied Revoire's face. Though his features were of a man in his thirties, he always looked concerned. Not anxious, but careworn, like a much older man. As if he carried the burdens of the world and worried that they'd never be set right.

"And you?" she asked.

He shrugged, and she felt the push of his Gift. Behind him, the earth opened and seemed to suck the casket down before closing up again—and leaving behind an undisturbed plot.

Taylor was impressed. As Gifts went, controlling earth and soil was one of the more practical powers a Guardian could have. Not as good as teleporting, but still handy.

"It might be a demon," Revoire said. "Now and again, there's one that comes through and challenges Basriel for territory. If I don't get to them first, he takes them out."

"Yay for Basriel?"

Revoire smiled faintly. "He's low-key now, changing locations and identities quickly enough that I can't get a lock on him, but once he's established his territory, I'm sure that'll change. He's got five hundred years before Lucifer opens the Gates again, and he wants to reign over something. The vampires would be a good start."

"So why kill them?"

"Exactly. And this doesn't fit his pattern. He's been focusing on maintaining his territory. Doing my job for me, half the time."

By killing those other demons. "How far does his territory extend?"

"There's a clear perimeter from the Canadian border down to Missouri, including the states on either side of the river."

That included the location of the double murder they were going to investigate. "Do you know if he's ever pretended to be a ghost, and urged a human to take revenge?"

Revoire narrowed his eyes, considering that. "It doesn't sound right. Maybe he has before, but not since coming into the area. Not that I've been aware."

So they might be dealing with another demon. Maybe one coming in to challenge Basriel, or one just looking to get his human-murdering jollies in.

Revoire must have been thinking the same thing. His wings formed, brilliant white feathers arching high over his head. "We need to stop by the community leader's place, let him know what I found here. Then we'd best head north, take a look around."

"Before Basriel slays another one out from under your nose?"

"Yes."

His wings opened, but Taylor stopped him with a discreet cough. When he glanced back at her, she held out her hand.

"I've got a faster way."

Revoire's wings vanished. His quick grin washed away the impression of care and concern that usually hung over him. Oh, he should do that more often.

"Good," he said. "I hate flying."

Considering that most of the Guardians she teleported with ended up dizzy and dry-heaving at the end of the trip, he might choose flying next time.

"You hate it because of the Icarus thing?"

He gave a short, surprised laugh, shaking his head. "No. That name came from where I did: an Icarian colony, in the 1850s. We'd just come up from New Orleans and settled in this area when I died."

"Oh." A commune. No wonder he looked like a farmer. "I thought you were French."

"Most of the Icarians were. I emigrated as a boy—and when I became a Guardian, they called me the Icarian. That eventually became Icarus, though the colony had no connection to the myth aside from the name of an island."

"And so you didn't have a freak flying accident as a novice."

"I had a few. Mostly, I just hate flying because it's so conspicuous. I like being up there. I don't enjoy feeling like a spectacle." He took her hand, and all of those cares and worries returned to his face, but this time she could feel the bittersweet ache behind them. "The name fits well enough now, anyway."

"You flew too close to the sun?"

She knew that feeling, every time she opened up to Michael—or he did to her. A strange combination of warmth, freedom, and impending disaster.

"I did," he confirmed. "And drowned for my troubles."

"Who was she?"

Or *he*, maybe. Hell, given that they could all shape-shift, it was possible that Revoire hadn't started out as a "he," either.

Taylor had tried it a few times. Enough to know that she didn't like the dangly bits.

Revoire gave her a little half-smile. He really should do that more often. Especially to the one who got away. "You've got a more important mystery to solve right now, Detective."

"So we do." Her hand tightened on his. "Hold on, Icarus. It's a bumpy ride."

* * *

Despite the two showers he'd taken since they'd arrived in Duluth and checked into the lakefront hotel, Nicholas St. Croix didn't get naked in front of Ash as often as she would have guessed.

The lodging itself proved to be exactly what she'd expected. The corner suite overlooked Lake Superior and offered an unobstructed view of the canal's aerial lift bridge, brilliantly lighted against the clouded night sky. Inside the rooms, yards of white upholstery and bedding rejected any suggestion that any previous guests sins' needed to be concealed with beige or paisley fabric. Ash's nose told her differently, however. Evidence of the former occupants' activities lingered beneath the harsh scent of bleach, and warned her not to sit on the bed, the love seat facing the flat-screen television, the two chairs at the small table, or a large portion of the carpet beneath the eastern window—at least not until she made certain that nothing flaky or crunchy remained stuck to the fibers.

She didn't warn Nicholas. What he didn't know couldn't hurt him, and the information might be useful later, anyway. When she told him, he might take another shower . . . and he might forget to bring his clothes into the bathroom and strip off in the bedroom, instead. No door separated the living space from the sleeping area, but the angle of the rooms and a short wall offered privacy. Someone in the main room would have to make an effort to see another person undressing near the bed.

If it meant seeing Nicholas naked, Ash would make that effort.

So, her first plot against him consisted of warnings about dried bodily fluids. He'd probably consider it small potatoes. Ash was pleased, however. Stripping off in front of her wouldn't destroy Nicholas's soul, but the plan might offer her a better glimpse of it.

As it stood, his reluctance didn't make sense, just as learning that he saw a therapist initially hadn't fit her impression of him. Arrogant as he was, she thought he'd also have a blatant disregard for modesty. He'd do as he pleased and not care whether she saw him.

Yet he'd undressed behind a door . . . just as he hid his emotions behind a shield of another sort. But what would his nakedness reveal?

Maybe he simply knew that she wanted to see him and chose to deny her. Ash didn't think so, though. Nicholas St. Croix had reasons for everything he did, and so far, Ash hadn't seen any evidence that his reasons were so petty.

So it was something else. Perhaps he hid something from her. If so, he must believe that revealing it would give Ash an advantage over him.

Fascinating. She couldn't imagine what that advantage could be, but she wanted to find out. Until then, Ash worked with what she had, and even a clothed Nicholas revealed himself in many ways.

In Madelyn's town house, she'd recognized that an obsession enslaved him after a single look at his bare chest, yet Ash hadn't realized the effort Nicholas put into it until she'd followed him down to the hotel's workout room just after midnight. Too icy to jog outside, he'd fired up the treadmill, instead. For an hour, Ash watched him run to nowhere, admiring his stamina.

She also discovered that she could easily heft a fully loaded bench press bar. She amused herself on each of the lifting machines after that, setting them to their highest weight and testing her strength.

The gym didn't possess any weight heavy enough to truly test her, but she found that her pinky finger could lift several hundred pounds. If her toes had been longer, she'd have tested them, too.

Then Nicholas had abandoned the treadmill, drenched in sweat and his chest heaving. Water bottle in hand, he prowled the length of the room, cooling down. After a few minutes, he'd straddled one of the weight benches.

Ash hadn't been able to interpret the look Nicholas had given her when he'd removed the pin and selected a lighter weight than she'd been using, but she thought he was—once again—struggling not to laugh.

He wasn't threatened by her strength as she knew some men would have been, and not chagrined . . . just amused. But why hide that amusement?

Several times on the journey, she'd also noticed that he'd

struggled against an attraction to her—but that made sense. She looked like his dead girlfriend, and he wouldn't want to feel anything sexual for a demon. Why not laugh, though? Ash couldn't understand that.

She took his place on the treadmill and pondered it while she ran. After another hour of that—in her boots, without a drop of sweat forming, and even though she'd set the machine to the highest speed, she wasn't winded—Ash still hadn't figured it out. And although Nicholas headed directly into the shower after they'd finished, he closed the door again.

At least now she knew how he'd developed every muscle that he hid from her.

She learned even more when he emerged from the bathroom, fully dressed in a tailored white shirt and dark trousers, wet hair neatly combed, jaw shaved. So formal, as if he wouldn't let his guard slip for a moment, not even at two o'clock in the morning. He'd ordered room service before the kitchens closed at midnight, and before heading to the gym—two broiled chicken breasts and a pile of steamed vegetables, now cold and limp—and read the *Wall Street Journal* while he ate. Standing by the window overlooking the lake, Ash watched his reflection as he paused over an article that mentioned his company. He reached for his phone, and she saw his frustration in the subtle firming of his mouth when he realized that making the call would possibly alert the Guardians.

No, she didn't need to see him naked. In a few short hours, his obsession had been laid bare to her. Everything he did was calculated to serve his purpose, down to each unappetizing bite of food he put in his mouth. She saw everything that mattered to him: making certain that he possessed enough money to pay for his revenge, and maintaining the physicality to carry it through.

Revenge wasn't just his obsession, she realized. It was his *life*.

Now Ash was a part of that life, that revenge . . . and she was glad of it. *Glad.* She could feel that emotion as clearly as she felt the window glass against her fingertips.

Something inside her had changed during the journey here. Everything she saw seemed so familiar now: the highway, the streets and buildings, even this nighttime view of the bridge—as if she'd visited this city many times. She could *almost* remember the summer wind from the lake hitting her face, the scent of barbecue and popcorn, the spray of fireworks against the sky.

Tomorrow, they'd travel north to Rachel's hometown. Ash could picture that road, too . . . but she couldn't picture the faces of Rachel's parents. She couldn't hear their voices in her head. She couldn't recall any of that—but maybe when she saw them, when she heard them, they'd be familiar.

God. She wanted to haul Nicholas away from the table, drag him out to their vehicle, and drive north now. The anticipation that had been building with each mile had transformed into a quivering excitement and impatience—and though she expected those emotions to fade, they only deepened.

None of her emotions faded as quickly anymore. Nor were they as shallow as they had been—as if every familiar sight and every association she made created a stronger foundation for those emotions, even though she still had no memories to base them on. She felt so much more now than she had even twenty-four hours ago. Excitement, amusement . . . arousal.

She glanced at Nicholas again. When they'd arrived, she hadn't only expected to see him naked; she'd have *liked* it, too. Perhaps appreciation for a beautiful form accounted for part of that enjoyment, but she also liked the feelings that the thought of his nudity stirred in her. She relished the warmth that spread through her body, the ache of her flesh—sweet and painful, all at once.

Of course, she didn't need him naked for that, either. She had full memory of his mouth closing over hers, the penetrating stroke of his tongue. She could see the precision of his hands wielding his knife and fork, and knew he'd be just as deliberate with a touch. But what would she like best? A rough caress or a gentle tease?

Both, she thought. Just imagining the glide of his fingers seemed to tighten her skin, as if in anticipation—and he didn't need to take his clothes off for her to feel *this.*

Perhaps she didn't even need to imagine Nicholas. Maybe it could be anybody.

Now that thought made her curious. Was her sexual interest a physical reaction or an emotion? How could she tell the difference?

Her gaze landed on the television remote. There was a

fifteen-dollar answer. Watching a porn movie and cataloging her physical response might help her find out.

Or she could skip that. Imagining a pimply-assed plumber rutting over a plastic actress wasn't doing much for her now.

Nicholas did something for her, though, and Ash didn't think his looks alone accounted for it. She *liked* spending time with him. She liked his snarly responses when he forgot to maintain his icy composure—or when he *couldn't* maintain it. She liked that she couldn't anticipate his reactions. She even liked his obvious *dis*like for her, particularly when he couldn't stop himself from laughing, anyway.

She liked that he didn't pretend anything. Oh, he lied, but that fascinated her, because it meant he thought the truth might give her an advantage. And he held back information, which was irritating—but even that provided an intriguing challenge when it forced her to figure out *why* he lied or held back info.

But he was also different from the majority of the people she'd met, particularly those at Nightingale House. Rare was the adult human whose words and actions weren't at odds with what they felt—adults who would stare at her tattoos and pretend not to notice them, who would carry on a conversation while completely preoccupied by some other matter, who would express some emotion when she *knew* they felt another. Nicholas didn't do that. And although he hid his emotions from her, they weren't difficult to guess: hatred and distrust, because she was a demon.

He lied, yes. But at the same time, he offered her a different sort of honesty, one that she hadn't known she'd appreciate until she finally met someone who was both open and hidden from her, at the same time. She couldn't read him, but he didn't pretend to feel anything other than hatred and distrust.

Ash supposed she should have been hurt, or even offended. The soap opera ladies would have been. *I've never lied to you; why won't you trust me?* But she suspected that *liking* would have to become *caring* before Nicholas could hurt her. Hopefully, her emotions wouldn't develop that far—and if they did, she hoped that they also came with a survival instinct: not of the mortal kind, but an emotional one.

No . . . Ash hoped that she had *already* developed that emotional survival instinct, because she had come to care about something: whether she'd see Rachel's parents. It mattered. She could barely tolerate the idea that the only obstacle preventing her from meeting them was her inability to shape-shift.

Determined, she focused on her reflection. How hard could it be? She didn't even have to think about her eyes turning red; they just did. Why would shape-shifting be any different?

She studied the shape of her face and imagined it changing. But into what? It was probably best if she resembled someone that everyone would trust, like the Brady Bunch mom. Concentrating on the tattoos, she pictured vermillion fading to a light tan. She pictured her chin narrowing, her cheekbones widening and flattening. She pictured hair of gold in a mod little pixie cut.

. . . and nothing happened.

Dammit. What kind of lousy demon was she? There had to be a trick to shape-shifting, but whatever that trick was, her procedural memory couldn't recall it.

Her attention returned to the tattoos on her face. Okay. So she couldn't make her face resemble Florence Henderson's, but she could find out what the symbols meant. Turning away from the window, she stripped off her jacket and tossed it over the back of a chair.

When she slid down her sweatshirt's zipper, Nicholas glanced up from his dinner and newspaper. He looked again when her T-shirt came off. For a moment, he didn't react, then that cold amusement overtook his expression. His lips thinned and tilted upward just at the corners, his eyebrows lifting a fraction of an inch.

He sat back in his chair, his gaze running the length of her naked torso and pausing on her breasts. "Dinner comes with a show?"

She bent over to haul off her boots. "It's so we can take pictures of these symbols and send them to the Guardians."

"That's not happening tonight."

"Why?" Barefoot, she straightened and unbuttoned her jeans. "You had to use a credit card to reserve the hotel. How long do you think it'll be before they find us?"

"Not long. We'll find another place that takes cash tomorrow morning, but stay checked-in here so they won't know we've gone."

"So it won't matter if we send the pictures."

"It will, because they might not have connected my name to

the card I used. We might have a few days. An e-mail would bring them in right away." His gaze lifted to her face as she lowered her zipper. "Whatever you're doing right now, it won't work. You can choose that body or any other. You look gorgeous, perfect—but I know you're still a demon."

Perfect. Ash liked that, too. And was it evil to be glad he thought so, despite his obvious desire not to? If it was, she didn't care. It felt good. Nicholas thought she looked gorgeous. Too bad he'd gotten the rest of it wrong.

"I didn't *choose* this body," she pointed out. "I have no idea why I look like this."

"Right."

Oh, yes. Her plot. "So you're attracted to me, just as you were to Rachel. And you think I deliberately chose this body to foster that attraction. I didn't."

"Don't compare yourself to Rachel. You look similar, but there's a critical difference: She wanted me in return."

Not much of a difference, then. "I do, too."

"Jesus. You expect me to believe that?" He shook his head, then dismissed her by returning his attention to the paper.

So he'd decided to take the irritating route again, conveniently forgetting the portion of their bargain that made it impossible for her to deceive him.

"I can't lie," she said. "You made certain of that."

Oh, that little smile again. But this time, he didn't bother to look at her. Now that was interesting. She knew he liked her body. Why *not* look at it, unless he felt her nudity threatened him in some way?

"I made it part of our agreement," he said. "That doesn't mean you haven't been lying. It only means that you're fucked if you do lie. For all I know, you've been lying since the moment we struck that bargain."

"So basically, I'm either lying about everything, or I'm not. But you *choose* to believe that I'm lying. You *chose* to believe that I was breaking our bargain from the word *go*."

"Making any other choice would be stupid. You're a demon."

Maybe he was right, and any other choice would be stupid; he did know more about demons than she did. But he also had to know that there was no middle ground here. Either she'd lied . . . or he'd made the wrong choice.

And if he believed that she'd lied, why keep her around? If she'd broken her bargain, Nicholas had no use for her. He *lived* for revenge. He discarded anything that got in the way of his goal, and a lying demon wouldn't be any different.

So despite his response, he must be allowing for the possibility that he might be wrong. That he didn't know everything. He might not admit it to her, but he must acknowledge the possibility to himself. Otherwise, he'd have already dumped her off on the side of the road.

She liked that about him, too.

Nicholas looked up. He'd been waiting for her to answer, she realized. Maybe waiting for her to argue. But when his gaze dropped to her bare chest and he took a long, slow breath, Ash decided she'd rather do something else.

"I want to have sex."

He met her eyes again. Aside from that small movement, Nicholas didn't react.

His body did. A slight darkening of his skin followed the increase of his heartbeat. A flush, a quickening. Born of anger or arousal? Maybe caused by both—and both pleased her. She liked provoking that reaction, whatever it was.

And even if it was physical arousal, it wasn't desire. He didn't *want* her. His cold blue stare communicated that perfectly across a room full of silence: *Don't fuck with me.*

Too bad, because she fully intended to. She didn't expect him to fulfill her request for sex, but she wanted—*needed*—to push him about this. To make him acknowledge that she felt something.

Holding his gaze, Ash arched her brows. She could do cool and amused, too—and she could stare longer than he could. Whatever he thought that icy look would accomplish, she wasn't capable of feeling intimidated or discomfited. She wouldn't back down, and he'd have to eventually respond.

What would he say? Would he tell her to go screw a stranger on the street? She would have, if the thought appealed to her even a fraction as much as the prospect of sex with him did, and even though she *knew* Nicholas wouldn't climb into bed with her. Telling him what she wanted and forcing him to respond satisfied a deep-seated need that she hadn't known existed until a few moments ago. And yes, it was a little evil, a little mean.

Maybe she was getting the hang of this demon gig, after all.

Finally, he set his knife and fork onto this plate, so carefully that she didn't detect a clink. *Oooooh*, such restraint. She could hear his blood raging through his veins, yet he was so determined not to betray anything he felt. Simply fascinating.

Honestly, what did he think she'd do if he *did* reveal his emotions?

Perhaps she was about to find out. Nicholas rose from the table, all coiled tension and deliberation. His eyes didn't leave hers as he crossed the room. Despite the icy threat emanating from him, Ash held her ground. The last time he'd come so close, he'd kissed her. He'd also electrocuted her, but he didn't carry a weapon now.

Unless that weapon was his hand—not to hit, but to hold. Her pulse leapt when he cupped her jaw, when she felt the faint rasp of calluses against her skin, the sweep of his thumbs across her cheeks. Too late, Ash remembered: She couldn't pull away until he let go.

She didn't him want to, not yet. Heart pounding, she held his gaze. His eyes so cold and his expression so flat, though his blood raced, too.

The same restraint and tension flattened his voice. "You say that you didn't choose this body on purpose, and yet you offer it to me."

"I'm not 'offering' my body to you. It won't be yours. I just want your penis in me, and to discover whether I'd enjoy it."

Almost imperceptibly, his fingers tightened. "You wouldn't enjoy it."

"You're so terrible in bed?" Ash doubted that. "Don't worry, I'll make the best of it."

The brief clenching of his jaw betrayed his frustration. Because she'd continued pushing, or because a part of him wanted to make the best of it, too? Either way, his reaction pleased her.

Despite his frustration, his voice remained smooth as silk. "You think I don't know, demon? You can't want sex, let alone enjoy it."

"What do you mean, I can't?" A spark of fear burned through her. "It's against the Rules?"

"You can't. It's impossible, physically." His head lowered, mouth hovering over hers. "I could kiss you, and you'd feel my lips and tongue. You won't feel the need that comes with it, when you don't know if it's your mind wanting or your body taking over."

Mind or body? Ash didn't know. She tore her gaze from his and studied his mouth. She only had to lift onto her toes, and she'd taste him. She wanted to.

She couldn't. Not without permission. Her hands had to remain fisted at her sides instead of drawing him down to her lips.

But no matter what Nicholas thought he knew, she felt this need. God, how she felt it.

"Look at you, Ash. Your eyes beginning to glow, your nipples hard. Pretend all you like, but I know that's not from wanting me. I could suck on them all day, and you wouldn't get hot. Not really hot." His voice roughened. "Maybe you could even make yourself wet. I don't know."

As far as Ash knew, she couldn't make herself wet. But she was now. Her muscles seemed to turn to water, all of her warm and liquid. She wanted to sway against him, feel the hardness of his chest against her breasts—and if his body had reacted like hers, to rub herself against the thrust of his erection. Nicholas obviously didn't believe that he could do this to her, but she could feel the slick need, the delicious ache.

Ash met his eyes again. "I am."

For a moment, desire flared through the cool amusement, before hardening to ice again. "So I could have you. You'd surround my cock with heat, like nothing I've ever had . . . and it'd be like fucking a blow-up doll. Every reaction, faked."

Her body didn't agree. "Then what is it I'm feeling?"

"Lies." He lifted his head. "Not from your lips, but pretending without words."

"No." Her nipples and sex ached for a touch. That wasn't faked. "This is real."

"It can't be."

"It *is*."

But Ash understood that he couldn't do anything but assume that she lied. She tilted her head, considering him, and his hands slid from her jaw to her shoulders. Still holding her in place—because he knew the Rules. Yet didn't he know that a demon could feel something like this?

"Are you certain your Guardian informant knows what she's talking about?"

"I'm sure." Almost absently, his thumbs stroked her collarbones. Nicholas didn't look at the skin he touched, however; his gaze continued to hold hers. "Don't try to discredit her."

Ash wouldn't. "And there's no room for exceptions?"

His lips quirked. Not cold, disdainful amusement this time, but the sort of smile that existed on the edge of a laugh.

"Is this your new plot? You'll persuade me that you're some kind of exception, different from every other demon, and that you want me in bed. And when I'm finally in there with you, you'll say, 'Oh, Nicholas! I wish I could touch you, but I have to follow the Rules!'—and moments after I give you permission, you'll punch through my chest and rip out my heart."

Ash blinked. His imitation of her accent had been spot on, and as for the rest— "You've given that scenario a lot of thought."

"I like to remind myself what will happen if I let my dick do my thinking." His fingers tightened, as if he thought she might pull away when he asked the next question. "The nurses from Nightingale House said that you suffered from a lack of affect. That you didn't feel any emotion or empathy. Three years of that. So don't try to change your story now and pretend to feel anything."

"I won't *pretend*," she said. Let him take that as he liked. For now, she was more interested in the rest of what he'd just told her. "You've already verified everything I told you about Nightingale House?"

"Of course."

"So you know I told the truth."

Nicholas shrugged. "My investigator might be a demon, too. Or Madelyn might have some kind of hold over him—or *you* might—and now he's just parroting your lies."

Holy good God, what a ridiculous response. Either Nicholas was a completely paranoid lunatic who thought demons had some awesome conspiratorial power . . . or he wasn't serious at all. Was he? Ash watched him struggle against a grin, and that was answer enough.

"So you know it was the truth," she said.

"At least part of it," he agreed. "But I still can't trust that all of it is."

Which was either a smart decision, or insanely paranoid.

Maybe both. Whatever it turned out to be, she already liked his sense of self-preservation.

No, it was more than that. She didn't just like the things he did and how he did them.

"I like *you*," Ash said. And she *enjoyed* liking him, so much that her enjoyment spread into a smile—a physical response to an emotion. How odd, that being around this cold and obsessive man made her happy. "I truly like you."

His expression froze, and she realized that either her confession or her smile had surprised him. He recovered quickly, with a mocking grin and an arid tone—a defense, Ash recognized.

"Demons also like torturing animals. So coming from you, that's hardly a compliment."

"What would be a compliment, then?" Something evil, she supposed. "Oh, Nicholas, you're looking so coldhearted and sardonic tonight, as if you're dreaming about punching a baby."

She saw it—the beginning of a laugh. Heard it in his sharp intake of breath. But he forced it back, his strong fingers digging into her shoulders.

"Don't," he warned.

Yes, God forbid. Oh, and she knew this emotion welling up within her now: irritation. She felt the change of her teeth, the odd pointed pressure of fangs against her lips. She saw the wash of red light across his skin, the pink glow on his white collar. Suddenly, she *hated* that he could hold her here like this.

"I've got an idea," she said—*hissed*. "Why don't you give me permission to smash your balls in with my knee? I guarantee you wouldn't like me after that, and wouldn't have to stop yourself from laughing."

His eyes narrowed. "That bothers you?"

"Yes." She couldn't lie. Nor could she hold on to the irritation and anger. They'd already faded—yet she still liked him. Why didn't that go away? "It also bothers me that my fangs apparently give me a lisp, and I don't know how to make them appear so that I can practice."

Nicholas didn't respond, and she couldn't read his expression again—which meant that he was thinking something that she could use against him. But she saw the moment when his thoughts turned to something that he didn't mind her knowing: That cold little smile formed again and his gaze dropped to his hands, still holding her shoulders. Icy satisfaction bled though the shield over his emotions.

"What is it?" she asked. No doubt more about how evil demons were, rinse and repeat.

"I was remembering what Rosalia once told me: Fill a room with hundreds of demons and Guardians who can each fly and throw city buses around, then add one human . . . and that one weak person would be the most powerful being in the room."

That was far more interesting than evil and lies. "Because of the Rules?"

"Yes. A demon has little physical power against a human. But a human can do anything to a demon."

Suddenly, though he'd loosened his grip until it would take little effort to step away from him, Nicholas's hold on her seemed like a threat. Was that what he wanted her to feel?

"You want me vulnerable?"

"I don't know if *vulnerable* is possible for a demon. I just wanted the upper hand—and I almost forgot that I've always had it." He let go of her shoulders and stepped back. His gaze swept from her head to her toes. "So do what you like, demon. Try to lure me into bed, try to make me laugh. It won't matter in the end. The only power you can ever have over a human is an emotional one, and I'll *never* care for you."

Oh. Well, she already knew that.

It was strange, though. He'd let her go, but she *did* feel suddenly vulnerable, experiencing the brief impulse to cover her naked chest, to back away from him. And she didn't know whether the sharp stab of disappointment came because he'd stopped touching her or because of his declaration that he'd never care for her . . . but she felt that, too.

Then those emotions passed, and she could only be vaguely dissatisfied that she had, once again, somehow messed up this whole demon thing. He'd just admitted to worrying that he'd lost the upper hand, and she hadn't even realized it or taken advantage of the situation.

Really, she needed to step up her game. The plots he imagined her forming were much better than those she came up with herself.

Except for the last plot he'd imagined. That was just dumb.

She watched him return to the table, distracted for a second by the fit of his trousers over his ass and the broadness of his shoulders. Only a slight dampness at his collar ruined the tailored perfection of it all—and she'd have loved to run her hands through his wet hair, messing up the neatly combed strands, then dragging him down to the floor to strip away every bit of clothing.

"You really thought I invited you to have sex so that you'd begin to care about me?"

He sat, looked at her over the top of his newspaper. "Didn't you?"

"I have amnesia, not a rampant case of the stupids. I'd have to be an idiot to think that any man mistakes sex for affection."

His short exhalation sounded like the precursor to a laugh, and she felt his grin down to her toes.

"So you would," he said. "What is your plot, then?"

"To tell you about all of the dried semen in this room. I'm hoping that it makes you feel skeevy enough to take another shower, and gives me another chance to see you naked."

He didn't seem that concerned. Slowly, he folded his paper, studying her all the while.

Finally, he asked, "Why do you want to see me naked?"

"Because you *don't* want me to see you naked. I want to know why." Though if she was completely honest, there was more to it. "I also think that I'd like looking at your ass, and I want to see whether you lied about your not-monstrous genitals. For all I know, the truth is that you really only have one leg, but you prop yourself up with a dragon-sized penis."

Nicholas closed his eyes. He seemed to choke out his reply. "I don't."

"So you say, but it's difficult to trust humans who aren't bound by a demonic bargain to tell the truth."

He gave a short laugh and opened his eyes. "So noted."

She couldn't detect a hint of coldness in his amusement. Good enough for now.

She turned away to collect her shirt, aware that he still watched her. Aware that her body reacted to that look.

Porno time, then. She could have a fresh memory of both responses, and better compare them.

He still watched her as she retrieved a recently laundered blanket from the closet and spread it over the love seat facing the television. She sat and picked up the remote.

"My chair?" Nicholas asked.

She didn't look around. "You'll notice I didn't sit with you during dinner."

He joined her on the love seat a moment later, newspaper in hand. He read steadily through the opening credits, but by the time the grunting and ass slapping began, his fingers had crumpled the paper's edges. Not even once did he glance at Ash.

A round of perfunctory sucking and moaning finally pushed him over the edge. With a muttered "Fuck," he rose and stalked into the connecting room. Shortly afterward came the sound of undressing and the spray of the shower. Ash would have bet anything that he'd turned the temperature to cold.

She switched off the video. Her test hadn't worked well; she still didn't know if the movie aroused her, or if her sexual tension had been created because she'd imagined doing everything she watched with Nicholas.

She liked to think that he'd been imagining the same. If so, her plot had worked, somewhat. She didn't see him naked, but she'd learned that he'd walk away from a sexual situation with her . . . which meant that despite his upper hand, she affected him more than he could tolerate.

That knowledge could be useful. So she'd had a productive evening, if a little evil.

And she'd enjoyed the hell out of it.

CHAPTER 8

Until Nicholas stopped at a bed-and-breakfast on the outskirts of Duluth, Ash forgot about his plan to mislead the Guardians by abandoning everything in the hotel room and remaining checked-in. When he'd mentioned paying for the new room in cash, she'd expected them to pull up to a flea-bitten motel, but the converted Georgian Revival mansion sat on two picturesque acres of snow-covered fields surrounded by a wrought-iron fence.

Maybe Nicholas saved the flea-biters for when he was truly desperate, and not just hiding from angelic warriors who'd cut off Ash's head the moment they saw her.

She waited in the rented SUV while he went inside, and listened to him spin a tale about hotel bed bugs, stolen credit cards, and lost luggage, charming the innkeeper into a quickie reservation. As it was winter, and a slow period for tourists, he might have gotten a room anyway, but the week he paid in advance probably helped his cause.

To pass the time, Ash counted the money left in his briefcase. It took her longer than she'd expected. No wonder he'd willingly abandoned a few thousand-dollar suits at the hotel. With this stash, he could buy and abandon them several times over.

Strange that she felt no urge to steal the cash. Once again, her demonic nature failed her. Now she only had to decide whether her impatience to travel north and meet Rachel's parents was rooted in some demonic need, too . . . or a human one.

Finally, Nicholas returned to the SUV. His gaze dropped to the open briefcase. Ash lifted her brows, inviting him to accuse her, but he only said, "There's always more."

Dammit. If he cared so little, she *should* have taken some. Next time.

Just north of Duluth, Ash tried to shape-shift again. When her face remained the same, she admitted defeat and climbed into the back, mentally urging Nicholas to drive faster. Perhaps it was best that he didn't, though. Even a Minnesotan deputy might question the number of weapons in the long black duffel on the backseat. Ash shared space with it, hunkered down below the windows.

Nicholas was probably right that she'd be easily recognized when they neared Rachel's home. The township numbered only a little over two thousand residents, the population distributed along four rural roads. Rachel's parents lived a few miles past the center of the township. Ash held her breath as they drove through, her heart pounding with anticipation, her throat tight and chest full.

She *knew* these roads. Outside the window, she only had a view of the pointed tops of pine trees, their limbs drooping beneath a heavy blanket of snow, but she could picture the two-lane stretch of pavement. She could almost see the dirty snow pushed to the side by the plows. And even before Nicholas began to slow, she knew that the turn onto the lane shared by the Boyles and their neighbors was coming up. When he did turn, she anticipated the crunch of gravel beneath the tires, because she knew the Boyles and their neighbors paid a private contractor to plow and sand the driveways after each heavy snowfall.

Her gut-deep excitement boiled over. "We're almost there."

Nicholas threw a glance over his shoulder—probably to check that she was still hidden. "How do you know?"

"It's familiar. It's *all* so familiar." She had to force herself to stay down. In just a few moments, the Boyles would be able to look out of their living room windows and see the vehicle approaching. She still couldn't picture their faces, but she could visualize the house. "It's the Craftsman with the red door. The driveway is marked with a gated entrance between two brick columns—but the gate is always open, and there's a concrete garden gnome on top of each column, because . . . because . . ."

"Because?"

Disappointment pierced her excitement. "I can't remember why. They mean something, but I don't know what. Will you ask them?"

He didn't answer for a moment . . . and then several moments. Ash tried to recapture her anticipation. They were driving closer, closer—but no, something was wrong. Something was *un*familiar.

Nicholas began to slow. Ash shook her head.

"No, this is wrong. You've passed the house—"

"On purpose. Now sit up and take a look before it's out of sight."

Ash turned in the seat. Through the back window, everything appeared as she'd expected: the columns flanking the driveway and the snow piled around them, the gnomes, and farther back from the lane, the house and the red door.

A red door cordoned off with yellow police tape.

Her fingers tightened on the back of the seat. "What happened?"

"I don't know." His voice had lowered to a murmur. As soon as the house was hidden behind a stand of pine trees, he stopped in the lane and cut the engine. "Can you hear anything?"

Only his heartbeat and hers and the ticking of the motor and a few winter birds and the cracking of branches beneath the ice and snow and the wind through the pine needles and the snuffling of some animal out in the woods and a neighbor's dog scratching at a door and the tumbling of an electric clothes dryer—

No. She could focus. She *had* to focus on the Boyles' house.

She recognized the sounds a moment later. "Two people are inside the house, talking," she said softly. "I can't make out what they are saying, but it's definitely a man and a woman."

"The Boyles?"

A man and a woman . . . maybe they were the Boyles. If so, they weren't familiar.

The realization brought an unexpected lump to her throat. *Their voices weren't familiar.*

"Ash?"

"I don't know," she finally answered. "They are— Wait."

She frowned, listening. Had they gone so silent? Why couldn't she hear anything at all from the house now?

Why didn't she *feel* anything?

"They're gone," she whispered. "They've left."

"In a car? There wasn't one in the drive."

No, there hadn't been—and she hadn't heard the garage door open, or an engine start. What the hell?

Frowning, she glanced back at Nicholas. "They're simply gone. And there's something more I just realized: I couldn't sense them at all. Their emotions were blocked, like yours are. Actually, *more* than yours. I can feel the barrier you put up. I couldn't feel theirs."

"Fuck." His heart sped up. "Guardians. We've got to go."

"No!" Ash scrambled into the front seat, snatching the keys from the ignition before he could turn them. She didn't give him time to become angry. Before he'd had more than a second to stare at the empty keyhole, she said, "Nicholas, something happened in that house. I *need* to know what."

"The Boyles aren't there."

"No, because something happened. I have to know." When he hesitated, she added, "Please."

"The Guardians might come back. If they do, you're dead."

She didn't care. "I need to look. *Please*."

It didn't matter if he agreed. In another second, she'd jump out into the snow and go, anyway. But he set his jaw and nodded, holding his hand out for the keys.

He needed to know, too, she realized. Discovery by the Guardians could jeopardize their bargain and his search for Madelyn, yet he'd agreed to go back to the house, anyway. Ash wished she could kiss him for that, but she settled for shutting up and letting him concentrate on reversing the SUV down the icy lane. He backed into the driveway, as if preparing for a quick getaway. Perhaps he was.

She leapt out before he cut the engine. Cold air bit into her face, her lungs. Her heel skidded out from under her, and the world seemed to twist, icy and dark and erupting with screams all around her, the dark tower spearing up into the red sky, not trees but worse, Lucifer looking down at them all, but he'd let her free and the agony would be over, and the screaming pain, her body gone, gone—

No. Ash planted her feet, stayed upright. Her stomach

heaved up a scream, but it couldn't get past the dread tightening her throat. The house was too still, too cold.

And she could smell the blood from here.

"Come on." Nicholas caught her elbow, pulled her forward. He carried a crossbow, the bolt already loaded and ready.

"Something's wrong," she whispered.

"I know."

She followed him to the porch, up the stairs. Nicholas swore at the locked front door. Ash found the key exactly where it should have been, beneath the blue cushion on the front porch swing. He took it from her without question, studying her face.

"Are you sure you want to go in?"

Ash couldn't imagine what she looked like, that he had to ask that. "Yes."

"You stay here until I've cleared the rooms, made sure no one is waiting."

"No."

He shook his head, but didn't argue. The police tape ripped away easily. Opening the door, he took a step inside—and stopped. Though his shields, she sensed the hot burst of rage, the hard bitterness of grief.

No, no, no.

Nicholas backed up, began to turn. "Let's go out—"

Ash ducked under his arm, was through the doorway before he could touch her, before he could stop her. *Oh, God*, she knew this house. The wooden floors polished to a high shine, the coatrack that looked like a bowling pin with arms, the pine chest beside it that was the perfect place to sit and remove a pair of boots. Emotions flooded her, so many things that she knew but couldn't remember. She couldn't breathe.

Then she did breathe, and smelled the blood again. She turned toward the living room and saw it.

The cornflower blue rug that should have been in the center of the living room was missing, and she knew, she *knew* that somewhere that rug had a huge, irregular stain on it. Because the rest of the blood was splattered and dried against the walls, across the marble fireplace, in handprints on the floor.

The scene blurred, and she suddenly wanted to stop feeling anything, wanted to go back to the way life had been at Nightingale House, where every emotion skimmed along the surface. Because now the emotions stabbed, and stabbed, and even though she held her stomach and tried to keep her guts in, she could feel how they ripped and tore with every drop of blood she saw in that room.

With her demon vision, she saw them all.

Then Nicholas was in front of her, holding her face, forcing her to see *him*. "Ash. We don't know what happened here. Who it happened to. And whatever happened, they might have survived."

She knew who it had happened to. She knew who'd been in this room. The knitting basket set beside the armchair and the haphazard tangle of a partially finished scarf told her that Rachel's mother had been here. The tray tipped over next to the recliner, the scattered pieces of a model train said that Rachel's father had been here, too.

"Ash." He shook her a little, and with effort, she focused on him again. "I'm leaving you here to check the rest of the house. All right?"

No. But she nodded.

As the sound of his footsteps moved down the hallway, she entered the living room. A framed photo sat on the fireplace mantel. Taken during the summer in the house's backyard, it depicted a smiling Rachel flanked by a middle-aged man and woman. Her parents.

They didn't look any more familiar than Nicholas had the first time Ash saw his picture. How could that be? How could she feel this much fear and dread, this terror that they'd been hurt—or worse—and yet have no memory of them at all? How could she recognize the location where the picture had been taken, but have no memory of being there?

"There's no one here," Nicholas said from behind her. "Ash, we have to go now."

Yes, they did. She joined him in the hallway. "We need to find out what happened."

"We will." His gaze dropped to the photo she still held, but he didn't tell her to put it back. Perhaps he realized she wouldn't have. "Who would have put that tape across the door?"

The township didn't have a police force. "The county sheriff. His office is in Duluth."

"We'll head back, then. Look, you can't go with me. There might be family, friends at the sheriff's or the hospital. People who'd recognize Rachel. So I'll take you to the bed-and-breakfast. I have to leave you there alone. Do you have any weapons in your cache?"

That mental storage space. "If I do, I don't know how to get to them."

"I'll give you some, then. What can you use?" He lifted his crossbow. "This?"

"I . . . don't know."

"A sword? I have one in the car."

She glanced down at her hands. Could she use a sword? "I don't know that, either."

His mouth tightened. "Can you fight hand-to-hand?"

"I don't think so. Why?"

"Because if the Guardians were here, they are obviously looking for you."

"And if they knew exactly where I was, they'd already be on me. Wouldn't they?" When he nodded, she said, "So chances are, they don't know I'll be at the B and B, either."

He must have agreed. With a nod, he said, "All right. I'll drop you off, and you stay in our room."

Easy enough. "And if they do come?"

Nicholas started for the door, his expression grim. "Can you run?"

"Yes."

"Then you'd better run faster than they do."

The crime scene photos were worse than the house had been.

Taylor closed the Boyles' murder file and passed it to Revoire. No longer the farmer, he'd changed into the same "federal agent" suit that she wore. Appearance was always important. Not many of the smaller law enforcement agencies had heard of Special Investigations, even though they were a legitimate division within the Homeland Security Department.

"They aren't pretty," Sheriff Brand said, nodding at the photos. He was the kind of cop Taylor liked: professional, courteous, damn sure of his job and how to do it. He hadn't put up a fuss when they'd arrived and asked to look at the Boyle case, claiming that the MO matched that of a serial killer they'd been tracking. He'd simply taken a look at their credentials, checked them out, and invited them into his office.

"No, they aren't," Taylor agreed. Horrific—and she knew

Brand felt the same. He wasn't interested in getting involved in a pissing contest with the feds. He reserved his anger for the man who'd done it, and his pity for the couple killed. "Did you know them?"

Brand shook his head. "I talked with them a few times after their girl, Rachel, went missing six years back. But she was working over in London at the time, so there wasn't much to do. A shame. Pretty girl, sharp as a tack. We looked at Steve Johnson then, just routine—she'd had some trouble with him—but they hadn't seen each other since she left that school in Chicago."

Rachel Boyle. Why did that name sound familiar? Taylor couldn't immediately recall, but she remembered the photo on the fireplace mantel at the Boyles' house. Just the three of them.

"No other family?"

"Nope. It was a neighbor who spotted Steve Johnson sitting on their front porch swing holding that butcher knife. No coat, no shoes, all cleaned up and just staring off into space. She didn't recognize him, so she called it in." Brand shook his head. "That part of the county, we get a hunting accident now and then. A few meth heads, a few missing hikers. Nothing like this. Sick."

So they had Steve Johnson pretty much red-handed, and with a confession on top of it. Case closed for the locals. Taylor and Revoire wouldn't be able to do the same so easily. They wouldn't pursue Steve Johnson. The courts could take care of him, and influenced by a demon or not, the man had made a choice. Free will mattered. He'd made a choice to seek out the Boyles. He'd made a choice to pick up a knife. He'd made a choice to murder them. At any point, he could have chosen differently, and there was nothing the demon could have done to force him.

But Johnson hadn't resisted, and his actions had served the demon well. The choice Johnson had made would probably send him to Hell, too.

Brand looked to Revoire, who'd finished flipping through photos and closed the file. "And you still think we have your guy in our lockup?"

"Probably not," Revoire said. "There's a distinct difference in the blood spatter. There's no control. This looks like he was angry. He knew the victims?"

"Not well." The sheriff sat behind his desk, removed his hat. "They're from up Lakewood, Steve Johnson has been here in Duluth for nine years now. Came in from Chicago. Says he was following Rachel, but when she moved to England and then disappeared . . . he found himself a few other girlfriends. He says that he never contacted the Boyles before Saturday morning."

"But he claimed that Rachel's ghost visited him?"

"Yes. Visited, and said that she hadn't gone missing. Said she hadn't been killed by some rich man. That her parents had done it, and she needed Johnson to get revenge for her." Brand sighed. "The defense is already working up their insanity plea."

"And what do you think?" Taylor wondered.

"I don't think it'll fly. He's been working up to this for years. Rachel had a restraining order on him after he stalked her on campus. We've had other complaints from other girls. No violence in the priors, so this is unusual—but he said flat-out in the interview that he knew it wasn't right, but he had to do it for her. So he's got something loose up there, but he knows right from wrong. He'll stand trial."

So the demon had probably known about Johnson's obsession with Rachel, had known exactly who to push. To know that, it had probably accessed court records and found the restraining order. There might be a paper trail.

Taylor and Revoire would start there.

They took their leave of Sheriff Brand, walked to the front of the building. Teleporting around a busy city in the middle of the day was out, except in an emergency. Taylor didn't mind. Growing up in San Francisco, she hadn't seen a lot of snow, but it was falling outside and she wouldn't get cold.

She didn't think Revoire was ready to teleport again yet, anyway. She caught his eye. "All right?"

"Fine. Just reminded of why I can't always tell the difference between humans and demons. That little shit deserves to burn."

Yes. Johnson had his issues, but when it came down to it, he'd wanted to kill the Boyles. Taylor had about as much sympathy for him as she did serial killers who blamed their mamas.

She nodded her agreement, squinting a little as they emerged from the dim office to the bright fall of white. The sun wasn't out, but the daylight and the reflection off the snow still glared on her sensitive eyes.

"Do you recall anything odd about Rachel Boyle? The name is nagging at me." And years on the force told her not to ignore those little niggles.

Revoire shook his head. "I remember when it happened. It caught the news in this area a couple of times. But nothing stood out. Most people thought her rich boyfriend did it."

Rich boyfriend. Taylor stopped as the niggle turned into a full-blown itch. "No, not the news. The dungeon."

"Dungeon?"

"Nicholas St. Croix." Oh, it was coming to her. She'd been distracted, but she remembered this. "He said that a demon killed Rachel Boyle. That she died in his arms after saving him. He'd wanted to know if she'd become a Guardian."

"Did she?" Revoire's brow furrowed, as if he was trying to recall the name now, too. "I don't know many of the novices—"

"She didn't. We still don't know why. And . . . speak of the devil. There he is."

Crossing the circular drive that served the government buildings, and still looking like the same cold, rich bastard. Taylor almost laughed. He hadn't noticed her yet, and she briefly considered shifting her form—but no, this was better.

His gaze lit on her, and she couldn't detect any change of his expression or a crack in his emotional shields. But he recognized her. His heart sped up. An automatic response, she thought. Though Nicholas St. Croix knew he had nothing to fear from a pair of Guardians, his instincts were shouting at his body to fight or get the hell out of there.

"Mr. St. Croix," she drawled. "How was your trip from New York?"

Cool amusement hardened his eyes. "How is Rosalia?"

"Concerned about you."

"Ah, yes. The mother to everyone."

Such icy disdain for one of the sweetest women she'd ever met. God, Taylor wanted to punch him. "Better than your mother?"

"Is she?" He shrugged. "She lies, she manipulates. I don't see the difference, personally."

"You wouldn't."

"Perhaps not," he agreed easily. He looked to Revoire, who was frowning at him—probably wondering if St. Croix was a demon—before addressing Taylor again. "If that is all . . . I don't recall your name. Detective something or other, was it?"

Oh, he was good. Playing up that British accent when she knew he'd spent over half his life in America. Deliberately shutting her out, pissing her off. Why?

"Special Agent Taylor of Special Investigations. This is Special Agent Revoire. Do you have time to sit down for coffee, Mr. St. Croix?"

"No."

She smiled pleasantly, but put steel in her voice. "Make time."

"Or what?" His gaze ran over her in a calculating assessment. "How could you possibly make it worth my time?"

"Because we've just finished looking at photos from a recent crime scene. Frank and Caroline Boyle. I believe you know them?"

Finally, a break in his shields. Just a fraction, but enough to feel his rage. His sadness. But no surprise.

"Yes," he said, and now there was bleakness beneath all of that coldness. "How did it happen?"

Taylor suddenly understood that this was why he'd come to the sheriff's office. He was looking for answers. He *cared.*

She hadn't expected that.

"Steve Johnson, an old boyfriend of Rachel's, did it . . . after he'd been visited by her ghost."

She saw the realization hit him. His dark brows lowered and his jaw hardened, cracking the icy cast of his expression.

"A demon?"

"Yes. We're looking for her now." She paused, hoping for any reaction, but didn't get one. She'd have to try again. "Rosalia thought that you might have run into a demon lately."

"No. I just had questions."

"Questions that brought you to Duluth?"

"I heard rumors that someone who looked like Rachel had been seen in the area. I never believed that she hadn't become a Guardian. So I came looking, because when I find her, I can finally clear my name." That cool amusement came sliding back. "I guess I'm not looking for a Guardian, but a demon. I don't suppose that you've slain her yet?"

"No." Was he lying? Taylor couldn't decide. He did have

good reason to follow up on any rumors. "But we will. Do you plan to stay in town?"

"Just long enough to make certain the ghost wasn't the demon I'm looking for."

His mother. Though that demon wasn't an excuse for him to grow up into such an asshole, she couldn't blame St. Croix for wanting to slay her.

"We'll let you know if she is," Taylor said.

"Not if I find her first."

Taylor smiled thinly. "Good hunting, then."

He nodded and continued past her up the stairs. Taylor waited until he passed through the doors before looking to Revoire.

"We need to contact SI. I want to know everything he did, looked at, bought, went online for in the past week. And we need a picture of Rachel Boyle." The demon had probably changed her shape by now, but maybe not. "If the demon impersonated Rachel once, it might do it again—especially if the target is someone like St. Croix."

Rich, ruthless, probably on the edge of sanity after a childhood in a demon's tender care. God knew how a man like that could be manipulated, or how dangerous he could be.

"I thought for certain I'd finally run into Basriel." Revoire shook his head. "He was human?"

Barely. "Let's go. We've got a demon to find, before Basriel does."

Or before Nicholas St. Croix did.

Nicholas returned to the hotel. If the Guardians tailed him, they wouldn't find a demon. They wouldn't find any evidence that she'd stayed in the same room the night before. Hell, even the porn rental suggested that he'd been alone. He ate lunch and watched the financial news, then hit the gym for two hours, giving the Guardians time to conduct a search of his suite.

If they were tailing him. Hopefully, they'd decided to focus on finding the demon who'd posed as Rachel, and hopefully they'd believed Nicholas when he'd told them Rosalia had been mistaken about his being with one. And if they hadn't believed him, hopefully they thought he was such a dickhead bastard that he deserved whatever a demon did to him, and left him to it.

He knew the Guardians didn't work that way, though. Unfortunately, they even tried to save the bastards.

In the afternoon, he completed the business-related calls and sent the e-mails that he hadn't the day before. No need to hide his electronic trail now. He tried to think of *any* way to contact the bed-and-breakfast without giving Ash away.

If they were watching him, he couldn't. Goddammit. He couldn't. There was absolutely nothing that they couldn't hear or trace or follow.

Was Ash still waiting in the room as he'd instructed? How long would she wait? She'd been desperate to know what had happened to Rachel's parents. If Nicholas didn't bring back answers, would she stay in the room? And even if she did, how long until the innkeepers worried and contacted the authorities? Probably overnight, he thought. Maybe into the next evening.

Maybe by then, he'd figure out whether she'd killed the Boyles, and whether her desperation had been an act.

An act? *God.* That he even considered the possibility it wasn't proved how she'd already gotten to him, somehow made him believe that she was different from other demons, made him wonder if the amnesia had affected her nature so strongly. But, Jesus—when she'd seen the Boyles's living room, she'd seemed so shattered. Lost. He knew that emotional reaction *had* to be a lie. Maybe the Boyles' murder had been her plot all along, and bringing Nicholas in to see the aftermath was just the icing.

But if that were true, why the hell would she still be playing along? Why would she pretend to care what had happened to them? Why wasn't she gloating?

He didn't know. But he needed to figure it out. And if she had been responsible for the Boyles, he'd let the Guardians have her—his bargain and his soul be damned.

Searching through his e-mails, he found Cooper's report, verified the investigator's timeline. A month ago, Ash had escaped from the hospital. Cawthorne had hung himself a week later; the same night, someone had entered Madelyn's town house. A few days after that, Rachel's ghost had begun visiting Steve Johnson. Then the previous night—Saturday night—Nicholas had found Ash at the house in London.

The Boyles had been murdered Saturday morning. Even accounting for the time difference, a demon could have easily watched Johnson kill them, then flown across the Atlantic to London.

Ash *could* have done it. But Nicholas couldn't make himself believe she had.

He tried. At the window overlooking the lake, he recalled how she'd stood here while he ate dinner, plotting to see him naked, with amusement and mischief taking their turns lighting her usually emotionless expression . . . and later, tempting him with her nudity and her claim that she wanted him. *Jesus.* That lust had to be a lie, too. But she hadn't lied about Nightingale House—and why would any demon stay there for three years? Why didn't she try to tear him apart with every opportunity? Why didn't she imitate Rachel more perfectly? Aside from a few mannerisms and her accent, nothing about the two women was similar.

He'd go mad trying to make sense of her. Demons were supposed to be creatures of habit, but there was nothing that he could see in Ash that resembled any other demon he'd heard of. Certainly not—

Oh, fuck. Creatures of habit. What the hell had he been thinking, wasting time worrying about one demon when he should have been hunting another? He knew someone else who preferred hotels like this—and there weren't many of them in Duluth.

And that someone might be looking for Ash, too.

Nicholas didn't have to go far. The clerk at the registration desk recognized Madelyn's picture. She wouldn't tell Nicholas the name Madelyn had checked in under, but he learned that she'd left two days before.

Fuck. He'd missed her by only a day.

And she had some balls, still using his mother's face. He scanned the hotel lobby and the adjoining bar. Shape-shifted, Madelyn could be any of the people here. The Guardians could be any of the people here. Just waiting for him to lead them to Ash. If Madelyn had waited a day, she'd have just run into Ash at the hotel, and wouldn't have needed to—

Realization hit like a punch to the stomach. *Two days.* Saturday. She'd left the hotel the same day the Boyles had been murdered.

Oh, goddammit. Now *that* made sense, sick as it was. Ash had escaped from Nightingale House, and if Madelyn knew Ash was searching for answers, she'd have assumed that Ash would eventually make her way to America and the Boyles' doorstep. But if Madelyn got to the Boyles first, Nicholas had no doubt that she'd have taken Rachel's mother's place. Within a few days, after the investigation died down, she'd probably have begun waiting at the house, planning to lure Ash in like a witch from a fairy tale.

For what purpose?

That didn't matter. Whatever Madelyn wanted from Ash, he'd see that she didn't get it.

Of course, it was damn hard to make certain of that when he was stuck in a hotel lobby, and Ash waited a few miles away. Did he risk going?

If he didn't, and Madelyn found Ash, he might lose his only chance to learn where his mother's body lay, and to slay the demon bitch who'd killed her, Rachel, and now Rachel's parents. But if he was with Ash, Madelyn would come to him.

And he knew exactly the place to wait for her—where the Guardians wouldn't find them, but Madelyn eventually would. When she did, he'd have his revenge, and Ash . . .

Ash. *God.* All right. She'd gotten to him. And though he'd planned to slay her after her usefulness ended and she led him to Madelyn, he wouldn't now. He *couldn't* now. He'd tell her what the Guardians looked for when they searched for demons so that she could avoid them, and then he'd let her go.

So what would he rather risk: staying away from Ash and possibly losing an opportunity to find Madelyn, or having the Guardians follow him to the bed-and-breakfast?

The answer came easily. Nicholas returned to his room, collected his computer and his keys, and left everything else. Hell, he should have done this earlier—this wasn't much of a risk at all. Even if the Guardians followed him, he'd get to Ash first. He'd protect her. As a human, the most powerful being in a room of Guardians and demons, he had no doubt that he *could* protect her.

And she was just too damn useful to lose now.

CHAPTER 9

Ash couldn't remember staying at a bed-and-breakfast before, but this one didn't fit the mental image she had of them. Instead of small, cozy rooms filled with overstuffed furniture and quilts, everything in their suite appeared spare and elegant. Just as well. Better not to have rooms that seemed to invite her to hide beneath the blankets, or curl up in a ball and eat a tub of ice cream. The Victorian restraint, the straight-backed wooden chairs, served as a guide for Ash. She, too, remained stiff and composed.

She'd thought the grief and fear would have faded by now. They hadn't. And she'd forgotten—or maybe she'd never known—how much effort it took to constrain them. By the time afternoon had come and gone, and Nicholas still hadn't returned with any information, that effort had crept into a soul-deep exhaustion. Never before had she wished that sleep would come to her; she wished it now, if only to make the time pass more quickly. If only so that she wouldn't feel this emptiness—an emptiness that, for the first time that she could remember, seemed hollow.

She wished Nicholas were here. Not only so that he could confirm the news Ash feared she already knew, but so that he would be here *with* her when she learned for certain. He made her happy. He also irritated and frustrated her, but any of those emotions had to be better than this unending dread.

Where was he?

Night fell. The innkeeper's wife knocked on the door and invited Ash down to dinner. Roasted chicken and garlic mashed potatoes, by the scent of it. She could taste the woman's sweet concern, and the piquant bite of her pity. Though she was tempted to join them downstairs for no other reason than to ask whether they had a newspaper from that morning, or even a computer and an Internet connection that she could use, Ash had to plead a headache and decline without opening the door.

Her eyes wouldn't stop glowing.

In the red wash of light, she studied the picture of Rachel and her parents over and over again, searching for a simple emotional association, any hint of familiarity. A little girl's tiara could remind her of Cinderella and send Ash on a search through her memories, but there were no similar connections to find here. Nothing in the Boyles' shirts, their smiles, the sparkle of the mother's wedding ring. Yet seeing their blood had torn her apart. *Why?*

She found no answers in the photo. Perhaps the answers were coming, however, as was the familiar sound of the engine that she'd listened to for a thousand miles. Nicholas. Unable to see the road from her room, she pushed through the doors leading onto the balcony, where she had a better angle on the winding street leading to the house. His headlights swept across the snow as he rounded the final curve. He wasn't even to the driveway yet. Minutes might pass before he arrived at the mansion and walked up the stairs.

Ash couldn't wait that long.

She dropped from the balcony, landing in a knee-deep pile of snow. Behind her, light from the dining room spilled across her body, casting a long shadow. She didn't give anyone eating inside time to see her. Up on her feet, she sprinted across the unbroken blanket of white. It should have been harder, she thought, but her legs churned a trail through the heavy snow, strong, unstoppable. Within seconds, she was at the driveway, racing in front of Nicholas's vehicle and into the splash of his bright headlights.

He slammed on the brakes. She heard his shouted curse—though she supposed even a human might have heard that. Rushing to his door, she pulled it open.

Nicholas was still yelling. "Jesus, Ash! What? Are you being chased?"

"No," she said, but he must not have believed her.

Grabbing a crossbow already in the passenger seat, Nicholas jumped out of the car. He turned, searching the empty field, then looked up at the sky. As if satisfied that no one was after her, he finally looked to Ash again.

"What the hell?"

He couldn't guess?

"I need to know," Ash said. His expression changed suddenly—and she knew. She'd been right. Oh, God. Pain hit her gut again, ripping, tearing. "What happened?"

"One of Rachel's old boyfriends did it."

"What did he do?" She didn't really need to ask. The blood had said it all. And a *boyfriend* had done that? "My God, did she just attract the psychos?"

Surprise and pained humor flashed across Nicholas's features. "Apparently."

No. No, not him. He wouldn't have done this. He wouldn't have torn them apart. Maybe a demon, but not a human. What kind of person did that?

Not the kind that deserved to live.

The stabbing pain hardened into something else. Ash didn't know what. But she knew what she had to do. "Where is the boyfriend at now?"

"They caught him. He's in the county lockup."

"All right. Move aside, and give me the keys."

Nicholas frowned at her. "Why?"

"Because I'm going there to kill him."

"What?" His confusion changed to disbelief as he looked at her face. "You're serious."

Completely. And since he wasn't getting out of her way, she went around him, reached for the driver side door. He caught her wrist.

"You can't. He's human. It'll break the Rules, and the Guardians will have you. You'll be the next one dead."

"I don't care." She didn't.

"Then care about this: You'll be breaking your bargain. Getting killed isn't helping me find Madelyn."

"Fuck that." The response sprang so easily to her mouth. "Release me from the bargain."

"Fuck *that.*" His hold tightened and he whipped her around, shoving her back against the side of the SUV. "You break away, you break our bargain, you'll end up in that frozen field. You want that, Ash? Tortured for eternity, all for a little piece of shit?"

Not for the piece-of-shit boyfriend. For the parents. Not even *her* parents. Ah, God—and the pain was coming back now. She could feel it welling up, closing her throat and stinging her eyes.

A wail of grief poured out.

Nicholas's eyes widened. He clapped a palm over her mouth, cutting it off. "Stop that."

She couldn't. She stared at him over the top of his hand. Heat itched over her cheeks. Crying. *Crying.* Why?

Nicholas jerked his hand away as if her tears burned. He stared at her in shock.

"Let me go," she whispered hoarsely. If he didn't, something was going to break. Maybe his hold on her. Maybe the Rules. Maybe just something inside her.

"Shut up."

He set his crossbow on the hood and shoved her face against his neck. Hard warmth wrapped around her shoulders. Was he holding her? Nicholas? The kindness hurt almost as much as the rest. She let it come up, the inexplicable rage, the grief, sobbing it out against his throat.

And when it was over, she was exhausted again. Her body strong, but something inside her just . . . tired.

She tried to pull away, but Nicholas wouldn't let her. Still afraid she'd take off for the county jail? That had passed. Now she just felt the cold coming in all around her.

"You have to be freezing," she said.

"Actually, no. You kept me warm." He drew back just enough to look down at her. "You don't remember the Boyles. Why do you care so much?"

"I don't know."

His thumb swept the lingering wetness from her cheek before he met her gaze again. "I won't believe these are real. Not from a demon."

Was he reminding himself or her? "Right now, I wish that you were right. I'd rather feel nothing than this."

A strange expression passed over his face—humor and sadness, all at once. "I've thought that before. Revenge is better."

"Then let me have it."

His gaze dropped to her lips. "Johnson isn't going anywhere. You can come back after our bargain is finished and do it."

She could do that. "Or maybe a quick death is too good for him. Maybe I could spend the rest of my life making his a living hell."

Nicholas grinned. "Now *that's* a demon talking—and it wouldn't break the Rules. Though I'm disappointed that your first good plot isn't designed to ruin me."

"Oh, me too." Ash laughed. Oh, that felt better. So much better. "I'll have to come up with something that—"

His fingers tightened and his expression changed so quickly that Ash was left reeling. Abruptly, he let her go, grabbed his crossbow from the hood.

"Get behind me, Ash."

Why? She turned, scanning the field. Nicholas had frozen beside her, his gaze fixed on a point at the edge of the driveway. In the dark, she easily made out the shape of the man standing on the wrought-iron fence, his feet balanced on two points.

Ash blinked. Dark haired, handsome, and slickly dressed, he could have been Nicholas's brother. Except Nicholas's blue eyes didn't turn crimson like that. Fascinating.

Her heart leapt as she realized: This was a demon. He might have answers. He might know who she was. Unless . . .

She edged back behind Nicholas. "Is it Madelyn?"

No, Nicholas didn't think so. Demons were creatures of habit, and that included the genders they preferred to adopt in their human forms. This was someone different . . . and he didn't want to wait around and find out who.

"Get in the car, Ash."

"In the car?" The demon hopped down from the fence. "Oh, she won't be safe there."

Fuck. Nicholas swung the crossbow up, the explosive bolts ready. He couldn't control the pacing of his heart, but as long as the pounding didn't shake his aim, he didn't care if the demon heard it.

Heedless of the weapon pointed at him, the demon walked forward. "I'll admit, when I felt your grief from across the city, I wondered what had struck one of my brethren so. A demon, pained by loss? I thought it might be a trap. But now I see it is worse. It's pathetic."

Oh, Jesus. Ash had brought this thing here? "You didn't shield your emotions?"

Her back pressed to the side of the rig, Ash shook her head. "I don't know."

Shit. *Shit.* That meant the Guardians probably felt it, too.

Though right now, that might be a good thing.

"And look at you." The demon's eyes narrowed to glowing crimson slits. "Why, you're not brethren at all, but a little halfling? I thought you all dead or frozen."

Ash drew a sharp breath. "What do you mean?"

"No, no. No questions. There's one that's so much more important." Five yards away, the demon stopped. "Lucifer must have let you out. Why?"

"I don't know."

God. Nicholas clenched his teeth. Why wasn't she lying to this demon? She needed to be. Did she not recognize the danger he posed to her?

"What use could you have been? And he must have bound you to someone. Not to himself, because he can't control you from Hell. Not now."

"I'm bound to him." She indicated Nicholas with a tip of her chin.

The demon's gaze raked over Nicholas and paused on the crossbow. With a laugh, he asked, "Do you truly think you can aim that fast enough, human?"

"We'll see."

"Keep up, then."

Nicholas blinked. The demon appeared beside him, breath hot on his cheek. *Jesus.* And gone before he could react, thirty feet away and laughing. Footprints in the snow marked every step that Nicholas hadn't been able to track.

They had to get out of here.

"Ash, get in the backseat, *now*. Grab a weapon. Any one."

He reached behind for the door handle. Ash turned to do the same. A hot wind rushed past him.

She was gone.

Nicholas spun around. "Ash!"

There, by the fence. The demon had her by the throat, was looking at her face, pulling back the collar of her jacket. She shrieked, rammed up her knee. The demon blocked it.

Nicholas ran to them, slowed by the heavy snow. "Let her go!"

The demon didn't even look at him, just angled his body to keep Ash between his and the crossbow. "The symbols, this spell. Is this for a Gate? Does Lucifer think he can return early? No, no, ha! No. Not if you're dead, halfling."

Gone again. Nicholas slid to a stop, chest heaving. Fuck. *Where?*

Up. Ash's scream pierced the air—abruptly cut off. Silhouetted against the dark sky, her limp body dropped to the ground. Lungs aching with effort and cold, Nicholas raced to catch her. Not fast enough. God. The snow billowed around her when she landed. She didn't move.

Rage gripped him, gave him speed. Almost to her—and no, not dead. Thank God. No blood on her chest, her head still attached. Her eyes open and staring. Her neck, twisted.

The demon had broken her neck.

"I like to play with them."

Leathery wings spread wide, the demon glided to a stop beside Ash's motionless body. His feet sank into the snow as he landed, facing Nicholas. The malevolent glee on his face churned bile through Nicholas's stomach.

Stay in place for one second, fucker. I'll give you something to play with.

He fired the crossbow. Too late. The bolt passed through air, and detonated thirty yards beyond the target in a muffled geyser of snow. Ash's body was gone, too—but a trail through the snow showed where the demon had dragged her. Nicholas turned, aimed again at the demon's grin.

And realized the demon wasn't just playing with Ash. It was playing with *him*.

"Aw. Is the human going to quit now? You were doing so well." The demon bent over Ash's body. "How about this: I'll give her back to you a piece at a time. You just have to ask nicely—"

The ground beneath the demon suddenly erupted, tossing him off balance. He recovered, just as the snow in front of Nicholas seemed to explode in a frenzy of metal and white feathers. The Guardians. Thank God.

Swords clashed. Demon and Guardian moved too fast—Nicholas couldn't see what was happening, only the blur of feathers and shapes. The dark-haired Guardian male was fighting the demon, he realized. And Taylor was . . . bending over Ash.

"No!" Nicholas plowed forward through the snow, finger tightening on the crossbow trigger. He'd kill the Guardian first. "Don't—fucking—touch her!"

Taylor looked up. Eyes of pure black stared back at him, like a glistening abyss. No . . . that wasn't Taylor. That was Michael. Nicholas had seen this before in Rome. He knew how Michael protected the woman . . . and Nicholas held an explosive bolt pointed at her head. Shock and dread rammed through Nicholas's chest, but he didn't stop.

"Let her go!"

The voice that came from Taylor's mouth wasn't hers, either, but a terrifying harmony of many voices, man and woman. *"She's ours."*

"She's bound to me!"

"She's bound to a demon. With you, she's a danger to all."

Fuck that. Nicholas dropped to his knee beside Ash, blindly searching for her wrist, holding the crossbow aimed at the Guardian. "Let Ash go, Michael, or by *God* I will shoot Taylor with this."

A grunt of pain came from behind them. Taylor turned her head.

Nicholas didn't look, but he could guess. "Your friend needs a little help, Michael."

Those obsidian eyes looked into Nicholas's for a long second. Then Taylor was gone, swinging her sword into the fray.

Not daring to put the crossbow down, Nicholas got his arm around Ash as best he could, began dragging her back to the car. Through the snow, it was like pulling a sack of lead. Two hours in a gym every day hadn't prepared him for this battle. His chest ached. His muscles felt ready to rip in half.

Behind him, the sounds of fighting stopped. He turned to look. The demon lay on the ground in two pieces. Taylor—herself again—was holding up an injured Revoire, who wore a bashful grin and was saying something about how goddamned slippery blood made the snow. Her eyes met Nicholas's.

He raised the crossbow again. "Explosive broadheads. You take your friend somewhere to be healed, and don't come back until we're gone. Or I'll blow you both to Hell."

Taylor began, "You don't even know—"

"GO!"

Firming her lips, Taylor stared at him for another second. Finally, she nodded. They both disappeared. Teleported.

Not wasting a second, Nicholas slung the crossbow over his shoulder and bent to pick up Ash. Her eyes were still open. He couldn't see any pain in them, just frustration and confusion. She blinked as he looked at her. He couldn't even try for a smile.

He trudged to the SUV, Michael's voice echoing in his head. *She's ours.*

Bullshit. Ash wasn't theirs to slay. She wasn't theirs for *any* reason.

She was his.

CHAPTER 10

A broken neck wasn't quite what Ash had in mind when she'd told Nicholas that she'd rather not feel anything.

Nicholas had laid her on the backseat, but she couldn't even feel the pressure of the cushion against her body. Terror began to set in then, but she couldn't make a sound. Trapped in her mind, she'd waited for him to stop at a hospital, to tell her that he knew how to help her. He didn't.

Then her toes began tingling, and Ash realized this was another of those times when he must have assumed she knew something that she didn't. In this instance, the something was that her body could heal a broken neck.

So she waited in silence for it to happen, her panic fading . . . just like it should. Her grief and dread had receded, too, though she could still feel them pressing against the corner of her heart, heavy and sodden.

And she had more to think about now. Not the memory of those obsidian eyes boring into hers, the powerful mind that had seemed to squeeze her brain in its grip, wringing out every one of her thoughts, or that terrifying voice echoing in her ears. *She's ours.* She'd skip that memory for now. It reminded her too much of that other dark figure—it reminded her too much of Lucifer.

But she liked to remember Nicholas fighting for her, even though he'd been outclassed. Far outclassed. Ash had been, too. She hadn't realized how fast, how powerful demons and Guardians were. Nicholas had warned her, so many times. She still hadn't understood, not really.

Was *she* that powerful? Maybe not. The demon had called her a halfling. It wasn't a stretch to think that meant she had half of whatever powers they did.

Still, even half as strong should have put up a better showing that the pathetic kicks she'd gotten in before he'd snapped her neck.

She had to do better. She had to *be* better. Stronger. Smarter. Starting now.

Carefully, Ash tested the movement of her fingers. All good. She drew a breath. That worked, too. She sat up. A two-lane highway lined with snow-covered pines stretched out in front of them. How long had they been driving?

Not long. The dashboard computer showed that they were only about thirty miles west of Duluth.

As if he heard her movement, Nicholas glanced back at her. "You're up already?"

"Seems so."

He returned his gaze to the road. "We've got to ditch this rig. They've seen what we're driving, so they can track us through that GPS."

Ash climbed into the front seat, found the owner's manual in the glove box. She located the necessary page, studied the wiring diagram. There was no easy access to the GPS connection. Well, that's why she was a demon.

"You've got insurance against damages on this thing?"

"Yes." He sounded amused. "Not that it matters."

"I guess it doesn't." She ran her hand down the front of the dash, curled her fingers under, and found the edge of the molded plastic console. She pulled.

A thick chunk of the facing snapped off in her hand. Perfect. Ash bent her head to look at the exposed wires, almost resting her cheek on Nicholas's thigh. Her hair spilled into his lap.

Since no Guardians came for her, she assumed her hair wasn't breaking the Rules.

He cleared his throat. "Do you need a light?"

"No." She could see perfectly. "I'm a demon."

His short laugh drew out her own smile. She consulted the wiring diagram again, reached into the dash, and yanked.

"Is the GPS offline?"

"It is. And you managed not to kill the rest of the computer system."

"Good." She sat up.

Nicholas glanced over at her again. Making certain she was all right? If so, he didn't ask whether she was, so she must have looked fine.

"Where are we headed?"

"West. I know a place that will suit our needs."

"Any more specific than that?"

"Not until I'm certain that no one's following or listening."

Ah. His paranoia at work again. Fine by her. "So what are our needs that are being suited?"

"Isolation until you learn to shield your emotions," he said. "And training. A lot of training. We were both too slow. Unprepared. I'm sure as hell not ready for Madelyn."

No, he wasn't. "How are you going to get faster?"

"Not faster. Better able to anticipate a demon's movements and speed. I've never been able to practice before. Now we can."

"So you'll try to shoot at me?"

"Something like that. And I'll teach you to fight, so that if a demon grabs you again, you can get at least a punch in." His gaze lingered on her face this time. "The way I see it, we're just fulfilling our bargains—because neither of us will be able to help the other with anything if we're dead."

"I'm not arguing."

"All right." He looked back at the road. Comfortable silence stretched between them, until his lips quirked and he said, "We got our asses handed to us, didn't we?"

Ash laughed. "Yes, we sure did."

"It can't happen again." Serious now, he glanced at her. "And time for the first lesson."

"In the car?"

"You won't have to move. This isn't fighting; it's learning to block your mind. I'll tell you exactly what Rosalia told me, but I can't test it for you. So understand this, Ash: You have to do it right, and have to keep your shields strong. Because if you don't, they'll find us again. So are you ready?"

She took a deep breath, nodded.

"I'm ready."

So Michael wasn't completely gone. But the shattering pain that Taylor had felt from him didn't make that knowledge reassuring. God. Whatever he was going through down there, whatever he'd been hiding from her . . . she had to get him out.

Revoire wouldn't return to SI to seek out a healer for his injuries, but they'd heal up soon enough, anyway. Taylor dropped him off at the cottage he called his home, where he could celebrate in his quiet, farmerly way that he'd finally taken down Basriel.

Taylor sought out another teleporter. Only a few other Guardians had the Gift, but Michael couldn't stop *them* from checking on him. Jake, maybe. In possession of two Gifts, including a powerful electric burst that could incapacitate most demons, he'd probably be safe—but he was also the youngest Guardian in active service aside from Taylor. Selah was older, more skilled, but at this time of night, she'd probably be with her vampire lover, and Taylor didn't want to jump into that.

That left Khavi, who was undoubtedly the best choice, anyway. As old and as strong as Michael, she'd been one of the first Guardians—and like Michael, wasn't completely human. Michael and Khavi were both grigori, the offspring of a demon who'd been made fertile with dragon blood and a human.

And after living alone in Hell for over two thousand years, combined with her Gift of foresight, Khavi was also either completely freaking nuts, or the most brilliant strategist the world had ever seen hiding behind a wall of crazy. Taylor didn't completely trust her, and was certain that Khavi had an agenda that she forwarded with her Gift. Her dedication to Michael was unquestionable, however—as was her ability to kick demon ass to Hell and back.

The only problem was finding her. The grigori often disappeared for weeks or months at a time, searching for a spell that might free Michael.

Or . . . her Gift of foresight had told her to return to the Special Investigations warehouse exactly when Taylor needed her. As soon as she teleported, Taylor found herself staring into Khavi's eyes—fully obsidian, just as Michael's sometimes were when he was angry, or suppressing deep emotion. Just as Taylor's were when Michael took over.

Khavi's voice was similar, too. A feminine harmony, like many voices speaking together, and didn't match the rest of her. A woman this powerful didn't walk around in ripped jeans and a powder blue tank top featuring a glittery unicorn prancing across her breasts. Yet Khavi did.

She said softly, "Who is it that you've met, Andromeda Taylor?"

"You don't know?"

"Not yet. Only that something has changed. Doors have opened." The beads at the ends of her small black braids tinkled when she shook her head. "But I cannot see what I do not already know. So tell me: Who have you met? Show me."

It could only be the demon, Ash. Taylor had met St. Croix and Revoire before. Closing her eyes, she pictured the blonde in her head, the vermillion tattoos along the side of her face, and projected it into Khavi's psyche.

The grigori's breath stopped. "Who is she?"

"St. Croix called her Ash."

"No. That is not her name. She hasn't found it yet." Khavi tilted her head a little, as if examining the image in her mind. "When she does, it all begins to end."

"What does that mean?"

"I don't know," she said, which Taylor knew just meant that Khavi didn't want to tell her. "Where is she?"

"Minnesota. For now. What do you see in her future?"

"Not *hers*. I haven't met her. I only see yours."

"And I'm doing what?"

The black cleared from Khavi's eyes, leaving them dark brown. Human, except that no human ever had eyes that looked so ancient. "Sacrificing her."

No. Taylor *really* couldn't imagine herself doing that. "I don't think so."

"Not even to save Michael?" Khavi smiled when Taylor's breath caught. "It is so amazing to me, the lengths to which people will go for love."

"I'm not in love with him. You said I never would be in love with him. You *saw* it."

"But I didn't say that I was speaking of you now."

No . . . she hadn't. Khavi had said "people." God. Taylor

hated talking to this woman, sometimes. "And what about Michael? I—"

"Want to ask me to teleport to the frozen field to check things out. I know. I already did."

Oh, thank God. "And?"

"And Lucifer found him."

The psychic reaction to that softly spoken announcement reverberated throughout the warehouse. Guardians, all with perfect hearing, all listening—a practice that most would usually consider rude, but not when the Doyen and the grigori were discussing Michael. Now they began to appear at the top of the stairs, at the edge of the hub. Leaving the gymnasium, gathering around. But all silent, all waiting for more.

Their horror echoed Taylor's. "So what's happening to him?"

Khavi closed her eyes, but not before Taylor saw the moisture glistening in them. "What do you think? No, no—that is the wrong way to put it. You *can't* think of what is happening, because you are not a demon. Because you are not Lucifer."

"So maybe I'm imagining worse."

But no. The truth was, she wasn't sure what could be done to him. Only his face was exposed, and that was a block of ice. Would they scratch him? Poke at him? Try to stab him? He was frozen solid.

She looked to the faces of the other Guardians. She was not alone, Taylor realized. They, too, knew it would be horrible. But they didn't know exactly what that meant. Only . . .

Taylor turned toward the director's offices—and yes, there was Lilith, standing at the end of the hallway. Her hand rested on the scruff of Sir Pup's center neck. Shape-shifted down to the size of a Labrador, he was rubbing his left head against the former demon's leg. Comforting her, though it was almost impossible to tell by her face that she needed it. But the hellhound knew.

So did Hugh Castleford. He'd come up behind Lilith, slid his hand around her waist.

"Lilith?"

Taylor's voice cracked when she spoke her name. She didn't *want* to know. But she had to. Michael had made this sacrifice for them. They would all bear it, too.

Lilith's hand found Castleford's at her waist, and she threaded her fingers through his before she began. "An ice pick would be first, because it's instant gratification. The eyes are open, so Lucifer would focus on those at the beginning, digging all the way in, but then he'd realize that pain was pain, and it didn't matter where it came from, so he'd start in on the rest of the face. Hammers, maybe to finish shattering the ice, and he's strong enough to do it. And when the face and eyes regenerate, he can do it all again."

Oh, God. Taylor covered her mouth, uncertain whether she'd scream or begin crying. A few of the novices already were.

"You go easy on them," Khavi said, and Taylor couldn't determine whether there was appreciation or accusation in her voice.

But how could there be more? How could there be *worse*?

She looked to Lilith, and knew that it was true. "How?"

"For fuck's sake, Taylor—" Lilith stopped, glanced up the stairs at the novices. "He's being eaten by *dragons* in Chaos. Over and over, chewed and devoured, and then torn apart and eaten again. Do you really think that an ice pick to the eye is worse? Lucifer *knows* it's not. Especially to someone like Michael. The pain is fun for Lucifer, but it doesn't really *hurt* Michael. It doesn't get to the heart of him. So he'd wait until Michael's eyes healed, and then he'd drag up humans from the Pit. Now imagine your favorite torture, then imagine it a thousand times worse, and then imagine it being done to those human souls. *That* is what Michael's watching right now. And once they're down there, it doesn't matter so much that they're murderers, that they are the shit of humanity. Down there, they are only people, they're in agony, *pointless* agony, because they aren't burning so they don't give Lucifer power and they won't find release, *and Michael can't help them.*"

Taylor stared at her. *Yes.* That helplessness would hurt him more than any pain. But, of all people, Lilith knew that? Lilith, who never had a word for Michael that wasn't dripping with sarcasm or disdain for the "golden boy."

"I thought you hated him," she said.

Lilith's eyes narrowed on her. "Fuck you, Taylor." Her focus shifted to Khavi. "And fuck you, too. Why didn't you warn him?"

"I did. Before he made his sacrifice, I told him exactly what it would mean."

"Then why the fuck can't you see how we get him out?"

"I cannot see what I do not already—"

"Oh, fuck you again."

The grigori tilted her head. "No, I do not see fucking in our future."

Khavi vanished. Lilith shook her head, met Taylor's eyes.

"You, my office." She looked around at the gathered Guardians. "All of you. Every spare moment, I want you at the archives in Caelum, in the libraries wherever you can find one, searching for any damn little thing that would help get Michael out of there. So move your asses now, or I'll have Sir Pup come bite them off."

Taylor loved her a little bit right then. She followed Castleford and Lilith back to the office, grateful that Sir Pup stayed behind in the central hub to carry out Lilith's threat. Once inside, Lilith ripped her hands through her hair and sat heavily in her chair.

"Fuck."

Castleford smiled a little and sat on the edge of her desk, crossing his arms over his massive chest. Without the glasses he typically wore, he looked less like the scholar and more like the warrior—an eight-hundred-year-old warrior who, even though he was human again now, could still see the truth in a person's answers as clearly as if he read them. Luckily, whenever Taylor lied in front of him, he usually didn't call her on it.

"'Fuck' again? Now you're just teasing me, Lily."

Lilith glared at him, but even Taylor could see that he'd just pushed Lilith out of her temper. With a sigh, she picked up a file from her desk and tossed it to Taylor.

"We found St. Croix's demon."

Taylor opened the file to a picture from airport security in New York. Crap resolution, but clear enough to identify them both. "What name did she use?"

"She went through as Rachel Boyle. Straight on through. She was flagged as missing, not dead—but she's obviously not missing anymore, is she? She's never been charged with anything, and she's a citizen, so they basically just said, 'Come on in.' Idiots."

"Why would a demon use an airport at all?" Taylor wondered.

"Maybe she's trying to convince St. Croix that she's human,"

Lilith said. "But I don't think so. He wouldn't fall for that, and she's got symbols all over her. So maybe he didn't trust her not to drop him."

Castleford frowned. "Boyle. The same as the double murders Taylor was looking at?"

"The same," Taylor confirmed. "We saw her tonight. She wore the markings then, too, but St. Croix called her Ash."

"So St. Croix went to Duluth?" He exchanged a glance with Lilith. "*With* the demon who was pretending to be Rachel's ghost?"

Lilith shook her head. "That makes no sense. No sense at all."

They'd only heard the beginning of it. "Let me tell you the rest," Taylor said.

She relayed the meeting with St. Croix outside of the sheriff's office, the burst of grief that had led them to the snow-covered field, Nicholas's defense of the demon.

"This is the crazy part, and I'm not really clear on it, because as soon as I saw her, Michael jumped in and began steering the boat," Taylor told them. "And he was . . . angry. Not at the demon, but that kind of anger that comes from realizing that something is completely fucked up, and someone got hurt, but there's nothing you can do about it. Then he told St. Croix that she was ours."

"As in, 'ours to kill'?" Lilith asked.

"No. As in, 'she belongs to the Guardians.'" Taylor took in their confusion. "Rachel Boyle died saving St. Croix's life, remember."

"Then she *was* supposed to be a Guardian," Castleford said. "So how is she a demon, instead?"

"No, that's the wrong question," Lilith said. "It's not: How did she go from being a Guardian to a demon? There'd have to be more steps. And the first: Why isn't she a Guardian?"

Castleford nodded slowly, as if in dawning realization. "A bargain."

Taylor shook her head. "I'm not following either of you."

Lilith sat forward. "It's like this: The only way Michael wouldn't have been called to transform her into a Guardian is if there was a prior hold on her soul. She must have broken a bargain—probably a bargain with St. Croix's mother."

"That would put her in the frozen field when she died," Castleford picked up the rest. "Her soul, anyway. Just like Michael's soul is in the frozen field, but his body is in your cache."

In Taylor's cache, and marked up with symbols that completed the psychic connection between them . . . and allowed for an eventual rejoining of his body and soul after he was released from Hell.

"St. Croix said that Rachel's body vanished. You think his mother had it in her cache?"

Lilith nodded. "And *she* would be in Hell, enduring her punishment for killing a human. So Rachel's soul is in the frozen field, her body is in a demon's cache . . . and Lucifer has access to both. So he makes a halfling out of her."

All right. Taylor could follow that far. Lucifer had pulled Rachel out of the frozen field, reunited body and soul, and then Rachel had completed the ritual that turned her into a demon. What she couldn't understand was *Why?*

Lilith didn't have an answer for that. "I have no idea. Obviously for some purpose. But I don't know what."

"Some kind of spell?" Taylor suggested. "The symbols on her face made Michael uneasy."

Lilith squinted at the airport photos, before shaking her head. "Even magnified, I wouldn't be able to read these. They're too pixelated. But symbols are part of the transformation ritual. I had them all over me. They defined my powers, my bargain with Lucifer, my name. They're normal. I only wonder why she doesn't hide them."

"The symbols I saw called for something to open."

"To open?" Lilith grimaced. "Not so normal. And Michael didn't like them, either?"

"Not at all."

"Okay. So let's assume that whatever Lucifer wants, he's going to get it through Rachel Boyle. The question is: Does Rachel share Lucifer's purpose? Does St. Croix?"

Castleford turned to Taylor. "Did you get a look inside her mind?"

"Yes, actually. A clear one." Which, thinking about it now, was strange. Beyond even "normal" strange. "And I do mean *clear.* I've never touched a mind like hers. She's wide open. And there's no conflict in her. Her emotions sang like pure notes."

Even children felt more of a push and pull—between love

and resentment, between desire for an object versus a desire to please.

"Demons aren't conflicted," Castleford said.

"But they're malevolent. She wasn't. There was only grief, confusion, pain—and joy, when St. Croix came for her."

"And what does he feel?"

"I couldn't get into his head. But he'd have killed me for her."

"So if we want to get to her, we have to get around him . . . and he's familiar with the Rules." Lilith considered that. "All right. And you say he called her Ash?"

"Yes."

"So Lucifer took her name and gave her a new one. If her emotions are that clear, too, he might have taken more than her name. Memories, associations—especially if they are connected to strong emotions—he might have taken all of that. If she's only just been transformed—and that would also explain why she couldn't fly into the U.S. by herself—she wouldn't have had time to create those new emotional connections yet. All those conflicting feelings that muddy everything up." Lilith heaved a long breath. "Which means that now is a good time to recruit her."

Both Taylor and Castleford stared at her.

"What? Halflings aren't the same as demons."

"I know that better than anyone," Castleford said. "But there's the matter of her bargain. She'd have vowed to serve and obey Lucifer during the ritual. We wouldn't be able to trust her."

Lilith shook her head. "Probably not sworn to obey Lucifer. Not with the Gates closed. He'd have bound her to someone else, someone who probably was charged to carry through whatever purpose he had in mind."

"St. Croix?"

"No." Castleford didn't hesitate. "Not a human. A demon. And he probably bound *that* demon to him, to make certain whatever he wanted from them was followed through."

"So we just have to kill the demon she's bound to," Lilith said. "And she's free."

"And Lucifer's purpose thwarted," Castleford added.

"Always fun, the thwarting. So we should definitely bring her in." Lilith pursed her lips. "Does anyone know where she is?"

CHAPTER 11

Nicholas thought he'd had enough of snow, but it wasn't so damn bad when it meant traveling by snowmobile with a furnace of a demon sitting behind him, her arms wrapped around his waist. The view wasn't a kick in the face, either. White-capped mountains thrust into the western sky. White stretched around them, framed by the trees climbing the valley walls.

Leslie often told him he ought to make an effort to study and enjoy the beauty around him. The land just east of Glacier National Park made it easy.

Beauty wasn't his reason for being here, though. This time of year, the only access to the cabin took two hours by snowmobile—unless a man could fly. Considering that most Guardians and demons could, the isolation wasn't Nicholas's primary reason for choosing his granddad's place, either. The old man's paranoia had been.

The afternoon sun cast long shadows by the time they reached the log cabin. An A-frame situated in a tiny clearing at the edge of a valley floor, surrounded by a stand of tall firs, the place wasn't an easy find unless a man already knew where it was. From high above, the snow piled on the steeply pitched roof would blend it into the surroundings. Inside, the main level housed two simple rooms: a living area, and a corner bedroom holding the toilet and a tub. A generator provided electricity if they wanted it. The cellar doubled as a nuclear fallout shelter, still stocked with weapons and supplies. Nicholas wouldn't need them; he'd brought his own in the snowmobile's sled. Still, he liked knowing they were there. A man couldn't be overly prepared.

The snow was almost level with the top step when he pulled up to the front porch, cut the engine. The sudden silence seemed almost heavy, until the quiet sounds of the forest around them began filtering in.

He was almost sorry when Ash got off. God, she was warm. Even the best wet-and-cold weather gear money could buy didn't compare to a demon at a man's back.

And her boots were as sexy as hell, but they weren't doing her any favors. One step, and she sank knee-deep in the snow. She didn't seem to notice. She only studied the cabin, looking as if she were freezing in that thin jacket and hoodie. A human would have been, but a demon didn't need to hunch into her clothes.

Why did she do that? She couldn't be cold.

"What is this place?"

"My grandfather's. This, and a hundred acres around it."

"He's not here?"

"Dead. Ten years. It's mine now."

She pushed her hands into her pockets. "Won't the Guardians find us, then?"

"No." Nicholas stripped off his thick outer gloves, began loosening the bungee cords holding the tarp over the sled. "There's a record of the land, but not the house. He didn't want the government touching him . . . and he was something of a survivalist. He didn't leave much of a footprint in paper, and nothing electronically. Just a post office box in town."

Ash looked doubtful. "What kind of survivalist?"

"He didn't get to the point of mailing bombs, if that's what you're wondering. He lived through the stock market crash in the eighties. My grandmother took too many Valium and didn't. He became convinced the world was out to fuck him over, so he gave it all up and came out here to live off the land."

Of course, being a St. Croix, he'd brought a hell of a lot of cash with him.

"So no one knows it's here?"

Madelyn did, though she'd never been here. When Nicholas had been a boy, his mother, father, and he had frequently visited the old man, but Madelyn never had. The summer she'd refused to go gave Nicholas his best, first clue of when his mother had disappeared. He and his father had gone without her that year. By the next, his father was dead, and Madelyn hadn't wanted to hear one word about visiting America.

Granddad wouldn't want a little boy underfoot who reminded him of his son. *Nicky, love, why won't you stop being selfish and think of that poor old man, instead? Let him grieve in peace, instead of bothering him about taking you fishing and running all over those woods.*

So Madelyn knew about the cabin, but it'd take her a while to figure out where he'd gone. She wouldn't expect this of him. For years, he'd been hunting her. Now, he'd sit back and wait—and prepare. Eventually, she'd come looking for Ash. He'd be ready for her.

"There's one in town," he said. "The son of the man who was Granddad's only friend. He uses the cabin in the summer and fall for his fishing and hunting—and in exchange, he makes any necessary repairs."

"So that's why it's not falling apart."

That, and because his grandfather hadn't skimped on the original construction. He'd had everything but the logs airlifted in by private contractors, and he'd built the place himself. For a man who'd spent most of his life on Wall Street, he'd ended up being damn good with his hands.

"The front door is unlocked if you want to go in," Nicholas said. After she took a step and sank to her knee again, he added, "There should be a pair of snowshoes hanging on the wall."

"I'll manage."

He followed her in, the bag of weapons slung over his shoulder. Cold, a bit musty, but not bad. The windows were shuttered, but provided enough light to see by when he opened them. No sofa, no comfortable seating—just the small handmade table with two chairs, and one cane-back rocking chair by the window. Rustic and simple. Nicholas had forgotten how much he liked it.

He hadn't visited since the old man had died. Then, he'd come with the intention of selling it, but he'd made arrangements for its upkeep, instead. Before today, the place had never been useful to him, but he hadn't been sorry for holding on to it—and he didn't need Leslie to explain why. This cabin was a part of his childhood, one of the few parts Madelyn had never tainted.

Would he hold on to it after she came? He didn't know. Finally having his revenge would be sweet, but this place, this land, wouldn't be the same afterward. He knew he'd never come here again.

But if he did have to give it up afterward, it was a price he'd be willing to pay.

A wood-burning stove provided heat for the rooms. It had been a while since Nicholas had started one, but it came back quickly enough.

No, not quickly enough. With the dry kindling crackling, he turned to find that the sled had already been unloaded, the boxes and bags stacked on the floor and the table. No need to ask when she'd done it—with a demon's speed and strength, she'd have had the task completed within seconds.

But he didn't like that she'd done all the work. "I'll unload it next time."

And there'd have to be a next time within a few weeks. He didn't mind roughing it, but he didn't have time to trap or hunt, and he preferred not to test the longevity of the supplies in the fallout shelter.

"You still have to put them away," Ash said. Her gaze fell on the stove behind him. "And I'm not cooking for you. Especially on that thing."

Nicholas wasn't looking forward to whatever he managed to produce on that stove, either. But as long as he could chew it, he didn't care. "I'll cook my own," he agreed. "I can't trust that you wouldn't pile on the butter, anyway. You'd make it a slow death, demon."

She smiled, an expression that came more often now. "Are you speaking from experience? Did Madelyn?"

Oh, hell. Nicholas hadn't been thinking of that at all, but after his father died, there were always "comforting" foods in the house. Always. And Madelyn had encouraged him to comfort himself as often as possible.

"She did. And I became big-boned very quickly." *Big-boned* was her way of putting it, too.

Ash frowned. "You really think she was trying to kill you?"

"No. I think it was more about the short-term fun of seeing how other boys treated the fat kid."

"Oh." Her gaze slipped over his body. "I see."

She probably did. Too much. And Nicholas probably shouldn't have offered her such a clear view, but fuck it. She'd already gotten to him. He'd let his guard down, and giving her a little more ammunition at this point didn't matter so much.

What mattered was that he still knew what she was, what she might do with the info he gave to her. She hadn't done it yet, but he had to believe she would, eventually.

"I still want to see you naked," she added.

God, and he wanted to be naked. With her. But that was a step he didn't dare take. Now, he could remember what she was: a demon. The second he believed that she *could* physically want him would be the second he started forgetting that.

"Then I'll make a point not to let you." He reached for his gloves. "You don't need to sleep or bathe. The bedroom is mine, and you'll stay out."

Her brows lifted. "So I'm stuck in this one room?"

"Not stuck." He gestured to the windows. "There's a lot of space out there."

God knew he'd be out as much as possible. Training, as they'd planned. And any other damn excuse he could think of.

"And a lot of cold."

"Oh, that matters to a demon?" Jesus Christ. He shook his head, and found a damn excuse. "I'm going to put the snowmobile in the shed. There are books and other shit in the storage upstairs if you want to look through them. Just knock yourself out."

Her expression remained impassive through his tirade, but now another little smile curved her gorgeous mouth. "All right. I will."

Uneasy, Nicholas waited for her to say more, but she didn't. So why did he have the feeling that he'd just exposed another bit of himself to her?

Fuck it. He pulled on his gloves, headed for the door. He'd go crazy trying to figure her out.

If he didn't go crazy with wanting her first.

* * *

Nicholas obviously didn't handle sexual frustration well.

Sitting opposite from him at the small table, Ash watched him sort through boxes of ammunition by the light of a kerosene lamp. In jeans and black cable-knit sweater, he didn't bother with the tailored perfection from the city. Out here, there was no point—and it would have been ridiculous. A man couldn't trot around snowdrifts in handmade Italian shoes, and he'd been working steadily since they'd arrived. All but ignoring her, but she didn't mind. She liked watching him, studying him—and she already knew that retreat was his favored way of dealing with his attraction to her.

Had he never been frustrated before, had no experience with it? She thought it was possible. With his money and looks, and as long as that need wasn't directed at a specific person, he could easily scratch a sexual itch with anyone. And if there'd been anyone he did want, but for some reason couldn't have, he'd probably have quickly moved on if the emotion—or the woman—didn't prove useful.

Ash didn't have any experience with it, either—not that she remembered—but she also wouldn't have called the desire she felt *frustration.* She wanted him so much that she ached, but there was no conflict. She liked him, she wanted him, but she didn't feel impatience. It was simple. On the other hand, although Nicholas desired her, he didn't want to. And although they had both begun treating her plots and any discussion of her demonic nature in a lighthearted manner, Nicholas became much more serious about it when sex entered the picture. It had become a recognizable pattern: He reminded himself that she was a demon and put physical space between them. Or he put a table between them.

But he was apparently finished with ignoring her. He glanced up, saw her watching him, but didn't look away. Instead, he reached into his weapons bag and set a sawed-off shotgun between them.

"All right. You can't fight yet, but you can pull a trigger—and for now, this will work best for you. Your aim won't have to be as good, and you can aim fast enough that it'll shoot in the right direction." He opened one of the ammunition shells, showed her the pellets inside. "And the birdshot will scatter, do the most damage."

Ash wasn't so sure. "I healed from a broken neck. Are those little bits of metal going to slow them down?"

"No. The hellhound venom is." He set a vial of golden liquid next to the shotgun barrel. "A trace amount of this will slow a demon down. A little more will paralyze one. I've got darts, and I've dipped my handgun bullets in this stuff—but for you, we'll make sure the birdshot is covered in it. So those pellets don't have to do much damage. They just have to pierce the skin."

"So it'll stop them before they get in close."

"Yes. The sawed-off barrel will make close-range shooting easier. But if they're already in that close—"

"Then I'm screwed."

"Yes." He pulled the box of shotgun shells toward him. "I'll fix these up for you now. We'll begin practicing tomorrow with regular ammunition so that we don't waste the venom, but when we aren't practicing, I want you to keep the gun with you and loaded with the poisoned shells. You keep it with you at *all times*, either right next to your hand or in your cache, when you figure out how to use that. All right?"

"Yes." Her very own boomstick. She liked it. "Thank you."

His gaze locked with hers. "Don't let a demon close to you again."

Her chest tightened, like a strange little coil straight through her heart. She didn't know what Nicholas had felt when the demon had been dragging her around like a rag doll. Afterward, he'd never asked if she was all right.

But she knew now that he never wanted to see it happen to her again.

"Thank you," she said again, even though "*I won't*" might have been a more appropriate response.

He nodded, stood. Her chest still caught in that sweet ache, she watched him cross to the bedroom. He'd left, but not because of sexual frustration this time. Would he hate for her to know that he cared? She thought he would.

He returned a moment later with a set of scales and a small, dusty machine. Except for the empty bottles on the top that fed into a steel tube, it resembled a standing car jack. A lever handle jutted from one side.

"What is that?"

"A reloading press. To seal the shells after I poison the shot."

"You didn't bring that with you?"

"No."

"But you've used it before."

"Yes." He glanced up from the press. "Why?"

"You've been here before, then—after you were old enough to handle guns, ammunition."

"A few times, in the summer after I came to America."

"So your grandfather wasn't a complete hermit."

"No."

He set out a line of empty cartridges—a perfectly straight line, she noted, that he gave his full concentration. But that wasn't *just* focusing; he was focusing on *not* looking at her.

Was he lying? Hiding something? She couldn't be certain, but she thought so.

She had no idea what he could be lying about, though. Perhaps he was just trying to conceal that he cared about someone again—but this time, that he cared about his grandfather.

"It took a while to hear back from him," Nicholas surprised her by offering. "He only checked his mail twice a year: at Christmas and tax time, in April. I finally heard back in May, and spent my sixteenth summer here. Chopping wood, mostly. Dropping about forty pounds."

"But you didn't stay?"

"Revenge isn't easily served while hiding at a cabin in the woods."

So he'd left to destroy Madelyn. "Wouldn't revenge also have been staying here, and completely forgetting about her? By proving that she hadn't destroyed *you*?"

His brows snapped together. He looked up from his line of cartridges. "She didn't. But she did fuck me up pretty well. Pretending she didn't wouldn't be proof of anything—it would just be denial. And sticking my head in the sand sure as hell wouldn't make her pay for any of it."

He had a point. And the demon had killed his mother, his father, and his girlfriend. Maybe forgetting about her *wasn't* enough. Ash wouldn't soon be forgetting about Steve Johnson; that was for damn certain.

The heat left his voice. "Anyway, whether I live or die, she doesn't care. Before I left England, I was kicked out of school, arrested for heroin possession, all kinds of shit. Whether I was first in my class or expelled, none of it mattered. The only thing that mattered to Madelyn was Wells-Down, and so the only way to get back at her was by taking it."

"And you did."

"I did. And then I found out she was worse, that the business wasn't enough. *She* has to be destroyed."

"And that's all you've done, all these years. What will you do when she's dead?"

Nicholas blinked, then stared across the table at her with an expression she'd never seen on him . . . but she recognized what it was. He was at a loss. A complete loss, as if he'd never even considered the question before.

"I don't know." His lips twitched, as if in sudden humor. "Eat a slice of pizza, probably."

Ash laughed, and his smile widened into a grin.

"Maybe two pieces," he said. "And I'd run for thirty minutes instead of the full hour, do half as many sets."

He could do zero, for all that Ash cared. "I'd still want to see you naked."

"If you end up helping me slay Madelyn, I'll shake my ass for you."

"*Naked* ass."

His eyes narrowed. "You drive a hard bargain, demon."

"I do." And she was relieved that despite the naked talk, Nicholas was still amused, still playing along, instead of putting distance between them. "Though I didn't ask for Reticle yet. Will you begin working again afterward?"

"Probably. I enjoy it. Though with Madelyn gone, I'd probably focus on more speculation, less takeover."

"Oh, speculation. I think I'd enjoy that, too." Just as she enjoyed reading financial journals. Just as she surfed to the stock listings the moment she got onto a computer. "So if you ever decide that you don't want to work anymore, you can pass the reins to me."

"I see." He sat back. "This is your plot, isn't it?"

"Taking over your company and making you a ton of money? Eeeeevil."

His laugh shook right through her chest, seemed to loosen pieces of her there. Was this how emotions deepened? They rattled everything apart, then rebuilt on a stronger foundation?

She didn't know. She only knew that her emotions were growing all over inside her now, like climbing vines that rooted deep and twisted around every available surface. There was contentment, as she sat and watched him drip a small amount of venom into the birdshot and stir it around. A hint of surprise when she smelled the venom's fragrance, sweet like a peach. And trepidation when she remembered that he'd said it affected demons.

"Does the venom work on Guardians?"

"No. That's why we'll also start working on your hand-to-hand, and I'll teach what I know of fencing."

Sword fighting? She *really* preferred her boomstick. No need to get near anyone, no chance of being cut into pieces.

Her doubt and fear must have shown in her expression. Nicholas glanced up, studied her for a long moment. "All right. We'll work on a little hand-to-hand now—and start with what will probably benefit you the most: avoidance and getting away."

She looked around the small room. "Here?"

"We won't need a lot of space." His chair scraped back as he stood. He held out his hand. "Come on."

She could get up on her own, but she couldn't pass up the chance to touch him. His fingers wrapped around hers, and he tugged Ash to her feet.

And let go.

That wasn't enough. She clenched her fingers together, trying to hold on to the feel of him.

He faced her in the center of the room. "You're a demon. That means you're thousands of years old, if not older. You fought in a war with Heaven—and this will come back to you, just like remembering that security code."

That made sense. That made a lot of sense. Her procedural memory *was* intact. If she'd ever known how to fight, she'd remember how.

Of course, she hadn't remembered how to fight when the demon had attacked her.

Nicholas raised his fists—a classic boxer's stance. She recognized that, at least. Maybe she wasn't a lost cause, after all.

"Wait. What about the Rules? How can I block you if I'm not allowed to touch you?"

A flat, icy tension moved into his expression, and she remembered: He'd been waiting for this. *You'll say, "Oh, Nicholas! I wish I could touch you, but I have to follow the Rules!"—and moments after I give you permission, you'll punch through my chest and rip my heart out.*

"I won't rip your heart out," she promised.

Some of the ice melted. "All right. I'll give you permission to block me, and to make a hit in return. A *soft* hit, by demon standards. Nothing that could seriously injure a man."

Because a demon wouldn't pass up the opportunity to hurt one, if he gave her permission. Ash couldn't imagine it. And with her strength, it might be easy to make a mistake and hit too hard.

So she couldn't make a mistake. She had to be careful.

"All right," she agreed on a deep breath. "I'm ready. What are we doing first?"

"Just avoiding me. It'll be easy for you—too easy, actually. But if you practice with someone slower, it'll still be more natural for you to react quickly if it's a demon or a Guardian."

Building up her reflexes. "Okay. I'm ready then. Go for it."

"Okay."

But he didn't throw a punch. He looked at her over his fists. His mouth firmed.

Silence hung in the air for a moment.

Then he whipped around, shoving his hands through his hair. "Jesus!"

"What?"

"Even knowing what you are, that you can cross the room in a blink . . ." He shook his head, turned back, raised his fists again. Still, he hesitated.

She supposed he wasn't used to punching women. She liked him for that. "Are you going to dick around like this when you're up against Madelyn?"

His eyes narrowed. "No. I do wish you could shape-shift, though."

"To look like her? No, thanks. You'd probably lose control and kill me."

"Hardly." He smiled a little. "All right. Are you ready now?"

Ash didn't point out that *she* hadn't been the one delaying. She only nodded.

His fist snapped toward her face. Oh my God, *so fast.* Her heart leapt . . . and his fist all but stopped. So he was pulling back anyway, throwing a little practice punch. It moved toward her at only a fraction of an inch every second or two—and okay, that was ridiculous. A baby could avoid that. Hell, a baby would be an old man before it hit him.

She frowned at Nicholas, wondering if he was just joking with her now. But no, he stared at her, his eyes and expression almost frozen. And she couldn't hear his heartbeat. She couldn't hear her own heartbeat. *What the hell?*

Her mouth dropped open as she realized: It wasn't that they had no heartbeats. They were *between* heartbeats. Either time had frozen . . . or her perception of it had really, really sped up.

Incredible. How long did it take to throw a punch? A second? Yet his fist had only traveled three-quarters of the distance between them. She could have run around the room several times before it would touch her. Maybe outside to the tree line and back. Was the clock frozen, too? She glanced at it. The second hand didn't move. Maybe next time, she'd try to time everything.

Unless her perception was stuck this way now? Oh, God, she hoped not. Maybe it had just been an involuntary reaction, like a spurt of adrenaline into her system. A reflex, kicked into gear by instinct. If so, how long would it last? Would Nicholas be stuck like this for what felt like forever, or would *Holy shit he was going to hit—*

His fist smashed into her mouth. Ash's head snapped back, and she staggered into the table. Pain shot through her lips, her teeth. Blood spilled over her tongue.

Gross. And, *ow.*

"Jesus fucking Christ!" His heart pounding—and her perception obviously back to normal now—Nicholas reached for her, cupping her jaw in both hands and raising her face to his. Horror and shock whitened his face. "Jesus. Are you all right?"

"Yes," she said, but the blood she could feel spilling from her split lip must not have convinced him.

"Ah, fuck. Goddammit. Come here into the light." Though his voice was rough, his fingers were gentle as he touched her lip, her teeth. "Why the hell didn't you move?"

Hot anger leaked through his shields. Not at her, though, she realized. Anger at himself. Guilt was mixed in with it.

"I meant to get out of the way, but I ran out of time." She ran her tongue along her teeth, didn't feel any broken edges. "Is my lip bad?"

"No. No, it's already healed. You just need to wash it." His gaze lifted from her mouth, but he didn't let her go. Still cupping her jaw in both hands, he said, "Don't do that again."

"It didn't hurt much," she said. "Either that or I can take more pain that I realized. And I didn't know how quickly a cut would heal. Now I do. It's better to know both of those things."

"Don't do it again."

She hadn't meant to this time. But maybe she should have. "I should have made it part of my plot: how to make Nicholas St. Croix feel bad."

His fingers tightened. That familiar flatness moved across his expression, the coldness into his eyes, as if to say that *No, Nicholas St. Croix didn't give a shit whether he hit a demon.* But he couldn't say that, because they both knew he did.

"Just don't do it again."

And now he wasn't talking about forgetting to move, she knew. He didn't want her to do anything that might reveal how much he cared.

She nodded.

He let her go, moving back to the center of the room. "What do you mean, you ran out of time?"

"My perception changed, all of a sudden. I was watching your fist come at me, and it was like in slow motion. It was strange. So I was looking around, seeing what else appeared different, trying to figure it out . . . and I didn't look back in time to miss your fist."

He closed his eyes. Stopping himself from laughing—and it had sounded pretty ridiculous. Which made her believe that he'd stopped himself from laughing only because he didn't want her to *feel* ridiculous, as if he were laughing at her. He need not have bothered. Embarrassment apparently hadn't taken root among her other emotions yet.

Still, it was nice.

"So . . ." He cleared his throat. "You sped up. Did you do it on purpose?"

"No. It just happened after you threw the punch. Like a reflex."

"Did it happen when the demon attacked you?"

Had it? "I don't know. How much time passed from the moment he grabbed me by the car to when he stopped at the fence?"

"Less than a second." A rough note entered his voice.

"It felt like forever. I tried to hit him about thirty times along the way. So maybe the reflex did kick in."

"I don't think it's a reflex for the others. They just speed up when they want to. Can you move fast on purpose?"

"Faster than anyone I know."

"I've seen that," he agreed. "But that's the problem: I've seen it. What about now? Bring to me a book from the shelf there."

He pointed across the room. Ash raced for it, slapped it into his hand.

"See? That was only a second."

"And I *saw* you. I couldn't see the other demon move, or I just saw a blur at other times. You weren't a blur."

Ash narrowed her eyes at him. "I can be a blur. I'm a demon."

"Then take the book from me," he challenged.

Too easy. Wondering if it was some kind of trap, she snatched her hand out. He jerked the book away from beneath her fingers.

His grin irritated her. "Lucky timing," she said.

"Then prove it. Grab it."

Her hand shot out. He moved the book just in time. Her nails scraped over the cover.

She felt the points of her fangs digging into the inside of her bottom lip. "So you've got good reflexes," she hissed.

"Ha! Look at you. Can't take it from me, demon."

Fuck that. Determined, she reached for it again. He jerked it back . . . and slowed. She snatched the book before he'd moved it an inch.

And for good measure, raced across the room.

Nicholas blinked, looking at the spot she'd been standing. He looked down at his hand, then found her standing by the stove. "Better," he said. "Now come back here, and we'll try a few jabs again. Don't you let me hit you. Either move or block every one."

She did—blocking most of them, just for an excuse to touch him, to catch his fist against her palm and slide her fingers against the backs of his. In the space of a half hour, using that different perception became almost natural. It wasn't so much that everything slowed, she realized; she just reacted more quickly. So quickly that it didn't matter when he changed up the hits he threw, faster and faster . . . getting his own workout, she realized. Well, this had worked out well for both of—

He spun and dropped, sweeping her legs with a kick. Ash shrieked and crashed to the floor onto her stomach. Prepared, Nicholas grabbed her wrists, pinned them over her head. His body came hard over hers, smashing her flat.

"No more permission," he rasped in her ear. Winded from the workout, probably boiling in that sweater, his chest worked like a bellows against her shoulders. "The Rules are in effect again. But try to get out, anyway."

And what if she didn't want to? He lay on top of her, and she could feel each hard muscle through her clothes.

Please let them disappear, she prayed. *And his, too.*

Apparently, God wasn't listening. Her clothes remained on.

Nicholas's grip relaxed slightly. "Ash? Are you okay?"

"Fine," she said, and realized too late that she shouldn't have replied. If he was determined to make her get out of this despite the Rules, pretending to be hurt would have done it. And it would have been pretty evil, too.

Next time, she thought, and then couldn't think at all when he shifted his weight slightly, lifting off her torso and trapping her thighs with his legs. As if he'd suddenly forgotten that she didn't need to breathe—or recognized a weak spot in his hold.

But she could have told him that there were no weak spots. Not a single inch of hard flesh against hers felt weak at all.

"Ash?"

"I'm thinking."

About Nicholas sliding her jeans down. About his thighs slipping between hers and pushing them wide. About him slamming forward, taking possession, filling her slick flesh with explosive pressure and heat.

She closed her eyes. Oh, God. She tried to open her legs, let his weight settle in between—but she couldn't. Her thighs pressed against his and if she moved him against his will, without permission, the Guardians would come and kill her.

Frustration bit, sharp and deep. Though she was strong, she couldn't move her hands. Though she was strong, she couldn't lift him off her. Though she was strong, she was trapped here, because she couldn't throw him off and she couldn't touch him even though he could do any damn thing he pleased . . . even *not* touch her when she so desperately, desperately wanted it.

Fuck this. And she knew exactly how to make him let go.

She opened her eyes, and crimson light shined through the

blond hairs curtained over her face, a glow against the wooden floor. "I want to have sex now."

Nicholas stiffened above her. His grip on her wrists tightened.

"I don't have sex with demons."

She knew. But suddenly, she also realized why she couldn't feel him *everywhere*. He'd shifted his weight, adjusted his legs, braced his knees. Why had he lifted part of his weight off her? She didn't need to breathe. But *he* liked to conceal information.

"But you want to. Your cock's as hard as steel right now, because you were up against me, and you liked it. And you started thinking about fucking me."

Only a guess, but the right one. He released her hands, let her up. Before she'd even gotten her feet under her, he'd stalked across the room. Putting distance between them.

And it had worked. Her breath came out as a sudden laugh.

He turned at the sound—and God yes, she'd been right about his erection, too. Confined behind denim, his penis might not have been monstrous, but that thick bulge looked exactly the right size to her.

She glanced up. Nicholas was staring at her in surprise, but also a reluctant admiration.

"So that was—"

"A plot, yes."

And now there was something else sweeping across his expression. Disappointment?

"But I do want to have sex," she added.

"Demon," he said, before joining her in the middle of the room again. "That wouldn't have worked against one. They wouldn't have felt anything."

"I think you're wrong about that." Because she sure as hell felt something. Her nipples hadn't just spontaneously hardened and she wasn't wet through to her core for no reason at all.

"Try it on a demon," he offered. "We'll see who's right, and who is dead. Demons can make their dicks hard, too, you understand? But they don't *want* it. And teasing them won't scare them off."

Ash didn't want a demon, anyway. "All right. Accepted. It won't work against anyone but you."

His lips thinned, but at least he didn't lie and say it wouldn't work on him, either. He turned and walked away. To put space between them again? But no, just to shake off the frustration. By the time he circled the room, he had his serious face back on.

"All right," he said. "You weren't ready for me to drop. So we'll do the sweeps again, and this time you avoid having your feet knocked out from under you."

Avoid it? Maybe not if he got on top of her again. "And the Rules?"

"Same as before. No injuries."

Well. She could just turn it around, then.

Ash dropped, sweeping her leg around just as she'd seen him do. He went down, hard—but no injuries, because she caught him, cushioned his fall with a hand behind the back of his head.

Before he could react, before his heart pumped another beat, she pinned his wrists, straddled his stomach. She lowered her face to his, and was looking into his eyes when she saw him realize what she'd done.

"Goddammit. That was . . ." His gaze fell, fixed on her lips. His throat worked as he swallowed. "Nicely executed. Good job."

"Thank you." Ash grinned, sliding her fingers down to grip his hands. She easily hauled him to his feet again. "Do you want to practice avoiding the superfast demon again?"

She did. This had become her only way of gaining permission to touch him. If he wanted to, she'd practice this all night and day.

Nicholas's jaw clenched, and she watched the struggle that played through him. He did want to. He didn't want to. But she knew which would eventually win, because only one would leave him better prepared to face Madelyn.

Finally, he nodded. "Yes."

But his answer didn't please her quite as much as Ash thought it would have. Maybe because *Yes* wasn't enough. Because although it was what she wanted him to say . . . she wanted him to say it because he enjoyed her touching him, too.

So maybe she was beginning to feel a little frustration, after all.

CHAPTER 12

Lying on his side, Nicholas half opened his eyes to a dark room. Sleep still heavy on him, he almost fell into it again before the noise that must have woken him came again: the opening of the stove, the low thud of wood being tossed in.

A familiar sound, and for a moment he was sixteen again, listening to his grandfather stir up the morning fire. Maybe Ash, then, starting early. She always had it roaring by the time he awoke, and the kettle on to boil. In the past week, she'd gotten into the habit of taking coffee when he did, sitting at the table and reading while he ate breakfast.

He'd gotten into the habit of looking forward to her company. Maybe too much.

But hell, who was he kidding? Now that he'd woken, he'd be out of the room within minutes, just so that she'd look up and smile at him a little earlier.

He rolled over, switched off the alarm on the windup clock. No need to have it now. And—hell, it was *really* fucking early.

The blanket slid to his lap when he sat up. Though his chest was bare, he didn't feel the nip of cold. A toasty warm room. He was used to that upon waking, because she always started up the fire well before the alarm got him out of bed. In the past week he'd come to appreciate that. Unlike when he'd stayed with his grandfather, his toes didn't freeze into ice pops before he could drag a pair of wool socks on.

He didn't need socks now. The floorboards weren't cold at all. And it was two in the fucking morning. God.

Scrubbing the remainder of sleep from his face, he opened the door. It took him a second to see her through the dark—sitting in the rocking chair near the window. Pale moonlight gleamed on the pages of the book she held, her blond hair, the barrel of the shotgun tucked beside her.

Then, as if she'd struck a light, her own crimson glow began shining from her eyes, washing her features in red. "Did the wolves wake you?"

That glow lit his way across the room. He struck a match to the table lamp, faced her again.

"What wolves?"

She tilted her head, eyes still glowing. "I can hear them. You can't?"

"No."

"Sometimes it's almost as loud as the city here. It's just loud in a different way. Not as many people noises."

"I heard people noises. And now I understand why the woodpile has been disappearing faster than it should have been." His grandfather would have skinned him. "You don't have to keep it hot in here at night. That's what the blankets are for."

The shining in her eyes dimmed, left only blue—human, and amused. "Not everything is about you, Nicholas. The fire is for me."

"And you could lie out on a glacier for twenty years, then get up and walk away without feeling any the worse for it. You're burning through our fuel—which I *need* if we're going to live out here—twice as fast as we should. And we didn't spend the summer stockpiling it."

She shrugged. "So I'll chop more."

"You don't need to," he pointed out. "So *why*?"

With a sigh, she set her book aside. "I don't like being cold."

"You also said that like and dislike don't matter. Only familiar does."

"The cold *is* familiar. Not the kind of cold out there, but colder. It's enough to be familiar, though, and I don't like it."

"Why?"

"Because it's different. Those other things that are familiar, when I feel them I want to chase them down. I want to find out where the familiarity came from. I want to know what memory I'm missing." As if suddenly agitated, she rocked up out of the chair, stood looking out of the window before turning to face him again. "With the cold, I don't want to chase down what's at the root of it. And I have memories, real memories that frighten me, and that I don't want to revisit—a memory of Lucifer cutting these symbols into me. The memory of that Guardian looking at me. When I do think of them, I'll shake a little. But when I think about the cold . . . I feel like if I ever reach the end of that memory, if I ever remember why it's familiar, I'll start screaming and screaming and I'll never, never stop—"

Her voice cracked. *God.* He didn't know what to say. He wanted to go to her, hold her. He didn't trust himself to.

"Ash?"

Shaking her head, she pushed her hands into the pockets of her hoodie. Wearing it, even inside. She *always* wore it, he suddenly realized. Despite the T-shirt beneath, despite the heat of the room and her own body. She took off her jacket sometimes, and he would see it tossed over the back of a chair, but then it would disappear until the next time he saw her wearing it again.

Hell, she was always fully dressed. Except for the time she'd stripped off in front of him, he'd never seen her boots come off. Like her jeans, they seemed to change now and then, especially if she'd ripped them during their training or they'd been soaked in melted snow or mud. She didn't launder them; they simply became new.

Maybe because they were familiar, too. And comforting, unlike the cold.

"Anyway," she said. "We train outside all day, and I make myself ignore that feeling as much as possible. But it's always there. So at night, I keep warm."

He could keep her warm. She didn't sleep, but she could read in the dark. The bed wasn't all that big. If she slid in right next to him, he'd keep her warm all night.

And she'd be hot. So fucking hot next to him. He could discover how hot she became, how wet, how loud when he buried himself inside all of that heat.

Or he could chop some damn wood, bring it in, and let it start drying out.

"Was she that bad?"

"Who?" Confused, Nicholas followed the direction of her gaze, realized she was finally seeing him naked. Or half-naked, at least.

And that he was just fine with that.

"Madelyn. Your wrists."

Oh. He couldn't remember why it had seemed so important to hide those scars from her.

"Yes," he said. "She was."

Her gaze returned to his face. A fierce emotion lit her eyes. "I'd help you find her even without the bargain."

She would help him find Madelyn just by being here, because Madelyn had some use for her. That was good enough. But he sure as hell wasn't going to release her, and risk having her leave or running straight into the Guardians again. Or maybe even chasing after Madelyn, if she discovered anything about Steve Johnson's ghost—which she *would* discover, as soon as she returned to make his life hell.

No. There wasn't a chance he was letting her go. "You're not getting away that easily, demon."

She smiled, and he drank in the sight of it before realizing that he was about two seconds from asking her to return to the bed with him. Jesus, what was he thinking? He needed to sleep this off.

Her voice caught him as he turned away. "Nicholas?"

He stopped, waited.

"What I said before, about like and dislike—I didn't lie. It was true then, they didn't matter. But they do now."

She'd also claimed that she liked him. *That* shouldn't matter to him. And so that's what he said.

"Whether you do or not doesn't make any difference to me."

But goddammit, it did. Too much.

Had she always been this stupid? Ash couldn't remember.

The slender tree top swayed beneath her weight. Maybe she shouldn't have climbed so near the top, but she'd wanted to have the longest drop possible, the longest time for her reflexes to kick in. She'd learned to use her speed that way; she'd also learn to fly.

She gripped the trunk tighter when a breeze slid through the firs, bending the tree top toward the ground. If it broke, the end result wouldn't be any different than what she'd planned, but Ash preferred to control when she fell. It might be the only thing she controlled in this experiment.

As soon as she got up the courage. Until then, she could at least enjoy the view.

She'd chosen the tallest tree at the edge of the clearing that surrounded the cabin. In the distance, the mountains rose against a clear blue sky. Gorgeous. The sun shone from directly overhead. The cold never felt familiar with the heat of the sun against her skin, and she lifted her face to it, soaking in the warmth.

The birds must have been enjoying the sunshine, as well. Though usually quiet, today they were twittering away in the trees around her. Grizzly bears inhabited this area, but she hadn't seen one yet—she supposed they were all in hibernation at this time of year. Ash was almost sorry for that. She'd have liked to have heard one, as she often heard the wolves.

A continuous, almost rhythmic thud was coming from beside the shed—Nicholas, chopping wood. Ash had volunteered to do it instead. She didn't tire, and strong as she was, the effort would go more quickly, but he'd grunted something that apparently passed for words in man-chops-wood language, looking disgruntled and almost offended, and so Ash had left him to it. From her vantage point, she could only see his back. He hadn't turned around yet, hadn't seen her climb the tree. Probably a good thing.

Oh, and now she was just delaying. She glanced down at the clearing, trying to choose the best landing spot. Tracks crisscrossed the deep snow, mostly from their training sessions, and she tried to recall if any one area had seemed softer than the others. Even if it wasn't, maybe it didn't matter. The demon had dropped her from a similar height, and it hadn't hurt too much. Of course, he'd also broken her neck, so she hadn't felt anything at all.

And maybe that wasn't the best thing to think about right now.

Anyway, the point of this experiment was *not* crashing into the ground. Her instincts should kick in, her procedural memory should take over. All right. She filled her lungs with a deep breath, and gave a small prayer that it wouldn't be smashed out of her at the bottom.

Gathering her body, using the tree trunk as a spring, she leapt out over the clearing . . . and began to fall. Quickly. *Oh, shit.* Something needed to happen here, her wings needed to pop out and—

The muscles of her back suddenly locked. Ash cried out in surprise. Sensation exploded through her, strange and new, in places she'd never felt anything before. Places that hadn't *been* there before. Cold air rushed over wide expanses of skin. New muscles strained against the onslaught of the wind. From the corner of her eye, she saw one of her wings. Black and leathery, it stretched over a thin frame, like a bat's wing.

How did she move them? Why weren't they flapping? Ash rolled her shoulder, tried to flex the new muscles. Pain ripped along the frame. She'd pushed something the wrong way, and like a fragile kite folding beneath a strong wind, her wing seemed to collapse. Unbalanced, she flipped over, went into a flat spin.

Oh, God.

Ash slammed into the snow. White erupted around her, a bit of a cushion but not enough. The impact smacked the breath from her lungs in a painful slap, a punch to the belly, and she didn't want to fly anymore but just curl up and not move again for a while, but she couldn't even manage that yet. Everything still spun and she couldn't quite focus.

Now the cold surrounded her. The pain wasn't the same but she could almost hear the screaming—

No. Not now. She wasn't going there.

More rhythmic thuds. Nicholas? These were different, not the sound of an axe, but boots smashing through the snow toward her. Dizzy shock began to fade into awareness.

Strong hands gripped her shoulders. "Ash!"

Her wings had already vanished again. Moving still hurt too much. So did breathing. She groaned an answer instead, and Nicholas swore.

"I'm going to turn you over. Tell me if I hurt you."

He didn't hurt her. Everything just hurt. He pulled her against him, half-propped up against his leg, and she opened her eyes. Tiny snow clumps clung to her lashes, framing her view with white flakes before they melted from the heat of her skin. His face taut, Nicholas brushed more snow from her hair, her jacket.

"What the hell were you doing? Trying to kill yourself?"

"No." Her voice came out thin and hoarse, but her chest was working again. "Trying to fly. But I only managed the worst belly flop ever."

He didn't laugh. His lips thinned, paled with anger. "Do you have any idea what it was like watching that? I can't even— God."

His fingers tightened in her hair. He stared into her eyes, wild emotions chasing across his expression, each one too fleeting for Ash to catch.

Then he bent his head, and captured her mouth in a kiss.

Surprise held Ash motionless, then flooded away the pain in a sweet rush. Oh, she'd waited for this. Wanted this. His lips parted over hers, searching out her response. Shuddering, she opened for him.

He swept in, taking possession. Oh, God. This was nothing like his first kiss. That had been controlled, and this was all searing hunger unleashed with teeth and tongue. Ash's fingers curled into his sleeves, holding on as his need fed hers, until she was moaning low in her throat, desperate for more.

But he must have mistaken the sound for pain. He lifted his head—and no, she couldn't grab him, pull him back down. She couldn't follow him up and take what she needed. And now that she'd had it, now that she knew the feel of him, the sweetness, the heat, only the fear of death and breaking the damned Rules held her back. She'd have crawled across the frozen field for more of this.

She could only ask. "More."

"No. I shouldn't have—" Nicholas broke off. Looking almost shaken, he drew back. "I'll help you inside. Are you still hurting?"

"Not really," she said.

He pulled her up, so close, and when she looked up, the world stilled again. Would he kiss her? She watched the struggle play across his face, the war between what he wanted and what he believed.

Belief won. He didn't put distance between them this time, but he might as well have. His expression hardened—not cold now, but solid . . . and effective.

Now she was hurting again, pain centered near her heart. Throat aching, she started back to the cabin.

Nicholas trudged through the snow beside her. "So what the hell were you doing?"

"We're here to train. But if I'm going to do it right, I need to fly."

"So you just decided to jump?"

"Yes. I needed to be fast, so we worked that out. Now I need to know how to make my wings appear, and if I can force them through some survival instinct, maybe eventually I'll just be able to control them—just like I can be fast whenever I like now."

"So you'll keep jumping?"

"Yes."

"God." A heavy breath clouded the air. "Tell me next time, then. So I can be there."

"I would have this time, but I thought you'd try to stop me."

His smile was grim. "I probably would have."

They reached the porch. Nicholas paused to stomp the snow off his boots. Ash's were already clean and dry. She didn't know how they did that. Sometimes she thought about what she'd like them to be, then looked down, and they were.

"There's something else," she said, and waiting for him to glance up. "They weren't familiar."

"What weren't?"

"My wings. They're completely new to me."

He frowned. "Do you mean you just don't remember—"

"No. There's familiar, and there's not. The wings were *not* familiar." And not in the same way the Boyles' picture had been unfamiliar. There had been no surprise when she'd seen them, no sense of something new. "And I was falling, falling . . . but I didn't know how to fly. It's not in my procedural memory. Just as fighting isn't, even though I supposedly fought in a war in Heaven. You'd think *that* would leave a stamp on someone's memory, wouldn't it?"

Nicholas's brows drew together. "So you don't remember that. All right."

"No. I'm saying that being a demon is *new* to me. How can I put in a security code or drive but not know how to fly? It doesn't make sense."

"It doesn't," he agreed, but she could see by the cold front coming in that the explanation that first occurred to him was:

If it doesn't make sense, then maybe the demon is lying. Even if he did agree, even if he believed her, Nicholas was reminding himself that he *shouldn't*.

Disappointment weighed on her chest. God, she was an idiot. Disappointment meant expectations, and that meant she'd expected something different from him.

That had to be stupider than jumping from a tree.

With a sigh, she left him standing on the porch and pushed open the cabin door, but stopped halfway through. She faced him again.

The expression he wore was familiar. Battling himself again. Well, she wasn't stupid enough to get involved in that fight.

"Do you know what else wasn't familiar? The way you kissed me. But maybe *you* can come up with an explanation for that, since I can't." The ache filled her chest again. "And because even if I could, you wouldn't believe it, anyway."

This wasn't working anymore.

Nicholas closed his eyes, forced himself not to go in after her. In the dark behind his lids, he could see her again: her wings twisting around, falling out of control, her wild spin straight into the ground. *God.* He couldn't stand this. He couldn't stand seeing her hurt like that, over and over again.

And she was right: She had no instinctive knowledge. Her fighting had improved, but only because they trained their asses off, until Nicholas dropped from exhaustion into the bed every night. She'd become astonishingly proficient with the shotgun—her boomstick, as she called it—but her ability hadn't come from some long-lost memory. She was building it, a single day at a time.

But she was still no match for Madelyn. That demon in Duluth had snatched her up *so* quickly—and although Ash might be fast enough to avoid that now, she couldn't wield a sword. She wouldn't last a second against either demon or Guardian. If Madelyn came, the shotgun and hellhound venom might give her a chance . . . but Nicholas was getting to the point where he wasn't sure he wanted to take that chance. To the point where he thought that running from Madelyn and protecting Ash was the far better choice.

Which was more important to him, revenge or Ash? A week

ago in Duluth, that answer had been an easy one. It wasn't easy any longer. He wanted revenge. More than that, he wanted Ash to be safe.

And fuck it all, he wanted to kiss her again. Kiss her until it wasn't just familiar, but the taste and feel of him had been branded into her memory—as hers was branded into his.

He'd kissed her before, but he knew why this one hadn't been familiar: He'd never kissed any woman like that. Not without calculation, not without considering the consequences or as a means to an end. He hadn't given a thought to anything but the need to have her mouth open to his, to know the heat and taste of her. To reassure himself that she was alive, unhurt.

But although she'd quickly healed, Nicholas wasn't so certain she was unhurt.

Something had changed in her. He realized now that the Ash he'd met in London might have very well fit the nurses' description of a flat affect, a lack of emotion. By the time they'd reached Duluth, however, there'd already been more—amusement, irritation, joy—all clear and easily readable, and all of them unaffected by what anyone else said or did to her, and always unoffended.

He didn't think that was the case any longer. Nicholas had begun to believe that her capability for emotion had expanded, deepened. He'd begun to believe that she could be hurt now.

And then he always wondered if that was what she *wanted* him to believe.

Jesus Christ, he was so fucked up. Perhaps that was Madelyn's legacy: He'd never be able to trust anyone, anything, even if he wanted to. Even if he knew that it was hurting Ash that he couldn't let himself trust her, that he couldn't let himself believe her.

Then again, maybe he was right not to.

God, this would all drive him mad—if seeing her dive out of the sky didn't do it first.

But whether he went mad didn't matter. All that mattered was protecting her, keeping her safe—and if safe meant watching her jump over and over, until she had the ability to fly away from a demon or a Guardian as fast as she could, then *by God* he would help her do it.

They still had hours of daylight left. Maybe she could be flying by the end of it.

She didn't look up when he came into the cabin. Sitting at the small table, she had the shotgun on her lap, cleaning the barrel with an oily rag.

"Do you want to try the tree again?"

"There's no point. I don't know how to fly. I'll just fall and fall and fall again." She popped open the chamber and removed a cartridge, replacing it with one of the shells prepared with hellhound venom. So she didn't intend to practice shooting, either. "You know what I want to learn, more than anything?"

"Tell me." And he'd do anything he could to help her.

"I want to know how to get around the damn Rules."

Shit. Nicholas couldn't do that. And the only being that could change those Rules hadn't been on Nicholas's side for a while now. "That requires a higher power than we have."

"No. I don't mean 'how can I break the Rules with no consequences.' I mean, how to get free, how to move without breaking them." She set the shotgun aside and stood. "Like before, on the floor. I didn't really try to get out from beneath you. I want to try again and see if I can think of a way to get you off of me without breaking the Rules."

"You want to get on the floor again?" With her body beneath him. It would be torture. But he'd suffer through it. "All right."

"Right here is good enough." Ash leaned forward, placed her hands in the middle of the table. "Grab my wrists like you did before."

Nicholas approached the opposite side of the table and pushed the chair out of the way with his foot. She wasn't a small woman, but his hands easily encircled her wrists. Her pulse pounded beneath his fingers, her skin hot against his palms.

Her hair slid forward over her shoulder as she studied their hands. "I can't lift up, because your will is to hold my hands down like this."

"Yes." Though he'd really like to hold her a lot closer than this.

If she heard the wry note in his voice, she didn't acknowledge it. "If I was human, what would I do? I'd pull, I'd try to scratch, I'd kick you in the balls. I can't do any of that."

"No." And thank God for the lack of ball kicking, at least.

Frustration flattened her mouth. Her gaze left their hands to search the tabletop. "Okay. But what if I'm not *trying* to get away? What if I'm not trying to impede your free will . . . I'm just making it difficult for you to keep holding me?"

"Make it so that you aren't stopping me from holding you, but so that I *want* to let go?"

"Yes."

"That would work. How would you do it?"

Her mouth twisted into a small, ironic smile. "If I could fly, I'd say: 'You can hold on to me if you like, but I'm going up.' It would be different than trying to lift your hands, because then I'm trying to break your hold. But flying, I wouldn't be trying to break your hold, I'd just be warning you that you'd be in trouble if you can't hold on when I'm a thousand feet high. Then if you let go—before or after I'm in the air—it's *your* choice."

The intention made a difference, he realized. That made a hell of a lot of sense. And good for him to know, too, if he ever did get ahold of Madelyn.

"But I can't fly," she said. "Here, I could say . . . I'm going to fall, Nicholas. Hold on to me if you like, but if you do, you might get hurt."

That might work next to a cliff. But here? "Where would you—"

With a crash, the table collapsed toward her. The support for her hands gone, Ash's weight suddenly pulled hard on him, hauling him off-balance. *Oh, fuck.* He couldn't compensate, not at this angle.

He held on anyway.

His gut slammed into the edge of the upended table, his arms stretched over the top, pulled halfway over by Ash's dead weight. She lay on the floor on her stomach, her torso lifted by the hold he still had on her wrists.

She hadn't gotten away, but she was laughing, triumphant. "Did you see? That was close."

"Close." It came out as a wheeze.

Her smile faded a little. "Are you all right?"

"Fine." Fucking proud of her, actually. A lot of people would have let her go.

"I'll fix the table. I kicked out the legs on my side." She got her knees beneath her, easing the pressure of her weight on his arms. She studied their positions, Nicholas overbalanced and bent over the upended table, her own proximity to the wall. By the time she spoke again, he'd gotten his wind back. "I think this would be the same thing: I'm going to fall backward. You can hold on to me, but that's probably going to pull you and tip the table right over."

"On top of you," Nicholas pointed out.

"Your head might smash into the wall."

He glanced at the wall. Yeah, it might. That would hurt like a fucker. "All right. Go."

She didn't, not right away. She was looking up at him, her bottom lip between her teeth. "Are you planning to let go?"

"No."

Her eyes narrowed. "Are you bluffing? Seeing if I'll do it?"

"I hope you'll do it. Because if you're in this situation with some asshole human, you damn well better."

"I *am* in this situation with an asshole human."

His laugh hurt his bruised stomach. God. He couldn't argue that.

Her smile faded, replaced by determination. "Nicholas, I'm going to."

She held his eyes. He could almost feel her willing him to let go as she slowly tipped backward—not actively doing anything, just not supporting her own weight anymore. He tightened his grip when she fell back as far as she could go without tipping the table over, and he hung there, suspended for an endless moment—wondering if her weight wouldn't be enough to bring him over anyway. Then her heels skidded. Her weight suddenly shifted, yanking him over. He twisted as he tipped, trying to avoid the wall, avoid smashing her. She gave a yelp of surprise as he crashed into the floor on his side.

Still holding on to her wrists.

"Dammit," she spat. Her breath came in short bursts. Her fangs had appeared. "Why can't you let go?"

A million reasons. "You *want* me to make it easy?"

Her anger was gone, that quickly. Frustration remained—not directed at him, but at the situation, he recognized. At the Rules keeping her there.

"No." Her eyes closed briefly. When she opened them again, she was back to studying their hands. They both lay on their sides, facing each other, Nicholas's fingers locked around her wrists. "All right. There's nowhere left to fall. So there has to be something else to make you want to let go."

"An exchange?" Nicholas suggested.

She considered that before shaking her head. "With someone else, maybe. If they're greedy, I could offer money."

"You could lie and offer anything," he reminded her. "Say you'll do something and don't. Unless it's a real bargain—a demon's bargain—you can lie."

"Trick them?"

"Yes. Maybe they'll believe you."

"And if it's someone like you, who doesn't trust demons? Who believes everything I say is a lie?"

That was a punch to the gut . . . but true. "You'd have to come up with something else."

"Something that they fear. Something that makes them sick, makes them want to get away." She looked at her arm. "I could start chewing on it. Blood all over. Ripping away the meat—Oh, God."

He watched her gag, turning her face against the floor. If he let himself imagine it, Nicholas was sure he'd be losing his breakfast, too.

"I'd let go," he said. "Because I couldn't stand to see you do it."

She nodded, her tattooed cheek scrubbing the floor. "But also because it's me. If Madelyn did it, you'd be disgusted, I think. But you wouldn't care if she hurt herself."

That was true enough. "Yes," he admitted.

"So if it was someone who hated me, who didn't mind the blood, it wouldn't work. But if it's someone with any humanity, I can hurt myself. I can see how much they could stand before they *have* to let go."

"Yes."

"So it's not about what I can do at all. It's about what the human can stand to do. If they are willing to risk being hurt. If they're willing to stomach a demon being hurt. Everything I did would really be about finding their limits."

"And yours," he pointed out. "You could stand knocking my head into a wall. But what if it meant throwing me in front of a bus? Into a fire?"

"No." She smiled a little. "But I already know your limits."

"The arm chewing? That's a sure thing."

"Not even that. Just, 'Oh, let's have sex.' And off you go."

God. *God.* Was it that easy for her? Teeth clenched, Nicholas reared up. Her eyes widened, but he still held her wrists. He shoved her back against the floor. He braced his knees alongside her thighs and pinned her wrists on either side of her head.

Looming over her, he ground out, "Try it now."

Ash swallowed, hard. "I want to have sex."

"But I'm not leaving."

Her gaze darted to her arm.

Nicholas shook his head. "Can't reach it with your teeth."

Her eyes began to glow. "I'll slam my head against the floor so hard that my brains will pop out."

That would do it. Anything that meant hurting herself would. But he didn't have to worry about that one.

"Go on, then."

Her lips flattened, as if in determination. He felt her shake beneath him.

"You can't," he said. "There's a limit for you, too. Maybe you can be pushed over it, but you haven't been yet."

"And you?" It came out as a hiss. "I'll push you past yours, and you'll let go."

No. He'd already been pushed past them, and he was still holding on.

He dipped his mouth closer to hers. "Try."

Trembling, she closed her eyes. "I want you to fuck me."

If she really did, he might oblige her. "Is that the truth?"

Her eyes flew open, and he saw the sudden, stark terror in them. Fear that she'd broken her bargain. That in her attempt to get him off, she'd inadvertently lied.

Jesus. He hadn't meant to do that. He'd rather release her from their bargain than ever see her in the frozen field. He'd rather give her permission to kill him than see her hunted down for breaking the Rules.

"No." She relaxed beneath him, a soft sigh escaping her. "It's not a lie. It wasn't something that I meant at that moment, it was just something I said . . . but it's not a lie."

And he believed her. Maybe he was a fool for it, but God—he believed her.

Smiling, he pushed her wrists up and over her head, held them together in his left hand. Ash drew a sharp breath.

"What is this?"

"We're going to see what my limit is. And yours."

Her lips parted. As he bent to them, she whispered, "How?"

"We'll see how long it takes before I have to let go. Before

I have to touch you with both hands. Before I have to let you touch me."

Her chest hitched with excitement. "Let me go now."

"No, you're still playing 'get away without breaking the Rules.'"

"I'm not trying to get away."

Playfully, he narrowed his eyes at her. "But how do I know it's not a trick?"

She laughed. God, he loved when she did that. So soft and clear. Pure enjoyment.

"Can you vanish your jacket?"

Her breath stilled. Her brow furrowed, as if concentrating. Then, "No."

With only one hand available to undress them both, that complicated things—but probably for the best. He should do better than fucking her on the floor next to a broken table, fully dressed except for what he'd been able to open one-handed.

So he'd just push to her limits, instead. How far he could take her. How fast. His hand slid down over leather, found the hem of her jacket, her hoodie, her T-shirt. So many layers, and he slipped beneath them all, found the hot, smooth skin at her waist.

"Your choice, Ash," he said, and watched her eyes flare with crimson. "Up or down?"

She didn't hesitate. "Down."

"Impatient?" God, so was he. He couldn't remember ever being this hard, and he'd barely touched her. And he wanted to touch all of her, but he wanted to please her more. He held her hands; he could at least give her control over his.

"Yes." She laughed again, as if delighted by that. "So impatient."

Watching her face, he unsnapped her jeans. He'd take her mouth in a moment, but right now he wanted to see her eyes as he slipped his hand beneath the denim. Her lids half-closed in anticipation, her lips parted, her breath coming in pants, she was beautiful. So incredibly beautiful.

And wet.

His fingers slid over slick, burning flesh. Nicholas groaned, already imagining his tongue delving through that soft heat, his cock sliding deep. He shook, his head bending under the effort not to rip her jeans open, spread her wide, take her now.

"Give me more." Ash's back arched. "More."

"More, yes. God. I can almost taste you." But not yet. Her eyes had closed, and the agonized pleasure on her face deepened as he circled her clit. The small nub had stiffened, the only part of her that wasn't soft, but still so wet, so hot. "Like this? Or faster?"

Her head turned to the side, cheek pressing to the floor. Her hips rolled, and she cried out.

Jesus, so beautiful. "Like that?"

"Yes. Don't stop that."

He never would. Frenzied, Nicholas bent his head, licked the corner of her mouth. Her lips parted under his. Her moans came from deep in her chest, pulled answering sounds from him. Her legs widened as far as his knees allowed, and his fingers slid deeper.

Oh, fuck. Nicholas shook, battling the need to rip off her jeans now, ram deep. Her passage squeezed at his fingers, so tight. With a soft cry, Ash rocked her hips, writhing, pumping against him, her wetness flooding his palm. Pinned by his hands above and below, out of control, her ecstasy so unadulterated, so clear, so obviously her only thought, she was the most incredible, sexiest thing Nicholas had ever seen. He could have watched her forever, taking his own pleasure just in this.

But she wasn't waiting for him. Her body jerked, stiffened. She cried out, exposing her fangs. Her sex clamped around his fingers, sweet fucking heaven. Her eyes opened, shining red—crimson swept across her skin. Obsidian horns erupted from her forehead, curling back to her temples.

Demon. Nicholas froze.

What the fuck was he doing? Had he forgotten what she was, or stopped caring? Had this been her plan all along, to *make* him stop caring?

Shaken, he slipped his fingers from inside her. He released her wrists. Ash trembled beneath him, then fell back to the floor, panting. A soft laugh erupted from her, and she looked up at his face. She stilled.

"Nicholas?"

"Well done. You got me to let you go," he said.

She blinked and half rose. Her head wobbled a little. Frowning, she reached up. Her mouth fell open when she touched the horns. She pulled her hand back, looked at her skin.

"Oh," she said softly. "I see. I found what disgusts you."

Disgust? Nicholas rose to his feet. Not disgust. His cock was still hard, aching. And he wanted her. He still wanted her. Even now, with all this on display, she was beautiful to him.

No, the problem wasn't that he was disgusted. It was that he *wasn't* . . . but he should have been.

He should have been.

"Nicholas?"

He shook his head. He couldn't. Rounding the broken table, he headed for the door. He heard her get to her feet, but he couldn't stop. Not until he got his head together again.

A soft noise made him look back. She hadn't come for him. She stared at herself in the small mirror over the sink, instead, her fingers tracing the reflection of the horns in the glass.

"This is who I am?"

His chest tightened. His heart told him to keep quiet, to figure this out, to work it through. He didn't listen to it. Didn't know if he could trust it.

"Yes. As I've said."

"So you have," she whispered. Her hand fell away from the mirror. "Again and again. So you were right . . . and now you've fulfilled your part of your bargain. I know what I am now. A demon."

"No." That wasn't all she was. "We're not done. We don't know your name. We don't know where you came from."

"The bargain was 'Who I am'—and I'm a demon. Anyway, it's not your choice. I'm releasing you."

God. She was right. He couldn't do a damn thing about that. But he didn't have to let her go. "You're still bound to me."

She fixed those glowing eyes on him. "Only until I find your limit. Then you'll release me."

No, he wouldn't. Not with Madelyn still out there, posing a threat. Not as long as he drew breath.

"I won't." He started across the room toward her—and she vanished.

No, not vanished. He heard the door open, and turned just in time to see her leave.

The tightness in his chest hardened to a deep ache. God, he'd fucked up. How many times had he seen her fangs, her glowing eyes? And only thirty minutes ago, her *wings*. But throw in the red skin and horns, and suddenly that mattered? Jesus. Yes, she was a demon. She was also the only woman who'd ever gotten to him like this . . . and he'd hurt her.

Somehow, he had to pay for it, make it right. He'd get his head on straight, so that he wouldn't hurt her again.

But he wasn't letting her go.

CHAPTER 13

Ash came back to the cabin when she heard Nicholas start the bath. Finally washing her off, probably. She was only surprised he hadn't done it earlier—and she wasn't sure she blamed him.

No, screw that. She blamed the hell out of him.

But it was difficult to stay angry, though she tried to nurture the emotion. After she'd looked in the mirror, Ash hadn't known what to think. She had *horns*. Heavy, shiny horns. The wings looked like a bat's, but at least they were useful. But horns were just . . . she didn't even know. For hours, she'd been trying to decide whether they changed anything, whether they mattered, or if they only bothered her because they'd bothered him.

If so, it was too bad she'd begun caring about what Nicholas thought of her. Eventually, though, it would probably fade. So really, the horns didn't matter at all, except that they'd finally driven home what Nicholas had been reminding himself about all along.

She was a demon.

Now, she planned to act like one. She was going to frustrate him, use him. And even though, judging by her experience, that sounded more like what Nicholas St. Croix would do than what any demon would do, it just made everything more fitting.

A splash sounded as he got into the tub. Though it would be

better if she could make the horns, wings, and fangs show themselves now, she didn't need them. Appearing human, but *feeling* like a demon must, Ash opened the door to his room.

The small clawfoot bathtub sat in the opposite corner to the bed. She knew Nicholas hated it, that he preferred a shower that washed away the grime and sweat rather than sitting in a shallow, diluted pool of it, but he'd been making do. He'd lain back against the sloped, rounded end of the tub, elbows hooked over the sides, his head resting against the upper edge as if he were exhausted, knees bent and his feet braced beneath the spigot. She'd hoped he would seem crunched up in there, his long body in that short space, but no—and the narrowness of the tub only emphasized the broadness of his shoulders, the long muscles of his thighs.

His eyes opened when she crossed the room toward the bed, and although he seemed tired, burdened, he immediately sat up, his expression alert.

"Ash? Are you all right?"

"Fine." She gripped the iron rail that served as a footboard, began dragging the bed to the tub. "I'm just coming in to see you naked."

"Ah." He smiled a little, but there wasn't amusement in it. Regret, maybe. Sitting back again, he said, "You deserve that much from me."

"Yes, I do."

The feet of the bed frame were scraping up a trail of splinters from the floorboards. She didn't care. She dragged it to the side of the bath, sat on the mattress, and leaned forward to rest her elbows on the edge of the tub.

"I didn't mean to hurt you, Ash."

She met his eyes. He appeared sincere. And since he'd never had any compunction against telling her how much he didn't want to care about her, he probably had no reason to lie now.

His lying had never been the problem, however. She finished the rest for him. "But also, you're not even really sure whether you *did* hurt me, or whether I just want you to think you did. Am I right?"

His silence was confirmation enough. And if that confirmation made her chest ache, it didn't matter. It would eventually fade.

And she was here to see him naked, so she looked. A thin

trail of silken dark hair ran down the defined line of his lower stomach. His penis lay against his thigh, thickening even as she watched. Her presence, arousing him—and he didn't attempt to conceal his reaction to her.

That might have mattered, if he'd attempted to conceal his reaction to her earlier.

"The red skin, the horns. That's what you've always seen when you look at me. Isn't it?"

"No," he said softly. "But I always remind myself that it's under there."

"And you have to remind yourself, because *I've* never done anything to remind you. Except for this one time, when I came around your fingers." She met his eyes, challenged him to say differently. When he didn't, she asked, "Do you think I faked that, too?"

He didn't. *He didn't.* She could see that he didn't. But he didn't know what else to think. He didn't have another explanation.

She had an explanation. She didn't know why, she didn't know how, but she knew: "You were *wrong* about me."

"I want to be," he said simply.

The constriction around her heart eased. *I want to be.* Before, he'd wanted to believe she was a liar. It was so much better that he wanted to believe she wasn't.

She looked into the tub again. His cock now stood fully engorged, rising up out of the water, though she wasn't even undressed. Though they hadn't been talking about sex.

He wanted to be wrong, and he wanted her.

And he was just shy of monstrous. The familiar ache started between her legs—something that she hadn't planned on feeling when she'd come here. She'd been plotting something else.

"I've been thinking about the Rules," she said. "And I've realized that it can't just be that I break them whenever I touch someone without their permission. I accidentally bumped into people in London all the time—especially in the Tube. But I didn't have any Guardians coming after me."

"Yes," he said, his gaze watchful. Maybe wary. She hoped it was wary. "In a situation like that, you're not impeding anyone's free will."

"Unless they've already said, 'Hands off.' Like you've made certain I know very clearly: Hands off, Ash."

His jaw tightened for a second. Then, "Yes. I did."

"But I want hands on. Right now, I want to stroke your cock. I want to take you into my mouth, suck on you until you come, drink you all down. I could do it now. I wouldn't even have to come up for air."

Nicholas didn't respond, but his heart began to pound, a flush sweeping beneath his skin. His fingers clenched on the edge of the tub.

Careful not to touch him, she slipped her hand into the water between his thighs.

"Ash—"

He broke off on a groan when she flicked her hand, splashing water against his thick shaft. Again and again, quick, sharp flicks with the tips of her fingers that transformed beads of water into a heavy massage raining over his cock, his chest. Nicholas set his jaw, dropping his head as he bore the onslaught. When the straining muscles in his thighs began to shake, when a thick drop of pre-come formed at the head of his cock, she stopped.

"Ah, God, *no*!"

His hips lifted, as if reaching for her hand to touch him, to finish him, before he clenched his teeth and settled back in. He watched her again, his eyes hot.

She'd planned to undress, lie back on the bed, spread her thighs, and make herself come without letting him touch her, but she couldn't look away from the thickness of his cock. She wanted him, still. She hadn't planned that—and she could only imagine how he'd feel inside her.

But maybe that would be familiar, too.

Frowning, she swirled her fingers through the water again, watching it run up in tiny waves around the base of his shaft. A hot emotion began to rise up from her stomach, almost choking her. Not desire. Something else, and it tasted like acid.

"Ash?" A soft query prompted her.

"I'm wondering," she said. "So far, almost everything of Rachel's has been familiar to me. Even you, that first time you kissed me. So I wonder: If I take you inside, would you feel familiar then? It might hurt a little. But then I'd take you so deep."

His voice roughened. "Yes."

"Maybe you'd feel familiar in my mouth, too. Did she do that? Did you let her go down on you?"

She looked at Nicholas for an answer, saw him watching her, his dark brows lowered, shadowing his eyes.

"Ash . . ."

He didn't want to say. And God—she didn't want to hear.

"Don't tell me." She stood abruptly, almost stumbled as the backs of her knees hit the bed frame. Nicholas sat up, arms extended as if to catch her, steady her, but she jerked her hands away, out of his reach. "This wasn't what I planned. I had a plot. I'm a demon. So I was going to come in, do this, leave you hard and frustrated."

"I know." He drew his hand back, his gaze searching her face. "I was going to let you. It would be torture. But it would be sweet, Ash."

It had been sweet for her, too. But now . . .

"I can't." She pushed her fist against her chest, trying to stop the bile that was still rising up, rising. Oh, God. She knew the word that fit this emotion. "Because I'm jealous. I'm jealous of a *dead woman,* because she got to touch you and I can't. And I don't want to feel this. I don't like this. I don't want to feel any more of this *shit* that hurts and tears at me. I want to go. I just want to go and let it fade away. I want to go back to feeling nothing again."

Nicholas stood, a cascade of water sheeting away from him. His face stark, he reached for her. "Ash—"

"No!" She slipped over the bed before he could touch her, before he could grab her and hold on to her. "Don't touch me. Just release me from our bargain. Let me go."

His hand dropped to his side, clenched into a fist. "I can't."

"Let me go!"

But she knew it was futile, even before he answered her again. He stood utterly naked in front of her, his obsession plain to see in every sculpted muscle. His body reminded her of everything she'd almost forgotten, what her need and desire had blinded her to: He only lived for revenge. And he wouldn't let her go as long as she was bound to help him get it.

"I can't let you go, Ash." His hoarse reply confirmed everything she already knew. "I need you."

But not for the reason she wanted him to need her. And she didn't want to see him naked anymore.

She turned and left the room, closing her ears to him when

he said her name. When she reached the front door, she kept going.

Lying awake in his darkened bedroom, Nicholas heard the cabin's front door open, and the familiar sound of Ash's boots against the floorboards.

Relief struck him like a punch to the heart, and he clenched his teeth against the need to get up and to seek her out now. He'd stayed up, waiting for her to come back, keeping the fire high and the cabin warm, but when 2 a.m. passed and Ash still hadn't returned, he realized she might not want to return until she was certain she'd be alone.

He probably should have realized it earlier. Leaving the house had made the message pretty clear: Even the cold was better than in the cabin with him.

But she had returned, if only because of the bargain. And since it was his only hold on her, Nicholas still wouldn't release her. It was the only reason the bargain mattered now. He didn't care if Madelyn came.

He just didn't want Ash to go.

But she already was. He shot out of bed when he realized her footsteps were crossing back to the door—as if she'd only come in to retrieve something, and was leaving again.

Not yet. "Ash?"

At his voice, she paused in the doorway, her shotgun in hand. The moonlight gleamed on her pale hair, left her face in shadow. "It's one of the wolves, I think. I'll take care of it."

The door closed. Nicholas shook his head. The wolves. What was she taking care of?

He crossed to the front door. The freezing air immediately bit at his bare skin. The moonlit clearing lay empty, and the darkness beyond the tree line impenetrable. She could have gone any direction, and the snow wasn't fresh enough to follow her tracks.

Disappointment eating a hole in his chest, he turned back—and heard the faint noise. A sharp, plaintive bark followed a series of ululating yips. An animal, obviously in pain. What was Ash planning to do? *Take care of it?*

Jesus. She shouldn't do that alone. Helping it might mean

getting close to it, and even as fast and strong as she was, an animal—a fucking *wolf*—could still hurt her, and one that was trapped or in pain would be more likely to lash out.

And if was hurt so badly it had to be put down, she shouldn't have to do that, either.

He headed back inside, hauled on his clothes in the dark. Grabbing a flashlight and his rifle, he slung the weapon over his shoulder and picked up the snowmobile keys. Outside, he listened, searching for the direction again. All was quiet. Was it already done?

No movement in the tree line—though he didn't know if she was coming back. Maybe he'd take the snowmobile out anyway, look for any recent tracks, make certain she was all right.

Halfway to the shed, he realized that the possibility she'd hurt the wolf had never even occurred to him.

Stunned to the core, he stopped, staring blankly into the night. It hadn't occurred to him. And even now that he realized it hadn't, not a single doubt existed within him. It was the perfect opportunity for a demon to torture an animal—isolated, with no one to hear and the evidence easily erased. But when he considered Ash, he rejected the idea as impossible.

Ash simply wouldn't. Maybe every other demon on Earth and in Hell would, but Ash wouldn't.

If he went out there looking for her, got lost in the snow, needed help, every other demon would ignore his shouts—or maybe even come in close enough to gloat while he froze to death. Ash wouldn't. She'd simply come. Even tonight, when she couldn't stand the sight of him, she'd come.

He'd been wrong, all this time. Not wrong to doubt at first, but to doubt for so long. He'd been waiting to get his head on straight, to figure out how to make sense of her, and now finally, finally, it did. She *was* an exception. He didn't know how, but he'd help her find out.

For now, he just needed to find her. Tell her. And pray it wasn't too late to matter.

Almost laughing at the lightness the realization left in him, he scanned the tree line again. And there she was. The soft red glow moving toward the cabin through the trees.

He went to meet her.

* * *

Up and down, up and down. Her emotions had gone through the most insane day of her life—that she could remember—and this was an up again. Her eyes glowed with it. She needed to learn how to control that, eventually. Right now, she didn't care.

She glanced at the dog limping along beside her. His foot had been caught in an old, rusty trap—probably one that Nicholas's survivalist grandfather had used, but hadn't been pulled up after he died. Not the wolf she'd expected, but a black Labrador, and friendly enough after eating the chunk of meat she'd collected from the cabin's icebox. Not a stray, either. Too well fed and wearing a collar, he'd obviously belonged to someone until recently, and had either gotten lost or had been dumped by his previous owners.

Too bad for them. He was hers now. She liked him—even if he had bitten her when she'd pressed the trap's jaws open. But she'd understood that, all too well. Being hurt made her want to bite someone, too.

Not just someone. Nicholas.

Who was in the distance, trudging through the snow toward her, almost like a wild man. What in the world?

"Ash!"

She'd never heard him call her name like that, an almost desperate note to the deep tones. Did he need help? She glanced at the limping dog. He'd already resisted when she'd tried to carry him.

"I'll be back for you. I'll be right back."

As if in reply, the dog chuffed. Her boomstick tucked beneath her arm, Ash gave a little laugh and took off through the snow. Slowing as she neared Nicholas, she searched his appearance for any sign of injury. No. His breathing was labored from plowing through the deep snow, but he moved with strength, speed. He just seemed . . . intent. Focused. On her. She reached him, stopped knee-deep in the snow, but he didn't. For an instant she thought he'd plow right over her, but then he stopped, and his gloved hands came up to gently capture her face.

He kissed her.

Not like before. Not like ever before. His lips icy from the cold, but firm, and sweet, he kissed her as if it were the first time, the last, as if it were the only thing that mattered.

His mouth broke from hers. His breath was ragged. "I'm sorry, Ash. I was wrong. And I'm so damn sorry."

She didn't understand—or couldn't believe it. "What?"

"You're an exception. Maybe *the* exception, I don't know." His pale blue gaze held hers. Not icy at all, and hers washed his face in a red glow, but he wasn't drawing away. "And I'm sorry."

She couldn't seem to catch her breath. This was a good feeling, the happiness bubbling through her. So why did it seem to crush her chest, sting her eyes, make her want to cry with it? She thought her smile wobbled a little, but it didn't matter, because he kissed it away, and this time there was more beneath it—more strength, more heat, more need. Almost perfect.

Except she couldn't lift her hands and hold him to her. Couldn't push her fingers through his hair.

A soft whine broke them apart. Nicholas frowned, looking through the dark.

He couldn't see the dog, she realized. She turned, and let her eyes provide the light he needed. "His leg was in a trap."

Nicholas nodded before crouching, pulling off his glove and holding out his hand. The dog came over, sniffed, and then seemed to groan when Nicholas's long fingers moved to scratch behind his ear.

"Is the leg broken?"

"I don't think so, but he's hurt enough that he lashed out at me, knocked me over onto my ass." And apparently broke open some of her shotgun shells in the process. She could still smell the sweet hellhound venom. "I'll look at his leg again in the cabin, see how bad it is."

Nicholas's eyes closed, almost as if in relief. His voice roughened. "So we are taking him in?"

"Yes."

"All right, then."

Nicholas stood, pulled on his glove. He gave her a hard kiss before pushing into the already furrowed trench he'd made through the snow. They made quick time back to the cabin, and Ash got the dog settled in with a blanket near the stove and a bowl of water while Nicholas changed out of his heavy clothes.

He returned to the living room wearing only his pajama

bottoms, and sank onto his heels next to her while she examined the dog's leg. "Diagnosis?"

"Just bruised, I think. I can't find any puncture wounds, and he doesn't react when I press on it."

"We'll take him to town tomorrow, have him checked out at the vet's. We'll need food for him, anyway."

The dog lifted his head at the mention of food. Nicholas grinned, scratching the pup behind the ears again, and Ash found herself looking at Nicholas instead, examining his every feature. Only a few hours ago, she'd been jealous, and horrified by what she'd been feeling. Now, she couldn't imagine not wanting to feel like this again.

He met her eyes, and his grin faded. Slowly, as if giving her the chance to retreat, he moved to her, brought her to her feet. His head bent, and he brushed his lips over hers. "I'm sorry for the bath, too."

"Nicholas—"

"And the floor."

She smiled against his mouth. "I liked the floor. Except the end."

"It won't happen again."

His lips pressed to her cheek. Again, and again. Her tattoos, she realized.

"Will you kiss every symbol?"

She felt his laugh, a soft rumble through his chest. "I'll damn well try."

His lips moved to her neck, and she let her head fall back. Her hands lifted to his shoulders—but she stopped. Her throat tightened.

She wanted this, so much. But she didn't want it like this.

"Stop, Nicholas. Stop." When he stiffened against her, she said, "I can't."

He immediately drew back, face carefully blank. Not cold. A mask of tension and pain. His gaze searched hers, and he finally closed his eyes and nodded.

"All right." His voice was the same, rough with strain. "But don't go back outside. I'll build up the fire again. Or you can stay in the bed. I'll keep you warm."

And torture her? "I can't do that, either. I can't *touch* you."

"Can't touch— No. No, Ash." He gave a hoarse laugh, shaking his head. "You can. Anywhere. Any way you like. Anything. Punch through my chest if you want. My free will, that's yours. Whatever you want to do to me, I want it, too."

Trembling, Ash looked to his chest. He offered a measure of trust that she hadn't expected. It wasn't even the qualified bending of the Rules they used in training. Her hand shook as she flattened her palm over his heart.

It pounded, but not in fear.

"For how long?" she wondered.

"Until you don't want to touch me anymore."

That might be longer than he thought.

She grinned up at him, and he'd just begun to smile in return when she was on him, her hands in his hair, dragging him down to her mouth. Hotter now, and his hands slid to her ass, lifted her against his rigid length. Ash's head fell back, and she panted.

"Naked," she said. "Get naked now. And on the bed."

Nicholas went out of order. Pants still on, he swung her up, carried her into the bedroom. She reached around, tried to shove down his waistband, and the moment he set her down beside the bed, she pushed him over. He fell back on the mattress, his laugh shaking the bed. She followed him down with her knee braced beside his thigh, and hooked her fingers into his pajama pants.

She paused. "Am I going too fast?"

He sat up. "Do you plan on going demon-fast?"

"No."

"Good. Because I'd like to see what's happening." He unzipped her jacket, pushed it off her shoulders. "I'd like to feel it, too."

"You will."

"We'll do slow next time, then."

He pulled her hoodie and T-shirt over her head in one motion. Her hair spilled down, slipping across her breasts.

"Sweet Jesus," he breathed, pushing the strands aside to expose the vermillion symbols again. "I'll kiss every one. Just so that I know I've kissed every inch of you."

His pulled her toward his lips, but not to kiss. Ash cried out as he drew her nipple into his mouth, sucking the hardened tip. Searing pleasure burned down her spine along the path of his fingers. Red light glinted against the dark of his hair. She gripped his shoulders, lost in the heat of his mouth, the tease of his tongue.

"I can't stop my eyes from glowing," she whispered.

He lifted his head, bent to press a kiss to the large glyph between her breasts. "Good."

"It doesn't bother you?" She had to ask.

"No." He rose up, kissed the corner of her mouth. "You're beautiful to me."

Her heart swelled. "I have horns."

"And I'm a bastard who should have known what might happen when you lost control. I saw you change in London. I should have been prepared for the same when you came."

"You have scars. And you have good reason not to trust demons."

"But not you." He pressed his lips to her temple. "And I don't care if your skin turns red. I don't care if your wings form. I don't care if your scales come out—"

"I have scales? Like a judging angel, or like a dragon?"

"A dragon." He held her face between his hands. "But for now, just shut up and let me tell you that you're beautiful."

Not with words. He told her with another kiss, sweet and thorough. He told her with each lick as he moved down her body, teeth tugging at her nipples, tasting his way down her stomach. He told her with his eyes when her jeans vanished and he parted her thighs, spread her open to his gaze, when looking wasn't enough.

His mouth covered her, tongue sliding between her slick folds. Fire shot through Ash's blood, burning every nerve. She cried out, lifting against his mouth. With a groan, Nicholas bent his head, took another long swirling taste that left her panting, writhing.

"God, Ash. So sweet and hot." Coming up for breath, he pushed her knee wide. "And we're going to go slow now."

So slow. An eternity of the thrust of his fingers and the flick of his tongue, the bed creaking with the desperate jerk of her hips, his hungry assault against her slick flesh, the raucous pounding of their hearts.

And then it all disappeared, narrowing down to just the ecstasy bursting through her, white-hot. She screamed with it, her back arching as it burnt her down.

Slowly, she built her awareness again, of Nicholas's soft kiss against her thigh, her stomach, moving up until she opened her eyes and he was there, too. She smiled up at him, and his gaze slipped to her mouth.

"Don't move," he said.

His head dipped, and he flicked his tongue across her lips before sliding between. Ash moaned at the subtle penetration, then stiffened when he licked the long point of her left fang. A shiver ripped over her skin, a sweet and painful tightening. She cried out in surprise.

He lifted his head again, studying her face. "Do you like that?"

"Yes." She licked her own, but it wasn't the same. "How did you know to do that?"

"I heard it about vampires once. But it looks like you get the benefits, with none of the bloodsucking."

She grinned, and realized that the fangs were already gone. A laugh escaped her when she saw Nicholas's disappointment. She'd make up for it. Rising up, she caught his mouth in a kiss, her fingers sliding down and curling around the thick shaft behind thin cotton. Somehow, he wasn't naked yet. But she—

Had to let the dog out.

Slipping out of the kiss, Ash groaned her frustration, hoping she'd been mistaken. The sound came again. A scratch at the front door, an anxious whine.

Nicholas froze, as if suddenly aware that she'd heard something. "Ash?"

"The dog. I'll be one second."

Or two, depending on how long it took the dog to slip out of the door. She left Nicholas on the bed, still aroused and his heart pounding. Hers pounding, too, so hot and thick that it seemed to echo in her ears. The dog sat in front of the door, tail wagging. She opened it and he merely looked up at her, giving her a doggy grin.

Cute, but she was standing there naked and the cold was seeping into her skin. "Out," she said. "Do your business. I'll let you back in. I promise."

He shook his head, flapping his ears wildly. Hope lifted when he rose to all fours, but he only snuffled at the edge of the doorway before padding back around to the middle of the room. The bed creaked, and she heard Nicholas coming to the door of the bedroom.

She looked at the dog. "I'm only going to have it open for a second longer. Then you have to hold it."

He chuffed at her.

Shaking her head, she turned back to close it—and stopped. Her boomstick should have been on that rack next to the door. It wasn't.

Neither was Nicholas's rifle, and the holsters that hung there were empty. Sudden dread filled her stomach, her heart began beating sickly thuds. And the rhythm of Nicholas's had changed, too . . . and there were still the echoes, but they were beating at a different time.

"Ash." Behind her, Nicholas's voice filled with a cold that she'd never heard before—the ice of fear. "Don't look around. Just run. Go. As fast as you can."

And leave him? She couldn't. She looked around, and her blood turned to ice water.

It wasn't a dog anymore. Standing as tall as the ceiling, it had three massive heads, jaws filled with gleaming dagger-teeth. Its eyes glowed, not steady crimson like hers, but flickering as if lit by the fires of Hell. Short fur as stiff as needles poked between crimson and black scales. She couldn't see Nicholas beyond its enormous body, but the monstrous creature was watching them, each of them to one set of eyes, and the third . . . was watching the door.

Pressing her back to the wall, she kept her eyes on the monster, let her fingers search for a weapon. A chair, a curtain rod, anything.

The head watching her growled, a long deep rumble. She froze.

"Nicholas?"

She heard the low noise he made, despair in the back of his throat. "*Go.* I'll distract it, keep it here. You have to go now or you won't have a chance. It's a hellhound. One bite can paralyze you."

It had already bitten her once. Apparently, she'd been lucky. Damn lucky. Ash eyed the size of its jaws. "One bite could kill either of us."

The hellhound chuffed, but this time it was a deep bellow,

from a chest as wide as a truck. She could almost taste the amusement behind it—

No. She *could* taste it. A little odd, but in the same way she sensed emotions in people.

"It's laughing," she realized.

"Ash. *Go*."

Not without him—but it was too late anyway. She heard a light thud from outside, followed by a second. A flutter, a flap. The sound of wings.

Feathered wings.

Her chest tightened. "Nicholas. The Guardians are here."

For a moment, there was only silence. Then a footstep from the porch seemed to break it, and Nicholas roared her name. The hellhound's heads swung around. Ash's heart stopped.

Nicholas was attacking the thing. Trying to get to her. Oh, God.

She sprinted forward, and though Nicholas's heart was between beats, she saw that the hellhound reacted just as quickly, that he'd already noticed her coming around and so she shouted, "I'm just protecting him!" before sliding beneath those enormous gaping jaws, across the floorboards and up. Nicholas seemed frozen, his expression contorted by fury and determination, and he'd found the only stabbing weapon the hellhound hadn't taken: the heel of her boot. Clenched in his raised fist, he was trying to protect her, but this would only hurt him, and if she didn't slow down, she'd hit him while going too fast and hurt him, too. She slowed, and caught his wrist as he stabbed down. She hadn't slowed enough. As her body hit his and they went flying, Ash managed to react, to twist, and take the impact.

She slammed back into the wall next to the bedroom door, holding on to him. It took him only a blink to realize what had happened, and then his arms were around her, shoving her behind him and putting himself between the hellhound and her.

Between the Guardians and her.

Ash slipped her hands around Nicholas's waist, ready to carry him away. She looked over his shoulder as the footsteps came nearer, as the resonance of their steps against the wood changed when they crossed from the porch into the cabin. "I hear two," she whispered. "One with heels."

The hellhound gave a happy chuff, an unmistakable sound

of greeting. His giant, slithering tail wagged. A woman answered him.

"Such a good boy. I love it when you look so mean. But you're taking up all of the room. Hugh can't even fit in here with me."

With a noise like a sigh, the hellhound suddenly diminished—looking almost like a Labrador again, but twice as big, and still with three heads—and revealing the man and woman standing near the door.

Tall, with a long black wool coat that buttoned to her throat, and a tangle of long dark hair, the woman regarded them with arched brows and a sharp amusement. The man gave less away, but Ash couldn't miss the calluses on his hands, the bulk of his shoulders. A man who had his own obsessions, was driven by some deep purpose.

That purpose was to kill her, Ash supposed.

"Just turn around," Nicholas said. His arms came back and his palms flattened against the wall on either side of her, as if to protect her from every side. "She's not like most demons. She's not evil."

The woman smiled and came farther inside. The man—Hugh, she'd called him—shut the cabin door.

"Different, yes. I know better than anyone," she said, her gaze narrowing on Ash's face. "You *are* new."

Easier to kill, Ash thought.

"And those symbols . . . Taylor was right. Those aren't for the transformation. They're a spell to create a new Gate. Fuck."

Ash trembled. *A spell.* The demon who'd attacked her in Duluth had said something similar, and there was a memory there, something she needed to know, but she couldn't trace it now.

The woman turned to look at Hugh, who seemed to shake his head without moving at all. She focused on Ash again. "I see you're all naked and cozy here, shacked up in the middle of nowhere, but unless the demon you're bound to is dead, you're not safe. *Nobody* will be safe if Lucifer opens that Gate. So you need to come with us."

Okay, that was easy. "We're safe then," Ash said, and since she didn't have a bargain with these Guardians, had no problem telling them, "The demon is dead."

Hugh spoke. "Lie."

She felt Nicholas's tension increase. The woman looked to him and grinned.

"You know what he is, don't you? He had a Gift to see the truth for eight hundred years, and he can still see it. So don't even try to lie." She glanced at Ash. "Or try, if you want. It's a lot more fun that way."

"Or maybe he'll lie even when he hears the truth," Nicholas said. "How can we know?"

"That's your first thought? Your mother really fucked you up, didn't she?" The woman studied him for a long moment. "He won't lie, not when he's here to see the truth. And not when I depend on him to tell me when you're lying."

"If he sees it, then he knows I told the truth when I said she wasn't like other demons," Nicholas said.

"Well, I don't need Hugh to tell me that. It's written all over her face . . . and from the little I can see, it's also written all over the rest of her. Lucifer named you Ash, is that right? Because after you sacrificed yourself to save St. Croix's life, you're not Rachel Boyle anymore."

CHAPTER 14

Through his own shock, the immediate denial, Nicholas felt Ash tense behind him.

"I'm not Rachel."

"Not anymore," the woman agreed, but her gaze moved between them, and Nicholas could almost see her calculating, weighing. "You don't know. Neither of you know."

"We know she's not Rachel," Nicholas said.

The woman's eyes flattened. "No, because Lucifer stripped most of Rachel out of her. Didn't he? Not everything, because she's talking, and I'm guessing she didn't have to relearn her ABCs, but the rest is gone, isn't it? Relationships, emotional connections, and the deeper they were the harder he dug. Then he ripped them right out, and took everything that made Rachel *Rachel* with it. And he made you with what was left."

Ash made a soft noise—of pain, of terror. The sound tore at his heart. Nicholas spun, caught her in his arms.

Behind him, the woman continued speaking. "You might not remember all of that, because it was Rachel who'd have made the decision. She's the one who'd have agreed to the transformation, the bargain. But you . . . you're the one who is stuck with it. The one with the spell on your face and the fate of the world on your shoulders."

Ash began to shake. Almost convulsing, her teeth rattling. Tears stood in her eyes. "I remember. I remember him tearing me apart."

Jesus. Nicholas wanted to rip the woman's tongue out. Couldn't she see what this was doing to Ash? Was this what the Guardians did? Fuck them. Fuck them all.

"What the fuck are you doing? What kind of Guardians are you? Just get out. Get the hell out."

"We're not Guardians. Or rather, Hugh isn't anymore. He used to be. But me, I used to be a halfling like her."

Ash's breath caught. "A halfling."

"We start out human, but are given the powers of a demon. Lucifer didn't take as much from me. Just my name. Now I'm Lilith. Even though I'm human again now, I'm still Lilith."

"Human again," Nicholas repeated, looking into Ash's eyes. "How?"

"Lucifer did that, too."

Her footsteps indicated her approach. Nicholas half turned, trying to shield Ash with his body, trying to make certain he could watch for any attack.

"So you see why we sent Sir Pup in here first to determine exactly what sort of demon she was and to take your weapons. It would have been a shame if Ash had shot either one of us. That would be breaking the Rules."

And that meant Nicholas couldn't use the Rules to his advantage, either. Fuck.

"I heard wings," Ash said.

"We needed a ride." Lilith looked up, as if through the roof. "Now they're up there, a full phalanx. Waiting. Because that spell on your face means that you are a danger to everyone. Ideally, we'd hide you in Caelum, but a demon—even a halfling—can't be teleported to that realm. So we'll take you to Special Investigations, where we can protect you until we hunt down the demon who holds your leash. Your choice is simple: Either you leave with us, or you don't leave this cabin alive."

Fury slammed through him. "Fuck you. You aren't touching her."

"I prefer not to slay her. But understand this, Nicholas St. Croix: I'm willing to sacrifice one to save the lives of many. That sacrifice won't be necessary, though, if she agrees to protection, so that the spell can't be cast."

"I'll protect her."

"You?" Lilith laughed. "I have a report that says a demon in Duluth almost ripped her apart while you waved a crossbow around. You didn't even know who or what she was. A woman *died* for you, and yet when she returns from the dead as a demon, you don't even question where she came from?"

"He did." Ash's fingernails dug into his biceps, her eyes glowing. Suddenly fierce, defensive. "He was trying to help me find out who I am."

"Was he? It's strange, though. That doesn't fit what I know of him at all. Raised by a demon, bent on revenge." Her head tilted as she studied him. "When you first met her, what did you think? That she was Madelyn, come to taunt you in Rachel's form? Or maybe a demon who'd been plotting with Madelyn."

Jesus. Whoever her sources were, they'd informed her well. But that was no secret. Even Ash knew that. "Yes."

"And then you intended to kill her."

His heart thudded. He felt Ash's fingers tighten, then her soft laugh. "No, he didn't. I was too useful to him."

Lilith's eyes narrowed. "Is that true, Nicholas? Say it."

God. What did it matter? "That was then," he said.

"So you did intend to."

Fuck. "Yes."

"Truth," Hugh said.

Ash's breath stopped. Obviously shaken, she looked up at him.

Nicholas shook his head. "I wouldn't now. I'd die before hurting you now."

No pronouncement of truth came. Somehow, the silence seemed damning. He touched Ash's face, her hair.

"Not anymore," he said, and didn't look away until she nodded. He turned fierce eyes on Lilith. "What the fuck?"

Her brows lifted. "I'm just trying to make sense of this. You didn't know she was Rachel, but you offered to help her. But Ash says that it's because she was useful. Useful for what? She doesn't know anything, either."

"I didn't know that."

Lilith looked at Ash. "You lied to him? There's hope for you, then."

"She didn't lie," Nicholas said. "And I was using her to find Madelyn."

"Truth."

"Madelyn," Lilith repeated. "Funny. You want to protect her, but you put her in the path of the demon who's most likely the one she's bound to obey. The demon who most likely intends to kill her in order to complete that spell."

Ash began shaking again. "Bound to her?"

"Yes." Lilith stepped closer, her voice softening. "I think you remember this, too—because Lucifer would need you to. Or Madelyn would have told you after the transformation. Did she bring you out of Hell? Was she the first person you remember?"

"Yes."

"And you're terrified of her now."

"Yes." She pushed her face against Nicholas's shoulder. Chest aching, he slid his hand into her hair, held her to him. "Yes."

"Because a part of you knows that if she speaks, you must obey. Any order she gives, you must carry through, or you'll break your bargain with her . . . and return to the frozen field."

Ash cried out, and he felt tears against his skin. Hot, burning, but he remembered her fear of the cold, her terror of the memory that was lost to it. Now he knew. She'd been down there, suffering. Tormented in ice, eaten by dragons. And even though she couldn't remember it, she carried that frozen field within her.

"Stop," he said hoarsely. "Stop what you're doing to her."

Lilith's gaze hardened when she looked at him. "That was Rachel, you realize. She and Madelyn probably had some kind of bargain. *Don't interfere between me and my son,* something simple like that. Something she probably agreed to, not understanding exactly what it meant. Then she saved your life, and paid for it—with death, and then with torture."

And that was enough. He didn't know what this woman was doing, but she wasn't helping Ash or protecting her in any way. And trying to use Rachel to guilt him into giving Ash over to Guardians who'd promised to kill her if her existence proved too dangerous wouldn't work. He wasn't a Guardian. And he'd see the whole fucking world burn before he sacrificed her life for anyone else's.

"Lucifer took your powers," he said. "But you're still a demon."

"Truth," Hugh said, this time with a hint of a smile.

Lilith's brows shot up. "And you've never been transformed, but you might as well be one, too. You brought Ash here, *knowing* that Madelyn would find you."

"You're throwing shit out there. You don't know that."

"But I think I do. Because there are a few other things that simply don't make sense. One is Cawthorne's suicide only a week after Ash left Nightingale House. Strange, don't you think, that someone entered Madelyn's code into her town house security system that same night?"

Ash lifted her head. "Cawthorne killed himself?"

"Nicholas didn't tell you? He knew. His private investigator told him the same day you arrived in America." Lilith caught his look and grinned. "You'd be *amazed* at how good some vampires are at hacking computer and phone systems. And you knew that Madelyn was probably looking for her, didn't you?"

"I knew it was possible."

"You counted on it. That's what made her so useful. And then there's the matter of the two demons running around with Rachel's face—one of them a ghost. *That* didn't make any sense, either, not at first. Not until I thought about Madelyn, and what I know of demons, and how she'd tried to get her hands on Ash."

"A ghost?" Ash's brow furrowed in confusion. "What ghost? Rachel's a ghost, too?"

"Oh, Nicholas. You didn't tell her that, either? Considering that they're her parents, don't you think she deserved to know?"

God. And he suddenly knew: Lilith had said that she didn't want to kill Ash, but that she'd sacrifice one to save many. And she was. But she didn't plan to sacrifice Ash.

In order to persuade Ash to come with her, she was sacrificing Nicholas.

"Nicholas?" Ash looked up at him, her expression a mixture of wariness and confusion. "What do I deserve to know?"

He couldn't answer, not yet. Tightening his arms around her, he desperately tried to think of some way to put it that wasn't damning.

There wasn't one. It *was* damning. And it was true.

"A demon took Rachel's face and goaded Steve Johnson into killing her parents."

Horror climbed into her expression. Not anger at him. Not yet. "A demon? The one who attacked us in Duluth?"

He picked his words carefully. "I don't know—"

"Lie."

Nicholas ground his teeth, faced the man. "I don't know *for certain*!"

"Who?" Ash's voice brought him back to her. "Who?"

He'd never wanted to lie so badly. He couldn't. Not now—and not because Hugh was listening. He simply couldn't look into her eyes and pretend he didn't know. "Madelyn. Madelyn killed them."

Everything in her face stilled. The hold of her fingers slackened. "You knew this and didn't tell me?"

"I didn't know they were your parents."

"But you *knew* they mattered. That they were important to me."

He wanted to plead ignorance. To say he didn't know, that he hadn't believed it, that he'd thought she was a demon who couldn't truly feel, that it was all a trick.

But he'd known. He'd held her while she sobbed for parents she couldn't remember, and he'd known that emotion was real.

"Yes," he said. "I knew."

"So you brought her out here," Lilith said. "And you waited for Madelyn to come to you."

He looked into Ash's face. He couldn't read all of the emotions there, but he recognized pain, horror, disbelief. God. She *had* to know everything had changed.

"Yes—"

"Truth."

"But not *now*! Goddammit, I wouldn't have used you as bait now! I can only think of protecting you."

And silence. Awful silence.

Ash's hands dropped away from his waist. And though the wall prevented her from backing away, he could feel her withdrawing.

"Ash," he pled softly. "Please. Believe me. Believe me."

Her voice was wooden, her face stone. "I don't know what to believe, Nicholas."

"I swear my only thought was protecting you," he said, but there was only more damning silence from Hugh. Did Ash see what they were doing? "They want you to leave with them, or he would say that is the truth, too."

"We can train her to protect herself far better than you can,

Nicholas," Lilith said. "You're only a man who needs to eat, to sleep. You can't protect her all the time. Can you? Because all it would take is a word from her, a letter sent, a shout from down the street, and Ash is lost to you."

Would it be that easy? Suddenly stricken, Nicholas looked down at her. Completely naked, she stood with her face set and her eyes averted from his, and though he knew Ash didn't care that the others saw her nude, though he knew her strength, she suddenly seemed so exposed, so vulnerable. *God.* Could he be so certain, when it meant risking her life?

"And Ash—if Madelyn finds you together with Nicholas, she'll order you to kill him. Because that would cause you the most pain, and because that is what a demon would do."

Ash shook her head. "But *I* wouldn't do it. I wouldn't obey."

"Then you'd be back in that frozen field as soon as she sacrifices you to the spell. And she wins either way."

Back in the frozen field. Ash continued to shake her head, but he saw the terror fill her eyes, the fear that would be her choice: to kill him, or to suffer an eternity of torment—a torture that she already knew too well.

No doubt, Madelyn *would* order Ash to do it. Nicholas wouldn't care if he died for her. But if Ash refused to carry it out, he couldn't bear the thought of her in that field, tortured for eternity for saving *him.*

He couldn't bear it. And if Lilith had been searching for his limit, she'd just found it. So what now?

It would be Ash's decision. It had to be hers alone.

Without taking his eyes from her, Nicholas said, "Will you two give us a minute? Let her take a breath, get dressed."

"So she doesn't run around like that all the time? That'll disappoint the novices," Lilith said. "But go ahead."

With a quick, grateful glance at Nicholas, Ash turned toward the bedroom. Nicholas's throat tightened. This wouldn't be the last time he was with her there. He'd follow—

"Ashmodei."

As if struck, Ash stumbled. She caught herself against the wall and slowly faced Lilith, her eyes wide. "What?"

"Your name. I finally saw it when you moved—it's written here." Lilith touched her own chest, and Ash mirrored the movement, flattening her palm over the large symbol between her breasts. "Lucifer named you after a demon who betrayed him. It would be considered an insult to Ashmodei, giving the name to a halfling. I take it a good sign."

"Ashmodei," she repeated softly. When she looked at Nicholas, a smile had transformed her face. "So you helped me discover it, after all."

"I didn't—"

"You're the one who stripped me naked."

God, and she made him laugh. He followed her into the bedroom, memorizing the sway of her blond hair against her back, the square of her shoulders, the dimples above her perfect ass. Then she looked down at herself and her clothes formed, with boots matching the one that still lay with a broken heel near the bed.

The Guardians could probably tell her how and why she did that. Nicholas hadn't even been able to tell Ash her name. They could train her, better than he ever could.

She faced him, and her smile had already gone, her eyes glowing crimson. He knew what her choice would be. What it *had* to be.

And he knew what his had to be, too. "I'll go with you."

"They'll lock me up, you realize. Not in a cell, but the effect is the same. They'll lock me up tight—and you'd be locked up with me, too, because Madelyn might find me through you."

"Then I'll stay locked up with you."

Her tearful smile gave him hope. Until she spoke. "You can't come."

Feeling sucker-punched, he shook his head. "What?"

"You can't." Her breath hitched. "The Guardians aren't perfect. They can be defeated. They have their limits. You forced one to leave us in Duluth by pointing a crossbow at her friend's head. They'll work harder than that to protect me, but there's always a chance Madelyn will get through and I'll have to choose whether or not to kill you."

And he'd make that choice as easy for her as he could. "You died for me once. I'd return the favor."

"That was Rachel."

No. He hadn't meant— "I *know* you aren't Rachel."

He'd never been this fucked up over her. Rachel had deserved better than she'd gotten, but he hadn't been able to give it to her.

"Yes, but that's my point. *That was Rachel.* She loved you."

His chest turned to lead. "And you don't."

But it didn't matter. He'd still protect her. He'd still die for her.

"Today I think I do," she said, but held up her hands, stopped him when he'd have gone to her. "Tomorrow, I might not."

"Ash—"

"It'll probably change. It'll fade." She drew her hands in, wrapping them around her stomach as if keeping herself warm, holding herself in. "Nothing I feel stays the same. My emotions are up, and down, and all over. Today, I know that if Madelyn told me to kill you, I wouldn't—even though there's nothing that terrifies me more than the frozen field. But tomorrow, I might kill you rather than be trapped there again. Tomorrow, I might hate you for keeping the truth about Madelyn killing my parents from me. Tomorrow, your life might not be my limit."

"I'd give it to you," he said hoarsely. "Whether you love me or not, and *not* in exchange for Rachel. Just for you."

"You might give it. But if I don't love you, I'd be *taking* it to save myself—and I'd become everything you finally believe I'm not."

If Ash was capable of becoming that, she wouldn't give a shit about whether she did. And Nicholas didn't believe she could be that, no matter how she felt about him. "No—"

"And you have to rescind the permission you gave me, so that you're protected by the Rules again."

What? She wouldn't be able to touch him as she wanted. She hated the restrictions the Rules put on her. If there was only one human in the world she didn't have to check herself with, it would be him.

Nicholas shook his head. *"No."*

"Yes. Not having to follow the Rules makes it too easy for me; there would be no consequences if I kill you. If Madelyn orders me to do it and my emotions aren't strong enough to stop me, maybe fear for my own life will."

And if her emotions did stop her, she'd end in the frozen field. So they were back to that again. If she loved him, if she was with him, then her soul was in danger.

Until Madelyn was dead.

So he had a purpose again—the same purpose he'd always had: destroying Madelyn. But this time, not for revenge. This time, it was for Ash.

"I'll find Madelyn," he vowed. "I'll kill her, just to release you. Then I'll find you again."

"But—"

"And I release you from our bargain. I won't take back the Rules' protection, but I'll stay away until she's dead."

"Nicholas," she whispered brokenly—and finally, she reached for him. He held her close, her body so strong, so warm. "I hope this fades. Because I *never* want to feel like this again."

Neither did Nicholas. Her mouth rose to his, and when she kissed him, Nicholas knew he wouldn't have a moment's peace until she kissed him again.

But it wouldn't be now. And when she drew back, he let her go.

CHAPTER 15

The Guardians' headquarters in San Francisco wasn't quite the prison Ash had thought it would be. She'd immediately had free range within the facility—and within two weeks, had been allowed to take walks around the neighborhood, with either a Guardian or Sir Pup by her side.

Today, Ash had chosen Sir Pup. Appearing as happy-go-lucky as any other dog sitting beneath a café's sidewalk table on a sunny spring day, he lay at her feet while she read and sipped her coffee. That appearance was deceiving. If Madelyn found her, tried to issue an order, the hellhound would shape-shift and bite off the demon's head before the second word passed her lips.

If Madelyn found her here. Ash knew the Guardians didn't think it was likely, or they'd never have let her outside. Except for changing between her demonic and natural forms, Ash would never be able to shape-shift. Lucifer's symbols carved into her body prevented any other shifting, probably just for this reason: so she couldn't hide from Madelyn. But stage makeup to cover her tattoos, scissors, brown hair dye, and a hat to shadow her features all worked well enough to keep attention away from her.

So did a Guardian named Radha, a master of illusion who

was currently in London and posing as a tattooed, miraculously-returned-from-the-presumed-dead Rachel Boyle. The story the Guardians came up with had been easy to follow online, caught in sensationalized headlines: Owing to some still-unknown trauma, Rachel had lost her memory for three years, which she'd spent at Nightingale House until she'd finally remembered her past . . . tragically too late to be reunited with her parents.

All close enough to the truth to be verified, and the remainder vague enough to mystify or frustrate anyone who tried to dig deeper. After two months, the news had lost interest, police investigations into those still-missing three years between Rachel's disappearance and Nightingale House were cooling down again, and Madelyn still hadn't made a move against Radha—she hadn't even made a psychic probe to confirm Rachel's identity.

Madelyn would probably do so soon, however. Since Rachel's tattooed face had first spread across the Internet and news feeds, other demons had come after Radha, all trying to prevent that spell from being cast and Lucifer's early return. The Guardian had slain them all—and Ash had no doubt she'd be able to slay Madelyn, too.

Until then, Ash remained a brunette who couldn't shape-shift, and who still couldn't fly. But she was working hard on that, doing the one thing that had never occurred to her while she'd been jumping out of a tree: reading.

Flying, she discovered, truly was for the birds. Humans-turned-Guardians—or halflings—didn't have an instinctive ability, and they had to make up for that lack in knowledge and understanding. In two months, she'd read her way through books and scrolls detailing bat and Guardian wing anatomy, piloting manuals for small planes and fighter jets, and texts loaded with information about the effects of wind currents and altitude—all in the hopes that when she was finally in the air, some of that knowledge had soaked deep enough into her brain that she understood the adjustments that needed to be made, and why she might need to change the angle of her wing in order to stop herself from crashing into the ground.

But the rest was simply familiarity. Inside the Special Investigations warehouse, Ash wore her wings constantly, and now she could maneuver them as easily as arm or a leg. She could flap them, hard and fast enough that she hovered—wobbling but upright—a few feet above the floor. In the next week or two, she'd be teleported to a desert for her first trial flights, with a Guardian standing by to catch her if something went wrong.

Much better than falling out of trees . . . but she wished Nicholas could be with her.

And her feelings for him hadn't faded.

She'd thought they would—or that they'd be replaced by some newer, fresher emotion. She liked several of the Guardians and vampires she'd met, but she hadn't stopped loving Nicholas, wishing he were there, trying not to laugh. Several other people she'd met were undeniably attractive. Ash didn't *want* them. When her body ached, her thoughts were only of Nicholas.

And she missed him. *That* was new, a longing that cut deeper with each passing day, instead of fading as it should have. Even her resentment had subsided, though it had burned hot when she'd first read through the reports Taylor had compiled on her parents' murder. For days, she'd been glad to be rid of him, glad to be surrounded by Guardians who gave her any information she needed, *especially* when it mattered. But her resentment hadn't been able to stand up against her understanding of him.

He'd been wrong to conceal Madelyn's involvement. He'd sacrificed her need for revenge on the altar of his own. But she also understood that he hadn't let himself believe in her need, or the grief that had driven it. He might have known it was real; he wouldn't let himself *believe* it.

That had changed. Given the same choice now, he'd have told her. Ash believed that to the root of her soul . . . and that belief didn't fade.

So she lived with a bone-deep ache that deepened with his absence, the hope that Madelyn would soon be slain—and the pleasure that the tiny contact she managed to have with him provided.

As promised, he hadn't attempted to reach her since she'd left the cabin. Though reporters had tried to find him after Rachel's reappearance had cleared him of suspicion in her murder, Nicholas hadn't made any public statements. But with Rachel alive and her accounts unfrozen, the Guardians had managed to liquidate and launder most of her assets, spread them across five different identities, and transfer them to Ash. With the substantial amount in hand, she'd begun buying up shares and taking over two of Reticle's outlying holdings—Ash's way of saying *Hello.*

Even distracted by his search for Madelyn, he'd eventually see her activity or be alerted by his staff, and look hard at her. And though he might not recognize who lay at the other end, she looked forward to his countermove.

No, that wasn't right. She looked forward to *everything.*

She loved the fighting practice, the unending fencing forms, and the continuous study of things she hadn't forgotten but had simply never known before. On the night she'd met Nicholas and he'd aimed his crossbow at her chest, Ash hadn't been certain whether she didn't want to die because of some deep survival instinct or a true desire to be alive. Not now. She *loved* life—as much as she still loved him. Preferably, that life would eventually include him again. But if it couldn't, she could at least be certain that she'd made the right choice by coming with the Guardians . . . because it meant she'd never have to choose between life or Nicholas.

A beep from her cell phone alarm warned that her time outside was up; if she didn't return soon, the Guardians would come looking for her. With a great huff, Sir Pup climbed to his feet. Ash collected her books and tossed her uneaten sandwich to the grateful hellhound—who'd already enjoyed two under the table.

"Pig," she said, and he grinned his doggy grin at her.

Her resentment against him had faded, too. And after she'd realized how smoothly Lilith and Hugh had manipulated her and Nicholas, it had taken longer to forgive them, but eventually that sense of anger and stupidity had gone, too.

Intentions mattered, and she understood why they'd pushed Nicholas away and brought her here: They simply couldn't allow a Gate to open and for Lucifer and his demons to spill out into the world. Ash couldn't feel the same urgency about the whole matter that they did, but she recognized the danger of thousands of demons, each pushing humans like Steve Johnson to their limits, and not enough Guardians to hold them in check.

The whole world would go mad. Ash preferred the world as it was.

Well, maybe it could be a little better—especially if Madelyn were dead. *Especially* if Ash or Nicholas were the ones to slay her. But she'd settle for dead, and be happy no matter who did it.

A block away from the café, she vanished the books into her cache. Easy now, just as forming her clothes or her wings were. Her eyes rarely glowed unless she wanted them to, and her fangs appeared with a thought. The only difficulty she had wasn't looking demonic, it was looking too much like herself—if she wasn't careful, her hair reverted to blond and grew to the middle of her back again. The Guardians had stopped buying the brown dye by the box and ordered it by the carton, instead.

Another two blocks of run-down warehouses and apartments brought her to Special Investigations' large fenced lot. The building didn't look any different than the others in the neighborhood—deliberately, she was told. Demons preferred to be surrounded by money and luxury, so they wouldn't come into this area unless necessary.

Ash didn't care about luxury, though it was nice. She *did* like money, however, so she'd gotten the demon thing half right.

A four-inch-thick steel door provided the first line of defense for the warehouse. Rigged with enough electricity to fry anyone with an elevated temperature on the spot, she avoided electrocution by swiping her keycard. As soon as she and the hellhound passed through the entrance, Sir Pup doubled in size and his two other heads appeared, tongues lolling from each massive jaw. Though her psyche and emotions were already shielded from detection, now she blocked all emotions coming from others. The Guardians had been surprised that she'd walked through London absorbing all of those human feelings, but even though they'd taught her to block them, she liked to open herself during the visits to the café. People were too fascinating to shut them out.

But although the Guardians and vampires at SI were fascinating, she couldn't bear to allow them to bombard her. Not anymore. It was all too painful.

From the first day, she'd sensed a tension hanging over the warehouse, related to the Guardians' missing leader, Michael. They'd been focused, determined. Fear and anxiety lay beneath that determination, but it hadn't been overwhelming.

Then, three weeks after Ash had arrived at the warehouse,

she'd been training with the novices in the gymnasium when a thin, spidery woman had stumbled through the Gate in the hallway—the portal that led to Caelum, but that Ash couldn't cross through or even sense. Bleeding from her head, the woman had fallen to the floor, her black dress billowing around her.

She'd looked at them, clearly dazed. "The whole of the Boreas shore has just crumbled into the sea. How very odd."

Her words had sent the novices swarming through the Gate to see. Ash had been left to help the Guardian—Alice—to her feet, and to make certain that she made her way to the main offices without tumbling over.

Since then, reports of falling spires and collapsing arches had been delivered to SI with increasing regularity, and the Guardians' growing terror and desperation pressed like a knife against Ash's tongue. She couldn't feel the desperation herself, but she understood theirs. Two enormous paintings of the realm hung in Lilith's office, an unimaginably beautiful city of sparkling marble domes and columned temples, set against the bluest sky Ash had ever seen. She also understood that their horror didn't just stem from the shattering of that beautiful realm, but that the destruction was connected to Michael, too—who was being tortured in the frozen field.

That horrified Ash. And though she'd gladly have given Lilith and Hugh information when they asked how Lucifer had brought her out of the frozen field, she had nothing to tell them. Ash simply didn't know.

Now, with her mind blocked, she waited for the various scans—temperature, fingerprints, retinal—to finish confirming her identity before forming her wings and heading toward the gym. The offices were busy, as they always were, with voices coming from every side. She'd learned to push them into the background, and typically only noticed when someone spoke her name.

Today, it wasn't her name that caught her attention, but a thread through the jumble of noise that made her breath stop, her heart pound.

—St. Croix attempted to contact her yesterday—

That was Taylor's voice, but it wasn't coming from the direction of the offices. Ash turned down the hallway to the tech room, where Taylor and Lilith stood behind a Guardian sitting at a long table topped by monitors and keyboards. Sir Pup trotted ahead to meet Lilith, who greeted him with a smile and a scratch at his ears.

At the computer, Jake glanced over at Ash. "You came back just in time. Whenever Lilith stands this close to me, I get the feeling that she's going to start using me as her dog and rub my head, instead."

"You wish, pup."

"No, I don't. I really, *really* don't." He put a protective hand over his shaved hair and edged away. "Sir Pup would probably bite my face off out of jealousy."

Ash thought the laughing chuff from the hellhound sounded like agreement. Taylor's lips curved faintly in response, but not enough that Ash considered it a smile. Of late, everything about the woman seemed faint, and though Ash couldn't see any measurable physical change, the impression of Taylor's fragility increased with every report of a cracked column and crumbling dome, as if she stood on the verge of collapsing herself.

From what Ash knew of Taylor, it wouldn't happen. The former detective would continue standing upright through sheer will—and chase down demons while doing it. Hopefully, that demon would soon be the one Ash most wanted to die.

"Was that Madelyn you were speaking about?" When all three lifted their brows in unison, Ash clarified, "I heard Taylor say that Nicholas tried to contact someone. Me? Because if he was, then that wasn't Nicholas. He wouldn't risk me like that. It would have to be Madelyn, fishing."

"It was St. Croix," Lilith said. "But he was trying to reach Rosalia."

The disappointment that slid across her chest didn't make sense. It was best that he didn't try to contact her. Still, Ash wished to hear the sound of his voice, the rough start of his laugh.

It wasn't all disappointment, though. There was also relief. "So that means you know where he is, and that he's okay."

"He's all right," Jake said. "And we've had a rough idea of his whereabouts since he left the cabin."

"Oh. Why didn't anyone tell me?"

"You didn't ask."

"I didn't think anyone would know."

But no, that wasn't precisely it. After all, the Guardians had found them at the cabin by sending Sir Pup after Nicholas's scent trail, all the way from Minnesota. Their computer techs had unearthed texts sent to unregistered phones. So, yes, if they wanted to, they could track Nicholas.

Yet now that she thought about it, everyone had carefully avoided any mention of Nicholas at all—so she'd equated their silence on the topic with a lack of information, a sign that they'd had nothing to give. They'd offered everything else so readily, so why not—

Oh. *Oh.* All right, so her emotions had taken a dive as soon as she'd walked away from Nicholas, and she'd been crying when she'd been teleported away from the cabin. There might have been a bucket of tears. It might have been ugly. But when had Ash given them the impression that *she* was fragile? Screw that.

"I'd rather you didn't conceal anything about him from me. I'd much rather know, no matter what it is." A thought occurred to her, seized her chest. Why had he needed Rosalia? Had they concealed the truth of that from her, too? "Is he hurt?"

"No. He's been busy." Amusement sharpened Lilith's features. "Looking for Madelyn, of course, but where he doesn't find her, he's doing a bit of cleaning along the way."

"What does that mean?"

"It means that he's been searching for Madelyn for a while," Jake said, "and while he did that, he must have come across other demons. Taking them out would have been pretty damn risky—the wrong bit of evidence, he doesn't hide a body well enough—so he likely chose to keep on looking for Madelyn rather than heading for jail. Now, he's going back and essentially tagging them and bagging them."

Oh, God. "Isn't that still risky?"

"Not so much when he's got Rosalia on speed dial. He shoots them full of hellhound venom, calls her up, she comes and takes care of it. Three that way so far, but this last one, he couldn't get ahold of her. So he finished slaying the demon himself."

"Beheading," Lilith said. "Effective. Then he finally got in touch with Rosalia, and she came to take care of it."

A first kill. Demon or not, that couldn't be easy. "How was he? All right?"

Taylor turned her back to the table, sat lightly against the edge. "Do you really think he'd let Rosalia know if he wasn't?"

"No." Ash would bet that he'd been all Stone Cold St. Croix. Maybe his therapist would hear what his response had been. She doubted anyone else would. "Why is he doing it, do you think? Why not just Madelyn?"

Had it become more important to him, seeing all demons destroyed for what they'd done—to prevent it from happening again? Or was there another reason?

"Why has he become a demon-bagging Batman?" Jake asked. "Speaking as a guy, I can give you three reasons right now. One: your hair. Two: your lips. Three: your tit—"

Too fast even for Ash to track, Sir Pup's right head shot out and his jaws snapped an inch from Jake's face. The Guardian's eyes widened. Smashing his lips together, he glanced at Lilith. A five-dollar bill appeared in his hand.

Lilith took the money with a smile. "I think what Jake means to say is that St. Croix's obviously crazy about you. Hugh told me all that stuff St. Croix said at the cabin about protecting you was true."

Ash didn't need Hugh to tell her that. "I know."

"So, this is probably part of it. Maybe's he's practicing to take out Madelyn. Maybe he's making certain that none of these demons come after you, like others have been going after Radha. Maybe he's just making certain the other demons don't kill Madelyn first—because if one did and we never found out about it, we'd never know whether we can let you go."

"He's a cold bastard—no offense, Ash." Taylor threw her a quick look before focusing on Lilith again. "But like Joe, he'd be one hell of a useful human here at SI. You should think about recruiting him after we settle this thing with Madelyn."

"I already plan to. Especially if we can get more out of him than his muscle—and in particular, his money. Which reminds me . . ." Lilith turned to Ash. "Jake tells me that you set up some kind of college investment fund for his granddaughter."

"*Great*-granddaughter," Jake corrected, grinning. "Because she's pretty flippin' great."

"I did," Ash said. "He brought in her piggy bank. I'll make sure she can go to Harvard, if that's what she wants—and her children, too."

"So you're good with money? I know Rachel was, but are *you*?"

"Yes. Probably better. Looking at her personal portfolio, it's obvious that she had a few pet causes, and that she often invested for nostalgic reasons. I think she really liked Barbies and Disney, especially the fairy tale movies. And she invested in an abnormally high number of companies that had unicorns in their name or logo. I won't have any of that baggage."

Taylor pressed her fingers to her lips, shoulders shaking. After a moment, she looked up and wiped her eyes. "Maybe we can get Khavi to help out, too."

Ash had heard that name before: a Guardian who could see into the future. She frowned. "What would be the fun in that?"

"With Khavi's help, you'd be surprised. Really, you would," Taylor said. "Not always in a good way."

"With Khavi's help, the quickest way to make a small fortune would be to start with a large one," Lilith said, and looked at Ash. "Which is what I want from you. You'll still be training, so it'd have to be during your off-hours, but I want Special Investigations monetarily self-sufficient within ten years. Right now, we're operating on government cash, and so far, they've only asked for stupid little things, like telling us to ship a nosferatu to one of their research facilities rather than slaying it. Or asking us to register the names and addresses of vampires we know. I've been able to put them off or ignore them—and if the requests stem from concerns about public safety, I give them what I can. But at some point, there's going to be something that we can't put off and can't ignore, and that won't necessarily be about safety, but about forwarding some other agenda. When that day comes, we need to be able to disappear off their radar, but still be functional."

Excitement had already begun sparking through Ash's veins. Now that was one hell of a challenge. "All right. I need your current budget, so that I know what I'm aiming for."

"You'll have it," Lilith said. "A few Guardians have pulled antiquities out of their collections, and those are going up for auction soon. We expect that you'll be starting with four to five hundred million dollars."

Ash suppressed her shudder of ecstasy. God. She was pretty sure she hadn't had a shiver like that since Nicholas had licked her fangs. "I can work with that."

"And spread it out. Don't become some visible megalith. We just want to quietly turn an asston of money into a fuckload."

She would. "Any limits? Anything I shouldn't invest in?"

Lilith pursed her lips. After a few moments, she came up with, "Sex trafficking."

Ash nodded. Yes, that would be bad.

"And I'll have a few more to add to that list," Taylor said dryly. Her focus shifted beyond Ash's shoulder, and her gaze flattened. "Hey, there are you are now. Nice of you to finally show up."

"Yes. Well, the sign said 'all-you-can-eat,' but they still kicked me out. So where else did I have to go?" The harmonious voice froze Ash's heart for two beats—so much like Lucifer's, like a Michael-possessed Taylor's—but the fear slowly let her go as the woman continued, "Plus I need to show the markings on this vase to Alice, so I hoped she'd be here. So now I ask Jake: Where's your wife?"

"Where's my wife?" Jake's jaw clenched. "Well, Khavi. Last week, she asked me to teleport all of her spiders back to Earth. You've seen some of these things, haven't you? How *big* they are? And you know I have to touch something to teleport it, right? I had my shirt off and those things all over me, so that *she* could focus on the Archives."

Taylor shuddered. "You really do love her."

"You think?" Though Jake snapped the reply at her, he still focused on Khavi. "So if you're looking for Alice, you'll find her and about six novices in the library, cataloguing all of the Scrolls, and putting them into indestructible, floating containers, just in case the goddamn building falls around their heads and the whole place sinks."

"Why is she doing that?"

Khavi sounded baffled. Not an emotion Ash expected to hear from someone who could see the future.

"Because we can't carry the Scrolls through the Gates, and because no one but Michael can vanish them into their cache."

"Taylor can."

Taylor's brows shot up. "I can?"

"Of course you can. They are written in his blood—and part of you is written in his blood, too. You can vanish the Scrolls or carry them through the Gates."

Jake wasn't mollified by that new info. "Oh, so *now* we

know. Would have been nice earlier. Where the hell have you been the past two months?"

"Eating. Like I said." The woman was frowning. With her black hair in neat rows of braids that marched back into an uncontrolled tangle and an air of leashed ferocity, Khavi was as slightly built as Taylor but possessed none of the other woman's fragility. Her gaze touched Ash for a brief moment, before she asked, "So Caelum's already falling apart? Where's Lyta?"

"With Alice," Jake told her. "Apparently chasing her own tail with one head, and slobbering all over the Scrolls with the others."

"I'll get her, then, and return shortly."

"Oh, no. Nononono." Suddenly tense, Lilith looked down at Sir Pup, who stood at attention, ears pricked. "You can't bring her here. You can't bring her to Earth. He'll run around the world, sniffing her out."

The hellhound's big body quivered, and he emitted a chorus of pleading whines.

"You can't," Lilith told him. "You'll kill her. You ate your way out of your mother, remember? So if it results in babies, you can't do it."

Sir Pup's heads drooped. With a sympathetic sigh, Lilith crouched and began scratching his ears.

"I'll find a place for her first, then—" Khavi broke off, glanced at Ash again. Her eyes widened. *"You."*

"Whoa." Jake sat forward, as if ready to teleport between them. "Oh, yeah. Khavi, here's Ash. She's a good demon."

"And she can bring Michael out of the field," Khavi said.

The warehouse seemed to fall silent. Then deafening again, as hearts began to pound—with Taylor the most silent and the loudest of them all.

Ash touched the tattoo on her face. "With this spell?"

That seemed rather careless of Lucifer, didn't it?

"No." Khavi began to circle her. "That is to open the Gate. The key to the frozen field is hidden somewhere else."

Ash looked to Lilith. "Did you see it?"

"I might have. But reading the symbols and knowing how Lucifer makes spells of them are two completely different things. Sometimes it's clear, like the spell on your face, where *open* and *Gate* overlap—yet even that spell is crowded with many more symbols that I can read, but I have no idea why they are arranged as they are."

"It is all arrangement and intention," Khavi said. "And I need to see the symbols to know what he has done. Take off your clothes."

Ash vanished them.

Jake choked. His face fiery, he edged toward the door. "Ah, okay. Alice probably wouldn't care that you're here, all naked like that. But I do. So I'll see you."

He disappeared. Nobody left in the room seemed to notice.

Khavi stopped circling, touched a series of symbols along Ash's ribs. "Here. This is how he unlocked the field, brought you out of it in exchange for another."

"He brought Rachel out," Ash said. *She* had never gotten out. Not all of the way. A part of her memory still lay frozen there, tortured, and leaving her sick with fear at the mere mention of the field. "What kind of exchange?"

"Probably a traitor. Someone who'd broken his vow to follow Lucifer. There are many tortured in the Pit or in his throne tower. It would have been nothing to sacrifice one." In a long, sweeping motion, Khavi's cool fingers traced one of the vermillion tattoos. "But it is not just the symbols—the power of that spell is still in you, your release from the field written into your blood, embedded as deeply as your name. *That* is why we can take him out."

Lips compressed, Taylor paced away from the desk, making a tight circle around Lilith and Sir Pup before turning back. "All right. You know, I want him out more than anyone, but we can't forget that he's down there *for a reason*: to strengthen the frozen field, so that Lucifer can't just can't slip through the barrier to the Chaos realm, and then open up a passage to Earth. Oh, and bring a few dragons with him. If we do this, we might as well just cast that spell on Ash's face now. At least Lucifer won't be bringing in dragons from Hell through a Gate."

"That's Michael talking through you," Khavi said.

"No, it's not." With a wild laugh, she shook her head. "He's not here right now."

"Of course he is, somewhere, so he'll hear me when I say that this halfling has opened doors that were closed to me before. And do not forget, Taylor, that there was another reason for his sacrifice: to prevent his sister from entering Hell through Chaos."

"And fat lot of good that did. She's down there, anyway. *He* took her down there. That was my body, but I wasn't jumping it."

"Exactly," Khavi said. "*He* did. Because a door opened there, too, and instead of wresting control over all of humanity, she only wants revenge on her father. Taking his sister to Hell allowed us more time here . . . and now Ash will give us more time, too. Her presence changes everything. With the proper symbols and spell, the barrier can remain as strong without Michael in it."

Okay. Ash didn't know half of what they were talking about, but the gist of it seemed to be: Michael got out of Hell, while Lucifer and Michael's evil sister remained trapped in the realm. That sounded good to her.

"So what needs to happen?" she asked. "What do I need to do?"

Khavi looked at Taylor. The other woman suddenly stilled, before turning stricken eyes on Ash. "She told me that I'd sacrifice you."

"Fuck that," Lilith said. "There's another way."

"No." Khavi shook her head. "There has to be an exchange."

An exchange—as in, Michael for Ash? Dread filled her chest. "No. I *won't* do that. Rachel's agreement with Lucifer released me from the frozen field. Forever. Even if I die now, I won't go back unless I break another bargain. Right?"

"Yes," Khavi said.

"Then I'm *never* going back there. The only bargain I have now is with Madelyn—and I won't break it."

She'd given up Nicholas so that she wouldn't *have* to break it. Nothing they said about Michael would persuade her to return to that icy hell now.

"Damn right." Lilith turned on Khavi. "Does it have to be a *willing* sacrifice? Shit like this usually has to be, because there are rules. Opening a Gate to Hell, you don't need Ash to agree to her sacrifice, because Gates can open on their own with enough pain and misery to fuel it. Rare, yet it happens—we had one beneath the fucking Golden Gate. But no one can get into the frozen field without willingly entering into a bargain first. By the time they're tortured down there, they're regretting that decision, but at some point they *did* make a choice of their own free will."

With a sigh, Khavi nodded. "Yes. It must be willing."

Ash's heart thudded with sick relief. "I'm sorry. But I won't."

"Are you so certain?"

In a blink, the seer's eyes filled with black from edge to edge. A surge of psychic power crashed through Ash like a wave. Khavi's Gift. Ash staggered. Already the surge was retreating, but felt as if it tossed little bits of her about in its wake, overturning stones along the path to her future as easily as churning through sand.

Ash didn't know what the woman saw. She didn't care. "The frozen field isn't part of my plan." It emerged as a hiss. "Only seeing Madelyn dead. Being with Nicholas. And making a fuckload of money."

Khavi tilted her head, looked at Ash through those blank obsidian eyes. "But Nicholas will soon be dead."

"What?" *Oh, God.* The room spun. Someone caught her arm, steadied her. Taylor, Ash recognized. "How? When?"

"Soon, as I said. I have seen it, and he is still young."

Ash pushed away, headed for the door. "Then I have to—"

"He will call," Khavi said. "He will need help."

No. No, he wouldn't. The ground seemed to steady. Ash shook her head. "He won't risk me like that."

"But I see him call. It is very clear to me. And that call *must* be answered."

"No," Ash repeated. "He wouldn't."

"Yes." Khavi paused, and another short, powerful wave swept through Ash's mind. "He will die . . . and yet your feelings will never fade. You will love him for the rest of your life. Are you sure that's what you want to live for?"

A horror of a future. Still better than losing Nicholas *and* an eternity in the frozen field. Both were unimaginable—and never could she choose them both. Unable to speak, Ash only shook her head, continued to the door.

"Ash," Lilith said softly behind her. "Save the naked traipse through the warehouse for a special occasion. I don't think this qualifies."

No. It didn't. Feeling suddenly old, broken, Ash formed her clothes and slipped out of the room, straight into a hallway filled with Guardians and their stares. Sympathy, horror, and resentment seemed to fill each one.

Ash kept her mental blocks strong, and kept on going.

CHAPTER 16

Jesus. Taylor waited for the door to close before swinging around. "What the fuck was that? 'You'll love him for the rest of your life'?"

"What?" Khavi frowned at her. "I did not say her life would be very long. I hope it is not."

"God. *We don't do this.*" Taylor looked at Lilith. When Ash had left, her eyes had been glowing red, but the flat stare Lilith leveled at Khavi looked twice as demonic. "Do we? Is this what we are now, that we sacrifice one life to save another?"

"That's what Guardians have *always* been," Khavi said. "Sacrificing our lives to save another's is how we become Guardians."

That wasn't the same at all. But Khavi had a way of twisting things about that made Taylor wonder, "Are you saying Ash will become one if she sacrifices herself like this?"

"No," Lilith said, and Taylor couldn't remember hearing such cold anger from the woman before. Usually, the former demon hid it behind a razor-sharp smile and a tongue that could slice to the bone. "It would be the same situation as Rachel's: She *should* become a Guardian, but the field would claim her first."

"She never becomes a Guardian," Khavi confirmed. "There is no door leading in that direction."

Fuck. Taylor pushed her hands into her hair, tried to search her mind for any sign of Michael. Was he *hearing* this? What would he think of this?

No, screw that. She didn't need to feel his reaction. She *knew* what it would be.

"He wouldn't want this," she said. "He wouldn't want us to guilt or coerce someone into sacrificing herself for him, especially a woman who should have been a Guardian, and who's literally been through Hell and torture, just because she sacrificed herself to save someone's *life*. And he sure as hell wouldn't want us to give that woman *nothing* at all to live for, to tear her heart out and then say, 'But hey, now that your life is total shit, you can save someone else and make your pathetic soul worth something.' That's what a demon would do."

"Yes," Khavi agreed. "He believes that free will should always be respected, and life protected. But he also knows that there are times when we must be more demon than man, and do what is necessary. Is that not what you did, Lilith, when you brought her here? Did you not tear her apart, so that she would willingly agree to come . . . and all because there were more lives at stake than hers?"

"Now there is only Michael's," Lilith said.

"Only Michael's?" Khavi laughed. "Oh, you lie. You know you do. You do not even see the darkness coming as I do, but you know that having Michael here would save many, many more lives than a halfling who can't even fly."

Jesus Christ. And who would be first? "Is St. Croix really going to die?"

"Yes," Khavi answered her, before looking to Lilith again. "If you want to help her, let her speak to him. Let the call go through to her. And maybe everything will change."

Change. A new door opening. Taylor latched on to that, tried to hope. "How would it change?"

"I cannot see what I—"

"What you don't fucking know. Yeah, I know." Taylor gritted her teeth and glanced at Lilith, who seemed to be making up her mind about something. Her mouth had firmed, and her gaze had slid toward the door, as if considering an object that lay beyond it. "What do you think about all this?"

"I think that certain people have a way of twisting things—and that to save St. Croix, Ash might *willingly* break her bargain with Madelyn and end up in the frozen field." She started for the door, Sir Pup at her heels. "So I think I'm going to tell her everything I know about how to get around breaking one."

Good. Damn good. Lilith had survived two thousand years of service to Lucifer without landing in the frozen field. If anyone had tips for the poor girl, it was her. Then Khavi murmured, "Good," and it took everything within Taylor not to rush after Lilith and bring her back.

Because maybe that was just what Khavi wanted.

And, Jesus, now she was beginning to sound like St. Croix. Fucking insanity. How the hell had she gotten into all of this? She'd jumped in front of a bullet for Joe, yeah, but that should have just made her a Guardian. Not a woman with an ancient half-demon in her brain and his blood written all over hers.

What the hell did that even mean?

"How is this any different than me?" she asked Khavi. "I signed up to be a Guardian, but not the rest of this, but I'm doing what I can. And Ash, Rachel made all of her choices for her, but now that she's thrown into this, she's trying to make the best of it, doing what she can to help—and even as a demon, she's a decent woman who hasn't hurt a single fucking person. Now she's being asked to kill herself? Is this the next step for me, too?"

"No. If you killed yourself, it would not free him from the frozen field. It would mean that even if he did get out, he couldn't leave Hell. Not without his body."

"That's not what I meant, and you know it!"

"Why do you even ask? If it were possible to free him, would you exchange your life for his?"

It wouldn't be possible. "He wouldn't let me. He'd do everything he could to stop me—even if it meant preventing my free will."

"That is not what I meant, and you know it." Khavi's smile was thin and sharp. "But since it is not even possible, the question of whether you'd sacrifice your life for his hardly matters. Does it?"

God. Taylor didn't know. She didn't know anything anymore. Except for one thing:

"None of this matters, because Ash isn't willing to do it."

"No, she isn't." Khavi's eyes deepened to black. "But only because she hasn't been pushed to her limit yet."

A halfling demon who could make her own clothes and carry everything she owned in a cache didn't need to pack, so Ash simply waited in her room, plotting, contemplating the best time to go.

The knock at her door told her she'd be waiting a little longer.

She opened it to find Lilith, who swept into the room with Sir Pup. No bigger than a dorm room, Ash had never bothered to decorate or add anything to the place, and only one chair had been placed next to a small desk.

Apparently, Lilith wasn't there to sit, anyway. She stopped in the middle of the room. "So?"

"So, what?" Ash settled back into her chair, the seat still warm from her waiting-to-go vigil.

"Don't fuck with me," Lilith warned.

All right. It probably wasn't hard to guess what Ash had been plotting. "Where is he?"

"I don't know, precisely. Last I knew, he was headed to New York. I don't know if he's there."

"I'm going to him."

"I can't let you."

"But will you *stop* me?"

Lilith's eyes narrowed. "Clever. That was the right question. So there's hope for you."

All Ash cared about was whether there was hope for Nicholas. "I want to take that call. Do you think he will place one?"

Her gut still said he wouldn't. But if he were hurt, dying—would he be in his right mind? Would he reach out to her? How could she *not* answer?

"He probably will," Lilith said. "Khavi's not always precise, but she's usually right. *But* she also has an agenda."

"Getting me into the frozen field."

"Yes."

Fuck her. And Ash couldn't sit any longer. She paced to the end of the empty room, back. "Do you know what I hate? What I really, really *hate*?"

Lilith's brows rose. "Short brown hair?"

God. Blond again. And Ash didn't care. "This." She gestured to the tattoos on her face. "And that shit downstairs. I'm so fucking tired of being the *sacrifice* to a fucking Gate, a goddamn frozen field. That there's barely any use in *doing* anything. No, it's what will be done *to* me. Oh, Ash, let's carve some symbols into you. Oh, Ash, you'll help us if you *die*."

Lilith didn't answer, only watched her with unreadable eyes. Ash stopped pacing, tried to get her temper under control.

With a deep breath, she said, "And it's not even death. It's torture, forever. And I will *not* go through it again. I'd prefer to let Madelyn have me. At least then, I really do just die."

"Actually, the preferable choice would be to live. At least, it would be preferable to me."

Yes. Yes, to her, too. Ash nodded. "That, too."

"Then listen. The Guardians are proof that the universe likes to reward those who sacrifice themselves for others—but I've never been interested in that martyr bullshit. I don't think you are, either."

"No."

"So the rest of us, we have to get that reward some other way. Me, I lied, cheated, and killed my way into it. I had the same fucking impossible choice to make: the frozen field, or Hugh's life. And instead of choosing either of those, I fucked up Lucifer's agreement with a horde of nosferatu, cut off his lieutenant's head, and lied so well that Lucifer lost a wager to Michael and released me from my bargain. I paid for it in blood, and so did Hugh—and I'd have paid more if I had to. But I'd be damned before I let that price be our lives or my soul in that field."

"So that's what a demon would do," Ash said softly.

"Only one of us so far. But I survived." Lilith pointed to the chair. "So sit back down. We'll talk. And when we're done, if I'm satisfied, I'll let them patch that call through to you."

Ash's heart pounded. "What about Madelyn?"

"It occurred to me on the way to your room that Khavi didn't mention one rather important thing happening in your future."

Oh, God. She'd missed that, too. "Being sacrificed to open a Gate," Ash realized.

"If that screwed up her plans to sacrifice you for Michael, she'd probably be doing something to stop it, don't you think?"

"I would if I were her," Ash said.

Lilith smiled thinly. "Me, too."

* * *

The waiting was endless. Ash tried to busy herself by looking through SI's budget, by buying up more of Nicholas's shares. Only a few hours had passed since Lilith had left her room, but the time already sat like a rock in her chest, weighing, weighing.

She wanted to go now. Wanted to leave these Guardians and their crumbling city and their shattered king behind, and just go. Wanted to hear Nicholas's voice, to find out where he was, whether he was all right. Wanted to find him, find and kill Madelyn, and do everything she'd planned—and now, save his life, too.

God. What was going to happen to him?

Her phone's ring shot her heart up into her throat. Ash stared at the glowing screen in disbelief. Snatched it up.

"Hello? Nicholas?"

"Ash." A novice's voice. "Lilith said to put him through if he called, and he's on the other line now. Do you want to take it?"

A choice to be made, now.

Fuck that. There was no choice at all.

"Yes," she said, and then— "Nicholas?"

"Don't hang up, love."

"I won't. I—" *Oh, God.* He'd never called her "love." And the accent was all wrong.

Now she couldn't hang up. But she could toss the phone away—

"Keep listening. Ah, there's my girl. I can almost hear your heart pounding. Been hiding from me, have you?"

Ash didn't answer. She didn't *have* to answer. Not unless told to.

What now?

Get help.

"Don't move. Don't go anywhere. Don't alert anyone. Is anyone with you, within hearing distance? Answer me."

"Yes."

"Answer me *truthfully.*"

Panic caught at her throat, almost prevented any answer at all. But no. No. She had to be quick. She had to be clever. She couldn't lose her wits.

"I'm alone," she said. "How did you find me?"

It didn't matter. Not really. But Ash needed to stall, needed to think.

"Well, love, it was the oddest thing. I saw you on TV, and so I flew to Duluth to see this Rachel, who was grieving her parents *so* deeply and putting their effects in order. And I thought: Oh, my poor little Ashmodei. Lucifer didn't rip out as much as he should have. But while I was standing there, I happened to overhear a *very* nice sheriff talking to one of the city police about a visit he'd had from two federal agents, who thought Steve Johnson might have been someone else. So I wondered, 'What kind of federal agents go looking into such a cut-and-dried case?' The answer seemed simple: Guardians *posing* as federal agents. So I started looking at Special Investigations. And since you're here, not in London where Rachel supposedly is, that's probably a good thing, too."

"I see," Ash said.

"Good. You do know what I did to your parents, don't you, love? Answer me truthfully."

"Yes."

"And how did you feel about that?"

Evade. "I didn't remember them."

"Oh, that's too bad. Well, my effort wasn't for nothing. They screamed so well. Your father tried to protect your mother and failed. It was so very lovely."

The edge of the desk cracked under her hand. Beneath her, Ash's seat trembled with the force of the rage shaking her body. And she'd thought she'd hated being a puppet? It was *nothing* to the hate she felt now.

She hoped Madelyn told her to get up, to go to her. Ash's boomstick was in her cache, and *by God* she would use it.

"I don't suppose you know where Nicky is? Answer me truthfully."

"He was in Montana a few months ago. I don't know for certain now where he is," she said, managing the truth. *Might be heading toward New York* wasn't certain.

"Oh, that's too bad. A pity, but we can do this without him. Now, listen carefully to me. Shield your mind, so tight that no one can sense any emotion from you."

God. *Fuck*. Why hadn't she thought of that? Every Guardian and vampire in the warehouse would have felt her terror, her rage, would have known something was wrong. Now they wouldn't.

"That done? Good. Now, at no time are you to attempt to kill or injure me, or encourage anyone else to do the same. Understand? Answer me."

Ash dragged in a ragged breath between her teeth. "Yes."

"All right. Now dump all of the weapons out of your cache. You will *not* collect any others, or vanish them back into your cache."

Oh. A mistake. With relief, Ash set her shotgun on the floor. *Everyone* knew that she wouldn't go anywhere without her boomstick. The moment they checked her room, they'd know something was wrong.

But how long before they checked?

"Now, do exactly as I say. When I give you the order, leave the warehouse and walk directly to the café that you were at with the hellhound today. Do not tell anyone that you've spoken to me. You will not give any indication that something is wrong. If they ask, you will only tell them that you talked to Nicky, and now you are going for a walk, that you need to be alone, because you need to think. You will not ask anyone to accompany you, and you will discourage anyone who offers. You will not stop for any reason, you will not write any kind of message, you will simply leave. Do you understand? Answer me truthfully."

"Yes."

"You will be at the café in one minute. Hang up and go now."

Ash cut off the call, stood up. *Think.* She'd leave the door open, but it was possible that no one would look into her room to see the boomstick until much later. Lilith *expected* her to leave SI after Nicholas's call, so she wouldn't believe that Ash was truly just going for a walk, but she'd also have no reason to think that Madelyn had been the reason Ash had left.

All right. Okay. Ash couldn't leave a message . . . but she could let everyone know that this was a *very* special occasion.

She vanished her clothes, walked out of her room. The low murmur of conversation died when she passed through the novices' common area. They stared at her in surprise, jaws dropped, eyes wide.

No one said anything until she'd almost reached the stairs. "Ash? You okay?"

"Fine," she said. "I'm just taking a walk. I just finished talking to *Nicky*, and I need to think."

"You want company?"

"No, thank you. I want to be alone."

Down the stairs, her breasts bouncing at every step. *Come on, someone.* She needed to run into an older Guardian. Any older Guardian. Even now, the novices were buzzing between themselves about her strange behavior, a thread of unease in their voices, but they wouldn't act quickly enough.

She didn't meet anyone through security, just answered the same questions when the novice at the desk saw her. *Are you okay? Do you want me to call someone to go with you?*

God, she wished.

Ash formed her clothes again just before stepping outside—no need to tip Madelyn off that someone might be quickly coming after her. And just before the door closed behind her, she heard a novice's voice—

"We need to let Lilith know."

Yes. *Yes.*

A minute had almost passed, but it only took her a second to run the three blocks to the café, already closed for the night. Her heart jumped into her throat. Nicholas sat at one of the darkened tables, but it was a poor version of Nicholas—handsome and slick, but not pared and hardened by his obsession; amused, but not burning with cold intensity. He'd crossed his legs at the ankles rather than his knee, tucked his legs beneath his chair. How strange. How strange and awful to see Madelyn in his shape.

"There you are, love, finally. We don't have all night, you know. We have places to fly." Madelyn's eyes narrowed. "Can you fly? Answer me truthfully."

"No."

"After three years? But I suppose halflings cannot help being incompetent and weak. I'm only surprised you came out of your stupor at all." She stood, uncoiling from the chair. "I will carry you, then, but there is to be no movement from you, no word spoken, no attempt to escape. You understand that you must obey me, no matter the order I give? Answer me truthfully."

"Yes."

"Let us see how well you understand." A dagger appeared

in Madelyn's hand. "Cut off your forefinger, and then give the blade back to me, handle first."

Which forefinger? Make the cut at which knuckle? *Evade, delay.* But Ash couldn't evade everything . . . and she had no odor, not really, but the scent of her blood would leave a trail to follow.

So without question, she took the dagger, and cut.

"So you let her go?"

"I let her go," Nicholas said, and it echoed through the hollow place in his chest. God. It *still* hurt to say, to think it. But he had let her go—*he'd had to.*

Leslie didn't immediately reply, and he could feel her studying his expression. Trying to read into him. Funny thing was, she didn't need to look that deep. He'd told her everything that had happened from the night he'd met Ash to the final day in the cabin, spilling his guts right out at her feet; the legs of her armchair might as well be swimming in them. But he waited, sitting on her couch, elbows braced on his knees and his hands clasped loosely in between.

Twenty years, they'd sat talking together like this. The salt-and-pepper in her hair had turned completely gray in that time. She'd moved offices, replacing drapes and soothing shadows with open blinds and pots of leafy flowers. Her two children had grown from gangly teens in a photo into a surgeon and an artist, now with children of their own. For twenty years, she's seen into him, understood him better than anyone.

Except for Ash.

She drew in a soft breath. "Nicholas, have you been reading the news at all in the past few months?"

"Every day."

"Then you know that Rachel Boyle has been found. That she suffered some trauma, lost her memory, but has spent the past three years at Nightingale House—just as you say this demon Ash did. Have you spoken to Rachel at all?"

"No, because that's not her. Rachel's dead, and Ash is what's left of her." And so much more. God, so much more than a woman stripped down to nothing. "The Rachel you've seen is a Guardian, drawing Madelyn out."

"Have you spoken to the Guardians? Have they told you this?"

"No. But I know. She looks exactly the same, but she doesn't move like Ash does. She doesn't speak like Ash does. It's close, but it's not perfect."

"I see," she said.

Nicholas grinned. When she raised her brows to encourage him, he said, "I know what you're thinking."

"Tell me."

"That whatever 'trauma' Rachel went through probably first occurred six years ago, the night that she and Madelyn disappeared. And that because I was with them, I probably suffered the same trauma—except that I repressed the events, and my mind created another scenario that seemed so real that I'm convinced that Madelyn shot Rachel, despite the lack of blood and other evidence. But now that Rachel has returned, I'm trying to fit the story from the news into the version that my mind has created. So I came up with Ash and all the rest."

Leslie didn't confirm or deny it. "Do you think that explanation is so impossible?"

"Not impossible. It's just not what happened."

"Nicholas, in our first session after you met the vampire who told you about the existence of demons, we discussed the possibility that you had constructed a mythology that not only eased your sense of guilt and responsibility for Rachel's disappearance, but one that also allowed for her return. A resurrection, of sorts."

"Yes, but this 'mythology' has never eased my guilt, and Rachel coming back never even occurred to me until I met the Guardians. *Bringing* her back was certainly never a goal. Only revenge was."

"Now Rachel has returned, and your desire for revenge has shifted into a need to protect her."

"To protect Ash," he said. "Not Rachel."

"Also, your mythology has deepened considerably," she said. "Once, there were only vampires, demons, and eventually Guardians. But in the time since Rachel has returned, there are now halflings, spells, symbols, and sacrifices that open Gates to Hell. Do you not think it at all possible that this layering of your mythology has simply been a way for you to incorporate Rachel's return into a form that you can accept?"

"I'm sure that's not what happened," he said, smiling. "And I know you hate it when I say that."

"Refusing to consider a possibility does cut off avenues of exploration." But though he recognized the faint exasperation at the corners of her eyes and mouth, she only said, "Let's continue then. You let her go two months ago. What have you been doing in the time between—when you were not canceling our weekly appointments, that is?"

Nicholas had to laugh. "I wondered when that would come in."

"I was very gentle," she said. "I did worry, though, especially when I saw the news about Rachel. You've never missed so many appointments in a row, and I assumed it wasn't a coincidence. Perhaps you can fill me in now."

"I was hunting demons. Madelyn, primarily, but there have been others, too."

"Other demons?" When he nodded, she asked, "You said that you had been wrong about Ash. How do you know these demons aren't like her?"

"Because there are no others like her. Rosalia never mentioned halflings because Lilith had been the last—and they didn't know about Ash." When he'd met with her, Rosalia had apologized to him in her soft, motherly way. It hadn't been necessary. She couldn't have anticipated the events that led to Rachel becoming Ash. Neither could Nicholas, and that was why he wouldn't take the risk of being wrong now. "But I won't take the chance again. So I make certain they aren't halflings."

"How?"

"The hellhound venom. Halflings aren't affected by it, just like Guardians and humans aren't." And Nicholas had verified that, too, by injecting himself with the venom. "But demons are, so I shoot them with the dart, and while they are paralyzed, I check their temperature. Then I call in Rosalia."

"And she takes them?"

"Slays them, then gets rid of the bodies. All but the last one." He looked down at his hands. "I had him down, paralyzed, but then I couldn't reach her on the phone. The venom would eventually wear off, so I had to make a choice."

"To slay him or let him go?"

"Yes. It was harder than I thought it would be. Maybe it'd have been easier if the demon had been fighting me, or threatening Ash like the one in Duluth had. It's for her protection, so I was going to slay it anyway . . . but her protection wasn't the only reason. I thought about Ash crying over her parents, I thought about my parents and Rachel. It's too many people, and if it's in my power, I'm not going to let any demon hurt even one more."

Leslie's brow had furrowed. "What did you do, Nicholas?"

"I chopped his head off with a sword." And *that* had been more difficult than he'd realized, too. Not just mentally, but physically. "Then after a while, Rosalia came and cleaned up."

He saw the slight tremble of her mouth. Maybe a man who hadn't known her for twenty years couldn't have recognized the alarm, the disbelief, the horror in her expression. Nicholas could. And he knew what she thought now, too—that despite his delusional paranoia, at least he'd always been functional. But now his delusions had either become a full-blown psychosis, or he'd become a serial killer.

She gathered herself. "Nicholas, I know that you've always rejected the idea of medication, but—"

"No." And because he'd always vowed to be brutally honest with himself in this office—and honest with her—he sat forward, took her hands between his. "Leslie, that's not what I need."

She squeezed his hand. "What do you need, then?"

Ash. But that wasn't possible yet.

"I need you to know that I can't express how valuable you've been to me. I know that I've not been the easiest man. You've probably saved my life more times than we both know." He took a long breath. "But what I also need now is someone who believes me."

She held his gaze, and he watched her struggle, the compassion and the acceptance. Closing her eyes, she nodded. "I don't know if I can find someone who will believe, Nicholas, but I know a few people who might be better able to help you. I can make some calls, give you a referral."

"Thank you."

"And Nicholas, you know that I will always— Oh, dear God!" She lurched back in her chair, her hand flying to her heart. Mouth open, she stared across the room.

Nicholas fought to cover his own shock. Wearing enormous black wings that arched up to the ceiling, a possessed Taylor stood . . . *No,* he realized. Not Taylor. Unless she'd shape-shifted, this woman with braided black hair and obsidian eyes wasn't Taylor, but someone more like Michael.

In a low, harmonious voice, she said, "Madelyn has Ashmodei."

God. Nicholas surged to his feet. "And you stopped to get me first?"

"Of course."

"You should have just gone after her, saved her." But since the Guardian was here, he wouldn't argue. "Where is she?"

"In some Roman ruins near old Fordham Castle in County Essex. There used to be a portal to Hell there—the weak spot makes it easier to open a new one."

By sacrificing Ash. Not if Nicholas had anything to say about it. "I have no weapons with me."

"Hold out your hand."

When he did, an egg-shaped grenade appeared in his palm. "You're only giving me *this*?"

"Why would you need anything else?"

He wouldn't, Nicholas realized. If this woman had half the power that Michael did, he wouldn't need anything. He probably wouldn't even be able to track the fight with Madelyn. "All right. Let's go. No, hold on."

He had just enough presence of mind to turn around. "Leslie, are you okay?"

Though obviously still astonished, she nodded.

"Oh," the Guardian said, peering around Nicholas's shoulder. "You are a psychotherapist? Are you taking new patients?"

Heart pounding, Nicholas stared at her in disbelief. "Ash is waiting—"

"And she won't be bleeding yet when we arrive, so whenever we decide to teleport, we'll still be in time." She looked back to Leslie. "Everyone thinks I'm crazy, just because I spent over two thousand years alone in Hell and I can also see the future. Do you suppose I could come and talk with you at some time?"

Leslie blinked. Her mouth opened, but no answer emerged.

"It's all right," the Guardian said. "I already know that you will say yes. Thank you. You will be very helpful to me, especially what you will have to say about coping mechanisms."

With a shaky nod, Leslie blinked again. "Yes. I— Yes. And

Nicholas . . . I think I might qualify for your new belief requirement. So, next week?"

"No, he won't be there. Shall I take his appointment, instead?"

Jesus. Whatever got them out of here, *now*. "Say yes, Leslie."

"Yes," Leslie said.

The Guardian smiled brightly, and took Nicholas's arm. Then the world dived, spun, and spit him out the other side.

CHAPTER 17

Even with his feet planted into the sodden ground, the world still spun. Only steadied by the Guardian's hand, Nicholas fought not to heave up his lunch, fought the darkness swirling around the edges of his vision, tried to focus. He stood in a large, flat field, with short grass that squelched with the swaying shift of his weight. The ruins near his feet were only distinguishable from any other weathered rock by the straight line of their formation and the ninety-degree angle of an ancient corner. He stood just outside the old building, the walls broken down to his shins.

Still dizzy, Nicholas lifted his head. Though he could focus more clearly now, he had to wait for his eyes to adjust. Twilight was leaching the light from a leaden sky.

Where was Ash?

"Nicky?"

Madelyn's name for him, but *his* voice? Nicholas gave his head a sharp shake. There, only ten feet away, in the center of what would have been a room of some sort, stood . . . Nicholas. He held two long, curving swords, and if the shadows playing over his double's face weren't misleading him, the demon was regarding the Guardian with abject terror.

The black wings, those obsidian eyes. Madelyn must know

she didn't have a chance, no matter whom she looked like. But where was Ash? He had to make certain Madelyn couldn't hurt her before this Guardian got a chance to tear the demon apart.

A crimson glow began to shine near Madelyn's feet, casting red light across the ground. Oh, Jesus. Ash lay on her back behind Madelyn, her face turned away from Nicholas. He couldn't see her expression or whether she was hurt, but those glowing eyes meant she was still alive.

Thank God.

"If you take a step toward me, grigori"—Madelyn shifted in an instant as she spoke, taking the form of his mother's dark-haired, elegant beauty—"I will kill her."

The Guardian's grip on his arm loosened. "Can you stand now without falling?"

"Yes." His fingers clenched around the grenade. When Madelyn was dead, he was going to shove it down her throat and pull the pin. "When you've finished with her, save me the head."

"What? Oh, no. I need to go feed my puppy. I'll be back when you're done."

She vanished.

Madelyn whipped around, as if expecting the Guardian to teleport in behind her. So did Nicholas. They waited with only the harsh sound of his breathing to disturb the silence.

Then Madelyn tossed back her head and laughed, cutting through the shock that held him frozen and threw him back to twelve years old again, humiliated and horrified after she'd walked into his room and caught him with his pants down. *Oh, Nicky, you don't even have enough there to play with.* God. It had taken him years to keep that mocking, nails-scraping-across-his-brain noise from echoing in his head. Now he feared it would never go.

Her laughter faded, but her amusement didn't. "Oh, Nicky—your expression almost makes up for all of the pain you've caused me. It almost makes up for that stupid girl throwing herself between us, even after she agreed not to. It almost makes up for *three years* in the Pit, with my skin flayed, and my flesh stripped from my bones and fed to hellhounds. Do you know what that is like, Nicky? Oh, but I would love *every* human to know."

Not just evil, Nicholas recognized. That torture had broken her. "You're mad."

"Mad?" Madelyn's laugh rang out again, wild, unchecked. "No, not anymore. Not after three years of searching for the right Gate, through every ruin in England. Do you know how many ruins there are on this cursed island? And when I finally found it, I learned that you've taken my little Ashmodei and have tried to hide her away."

Not well enough. "I'll destroy you, any way that I can. If it means you fail to sacrifice her and break your bargain with Lucifer, all the better."

"We'll see if someone will break their bargain—but it won't be me. Oh, Ashmodei," she sang out, and vanished her swords. "You can stand up now, love. You can also speak again. I think it's time to play a little game with Nicky."

Ash rose, naked and lean and strong, with her eyes shining fiercely red. Mud tangled in her hair and concealed half her tattoos. Leathery wings folded at her back.

She was absolutely beautiful . . . and she'd been going to let Madelyn sacrifice her. She'd been willing to die, just to keep from returning to that frozen field.

Nicholas would give everything he could to make certain she didn't have to do either.

He smiled, his arrogant son-of-a-bitch smile that had led to Madelyn trying to shoot him once before. "What game will we play? 'Make Ash kill Nicky?' There's only one problem with that, Madelyn." He showed her the grenade in his left hand. "You let her get close enough, and I'll blow her to Hell. That means you wouldn't be able to fulfill your bargain with Lucifer, and you'd end up screaming in the frozen field."

Madelyn's eyes narrowed. "You wouldn't."

"Try me. You're going to kill her, anyway. I'll take a lot of fucking pleasure knowing that you'll pay for it."

"And that close to the explosion, you'll die, too." Madelyn tilted her head. "But let's see what happens, make a little test. Ash, take that grenade from him and bring it to me."

"That will break the Rules," Ash said softly. "It'll bring the Guardians. By 'take,' do you mean that I should persuade him to give it to me?"

"Are you disobeying me, halfling?"

"I'm simply verifying exactly what you want, so that I can obey to your satisfaction."

No, Nicholas thought. Ash was lying. She could do anything she wanted to him. But if Ash could do anything she wanted to Madelyn, she'd probably have already done it. He had to assume she was bound not to hurt the demon.

So that would be up to him.

He slipped his finger through the pin. "She can take the grenade straight back to you. You better hope that she holds down the safety lever."

"Ash, bring me his finger, too."

"Of course. Which one?"

Madelyn frowned at her. "The left forefinger, the one in the pin. And that way, his hand will be a match to yours."

"What?" Cold fury spiked through him. "Show me."

Ash didn't. Laughing, Madelyn grabbed her wrist, lifted Ash's hand into view, and flicked a long fingernail against the stub of a knuckle. Jesus.

"Nicky, love. You always give yourself away. You shake with rage because of a finger and yet threaten to kill her? I don't think so."

Ash closed her eyes. "If you let me go, I'll bring the grenade to you now."

"No, no. Just kill him. And we'll finish the sacrifice before the Guardians come."

"Of course, Madelyn." Her voice was flat. "How should I do it?"

The demon pursed her lips, her gaze running the length of Nicholas's body. "So many possible ways. But I can't ask anything complicated of a halfling and expect it to be done right. So let's keep it simple: Break his neck. Then come back here and lie down again, so that we can finish this ritual."

Without hesitation, Ash stepped forward. Over the sick beating of his heart, he held her gaze, tried to let her know that this decision was right. Anything to keep her from the frozen field. Anything to bring her a few steps away from Madelyn, where maybe, maybe, he could think of some way to give her time, to help her escape.

"Just make sure you kiss me first," he said.

A sad little smile curved her lips, the first real expression he'd seen. She paused, midstep. "Madelyn, when I'm breaking his neck, should I twist to the left or to the right?"

"What does it matter? To the left."

"My left or his left?"

"His. You idiot."

"I am just trying to be precise as I carry out your orders," Ash said, and this time her eyes narrowed slightly, in the same way she had when they'd trained together and she was considering her next strike. "There are several vertebrae in the neck. Which one should I aim to snap? I've never killed a man in this way before."

"I don't care. The third."

"Oh." Ash's smile turned slightly apologetic. "I'm sorry, Nicholas. I have to ask you to face away from me before I can break your neck, because I first have to feel along your spine and count your vertebrae. I must find the location of the third, you see. I cannot disobey her."

What was she doing? Simply delaying?

"Are you delaying, halfling?" Madelyn's voice filled with threat.

"Obeying," Ash corrected. The crimson glow of her eyes faded, and through the dusk, her gaze sought Nicholas's. "I know that as long as I am in the process of carrying out your orders, I am obeying—and that in this sort of bond, it is not the completion of the task that matters. All that matters is that I am acting to fulfill it. So even if one of us dies before I finish, I am not reneging on our bargain."

No, not simply delaying. Trying to tell him—

"Are you trying to tell Nicholas to kill you?" Madelyn's laugh rang out over the field again. "Answer me truthfully."

"I'm not," Ash said. "I know he would not, even though it would stop the ritual."

He wouldn't have hurt her for any reason. She had to know that. What did she need from him, then?

"Are you telling him to kill *me*? Answer me truthfully."

"No such words have passed my lips. That would be disobeying. I only obey, as I walk to him now with the intention of finding his third vertebrae." Her gaze fell to the grenade in his hand, lifting to meet his eyes again. "I would never disobey."

Oh, Ash. He realized now that she wanted him to throw it toward Madelyn as soon as she reached him, and hope that the distance—and a small, ruined wall—would be enough to shield them both. A desperate, last-ditch attempt . . . that didn't have a chance. Madelyn was too quick. She could be halfway across the field before the toss he aimed landed at her feet.

When the explosion failed to destroy Madelyn, Ash would refuse to kill him, and she would be lost to the frozen field. Only the miracle of the Guardians' arrival might stop any of it.

Nicholas wouldn't count on a miracle to save her.

"Stop," he said. His throat had thickened, his lungs filled with burning lead. He pushed the grenade into his pocket, held up his empty hands. "Stop, Ash. I'll come to you. I'll let you kill me of my free will."

"What?" Horror filled Ash's face. "Nicholas, no."

"I can't bear knowing what will happen if you do this." Hoarse truth. He stepped over the low wall. "I just want to kiss you. Just let me kiss you, one last time. It won't break the Rules. It won't bring the Guardians to kill you. Madelyn, *please*."

"No, Nicholas. You have to—"

"Be quiet, halfling." Madelyn regarded him through narrowed eyes. "In exchange for a kiss, you'd let her kill you?"

"I'd let her kill me for less than that, but if I'm to die, I want the kiss."

"Why not ask to fuck her in the mud like a pig? I'd let you. I remember a time when it would have been fitting."

"I remember when I had a mother worthy of the name."

"Ah, yes." Something in Madelyn's eyes shifted. Nicholas recognized that look. He wouldn't know if it was a lie or truth, but it would be designed to hurt him. "She was a lucky find—young, beautiful, and *so* unhappy. It's always such a hassle to arrange for a death, but she walked to hers. That holiday in Brighton, Nicky, do you remember? One early morning I was strolling along the beach, and I saw her strolling into the sea. I watched her stroll farther and farther out . . . until it was done, and she began to float back in."

"You're lying."

"Am I? I still have her body in my cache. So fresh, so beautiful—and still dripping with seawater. I wondered, What could possess such a woman to walk into the ocean? So I followed her scent to your rented cottage, where both you and your father still lay sleeping, and found the note. She just couldn't live with either of you anymore, Nicky."

No. A demon's lies, piled on. Maybe his mother had accidentally drowned, and Madelyn had taken advantage. But the rest was simply too much.

"Produce the note, then. Of course you vanished it into your cache. You wouldn't have left any evidence where it could be found."

"I burned it."

Now that was a pathetic lie, and he let his disdain harden his face, his smile. "So I know the truth, then."

"What does it matter, anyway?" Madelyn hissed. "Do we have an agreement? You get one kiss—and you keep your hands out of your pockets while you do. She can't touch you until the kiss is done, then you give her permission to do anything she likes without breaking the Rules. Then I'll order her to kill you. And she will, with no more clarifications or delays. Is that understood, Ashmodei?"

"Yes," she whispered, and the despair and fear in the answer cut him deep. Already seeing herself in the frozen field. Thinking that he'd completely bungled the one chance they'd had.

He crossed the distance to her, coming up against her hard enough to send her stumbling back. Catching her face between his hands, he moved with her—closer to Madelyn, who watched with a twisted smile.

But for this moment, he would shove the demon from his mind. There was only Ash, looking up at him. There was only the trembling of her mouth, the desperation as her gaze searched his.

"Believe in me," he said softly.

His lips caught hers as she nodded, and there was only her sweet heat, the softness of her mouth. Only her surprise when he could no longer remain gentle, but hard and demanding. Only the squish of mud as she fell back beneath the force of his kiss.

Closer to Madelyn.

He judged the distance between Ash and Madelyn. God, he'd have to be fast. Angling his head, he kissed her more deeply, forcing Ash into a half-turn. Any closer, and Madelyn might step away. It had to be now.

But first, one more second with her. He gentled the kiss—he

wanted her to remember him like this. Not pushing, not shoving her around, not *using* her . . . but this.

He lifted his head, and smiled at her. "I think all the delaying worked, Ash, because here they come."

Ash's brows pushed together in confusion, then her eyes flared with sudden hope. From the corner of his eye, he saw Madelyn's swords appear. Saw her turn her back to them, searching the skies.

He leapt.

His chest slammed into Madelyn's back, sent her stumbling forward. He hooked an arm around her neck. She froze.

"Ash, kill—"

His hand slapped over her mouth.

His chest heaving, he waited, making certain. His hold was secure, standing behind her with his left forearm crushing her throat and his right hand over her mouth. She couldn't shake him off without breaking the Rules. And as long as his hand prevented her from speaking, she couldn't give Ash an order.

Madelyn was caught.

A harsh, disbelieving laugh boiled up from deep in his gut. God. After twenty fucking years, he had the demon right where he wanted her.

He looked at Ash, laughed again. Shock, joy, and hatred aimed at Madelyn—they were a gorgeous mix. "Do you have a weapon?"

Even as Ash shook her head, Madelyn's swords vanished. Not taking any chances. And Nicholas couldn't move his hand from her mouth, not even for a moment.

He fought the sinking in his stomach. All right. He'd known this might happen. He'd kept the grenade for this reason, as a fail-safe to keep Madelyn in line. Now, they had to count on the Guardians. He'd wait here with Madelyn while Ash made a run for the nearest phone. It wouldn't take long.

"Ash, reach into my pocket, give me the grenade—"

He broke off as a leathery membrane slithered against his chest. Madelyn's wings formed, snapped wide—not hurting him, not trying to dislodge him, not breaking the Rules. Still, he didn't like it.

They flapped once, twice. Though Madelyn couldn't speak, the intention was clear: She was going up, and Nicholas could hold on if he wanted to.

Ash's eyes widened. "Nicholas, let go. Let go now!"

Not in a million fucking years. Not when her soul depended on Madelyn's silence. He'd hang on even if the trip took him all the way to Hell.

He felt Madelyn's laugh against his hand—and his arm was almost yanked from the socket as she launched straight up. Ash's scream of rage and fear followed them, ripping through the night, then drowned in the rush of air, the slap of wings. Madelyn dove. Nicholas's weight shifted, almost broke his hold. *Jesus.* His right leg caught her waist, gave him another anchor. In his pocket, the hard bulge of the grenade dug into his thigh.

The wind whipped her hair into his eyes, his face. He could barely see anything below, just darkness beneath them. Darkness . . . and a faint crimson glow. Ash, racing along the ground, tracking their flight.

Madelyn laughed against his hand again. Calling in her swords, she dove—toward Ash. Oh, fuck no.

Without hesitation, Nicholas tightened his hold on Madelyn's mouth, his leg at her waist, and unhooked his arm from her throat. He shoved his hand into his pocket. Yanking the pin with his teeth, he released the safety lever. How many seconds? Three? The dark ground rushed toward them—and Ash was there, Ash with no weapons to defend herself against Madelyn's swords.

He wrapped his arm around Madelyn's chest, shoved his fist against her heart.

Two . . .

At least it would be like this, knowing Ash was safe. That she had nothing left to fear. He wished he could have given her more.

One . . .

He hoped that crazy Guardian hadn't given him a dud—

The explosion burst through Ash's head, an agonizing crack through her ears . . . and then only a faint, ringing silence. Her scream echoed in it, a silent eruption of pressure that squeezed her chest into nothing. She ran, but not fast enough to catch him.

The impact into the ground vibrated against her feet. Nicholas, on top of Madelyn—maybe she'd broken his fall. Maybe her body had shielded his from the shrapnel. Maybe there was hope.

But she couldn't feel a heartbeat, and her scream echoed in the empty silence again when she separated him from the mess that had once been a demon. Hauling him to her chest, she tried to breathe life into him, only tasted blood and death.

Oh, God. He should have let go.

She couldn't let him go. Even now, though someone was coming, a white light through the darkness. Probably humans, investigating the explosion. They could have Madelyn, wings and all, and the Guardians would cover up the truth somehow. She'd take Nicholas, and she'd . . .

She didn't know. Nothing seemed to matter now.

A touch at her shoulder. She could feel the vibration of a heartbeat now, though it wasn't the one she wanted, the punctuated hum of a voice through the silence. The white light grew brighter, washing out the red glow cast over his skin.

She looked up into Taylor's horrified face. Taylor's lips moved, and Ash realized the glow was coming from the Guardian, brighter now, impossible to look at.

Ash only wanted to see Nicholas, anyway.

Taylor sank to her heels on the opposite side of his body. She touched his forehead, and the light was everywhere except in the blackness of Taylor's eyes. Her voice hummed again in the silence, and echoed in Ash's head.

Nicholas, you have given your life to save another's, and so now you have a choice: Will you continue on to what awaits at Judgment, or will you serve as a Guardian?

And impossibly, impossibly, though he had no breath to speak, no life to shape the words, his voice, his reply—

I will serve.

Taylor's laugh came from nowhere, everywhere. *Well, this is my first, so let's hope I get this right. Ash, stand back.*

She did, not even moving but suddenly outside the light, looking into the blinding brightness, still holding Nicholas's body to her chest. Her heart seemed filled to bursting, aching with joy that couldn't have possibly come so close after the devastation, but she was overwhelmed with it, the highest up after the lowest down.

He'd be a Guardian.

She flattened her palm over his chest, waited for the beat of his heart. Oh, it was already there . . . so faint, almost undetectable. The light was growing dimmer, still so bright but no longer shining outward—it was being sucked into the blackness of Taylor's eyes.

Taylor's lips formed another word, unmistakable: *Michael.* Then, *Help.*

Nicholas's body jerked. His eyes flew open, staring sightlessly into the sky, his mouth shaping into a soundless scream.

And he vanished from her arms.

CHAPTER 18

After two weeks, he could finally walk.

The pain still ate through to his bones, but Nicholas could stand without crumpling, move one foot in front of the other. Slowly, he made his way to the enormous marble slabs that served as the temple doors. He just had to pull them open, and he'd be in Caelum. Then there would be a Gate—somewhere—that would take him to Earth. A Gate that would take him to Ash.

He just had to pull them open . . . but Nicholas didn't yet know if he could do it.

Strength wasn't the problem. Earlier that day, he'd lifted with a single finger the red sofa on which he'd spent the past two weeks. But two weeks ago, he hadn't even had two hands.

The left had regrown into the shape of a hand, but was still fragile. His guts and ribs, shredded by shrapnel, had almost completely pieced together—by the second day, his lungs had mended enough that he could take a breath. Tendons and muscle worked as they should, but the shattered bones beneath were still laced with cracks. Pim, a novice Guardian with a healing Gift, had predicted a full recovery within one or two more days. Of course, she'd said that four days ago, too.

Not completely healed, but he didn't look like a horror show any longer. He could close his eyes without being bombarded by the screams inside his head, the torturous bite of ice. So it was time to go.

He braced his feet and hauled back against the door. For a moment, a pain lancing through his ankle gave him visions of his leg snapping and folding over on itself inside his pajama pants. He was able to slowly open the door. Light poured into the temple, blinding him.

Nicholas stepped out into a ruin. As far as he could see, columns lay like tossed matchsticks, domes had collapsed into piles of rubble. No single building stood intact, and the towers that were still upright appeared sheared apart, pointed like jagged teeth. Beyond them lay a brilliant blue sky that stung tears from Nicholas's eyes.

"Not much left, is there?"

Because they never left him completely alone, helpless in a crumbling realm, Taylor sat on the temple's marble steps. The sun glinted against the gold and copper in her hair, and sparked like fire. It was almost a relief to look away from her, to the soothing white of the broken city again.

"No," he said.

"You'll get used to color in a little while. Too much at once is like a kaleidoscope jabbed into your brain. And then later comes the Enthrallment, where one color is so beautiful, you just want to stare at it for hours. Of course, sometimes it just takes a smell, or a sound. Sometimes it's just a combination of everything."

"So that's why I'm still here? To give me time to adjust?"

"That, and your freak hand." She said it like a joke that didn't come out right, and finished with a grimace. "Sorry. It doesn't look bad now anyway. Almost normal. Just—"

"Weaker," Nicholas said.

"That's all on me. When Michael transforms someone, he usually can't heal them with his Gift—just like Pim couldn't heal you—because most of the time, those wounds are somehow self-inflicted. But during the transformation, he's altering those people anyway, so he alters the body so that it's healed. I didn't know how to do that. It never occurred to me to study anatomy or how to rebuild someone. I thought he'd always be there to give it to me."

"But instead, he's like that." Nicholas nodded toward the city. "Broken down."

"Yes," she said, and when Nicholas turned to look at the temple behind them—still strong, still standing—Taylor added, "I think that one is me."

"I'm glad you didn't crack while I was in there, then." And because another pain shot through his ankle and up to his knee, he eased down on the step next to her. "Is she all right?"

"You ask that every day."

"I wonder every second."

"Ah, well. She's still not sure that we aren't all just lying to her. After Khavi . . ." Taylor shook her head. "It could be argued that she left you alone to die. Or that she single-handedly arranged events so that every decision you, Ash, Lilith, and I made led to your becoming a Guardian. We don't even know if the stuff about Ash being able to get Michael out of the field was true, or if that was just designed to put everything in motion. And I don't know what we're going to do when she comes waltzing back in, but you're one of us now, and your input will have weight."

He didn't care about that. Group decision making wasn't his style. They could what they liked. He'd do as he liked . . . when he could.

"Why am I not healing right?"

"We've got theories. You want to hear them?"

"Yes."

"One is that I fucked up the transformation."

"Did you?" If so, he could live with it. Some of it had obviously worked. He had strength. He could hear her heart beating. He could see a tiny fleck of quartz in a toppled marble column lying one hundred yards away. If he healed a little more slowly than most Guardians, then he'd just train hard enough, get so damn good with his weapons that he'd be hurt less, too. Hell, he'd do that even if he healed normally from this point forward.

Either way, problem solved.

"I think it went okay. Things only went bad when I tried to heal you. That's when Michael came in, and that didn't exactly go so well. So, that's the second theory—that the trauma of his mind slipping into yours was a shock to your whole system, and on top of the transformation . . ." She sighed. "Most Guardians are up and aware the second they are transformed. Me, I was in a coma for three months after he first got into my brain.

You were only unconscious for about six hours, which might have just been the time your brain needed to heal, anyway. So you came through better than I did."

"Or maybe I came through better because you shielded my mind from his."

"I—" She looked at him in surprise. "That is kind of you, St. Croix."

"I'm healing and vulnerable. It probably won't happen often."

Taylor laughed, and Nicholas bore the pang against his heart, the longing for the laugh he most wanted to hear. God, he missed Ash.

"Any third theories?" Anything to get him back to Earth more quickly.

"Two more, and both of them a bit more mental than physical." When he frowned at her, she said, "It matters, you know—the way a person perceives himself. Like, I've heard there were some novices who literally fell apart when they tried to shape-shift, because they couldn't hold an image of themselves in their mind. Then there's someone like Drifter, who can barely hold any shape other than his own, because his image of himself is so fixed. The funny thing about Drifter, though, is that last year, he had his leg bitten off by a dragon. Gulp! and everything from the thigh down was gone. That should have taken him a month to regenerate. He was walking around in two weeks."

Nicholas had to laugh. "So you think I'm not sure of myself? That I don't know myself? I should introduce you to my therapist." A thought occurred to him. "Where, by the way, you might find Khavi."

"But she'd know we were coming and skip her appointment that day."

"That's . . ." Nicholas trailed off, frowning. He didn't know what to call it. *Difficult* didn't seem to cover it.

Taylor nodded, as if reading his expression. "Now try a year of that."

"I will be, apparently."

"Yeah." Taylor abruptly sobered, and looked out over the city. "Which brings me to the fourth and final theory: You don't give a shit about being a Guardian."

"I don't give a shit about a lot of things."

"I know. You don't let anything get in your way when you

want something. Death almost put a big fucking obstacle in there, but it just so happened that the one thing in the world you care about needed saving, and so you got another chance. You lucked out."

Nicholas had nothing to say. He couldn't argue that.

"I know you have Ash. That's a pretty damn good reason to want to come back, to want to live. But it has nothing to do with being a Guardian. And I know what it's like not to want the transformation, but taking it anyway, because someone's counting on you, or you just don't want to die. Those are all good reasons for saying yes to the transformation. But to keep going? It's not enough. Take it from someone who has a God-knows-how-many-thousand-year-old guy hanging out in her head—it's simply not enough to serve as a Guardian just so that you can do something else, so that you can keep hanging in there until the world falls into the sun. You have to make being a Guardian serve *you*."

Like his money had always served him, giving him the ability to keep pursuing his revenge. He didn't have that now. The money, yes, but no Madelyn to keep hunting down—and no amount of money in the world would make him heal faster.

But he'd never been afraid to ask for help when he needed it. "How? What do I have to find?"

"We all have something. We all have some reason that being a Guardian matters. The woman who's leading us right now, Irena, she pretty much lives to smash demon heads in. Rosalia cares about everyone, so as a Guardian, she can help everyone in ways they can't help themselves. Jake likes to fly around and blow shit up, but he's also making certain that nothing like a demon can ever touch his family, or anyone else's family."

Nicholas had that. He had his parents, and Rachel, and the Boyles. Newer, and different than his need for revenge—the determination to see it never happen again. To anyone.

"I have something," he said.

"Good. Then cultivate the hell out of it. Make it matter."

Strange. For two weeks, he'd only been thinking about Ash. About getting back to her. But now, realizing what he'd be able to do, the demons he'd be able to stop . . . *God.* And his eyes were stinging again.

"St. Croix?"

Make it matter. "I think it already does," he said.

* * *

Taylor had been right about the colors, but she hadn't mentioned the sounds. Within a few seconds after she teleported him to his grandfather's cabin, Nicholas was on his knees with his eyes closed, covering his ears, certain that he was on the verge of vomiting a rainbow. *He could hear the snow melting beneath his knees.* He'd begged for her to leave him alone, and she had.

Jesus. So certain that he'd be able to go straight from Caelum to Ash, to a warehouse in the middle of a city. Now he was glad Taylor had suggested a test run at the isolated cabin, instead.

At the end of the week, when he could walk outside without flinching when a twig snapped under the weight of an icicle, he thought taking that trip might be possible. All of his lingering scars and new pink skin looked like his own; his left hand was strong and finally the same size as his right.

But rather than using the satellite phone Taylor had left for him and telling her to come, he began chopping wood, instead. Later, she brought in a load of books for him to read, but didn't mention going to San Francisco. He let her leave without mentioning it, too.

He didn't know what the hell he was thinking. He didn't know what the fuck he was doing. But despite the ache that was a constant companion, the desperate desire to see Ash, he wasn't ready yet.

And he didn't even know what he was getting ready *for.*

Another week passed, and Nicholas felt he was finally getting there—wherever *there* was. He'd read through all of the books on birds and flight, and started on his grandfather's collection—the collection that Ash had read through in her week here, though he preferred to read reclining on the bed rather than the stiff rocking chair. He wished she'd left notes in the margins. What had she felt and thought, reading these? Probably nothing like she'd feel and think now. She'd changed so quickly that week, but so had he, and—

The forest had quieted.

Nicholas sat up in the bed. The twittering and chirping of the returning springtime birds had become easily ignored background noise in the past few weeks, but the sudden hush seemed as loud as an alarm. He grabbed his shotgun—he still hadn't figured out his cache yet—and waited at the door, listening.

Nothing unusual.

Except . . . he tilted his head, focused on the odd, rhythmic sound coming from above him. Almost a gallop, but muffled. Almost like his own heartbeat.

Someone was on the roof.

His heart pounding now, too, he edged backward out of the door, backed away from the porch. The height and pitch of the A-frame made it difficult to get an immediate look at the top. When he did, his heart stopped.

Ash.

Leathery wings spread wide, she perched on the ridge, crouching like a gargoyle. Horns curled away from her forehead; crimson scales covered her body. She gripped the forward projecting edge of the roof with a taloned claw.

Her eyes began to glow. "Hello, Nicholas. You look well."

He hadn't been well. Not until this moment. "You look beautiful."

Fangs glinted in her smile, and his heart tightened, a painfully sweet ache. God, how he'd missed her.

"I thought I'd try to scare you," she said. "The birds gave me away. It makes me wish that I liked to eat chicken."

"You probably scared *them*."

"But not you." She rose and stepped off the roof. Her wings caught the air, and she glided to Nicholas, landing easily just in front of him. The glowing crimson faded to human blue. Scales slid back into tattoos and a tan; her horns vanished. Jeans and her hoodie formed over naked skin. "I've missed you. But is it too early yet?"

He knew exactly what she meant, but still didn't know how to answer it. So he gave her what he had to give. "I missed you, too. So damn much."

The joy in her smile slipped into him, through him. "It took me two years just to remember part of my name, Nicholas. If you need me to go, I can—"

"No." He'd missed her, he'd wanted her in his arms and to see her smile, but he hadn't known how much he *needed* to see her. And now that she was here— "I need you to stay."

Holding his gaze, she lifted her hands to cup his face, to slide her fingers through his hair. "You feel the same. And so familiar. I've touched you more in my imaginings than I ever have for real. I'd begun to fear that I'd forgotten, or that I remembered wrong."

"And you are just as . . . just as . . . *everything.*" It hit him like a punch to the chest. "Everything."

"So." She grinned. "Even you can't manage eloquence when you've just spent six weeks living like a hermit."

"No." He shook his head, and her smile faded. "Don't you see? It's—"

Too much to say. Too big.

So he kissed her.

This wasn't familiar. The urge to cry and to laugh, and the painful effort to hold it in, to keep her emotions from overwhelming him. She rarely took such care. Only once had she fought so hard to contain them, but that was when she'd been full of desperation and fear, but trying to prevent Madelyn from using those emotions in any way, trying to keep from giving herself away with every lie, every evasion.

And now, his mouth on hers, she felt the same thing from Nicholas—an explosion of emotion, somehow contained, but that couldn't be any longer. *Oh, God.* She lifted to him, welcomed the possessive surge of his tongue, touching his shoulders, his arms, the broad sweep of his back and the delicious tautness of his ass, claiming all of him for her own.

He lifted his head, breathing raggedly. "Everything, Ash. This is what I want to be. I thought you needed to be separate from what mattered, but it's not. You're the reason for it all. You're the reason I can *feel* that anything else matters at all."

"Nicholas." Smiling, she trailed her fingers from his temple to his jaw. "I have no idea what you're talking about, but I feel the same way. How is that, do you think?"

He grinned. "I have no idea. Hold on. And vanish your wings."

She did, then laughed aloud as he bent and swept her up against his chest. Her arms circled his neck. "They *are* a pain in the ass through doorways. Are you taking me to have sex? Because if your answer is no, I want you to put me down—so that I can pick *you* up, and take you to have sex."

"You'll have to come up with a better plot than that."

She could, easily. "Oh, Nicholas! My clothes just fell off."

The fabric between them vanished. With a single glance, his eyes flared with pale blue light. Ash caught her breath.

"Oh," she whispered. "Oh. You are . . ."

His arms tensed. "Different?"

"Beautiful, I think." Her chest filled with it. "It is sometimes hard to decide whether something is known or felt. I have always known how handsome you are. But you have never been so beautiful to me as you are now, naked like this."

"I'm not naked yet."

"You wear clothes, Nicholas. But I see you. Better than I have ever seen you before, with some of you that is new to see. Not just the glowing eyes; it was not just a transformation. You *are* a Guardian now."

His throat worked, and his answer was rough. "Yes."

"Just as I'm a demon—though I am, of course, the best kind. The only kind of demon worth being. So we're perfect together, I think."

She paused as he angled his body to carry her through the door. His face had hardened, as if containing some emotion again. Not hiding, as he often had before—just holding it in. A shudder ran though him when she leaned in to lick his neck.

At least he did not hold that in anymore.

"Take me to the bed. We'll talk more when your penis is inside me." She tightened her arms around his shoulders. "And you'll tell me why, when you have such purpose burning inside, you are still here . . . waiting."

"I didn't know why until today. I was waiting for you."

The bed creaked when he laid her on it, and again when he climbed in after her, bracing his knees on either side of her thighs. He leaned over, his hands flat beside her shoulders. His lips grazed her cheek in a soft caress.

That was not enough. Not enough after months.

"Feel me, Nicholas. Use your fingers to feel me. I'm wet. Already so wet. I only had two thoughts as I flew here: Wondering whether you were all right, and how much of your almost-monstrous penis I can take."

Eyes on hers, he slipped his hand down. Ash lifted to his touch, panting in anticipation. He didn't stop at the first sign of heat and moisture, but delved between her drenched folds, then pushed deep. She cried out, thighs clenching, squeezing his wrist. His groan filled the small room.

"Ah! Yes." Her fingers curled into the bedsheet. "Do you remember the bathtub? Do you remember how I tortured you there?"

A thrust of his fingers answered her. His head bent, his tongue flicking her nipple into turgid arousal.

"Like that, yes. Except I teased you with water instead of my tongue. And in my mind, I've tortured you a hundred times in the same way. But never to finish. Each time, I climb in and fill myself with you, and ride until we are both dying of it. I want to die now."

He breathed her name against her skin, rose to take her mouth. Hot and wet, each slow kiss killed her a little more. His hand worked at his belt, his button, his zipper. Ash used her toes to push his jeans down before running her feet up the backs of his heavily muscled thighs.

She pulled at his hair until he lifted his head. Cool blue light spilled across his cheekbones, glinted in his dark lashes.

"Why did you know today? What changed?"

"You came." His gaze held hers. "And I knew that you are not useful to me, Ash. Not anymore. Except as a reason to get up in the morning—"

"You don't sleep anymore," she reminded him, smiling.

"Except as a reason to keep breathing—"

"You don't need air."

He narrowed his eyes at her. "I'm still new at this Guardian thing. So just shut up, and let me tell you that I love you."

All happiness. Her laugh erupted, and she pulled him down for another kiss, but he lowered his body and shoved forward instead, his thick length filling her all at once. Agonizing pleasure lashed her nerves, whipped her muscles tight. Ash cried out, arching her back as her inner muscles clamped around his invading shaft, as deep as she'd wanted him, needed him.

His hand fisted in her hair, and he ground his hips against hers, until she was squirming against him, crying out for another heavy thrust. He froze, instead.

"I was waiting for *this*." His voice was a tortured groan against her ear. "To know that your feelings hadn't faded. To know that I was still a man that you'd want—even though I'm a Guardian now, too. I was too afraid to find you, Ash. Too afraid of what I'd see in your eyes, when you saw the change in me . . . even though you're the reason for it."

Her throat tightened. "I would not give you up so easily, Nicholas St. Croix. You should have more faith in yourself than that."

"I've given you little reason."

"You blew yourself up to save me. Which, so you know, tore my heart out. I've spent six weeks building a new one, and you are still stamped all over it." She wriggled her hips, gasped. God. So full. So *frustrating*. "And we were supposed to talk when you were inside me, but that did not mean you were supposed to stop everything to talk."

He levered up on his elbows, the strain of keeping himself motionless visible in the tendons of his neck, the clench of his jaw. "I can't do both at once."

"So you *do* have another limit."

His eyes narrowed. "We'll see."

Ash burst into a laugh. He was so easy. Then her laugh strangled itself on a moan as he slowly withdrew, began an endless thrust inside her again.

"Oh!" she cried out, and though she couldn't remember thinking that her toes needed to curl, now they were, and her heels were sliding up to dig into the muscles flexing in his ass. He drove deep again.

"*This*, Ash." His fingers interlocked with hers, he drew her hands over her head, stretching her body upward even as her flesh stretched to receive him. "Deciding what matters. You do, more than anything. Being a Guardian does. But there's more than that."

"I can't . . ." A long thrust drew the thought to nothing.

Again, and her only consolation was that his voice was as tortured as hers, his breathing as ragged. "What was that, Ash?"

"I can't imagine . . . what more."

He dipped his head, and she opened her mouth for a kiss. His tongue swept up the length of a fang. Body bucking upward, she cried his name as the movement drove him deep, hard. He caught her hip up off the bed, thrust again. She couldn't stand any more.

Hooking her leg around his, she shoved at his shoulder, pushed him over, and straddled his hips. Sank deep.

Head thrown back, Nicholas arched his long body, lifting her, driving deeper. His muscles locked in stark relief, he hung there. Ash battled between the need to remain still and absorb the sheer beauty of him and the urgent need to move; urgent need won.

Hands braced on his chest, she rolled her hips. Nicholas's breath hissed from between clenched teeth. His fingers gripped her thighs, swept inward. His thumb found her clitoris, began a slow circle.

"Oh, God." Fire coiled through her, a heated twist of every nerve. "That's . . . so evil."

"So *good*," he countered.

Yes. She couldn't stand it. The fire burned hotter, sizzling inside her, white-hot.

"Nicholas . . . Harder now. *Now*."

The world spun wildly as he turned, pushed her onto her back again. Hooking her leg up over his hip, he drove forward, deep. Ash cried out, her nails digging into his shoulders.

"Again."

"For how long?"

He had to ask? "Forever," she said.

"Please, God," he groaned, and when he raised his head, his eyes shone full blue. "Because there's more."

Chest heaving, he angled her hips up, thrust hard again. Her body bowed, a scream locked in her throat. How could she survive this?

Only over and over again.

"More." It emerged on a sobbing breath, and he obeyed, until she burned, burned, clinging to him as it raced through her, screaming as it left. Nicholas's mouth crashed down over hers, and his tongue thrust with the stroke of his body, until he suddenly stilled—shook. Wings erupted from his shoulders in a long, elegant arch. Heavier, suddenly blanketed by feathers, he settled over her. Still inside her, and despite his orgasm, still hard.

Oh, she could become used to this. She wrapped her arms and legs around him, wouldn't let him move.

"I love you," she said, in case he hadn't realized it yet. "I came here to tell you, but I was distracted by the sex."

His kiss was long and sweet, and muffled her noise of protest when he began to roll over. He didn't stop kissing her until she lay atop his body—with him still hard inside her, and so she was satisfied.

"I don't need to breathe," she reminded him.

"That's not the point." His new wings vanished, but a single feather lay on the sheets. She picked it up as he said, "I don't want to ever hold you down in *any* way."

"I think I'd like you to hold me down and just fuck away sometime. We could play 'demon almost broke the Rules.' "

"Only if we follow up with 'Guardian almost broke the Rules," he said, but the stirring of his flesh told her that a part of him wasn't averse to her idea now. His expression turned serious, however, so she assumed that wasn't in store just yet. "That's not what I meant, though. I can't bear the idea of you beneath anyone, Ash."

She didn't really want that, either. "Unless I'm beneath you, and you're inside me."

"That's different. Sex and play are different. But this is . . ." His brow furrowed slightly, as if trying to find the right way to express it. "This is the *more*, Ash. What I'm waiting for—what I might *always* be waiting for, but that I'll do everything I can to get there."

"Where?"

"To become the man who deserves you. Who is worthy of you." When her mouth fell open, he shook his head, swept his thumb over her lips as if to seal them closed. "You can't say anything. I've hurt you, Ash. I can't take that back. And you might have forgiven me, or you might say that the grenade made up for it—"

"I did. I would."

"But it's not yours to give. Not this one. It has to be me, doing my damn best to be the man *I* think might deserve you—not just some bastard who got lucky enough. As it is, it's almost impossible, but I'll spend forever trying."

Well, Ash thought that was *totally unnecessary*, but it obviously made a difference to him, so much that during his explanation, the determination filling his words seemed to fill his physical form, too, shifting and changing his—

"Oh," she gasped at the same time his eyes closed, a tortured moan rising from his chest. The feather fell from her suddenly nerveless fingers. "Nicholas, you—I think you shapeshifted. Not much, you just became . . . more."

Monstrous.

Stretching. Almost painful . . . but not. She sat up and cried out as his cock pushed deeper. Her nails dug into his chest.

His eyes were already shining. His hands moved to her hips, tried to lift her off. "I'm hurting you."

"You're *not* hurting—" She broke off as he managed to slide her up over his length. Ecstasy shot through her veins, sparking new fires. Her inner muscles clamped around him. Her head swam with the unexpected, overwhelming pleasure of it. "Oh, my God. *Stop.*"

He froze. Already needing more, she pushed down, and his entire body clenched, a groan ripping from him. Trembling, she waited for him to recover.

He looked up at her. She leaned forward, braced her hands, and gave him her wickedest grin.

"So, Guardian. Let's see just how long you can hold on."

CHAPTER 19

Nicholas could hold on for a long time, as it turned out. He'd adapted well to his heightened senses, though his glowing eyes and abruptly appearing wings showed the same lack of control that Ash once had.

She'd never experienced Enthrallment, though, and had only sensed it once, when a novice became fixated on the fragrance of baking bread wafting from a sandwich shop near the warehouse. That Guardian's psychic scent had gone into a long, slow spin—as if he were dizzy, and the bread formed his only remaining anchor.

When it happened to Nicholas, that anchor was the taste of her, as if his world had narrowed down to her flavor against his tongue. Ash held onto him through each searching lick, crying out again and again, and though her body remained strong, inexhaustible, by the time he came back to himself she was wrung out with the ecstasy of it.

Then he lifted his body over hers, pushed deep inside, and wrung her out again.

When they finally emerged from the bedroom, night had long since fallen and the fire had died down, leaving the cabin stone cold. From her rocking chair, Ash watched him lay the kindling in the stove, the lamplight playing over the muscles of his back.

He *had* gotten bigger. Not in any one direction, but overall taller and wider, and proportioned in exactly the same way. Without anyone standing next to him as comparison, the difference was hard to immediately see. The only evidence of it was in the tighter fit of his pajama pants, the higher hem.

"Unless you figure out how to shape-shift back or make your own clothes in the next few weeks, you're going to have to buy a new wardrobe."

"I'll hire someone." He reached for the lighter. "So you already have a penthouse in San Francisco?"

"It's awkward masturbating to my fantasies of you in a warehouse full of Guardians with superhearing," she said. "So I split my time between training and the penthouse, where I've been setting up these accounts that Lilith wants, and taking over your company."

The icy challenge in the glance he shot her sent a thrill through her blood. "You can try, demon."

She would. "You'll be training, too, but I'd love it if you'd work with me on these investments. I could use another eye and another brain, especially at this stage."

"Is sex included?"

"Yes."

"That easy? No negotiation?"

"I'll throw in a *lot* of sex."

"Then I'm in."

Perfect. "It's almost like training, anyway. Investing and trying to negotiate with a demon both mean a lot of waiting for the right opportunity, making the right queries to discover what they're not saying or reporting, and deciding whether the high-risk moves are worth the reward."

"I think the last high-risk move that I made was," he said softly. The kindling began crackling a moment later, and he stood, regarding her with his serious face. "When the training's over—thirty or so years, I guess—I'll probably hand Reticle over to you, start fighting full-time."

"I know," she said.

"I won't leave you, but—"

"I know, Nicholas." She'd seen the new purpose in him, and his company wouldn't serve it the same way the money had supported his revenge. "I'll hold on to it for when you need a cover or any other reason. As long as we're together, I'm happy.

Especially since I plan to own half the world in the next two or three hundred years, but very few people will know. All that matters is that you're with me, and you're impressed by my financial acumen."

"Everything about you astonishes me, Ash."

"Because you love me."

"No, because *you* love *me*. I'm coming to you a completely different man than you knew before. I shouldn't expect anything, and you give me forever."

"That's what I want, too. Anyway, you're wrong. You weren't a man when we met. You were like me—essentially a child in many ways. Maybe a teenager."

Nicholas shook his head, but she knew he wasn't disagreeing. He knew himself too well. His life had stopped when he'd decided to pursue his revenge.

"The essentials are the same, though," she said. "You sought revenge as a way to right the wrongs Madelyn did to you. Yes, you were myopic and obsessive and incredibly paranoid, but there wasn't any cruelty in you, just as there isn't now. And I like to think we grew up a bit together, that week we spent here."

"You are amazing." He bent and kissed her hard. "And fantasies in the warehouse, really?"

"Only once. What do I care, right? But apparently it makes everyone uncomfortable, so they told me about the spell that can keep anyone from hearing what's going on inside a room. Did you offend the bears?"

"I didn't. I don't."

"Think about me?" Impossible.

"All the time. But not . . . I can't." He turned away, set the lighter on its shelf. "I see Madelyn, walking in on me. Laughing."

Oh. When he faced her again, his features were washed in red light.

"I'm so glad she's dead," Ash said, and he gave a short laugh of agreement. "And that reminds me, I have something for you, thanks to Jake the teleporting Guardian. Straight from a brick oven in New York, to his cache, to my cache, and now to your table—still piping hot. Now you can celebrate the end of Madelyn as you planned."

The cardboard box appeared in her hands, bringing with it an explosion of scents: cheese, charred crust, tomato, and spices.

Nicholas didn't even allow her time to open the lid. He tossed the box aside, and it slapped against the floorboards. He hauled her out of the chair, his mouth all over hers, sweet possession, gratitude, and wonder filling his kiss.

He let her feet touch the floor again, following her down, his forehead against hers and his breath ragged. "I love you. I don't deserve you, but I won't let you go. Ever."

Another voice answered him—a harmonious voice. "Make sure that you don't."

Khavi. Ash whipped around, boomstick coming to her hand. She froze. Khavi stood near the door, and she'd brought a hellhound with her. Not as big as Sir Pup, but it didn't matter—the venom in Ash's shotgun shells wouldn't affect either of them.

Human in appearance except for brown eyes that never appeared so ancient in so young a face, Khavi looked at the pizza box. "Oh, I came just in time. You will be very, very glad not to have eaten first."

"What do you want, Khavi?" But Ash feared she knew. Vanishing the boomstick, she said, "If this is about the frozen field, I am *not* exchanging myself for Michael."

"I know. Your unwillingness has been noted, and adjustments have been made." She looked at Nicholas, who watched her warily. "You are finally healed, I see. Strong. And I am very sorry—I intended to wait until your Gift manifested itself naturally, but I cannot any longer. He will pull it from you anyway, just to determine whether you're useful. When he does, you'll have to look deep, and *see* what I cannot."

"What does that mean?" Nicholas pushed in front of Ash, shielded her. "Why are you sorry?"

"Because I have seen. But it must be done." Determination replaced the regret in her voice. "You need to call Special Investigations, Nicholas. Now, because you will need their help."

Dread filled Ash's chest. "Why?"

"Because I'm taking you both to Hell and giving you to Lucifer." Khavi sighed when Ash's crossbow was suddenly in her hand, aimed at the grigori's face. "No, no. Do not fight. It is no use—I will easily defeat you. I have already seen it."

Ash staggered, fell to her knees in the hot red sand. The world tilted wildly. God. Her stomach heaved, and she heard Nicholas fighting the same dizzying effects of the teleportation. She drew in a deep breath, almost retched again. *The stink.* Rotten, burning flesh.

No more breathing. Not here. Just listening, making certain . . .

They were alone for the moment. No heartbeats nearby. Only his.

Nicholas's arm slid around her. Though still not steady, he lifted her, waited until she planted her feet. "Are you okay?"

No. But there was no other choice to nod. "Next time, we'll know better than to try fighting a crazy teleporter who can see the future. Are you hurt?"

"She never even touched me, except to bring us here. And—" He broke off. "Ash, look."

She heard the bleakness in his voice, and didn't want to turn. In the direction she faced, there was only an endless stretch of red sand, a bruised crimson sky. But she couldn't pretend. Bracing herself, she turned.

Oh, God. Terror caught her throat, her heart in an icy, clawed grip. They stood at the edge of the frozen field. A few steps away, red sand bled into open mouths and eyes, a frozen carpet of faces locked in ice. So many locked together, with no space between. *So many.* She couldn't see the borders on the sides, only Lucifer's tower rising in the center like an enormous black spear. *How long had she stared at that, screaming, screaming?* Forever. And they were all there now, screaming, and she knew that there was no other sound, only silence, and just the tortured, endless screaming of the millions trapped—

Her knees collapsed. Nicholas caught her, drew her against him, and she muffled her scream against his chest, trying to hold it in, *don't let anyone know we're here*, but it had to come out before it ripped her apart inside.

She cried, hot tears. For herself, for Rachel, for all of them. All the same.

"I didn't know." His throat sounded as rough and broken as hers. "I didn't know there were so many."

Ash wiped her face, made herself look again. So many. "All like Rachel, just because of a choice. Maybe not even a bad choice, or an evil one."

"Yes." Khavi's voice came from behind them. "It's not like the Pit, where the judged go to be punished. And the majority of those in the field are demons—Madelyn is there, somewhere—and some humans who probably deserve it. But most of the humans, most of the halflings . . . They made the wrong agreement with a demon, and it doesn't matter at all how good their intentions might have been."

Ash shook her head. Through the ache in her throat, she still managed, "I'm *not* going back in there."

Khavi pursed her lips, looked at Nicholas. "I made the call to Taylor using your voice. It was important. You should have done it."

"Does your doing it change anything?"

"No." Giving her hellhound a pat on its enormous head, she looked out over the field and said, "There's Michael, by the way."

Khavi pointed. Unable to help herself, Ash looked. When she didn't see anything, she looked farther out . . . farther. Just visible on the icy horizon, a crowd of demons stood.

"Michael's the entertainment," Khavi said, and a rough note entered the smooth harmony of her voice. "Michael, and those from the Pit who are tortured with him. You cannot see, so I will help you see."

Ash cried out as a sharp crack opened in her psychic shields, saw Nicholas's suddenly white face. The image pressed against the backs of her eyes, every detail in clear focus: Michael's shattered face with his eyes open, seeing, aware—and the human, stretched between two poles, stretched more than a human could, the razor wire, the hellhound's thrusting haunches and bloodied jaws—

"Stop!" Her tears burned, and Nicholas pulled her back against his chest. She felt his own shuddering horror. "And you want me to be there? How can you do this? How can you say this?"

"That is not what I want now. I just wanted you to see. You have a different role—" Khavi stopped suddenly, her head cocked. "I know this moment."

She ducked.

Taylor appeared in front of her, fist jabbing the air over Khavi's head. Faster than Ash could see, Khavi was up again. Her arm swung, a backhand that caught Taylor full on the side of the head. A resounding crack—Taylor vanished.

She reappeared directly in front of Ash and Nicholas, blood spilling from her mouth. She reached for them.

Khavi teleported between, smashed her foot into Taylor's chest, knocked Nicholas's arm aside. Ash leapt at her—leapt into nothing. Unprepared for Khavi's disappearance, she sprawled on the sand. A growl froze her in place. Khavi's hellhound. A clear warning not to attack again. Ash looked for Nicholas.

God. He'd been knocked back into the frozen field. Already making his way out, his bare feet on those icy faces, and not even the flat determination in his expression could hide the pain of those screams that echoed in his mind, that awful silence.

He crossed over onto the sand, ran to her. Ignoring the hellhound, he crouched beside her, half shielding her body with his. "Just keep out of their way, or we'll be smashed. We'll try to get to Taylor if we can—and hope that someone else is coming, too."

A shriek pierced the air. Khavi's. Ash looked around the hellhound as an impact shook the ground. Taylor lay on her side, her head bleeding, her eyes dazed, but quickly regaining focus. Only ten feet away. At the same time Ash reached for him, Nicholas grabbed her hand, began to rise. They just had to—

Black wings extended, Khavi landed beside Taylor, stroked a lock of bloodied red hair from the woman's forehead. "Michael," she said softly. "You have to make her go now. Lucifer's coming. And if he finds her . . ."

"Michael, *no!*" Rage filled Taylor's voice. Her eyes opened wide, filled with black. She began to shake. "No! You fucking liar! You promised you'd never force—"

She vanished.

Forced away by Michael. And now Ash could feel Lucifer approaching, too, like a dark pressure on the edge of her mind, a stain scudding across the sky.

In horror, she turned to Nicholas. "Taylor will tell someone else. They'll come."

Holding her tight, he nodded. Kissed her once, hard. Looked into her eyes. "Do everything you can to survive. Promise me, now."

"I will. Promise me, too."

He kissed her hard again, and she took that as his vow.

Lucifer came alone, which told Nicholas everything he needed to know about their chances of escaping without help. It could have been that the demon was just too arrogant to bring backup against a Guardian like Khavi, but Nicholas didn't think so. Given that Khavi's elephant-sized hellhound began to shudder in silent terror as Lucifer approached through the frozen field, he thought that arrogance might be well deserved.

At his side, Ash shook, too. Waiting with him behind Khavi and her hellhound, Ash stood tall, her eyes dry, and her fingers all but crushing Nicholas's hand. *The dark figure*, she'd called Lucifer. Though big, much bigger than any other demon Nicholas had seen, Lucifer's scales weren't any darker than the crimson of Ash's scales. His eyes glowed the same red, his wings the same leathery span. The same obsidian horns wrapped back from his forehead. But he *was* darker, as if even the light avoided him, and instead of Ash's beauty, Lucifer's appearance only suggested that a great, horrible power lay beneath his scales.

More darkness seethed in the power pressing against Nicholas's psyche. This demon could crush his mind with barely a thought, he realized. Not just tear apart his body, but tear apart the rest of him, too.

And Nicholas *should* have been terrified. He knew that. The fear lurked within him, he could feel it—but he didn't *feel* it. Just as he'd always done when something stood in his way, he'd discarded it. This time, he'd frozen his fear into a hard, immobile chunk, and tossed it into the back of his mind.

He couldn't let anything get in the way of his protecting Ash, helping her. He'd withstand *anything* that Lucifer had to throw at him—starting with fear.

The demon landed on cloven hooves and knees that jointed backward. Not the same as Ash, then. Even fully changed, her body maintained a human shape. His gaze swept over them. Ash's trembling increased. In front of them, Khavi's hellhound whimpered with three heads.

Lucifer focused on Khavi, spoke. Nicholas didn't know the language. When he glanced at Ash, she gave a tiny shake of her head. She didn't know, either.

"I want Michael out of the field," Khavi replied in English. She reached out to her hellhound's shoulder, soothed the trembling beast. "The halfling refuses to exchange places with him, so I've brought her to you with the intention of making a bargain."

Lucifer's laugh chilled Nicholas to the bone, started the pounding of his heart. Not fear, but survival instinct warning him of the danger, urging him to flee.

Lucifer spoke again.

Khavi shook her head. "She isn't worthless to you. She has your Gate on her face—which I understand you *needed* because Michael won a wager that forced you to close your other Gates. You needed her because of Michael; now I need her because of Michael. Her worth to us is equal."

Ash's tremors ceased. Though her eyes didn't glow, the look she gave Khavi was nothing short of murder. Furious, Nicholas saw. Suddenly so angry that it had smothered her terror.

Because she hated being the puppet, he realized. Just as she'd hated the Rules that prevented her from acting of her own will, she would hate anyone who jerked her around like a marionette on strings . . . and that was what Khavi did now.

Lucifer didn't seem to mind Khavi's use of a demon, however. After a long, considering look at her, Lucifer gave a short reply.

Khavi responded, "The bargain I propose is simple: If you release Michael from the field by sacrificing one of your demons, when it is done and Michael has been released from Hell—completely away from this realm—then before one day passes, I will sacrifice this halfling on Earth and open the portal for you. It is a sacrifice for a sacrifice, and we each receive something of value to us."

No. Rage pushed Nicholas forward. Before he'd gone a step, Ash stopped him with a hard squeeze of his hand. Her lips moved.

Opportunity.

Waiting for an opportunity. She was right. Though almost impossible not to race forward, to tear both Khavi and Lucifer apart with his hands, it would be suicide. Surviving was more important than acting on his anger right now.

He hardened his rage, fought to toss it away. Fear, anger. He would *not* be controlled by either. Not when it risked their lives.

"Yes, with Michael's release, you also lose something of value to you," Khavi said to Lucifer. "So it is not completely equal. To balance that loss, I would also offer this novice Guardian. You lose one Guardian to torture, and gain possession of another."

Him, Nicholas realized, and then it was his turn to clamp his hand around Ash's wrist, to prevent her from reacting.

"No, he is nothing like Michael," Khavi agreed. "But it will be an exchange of the oldest Guardian for the newest one. There is something elegant about it, is there not? His transformation offered hope and strength to the Guardian corps, belief that our future could be strong. I am giving you the opportunity to destroy that; even Michael's return will not heal that injury."

Lucifer's powerful gaze swept over Nicholas. He spoke.

"His Gift has not yet manifested," Khavi responded. "And I cannot see what I do not already know. His Gift might be useful to you. I cannot say."

Lucifer regarded her silently for a long moment. When he spoke, she shifted uneasily.

"I'm willing to give you a day to consider it," she said. "But I won't leave them here with you without a bargain."

He spoke again, and Khavi snorted a laugh.

"You don't *have* any goodwill."

His gaze moved to her hellhound.

Khavi went still. "I won't leave Lyta."

Lucifer's smile said it all. Either she would choose to leave Ash and Nicholas, or the hellhound—but there would be no bargain if she didn't choose one to stay.

"Let me take Ashmodei," Khavi said. "She's the more valuable to both of us. I'll leave the Guardian here."

Yes, Nicholas thought.

Lucifer turned away.

Khavi called out, "Both of them, then! But only four hours to consider my offer. And you'll return them to me, *unharmed*, if you do not intend to accept our bargain."

Nicholas didn't know what Lucifer said, but the triumph in the demon's face told him well enough: He'd agreed.

Her hand on the hellhound's shoulder, Khavi didn't even turn to look at them. She vanished.

The details didn't matter. Bargain or not, they were dead.

Unless they got the fuck out of here.

Nicholas focused on that thought as they raced across the frozen field, surrounded by a troop of armed demons. Lucifer had finally called for them—not as backup, but as herders. No one but Lucifer could fly across the frozen field; their wings wouldn't even form. Nor would Lucifer carry them. So running it was, his feet burning from the cold. Ash's might have been, too. She'd vanished her boots after her heel had struck one of those frozen eyes, but her heated skin might save her some of the pain.

He didn't think that mattered, either. In the frozen field, surrounded by silence and screams, Ash probably wasn't thinking of her feet. But just as she had when Madelyn ordered her to kill him, Ash had concealed her emotions. Terror and anger had to be hidden behind her blank features. She wasn't going to let the demons know it.

The black tower rose ahead of them, spearing into the red sky. With a base the width of a small city, Nicholas couldn't see around it. They passed out of the silent, frozen field into a cacophony of flapping wings and demon tongues, the growls of hellhounds. Jeers and laughter followed them to the entrance.

Unharmed, so far. Lucifer didn't have to keep them that way—his agreement with Khavi at the end hadn't been a bargain. So Lucifer must be saving the pain up for something bigger than whatever a random demon threw at them.

They passed into the tower—obviously not through the main entrance. A small arch opened to a dark stair, and they were urged up, up, around and around. Nicholas counted steps until they stopped. Eight thousand four hundred and fifty-six. Thank God he didn't tire anymore.

Pushed out into an unlit stone corridor, they were assaulted by screaming, sobbing. Not the screams of the frozen field, echoing only in his head, but of terror and pain.

"Torture rooms," Ash said. "How fun."

Nicholas had to laugh. A demon's head turned sharply. Never heard a laugh in this place before? Well, he was sure it would be hysterical, sobbing laughter pretty soon.

Lucifer waited at the end of the corridor, a smaller demon at his side. No, not as his side. Just behind him. Clearly subordinate.

The second demon smiled and gestured to a stone door. "The honeymoon suite."

The what?

Ash closed her eyes. "I'm going to wake up tomorrow and find this is all an absurd trick played by Khavi."

"You won't wake up tomorrow," the demon said. "Go in."

The small chamber had been constructed of the same black stone as the rest of the tower. But not even black stone, he saw—it was marble, corrupted and pitted, as if after thousands of years of smoke and fire. Not the medieval torture chamber he imagined. Instead of cutting instruments, Iron Maidens, thumbscrews, there were simply two pairs of manacles, hanging from the ceiling by chains, ten feet apart.

A spear at his back urged him forward. But not a spear for Ash, he saw. The armored demons used their hands.

Why the difference? Kinder to a halfling? Something else?

They lifted her. A demon flapped his wings, tightened the manacles—thick steel or something similar. Not much different than the collar Nicholas had used around her neck that first night, he'd wager anything it was too strong for a demon to break. The demons holding her up let go. She fell, hung—her feet suspended above the floor.

God. "You all right?"

"Fine."

No. No they weren't. But they couldn't fight yet. They had to wait. An opportunity *had* to come.

They lifted him next—and no, it wasn't bad. This couldn't strain a Guardian's muscles, or a halfling's. Then they turned him around, positioning him to face her, and he knew:

It would be worse than anything he'd imagined.

"The honeymoon suite," the demon said again, and a short, curving knife appeared in his hand. The others filed out of the chamber, leaving only Lucifer and his subordinate. "Now and again, we're fortunate enough to receive humans in the Pit who are a matched pair—who truly love each other. For those souls, the torture in the Pit is never as rewarding as it should be. They are able to put the pain away, to take their minds elsewhere. Except, of course, when the person they use to escape the pain is hanging right in front of them. The only sweeter sound than the scream of a human whose gut is being ripped open is the sound of his scream when we rip his loved one open."

His gaze on Ash, Lucifer spoke.

The demon bowed and scraped before looking to Ash. "He cannot stand the sight of you. Change to your demon form."

She almost obeyed. Nicholas saw it, the almost immediate acceptance. But Lucifer wasn't her master; Madelyn had been.

"I don't know how," she said.

Not even a refusal. A lie. A clever lie. Because if they escaped this room, her demon form might allow them—*her*—to escape a little more easily than a human could.

And it was a test. Would Lucifer know?

If he did, what would he do?

"Halflings," the demon said, and looked at Lucifer. He nodded.

Realizing he had to try, Nicholas said, "Will you consider a bargain that lets her go?"

The demon whipped his knife around, made a long, deep cut across Nicholas's stomach. Oh, fuck. Painless, for an instant, and he only heard Ash's scream, the rattle of her chains, felt the warm slide of blood. Then agony struck.

"Do not speak to him," the demon hissed. "He will not answer. He will not foul his mouth with a human tongue for the likes of you, Guardian. Bad enough that you foul his tower by speaking it, by the spill of your blood."

All right. Breathing shallowly, using the anguish tightening his muscles to still every other movement, Nicholas nodded. Best not to point out that Lucifer was the one who'd brought them here.

But Nicholas got that now, too. This was a room intended for humans. Just like Ash's name, to bring them here was an insult. It said they were worthless, nothing, not even strong enough to escape a torture chamber made to hold humans.

And that was why they'd believed Ash. Halflings were stupid, incompetent. When she claimed not to have abilities, they took it as a confirmation of what they thought they already knew, compounded by their belief that a young halfling demon wouldn't have the balls—or the skill—to lie to them. They only saw what they expected to see.

Just like Nicholas had, when he'd believed Ash's every action was part of a plot to destroy him. God. The irony was a killer. But at least he understood it. He could use that knowledge . . . hopefully.

Lucifer spoke. The demon looked up at Nicholas, knife in hand. "Did Khavi ever tell you what your Gift would be?'

"No." He'd have answered the same, even if she had.

The demon translated Lucifer's words again. "Then we'll find it."

Khavi had said that. *He will pull it from you.*

She'd known this. She'd known. What did that mean? More than anything, Khavi wanted Michael out of the field. So what did it mean that she'd known this would happen—and that she'd hoped for his Gift to manifest itself?

A Gift that he'd never have had . . . except that she'd also left him with Madelyn. So was this some kind of fucked-up plan? Was this not about an exchange or a bargain with Lucifer at all, but using Nicholas's Gift to free Michael? She couldn't have warned him, told him what she was looking for—or even what his Gift would be?

And what the fuck did it mean that Lucifer would pull it from him?

Lucifer approached him now. Ash's expression cracked, filled with horror. She pulled at her chains. Nicholas looked across the room, held her gaze. He'd make it through this. She'd make it through this.

He hoped his Gift would be the ability to tear demons apart with his mind.

Her eyes narrowed, her ferocity a bite through each word. "It'll be something you can use to kill them."

God, he loved her.

Pain ripped through his chest, as if his left pectoral had been shredded. He held Ash's gaze, refused to look down—but he could feel, could feel what Lucifer was doing: carving symbols into him.

The demon said, "These will only encourage the Gift to come, to stay, to be easily controlled, of course. To actually manifest, we must produce *trauma*." His mouth seemed to caress the word. "We must shock your body into thinking it will die, or shock you into saving someone else—"

Lucifer spoke sharply, cut him off. The demon fell to the floor, begging. Lucifer merely looked at him. The demon nodded, stabbed himself in the gut. Staggered to his feet.

"So," he continued, and held up his knife. "I will create that trauma now."

CHAPTER 20

She'd destroy them. With God as her witness, Ash would do *everything* in her power to see them dead.

She didn't know the demon's name but she would hunt him through the bowels of Hell, rip him apart with her teeth. And Lucifer, Lucifer . . . oh, death would not be enough. She would see him destroyed, beaten, crawling until he *begged* for mercy.

They had to be close to stopping. Nicholas couldn't have much blood left, and if they drained it all, he would die. Lucifer still hadn't gotten results. Just a few flares of Nicholas's Gift, bursts of power that carried his emotions with them—pain, fear. So much fear, it sank into her mind, made her scream and scream.

Music to their ears, no doubt.

Finally, Lucifer stepped away. The demon cowered again—fearing that he'd be punished for the failure?—but the demon lord only turned to Ash. He towered over her even though she hung above the floor, forcing her to look up at him, allowing Lucifer to look down at her. Trembling, Ash stifled the impulse to stare defiantly into his eyes, as if to say she wasn't afraid.

This wasn't the time. She *was* afraid, and surviving—escaping with Nicholas—was more important than defiance.

Lucifer's terrifying gaze raked over her body, and he spoke.

The demon translated, "He makes an offer, halfling. He will return your pathetic human memories of your parents, your childhood. He'll return your life to you, if you will agree to kill the Guardian. Your life in exchange for the Guardian's, and then he will let you go."

Not at the price of Nicholas's life. Never at that price.

For a moment, however, she let herself consider the rest. Rachel's parents, and their love for her. Oh, how she wanted to remember that. To have all of those missing pieces, filled in. But those weren't *her* memories; they were Rachel's. And if Rachel's past returned, so would she. Ash would be lost, ripped away on an incoming flood of memories.

Ash didn't need her life returned to her; she *had* one. And she recognized the irony that, when Lucifer had been creating her from Rachel's remains, he'd torn away the one thing that might have made her stop and reconsider, the one thing that could have left her uncertain as to whether she *should* sacrifice her life to save Rachel's: guilt. She was sorry for Rachel, but Ash refused to die to bring her back, and couldn't feel sorry for that.

In any case, Ash didn't believe for a moment that Rachel would make it out of here alive—or manage to save Nicholas. Whatever the reason behind Lucifer's offer, it wasn't to let her go. His offer had to be part of a plot.

After all, Nicholas hadn't been wrong about *all* demons. He'd just been wrong about her.

"No," she said.

Terrible silence reigned for a long moment. Finally, Lucifer spoke and left.

That was it? No gutting, no screaming? Ash couldn't believe that Nicholas's pain had been enough. So why not do the same to her?

The demon waited until the door shut, and his cower became a gleeful grimace. "I'm to sew up the Guardian and wait for him to heal," the demon said to her. "Then we start all over again. I am truly favored."

Ash bit her tongue. She'd seen the demon's reaction when Nicholas had spoken of Lucifer. She wouldn't give him any excuse.

His eyes narrowed, and he stepped closer, examining her

face. "We are not to spill your blood in this realm. Not even a drop. Do you know why? If your answer gives me power, I can reward you."

So that was why she wasn't being gutted. But she would not foul her mouth by answering him.

The demon shrugged. A roll of wire appeared in his hands—thin barbed wire. "So I'll sew him up, then."

God. And Nicholas was still conscious. He couldn't always hold her gaze; he was still awake. His jaw clenched now as the demon moved in front of him. Pain.

She had to get free. She had to get free now, while the demon's back was turned, while he worked. This might be their only opportunity.

The chain was fastened to the ceiling with some kind of big bolt. She wasn't sure she could break either, not just by swinging or moving. She'd have to brace herself, use her full strength—her feet against the wall, maybe. She couldn't swing that far. Pull herself up the chain, then, brace her feet on the ceiling—except the manacles held her hands too far apart. She couldn't grasp the chain between them. She already knew the steel wouldn't break.

. . . but her hand would.

God. Like a wolf chewing off his leg to get out of a trap? She would do it, she would do it.

But she didn't need to. She only needed her hand to fit through a hole the size of her wrist. So there was just a choice to make: What did she need more, her smaller fingers or her thumb?

She thought of her weapons in her cache. Chose the thumb.

The first bone snapped. Ash held in her cry, watching the demon for any sign that he'd heard it. No, she'd been making too much noise, rattling and screaming this whole time.

And he'd never believe the halfling would get free, but she had to hurry. He'd almost finished sewing, would turn around, and the opportunity would be lost.

Now the second bone. *Snap!* Oh, God. But it was working. Her hand slipped a little in the manacle. Nicholas's head came up. His eyes opened and met hers. His Gift flared.

The demon snipped off the end of the barbed wire and looked at him. "There is your Gift. I will tell—"

"Don't you want to be the first to know what it is?" Though

he was barely able to speak, Nicholas's voice covered the next *snap!*

"Tell me."

"I see fear. Yours. It's like a black ribbon, all around you. You fear Lucifer."

"As all demons do."

Snap!

Her hand slipped through. The chains rattled as she swung, unbalanced.

Nicholas smiled. "You should have feared *her.*"

Ash called in her boomstick. Thumb, forefinger. That was all she fucking needed.

The demon turned. Very close range, hellhound venom. She pulled the trigger. The boom echoed through the chamber. His face exploded.

"Loud," Nicholas said. "Go fast."

"I know." Before the demon had even collapsed to the floor, she'd vanished the weapon again, reached up for the chain. It took one good pull to haul herself up. Bracing her feet against the ceiling, she yanked. The bolt tore from stone in a shower of chips—she fell.

Between heartbeats, she flipped around, got her feet under her. Landed.

"My God, you're amazing."

She formed her wings, leapt for his chain. Pulled it free. He dropped—even she couldn't outrace gravity and catch him.

But he was sewn up, so nothing fell out.

He stood, his hands locked together in front of him. "Manacles?"

"No time. Here." She placed a crossbow in his hand. It would be awkward, but he could fire it. "Come on."

She shifted into her demon form, vanished her clothes—and vanished the manacle and chain, too.

Nicholas stared. "What the—"

"They aren't connected to the tower anymore," she realized. "They're ours now, so we can take them."

"Take mine."

Oh, that made it so much easier. She vanished the manacles, his chain. Facing the door, she took a deep breath. "We really need more training before we do this."

"We'll get it. After we get out."

She shoved open the door, ducked into the corridor. No glowing red eyes. Just screams.

A lot more screams than there had been before. The smell of ozone and charred flesh choked the air.

She expected the charred flesh. Not the ozone.

Oh. Oh . . . *She knew who that was.*

"Open your mental shields," she said. "Now. Let them find us."

Three pairs of glowing red eyes appeared in the middle of the corridor. Sir Pup. Jake stood in front of the hellhound, electricity arcing between his hands. Holding a bloodied sword, his skin blackened with soot, Hugh stared through the darkness toward them.

"Say your names," he said.

She started forward. "Ash and Nicholas."

"Truth."

Jake nodded. "Then get your asses over here, hang on to me. Let's get the fuck out of— *Oh, Jesus flippin' Christ.* St. Croix, what did they do to you?"

Nicholas took Ash's hand, reached out to touch Jake's arm.

"Strangely enough, they gave me a present. And Lucifer gave more than he bargained for."

They found a healer first.

Jake teleported them straight to Pim, sitting in the novice common room on the second floor of the Special Investigations warehouse. When she saw Nicholas, her *"Oh, my God!"* brought others running.

"Help him," Ash said.

Pim recovered a moment later, knelt in front of him. "All right—"

Nicholas shook his head. "Her hand, first."

"But—" Ash broke off when his mouth set. Okay. So he couldn't bear being healed while she was hurting. One day, she'd point out that she felt exactly the same way—but not today, if agreeing meant no more delay. She held out her hand to Pim. "Go."

The novice touched her palm. Warmth spread through Ash's fingers; she felt the bones shift back into place. When Pim drew her hand back, Ash bent her fingers—painlessly. Incredible. But would it be that simple for Nicholas?

Pim looked to him. "All right. You have to give me permission to vanish this wire first. It's yours."

"Then it's yours now," Nicholas said. He closed his eyes, clenching his teeth—bracing himself.

Taylor appeared next to Ash, gasped. Her hands rose to cover her mouth. "Oh, God. I'm so sorry. I'm so sorry I couldn't—"

Ash touched her shoulder, stopped her. "You tried. We appreciate it, very much."

"Okay, just relax. This won't hurt a bit." Though focused on Nicholas this time, the power of Pim's Gift spread like warm fingers against Ash's psyche. The wire vanished. The jagged wounds left behind smoothed into tanned skin, hard muscle. "All done."

Nicholas blinked his eyes open. "That's it?"

"Yep." Pim nodded. "That's it."

With a wild laugh, Ash threw herself at him. His arms wrapped around her, held her tight.

"I love you," he said against her hair. "And my God, you're amazing."

Easy for her. She hadn't been the one ripped open. Pulling back to look up at him, she made certain that everything was in place, that he hadn't hidden any lingering pain. But, no. His eyes glowed blue, and he was just as beautiful as ever.

She looked over at the sound of heels running up the stairs. Lilith appeared, her gaze searching for Hugh, for Sir Pup, and the tension in her face eased when she spotted them both. Her mouth softened into a smile.

"You made it back, then?"

"As I told you we would," Hugh said.

"So you did, martyr." She said it fondly, and her brows arched when she saw Ash with her arms wrapped around Nicholas. "You made it, too. Both of you. I'm impressed. Now, can you tell us what the fuck Khavi was thinking?"

"I think so," Nicholas said, and Ash felt the sudden, subtle tightening of his body against hers. "Or you can ask her."

Heart pounding, Ash glanced around. Khavi had appeared in the common room, standing at the end of the hallway leading to the novices' quarters.

A gun appeared in Taylor's hand. "Get out," she said. "Now."

"What did Lucifer fear?" Khavi looked to Nicholas. "We need to know."

"Not much." Nicholas surprised Ash by answering. "Not much at all. But there were two things I felt clearly: He fears Michael, and he fears that you'll discover that Ash can free everyone in the frozen field. He didn't intend to enter into a bargain. But he also didn't dare to spill her blood."

"How?" Khavi whispered, stepping forward.

Taylor shook her head.

Khavi looked from Ash to Taylor's gun. "I can't see everything, but I *can* see the symbols from here, if you shift to human form again."

After a glance at Nicholas, who nodded, Ash shifted.

"And she's naked again," Pim said.

Ash grinned. Nicholas laughed, kissed her brow.

"There it is," Khavi breathed. "The symbols are necessary for her transformation, so I looked before, but I did not see them as part of this arrangement. The symbols are not *meant* to work together as they are written, but they *could* be put together—and if you had agreed to reverse the transformation, the proper arrangement would have been gone."

"He asked if I wanted to be Rachel again," Ash said. "I think he meant to torture Nicholas until I agreed."

"Oh, yes. Probably so much that you would agree to kill Nicholas just to put him out of his misery. That sounds very much like Lucifer." Khavi's focus dropped to the symbols again. "I can make the proper spell from these, one that would free everyone in the field. But why does he fear releasing all of them *so* much? Michael, I can understand. But the others? I do not know."

Did it even matter? Lucifer feared it. That was good enough for Ash.

"It will free *everyone* in the frozen field?" she asked. "Everyone? Even someone sacrificed at the same time the spell is cast?"

"Yes," Khavi said.

Hugh spoke. "Truth."

Ash looked at Nicholas, who was shaking his head.

"No, Ash. We can't risk—"

"You saw them," she said. "You saw *all* of them. Tell me again that I shouldn't risk this."

He couldn't. So he tried something else. "It would free a lot of demons, too."

"Who are trapped behind a Gate." Ash's gaze searched his, saw the denial there. "In five hundred years, you can kill Madelyn again."

He didn't even smile. "That's not—"

"I know." She caught his face between her hands. "I know that doesn't matter. But the others trapped there *do* matter—those who are like Rachel. And it will hurt Lucifer. There is such high return on this risk . . . and we know Khavi speaks the truth. I'll be freed again, too."

"But you'll return to the field first. Only for a moment, perhaps—but that is an eternity too long. You tell *me* that it is worth the risk. You wouldn't do it before."

"Maybe," she said, and ran her fingers over his newly healed skin. "But I have another reason now. Revenge. You got Madelyn. Let me have Lucifer. It won't kill him, but if it hurts him, I need to do it."

"I can't watch you die," he said hoarsely.

Of course he couldn't. Even though he was a Guardian, even though it would free so many, her life was still his limit.

"I'll come back. Believe me, Nicholas. I've been creating too many naked plots involving you to even think about dying now. But if you hold on to me through it, I'll have reason to come back even faster."

"God." He buried his face in her hair. Breathed deep, as if drawing her in. "You need me. I'll be damned if I ever let you go. Believe that, Ash."

She did. If there were only two things that would never change, would never crumble or fade, she knew what they were.

"I love you." She kissed him. "And I do believe."

Taylor's voice came from beside her, full of disbelief and something else. Hope? "So you're actually doing this?"

"Yes," Ash said. "As soon as possible, before I feel differently."

"We'll have to prepare," Khavi said. "I'll need to cut the proper symbols into your skin to cast the spell—and to draw you back to your body when it is done. And you'll need to break a bargain first."

Simple enough. "Nicholas," she said, and when he looked at

her his eyes glowed so fiercely, Ash's own eyes burned. "I need to make a new bargain with you."

"How can I?" he said hoarsely.

"Because you love me. Because you're strong. Because you're a Guardian now. And because of all that, I'm not afraid to do this."

"You will rip my heart out." He closed his eyes. "And I would tear it out myself for you. What will the bargain be?"

Not his death sentence, as his tone suggested. Ash smiled up at him. "You will tell me that you love me, and I will *not* kiss you. Agreed?"

"If it were true, I'd never say that I loved you again."

"I know. And since I need to hear it and to kiss you, I will gladly break this one. Are we agreed?"

His lips parted. His throat worked. It was still another moment before he said, "We are agreed."

Bound in another bargain. She stared up at him, waiting for the fear, the delayed terror, the regret. She could change her mind, and he would instantly release her. He probably hoped she would now.

But she couldn't. "Nicholas?"

His eyes blazed. He caught her face, stared into her eyes—and though he hadn't said it yet, she felt the love blasting through his shields, filling her mind, wrapping around her as if to hold and protect.

"I love you," he said. "I will *always* love you."

Little wonder there was no fear in her. There couldn't be, not in the face of this. Smiling, she pulled him down to her lips.

And gladly damned herself with a familiar, perfect kiss.

CHAPTER 21

When she'd been a girl, Taylor had believed that, one day, someone would hold her like Nicholas St. Croix held his halfling demon at the edge of the frozen field. Someone would look at her with the same fierce love, that he would hold her through anything, even if it killed him. She'd wanted that for herself.

She didn't want that now. She just wanted to be free of Michael. Wanted to be free of the man who would prevent her from helping two people desperately in need. Wanted to be free of the screaming, the shattering, the darkness that never left.

She wanted it more than anything. He'd pushed her past her limits.

It was the only explanation she had, for how she ever lifted a knife, and plunged it through the symbols marking a good woman's back.

The woman and her man cried out together, and his tears ran as hot as her blood. Taylor staggered away from them, sank to her knees in red sand. They'd trusted her to do it. They'd asked her to be the one. Killing a demon—even a good one—wouldn't break the Rules.

But until now, Taylor would have said that it broke *her* rules.

She'd had a choice. She could have said no. But she wanted freedom too much.

The first crack appeared when the first drop of blood hit the sand. Taylor heard the drop, she heard the crack—though she'd never heard any sound from that frozen field. Louder than the rain of blood falling, louder than Nicholas chanting Ash's name, begging her to come back now.

Another crack, then more, thin lines spidering between the faces. Frozen lashes blinked. Screams began, loud now, from thawing throats.

Far away, a large crowd of demons were scattering across the ice. She thought that if Nicholas had looked with his Gift, those demons would be trailing black ribbons of fear.

But he wasn't looking. He was staring into Ash's eyes, searching desperately for new signs of life in a body that Taylor had killed.

A fist punched through the ice from below, a fist that had never been frozen, only devoured again and again. And suddenly, that was the only sound—of the damned, breaking through, climbing out of their eternity of torture. Some wandered, dazed. Some grabbed the hands of others, helped lift them out. Others screamed and screamed, as if it were too late to feel anything different.

Taylor wondered if she should tell them now that they weren't free, not truly. Unless they went to the Pit, they were never leaving Hell. Unlike Ash, they didn't have a body with symbols inscribed on it to bring her spirit back to the right place—they *only* possessed their spirit, and that could only take physical form in Hell. Unlike Michael, they didn't have someone waiting at the edge of the frozen field, waiting to take his body out of her cache.

So that she'd be free.

Why weren't any demons coming out of the field yet? Where were their *faces*? Despite the thousands, hundreds of thousands in the field, the only demons were those who'd been torturing Michael.

All the demons gone. What would that mean for a demon halfling?

Oh, God. Had Khavi lied? Had Ash agreed, not knowing that Khavi meant a twisted version of 'free'?

"Ash? Oh, God, you're amazing. I love you." Joy filled Nicholas's voice, and quelled Taylor's sudden panic. "Jake, get her to a healer, now!"

Then the sound of his hard kiss against soft lips before they disappeared.

Michael had kissed Taylor, too. That was how all of this had started. The strange insanity of it.

Soon, she'd go back to normal.

At the back of her mind, the darkness suddenly eased. Not so much hidden pain. A deep, feral joy. Michael, climbing free.

Finally.

From behind her, she heard the sharpness of Khavi's indrawn breath. It must have been nice, watching everything that she'd worked for become true. No matter who it hurt, no matter who paid in blood and pain and the horrifying sacrifices they ended up making—

"I did *not* see this coming," Khavi said.

An enormous, terrifying figure rose in the distance, amber scales glistening. Fire roared. Taylor heard the screams begin again, flying toward her, almost with wings of their own. Demons took to the sky, desperately trying to flee. A rush of fire caught them, sent them spinning, burning to the ground.

"A dragon?" Instinctively, she drew back. No need to run, not yet. "Did it break through from Chaos?"

"No." Khavi's gaze followed the dragon up, up. "That's Michael."

Michael?

The dragon dove, began banking toward them.

"Taylor, teleport now."

"But—"

"Trust me."

Taylor didn't. She wouldn't ever trust Khavi again, but as another roar of fire roasted a swath of fleeing demons in a path toward them, she saw Khavi's point.

She called upon the power of Michael's Gift . . . and got nothing. It was there, in the back of her mind. She could feel it. She couldn't use it. A tumble of emotions rioted through the space he used to occupy, but there was only one rising above all the others.

Hunger.

Oh, Jesus. Taylor stumbled back, searched for the Gift again and again. "He won't let me go!"

And was it just her, or was that dragon coming really fucking close?

Khavi's Gift rolled out. The dragon shrieked. Enormous wings folded against its back, and he dove.

Straight toward her.

"Khavi!"

The woman grabbed Taylor's hand—and they were standing in Caelum, watching Michael's temple fall. Columns cracked. Marble walls buckled and collapsed, crashing together in a billowing plume of pale dust.

Taylor pushed her hands into her hair, tried to push her brains back in. That had not just happened. Had it?

And what now?

One person would know the answer to that question. Taylor spun around to face Khavi. "You used your Gift. What did you see?"

Mouth open in shock, Khavi shook her head. "I didn't see anything in its future at all."

Oh, God. So, the oldest and most powerful Guardian, the man stuck in her brain, had become a hungry dragon . . . and they had no idea what was coming next.

Was that strange or normal? Taylor couldn't decide if it even mattered. She only knew that she wasn't free.

Not yet.

Either the meeting in Caelum had run longer than the Guardians had anticipated or Nicholas was Enthralled again.

Last week, only a few hours after they'd returned from Hell and Pim had healed the stab wound in Ash's back, the sparkle of broken glass against asphalt had kept him in the Special Investigations' parking lot for almost forty-five minutes. There hadn't been another Enthrallment since—and even if there had been, Ash trained during the same twelve hours that he did, so she'd always been there to make certain the infrequent Enthrallments didn't leave him vulnerable as they traveled between the warehouse and their apartment downtown.

Not today. She couldn't travel to Caelum with him, and the warehouse was empty of Guardians, so she'd remained at the penthouse and worked, instead.

Now she worried—an emotion still new to Ash, and one that, rationally, she knew shouldn't be affecting her. He'd make it home. Of that she had no doubt. The Guardians took care of their own . . . and the halflings that they called their own.

Standing in her private rooftop garden, Ash searched the cloud-darkened sky one last time. She loved the height of the building—at night, she could easily fly off the edge without attracting notice, and soon Nicholas would be able to come and go as he pleased, too. Now, she hoped to see the approach of a Guardian bringing him in, but aside from the distant planes and nearer birds, the sky was empty.

With a sigh, she forced herself to return inside. Sparsely furnished, simplistic, and a little rustic, the penthouse wasn't as slickly decorated and no longer looked as contemporary as the day she'd moved in, but Ash liked it. All that she and Nicholas needed was an office and a bed—and the bed was usually optional.

So was the floor, the bath—and once, the ceiling. If there was one thing to be said for her demon form, her talons could *cling.*

The ding of the elevator made her pause in the middle of the living room. Nicholas. Her heart began pounding, anticipation building a slow burn through her veins. Would she always feel this with him?

God, she hoped so.

But for now, a quick plot: She would keep her distance from him until he couldn't stand the separation any longer. How long would it take?

Not long, she thought. Not long at all.

She vanished her clothes as he came through the door—mussed. What the hell? They hadn't been training today. He'd left looking like Stone Cold St. Croix, and now his tie was askew, his hair slightly disheveled.

"Is everything all right?" Forgetting her plot, she went to him, instead. "Did you run into a demon? Did the Guardians have a brawl in Caelum?"

Shaking his head, he grinned and closed the door, leaned back against it with his hands in his pockets. Playing hard to get? She could win this. Ash pressed up against him, lifted her mouth to his neck and began to nibble.

"No, that went well," he said, and his voice was a delicious reverberation against her lips. "The whole place is still rubble, and we've started a revolution among the novices. Now that they have nowhere to go in Caelum, they all want their own apartments instead of being stuck at the warehouse twenty-four/seven."

Good for them. "Most of them are older than us, anyway. And Michael?"

"Still a dragon, as far as anyone knows. Khavi mentioned using Taylor as bait. Taylor wasn't thrilled."

"I'm not surprised." Ash breathed in—stopped short. "Why do you smell like dog?"

His laugh shot out, echoing in the room. "Would you believe that I was Enthralled by one?"

"No, not really." She pulled back to look at him. Beneath the laughter lay something else. The love, she recognized. Not the shame. "What happened?"

"I went to a shelter." He closed his eyes, tipped his head back against the door. "I planned to bring home a puppy for you. And I found one, a little Jack Russell. God, it was almost like Enthrallment. He licked my face and I fell half in love with him right there in the kennel. But then I realized—I couldn't."

Something inside her froze. But he wouldn't think that she'd hurt it—he didn't believe that any more. Did he?

"Why couldn't you?"

Something in her voice must have betrayed her. His eyes flew open, suddenly blazing blue. He caught her face in his hands, shook his head. "No. Not that. Never that."

Her throat felt thick. "Then why?"

"Ash . . . I swore I'd never hurt you again. Ever. But a dog won't live forever. In fifteen, twenty years, you're going to be hurting like hell, just because I brought a puppy home today. I can't do that to you."

"Oh." Now the ache moved from her throat to her chest, so sweet, so perfect. "It'll hurt. But I think I'd rather have fifteen or twenty years with him. I think he'd prefer that, too."

Nicholas slipped her hair behind her ear, studying her face. "Are you certain? I'll call them now, and we'll go back tomorrow morning. You can see him first before you decide."

"I'm certain," she said. "Wouldn't you prefer it, too? Any amount of pain is worth feeling like this, no matter how short of a time we have."

"It's worth it." He drew her in, kissed her hard. "I'd have gone to Hell and picked you out a hellhound puppy, but I think Sir Pup would eat it, defending his territory."

God. "He won't eat a terrier puppy?"

"I asked Lilith. She said we should bring the puppy in during training, that it would do Sir Pup good to learn restraint, and that he could teach the puppy how to be a halfling's companion."

An evil puppy at Ash's heels? She could get used to that.

"She's grooming me," Ash said. "I'm going to be just like her in two thousand years."

Nicholas's face darkened slightly. "I hope not."

Oh. She looked up at him, and knew he was remembering the cabin, Lilith's manipulation. "I think she lied, you know."

"Which time?"

Ash had to smile at that. Yes, that fit Lilith very well. "When she said that she'd sacrifice one for the good of all."

"You don't think she would?"

"Maybe." If pushed to her limits. "But she's not stupid—and the smartest thing she could have done in that cabin would be to let Sir Pup kill me, then and there. To not take any chances that Madelyn might find me, that the Gate might be opened. She didn't do that. I *believed* she would, though."

"So did I," Nicholas said.

"And why wouldn't we? Two thousand years, that's a lot of people who must have died around her. So what's one more person? It wouldn't mean anything, right? But I think that's where we went wrong. Because when you see all of those people die—or just a few like the Boyles, like Rachel or your parents—then one more person isn't *nothing*."

"It's everything," he said. "One more person means everything."

"Yes." She rose up, kissed him. "So I wouldn't mind being her in two thousand years."

"I think you'll be better."

"Because you love me."

"I do." Palms sliding to her ass, he lifted her against him. "So what's your plot today?"

She ran her fingers down his stomach, closed over his thick length. Hard, ready for her. "I plan to see whether I can reach your limit with just my hands."

Keep reading for a special preview of Meljean Brook's next Iron Seas novel

HEART OF STEEL

Coming November 2011 from Berkley Sensation!

CHAPTER 1

Yasmeen hadn't had any reason to fly her airship into the small Danish township of Fladstrand before, but her reputation had obviously preceded her. All along the Scandinavian coast, rum dives served as a town's only line of defense against mercenaries and pirates—and as soon as the sky paled and *Lady Corsair* became visible on the eastern horizon, lights began appearing in the windows of the public houses alongside the docks. The taverns were opening early, hoping to make a few extra deniers before midday . . . and the good citizens of Fladstrand were probably praying that her crew wouldn't venture beyond the docks and into the town itself.

Unfortunately for them, *Lady Corsair*'s crew wasn't in Fladstrand to drink. Nor were they here to cause trouble, but Yasmeen wasn't inclined to let the town know that. Letting them tremble for a while did her reputation good.

Dawn had completely faded from the sky by the time *Lady Corsair* breached the mouth of the harbor. Yasmeen stood behind the windbreak on the quarterdeck, her spyglass aimed at the skyrunners tethered over the docks. She recognized each airship—all of them served as passenger ferries between the Danish islands to the east and Sweden to the north. Several heavy-bottomed cargo ships floated in the middle of the icy harbor, their canvas sails furled and their wooden hulls rocking with each swell. Though she knew the skyrunners, Yasmeen couldn't identify every ship in the water. Most of Fladstrand fished or farmed—two activities unrelated to the sort of business Yasmeen conducted. Whatever cargo the ships carried probably fermented or flopped, and she had no interest in either until they reached her mug or her plate.

When *Lady Corsair*'s long shadow passed over the flat, sandy shoreline and the first rows of houses overlooking the sea, Yasmeen ordered the engines cut. Their huffing and vibrations gave way to the flap of the airship's unfurling sails and the cawing protests of the seabirds whose flight paths had been interrupted by the balloon. Below, the narrow cobblestone streets lay almost empty. A steamcart puttered along beside an ass-drawn wagon loaded with wooden barrels, but most of the good people of Fladstrand scrambled back to their homes as soon as they spotted *Lady Corsair* in the skies above them—hiding behind locked doors and shuttered windows, hoping that whatever business Yasmeen had wouldn't involve them.

They were in luck. Today, Yasmeen only sought one woman: Zenobia Fox, author of several popular stories that Yasmeen had read to pieces, and sister to a charming antiquities salvager whose adventures Zenobia based her stories on . . . a man that Yasmeen had recently killed.

Yasmeen had also killed their father and taken over his airship, renaming her *Lady Corsair.* That had happened some time ago, however, and no one would consider Emmerich Gunther-Baptiste *charming*, including his daughter. Yasmeen had seen Zenobia Fox once before, though the girl had been called Geraldine Gunther-Baptiste then. As one of the mercenary crew aboard Gunther-Baptiste's skyrunner, Yasmeen had watched an awkward girl with mousy-brown braids wave farewell to her father from the docks. Zenobia had been standing next to her pale and worn-looking mother.

Neither she nor her mother had appeared sorry to see him go.

Would Zenobia be sorry that her brother was dead? Yasmeen didn't know, but it promised to be an entertaining encounter. She hadn't looked forward to meeting someone this much since Archimedes Fox had first boarded *Lady Corsair*—and before she'd learned that he was really Wolfram Gunther-Baptiste, not the writer she'd been led to believe he was. Hopefully, her acquaintance with his sister wouldn't end the same way, with Yasmeen throwing Zenobia to a mob of zombies.

A familiar grunt came from Yasmeen's left. *Lady Corsair*'s quartermaster stood at the port rail, consulting a hand-drawn map before casting a derisive look over the town.

Yasmeen tucked her scarf beneath her chin so the heavy wool wouldn't muffle her voice. "Is there a problem with the directions, Monsieur Rousseau?"

To avoid the ridiculousness of asking around town for Zenobia's location—and giving someone a chance to warn the woman that a mercenary was coming for her—Yasmeen had overpaid a Fladstrander fisherman for the information, instead. If he'd misdirected them, Yasmeen wouldn't hesitate to ask for her money back.

Rousseau pushed his striped scarf away from his mouth, exposing his short black beard. With gloved hands, he gestured to the rows of houses, each one identical to the next in all but color. "Only that they are exactly the same, captain. But it is not a problem. It is simply an irritant."

Yasmeen nodded. She didn't doubt Rousseau could find the house. Though hopeless with a sword or gun, her quartermaster could interpret the most rudimentary of maps as if they'd been drawn by skilled cartographers. That ability, combined with his expressive grunts and eyebrows that could wordlessly discipline or praise the aviators—and a booming voice for when nothing but words would do—made him the most valuable member of Yasmeen's crew. A significant number of jobs that Yasmeen took in Europe required *Lady Corsair* to navigate through half-remembered terrain and landmarks. Historical maps of the continent were easy to come by, but matching their details to the overgrown ruins that existed now demanded another skill entirely—that of reading the story of the Horde's centuries-long occupation.

Though not ruins, Fladstrand's identical rows of houses told another tale, one that Yasmeen had seen repeated all along the Scandinavian coastlines.

In one of her adventures, Zenobia Fox had written that the worth of any society could be judged by measuring the length of time it took for dissenters to go from the street to the noose. Zenobia might have based that statement on the history of her adopted Danish home; a few centuries ago, that time hadn't been long at all. Soon after the Horde's war machines had broken through the Hapsburg wall, the zombie infection had outpaced their armies, and the steady trickle of refugees from eastern Europe had opened into a flood. Those who had the means bought passage aboard a ship to the New World, but those without money or connections migrated north, pushing farther and farther up the Jutland Peninsula until they crowded the northern tip. Some fled across the sea to Norway and Sweden, while others bargained for passage to the Danish islands. Those refugees who were left built rows of shacks, and waited for the Horde and the zombies to come.

Neither had. The Horde hadn't pressed farther north than the Limfjord, a shallow sound that cut across the tip of Jutland, separating it from the rest of the peninsula and creating an island of the area. The same stretch of water stopped most of the zombies; walls built near the sound stopped the rest. And although poverty and unrest had plagued the crowded refugees, and the noose had seen frequent use, the region slowly recovered. Rows of shacks became rows of houses. Now quiet and stable, many of the settlements attracted families from England, recently freed from Horde occupation, and from the New World. Zenobia Fox and her brother had made up one of those families.

"We are coming over her home now, captain." Rousseau's announcement emerged in frozen puffs. "How long do you intend to visit with her?"

How long would it take to say that Archimedes had discovered a valuable artifact before Yasmeen had killed him, and then pay the woman off? With luck, Zenobia Fox would send Yasmeen on her way in a fit of self-righteous fury—though it might be more entertaining if she tried to send Yasmeen off with a gun. In both scenarios, Yasmeen would hold on to all of the money, which suited her perfectly.

"Not long," she predicted. "Lower the ladder."

Rousseau relayed the order, and within moments, the crew unrolled the rope ladder over *Lady Corsair*'s side. Yasmeen glanced down. Zenobia's orange, three-level home sat between two identical houses painted a pale yellow. Unlike many of the houses in Fladstrand, the levels hadn't been split into three separate flats. The slate roof was in good repair, the trim around the windows fresh. Lace curtains prevented Yasmeen from looking into the rooms. Wrought-iron flower boxes filled with frosted-over soil projected from beneath each windowsill.

Large and well tended, the house provided ample room for one woman. Yasmeen supposed that much space was the best someone could hope for when living in a town—but she couldn't have tolerated being anchored to one place. Why would Zenobia Fox? She had based her adventures on her brother's travels, but why not travel herself? Yasmeen couldn't understand it. Perhaps money had been a factor—although by the look of her home, Zenobia didn't lack funds.

No matter. After Yasmeen paid her off, Zenobia wouldn't need to base her stories on Archimedes's adventures. She could go as she pleased—or not—and it wouldn't be any concern of Yasmeen's.

As this was a social visit, she'd removed the guns usually tucked into her wide crimson belt. At the beginning of the month, she'd traded her short aviator's jacket for a long winter overcoat, and the two pistols concealed in her deep pockets provided enough protection, backed up by the daggers tucked into the tops of her boots, easily reachable at mid-thigh. She checked her hair, making certain that her blue kerchief covered the tips of her tufted ears. If necessary, she could use her braids to do the same, but the kerchief was more distinctive. There would be no doubt exactly who had dropped in on Zenobia Fox today.

The ladder swayed when Yasmeen hopped over the rail and let the first rung catch her weight. Normally she'd have slid down quickly and landed with an acrobatic flourish, but her woolen gloves didn't slide over the rope well—and Yasmeen didn't know how long she would be waiting on the doorstep. She wouldn't risk cold, stiff fingers that made drawing a knife or pulling a trigger more difficult, not for the sake of a flip or two.

The neighbors might have appreciated it, though. All along the street, lace curtains twitched. When Yasmeen pounded the brass knocker on Zenobia's front door, many became bold enough to show their faces at the windows—probably thanking the heavens that she hadn't knocked at their doors.

No one peeked through the curtains at Zenobia's house. The door simply opened, revealing a pretty blond woman in a pale blue dress. Though a rope ladder swung behind Yasmeen and a skyrunner hovered over the street, the woman didn't glance up.

A dull-witted maid, Yasmeen guessed. Or a poor, dull-witted relation. She knew very little about current fashion, but even she could see that although the dress was constructed of good materials and sewn well, the garment sagged in the bodice and the hem piled on the floor.

She must have recognized Yasmeen as a foreigner, however. A thick Germanic accent gutted her French, the common trader's language. "May I help you?"

"I need to speak with Miss Zenobia Fox." Yasmeen smoothed the Arabic from her own accent, hoping to avoid an absurd comedy of misunderstandings on the doorstep. "Is she at home?"

The woman's eyebrows lifted in a regal arch. "I am she."

This wasn't a maid? How unexpected. Despite the large house and obvious money, Zenobia Fox opened her own door?

Yasmeen liked surprises; they made everything so much more interesting. She'd never have guessed that the awkward girl with mousy-brown braids would have bloomed into this delicate blond thing.

She'd never have guessed that her first impression of the woman who penned clever and exciting tales would be "dull-witted."

Archimedes certainly hadn't been. Quick with a laugh or clever response, he'd perfectly fit Yasmeen's image of *Archimedes Fox, Adventurer.* She could see nothing of Archimedes in this woman—not in the soft shape of her face or the blue of her eyes, and certainly not in her manner. Zenobia had either grown to resemble her mother, or her mother had dallied while Emmerich had been away.

"I am *Lady Corsair*'s captain." Kerchief over the hair, indecently snug trousers, a skyrunner that had once belonged to her father floating over her house—was this woman completely blind? "Your brother recently traveled on my airship."

"Yes, I know. How can I help you?"

How can I help you? Disbelieving, Yasmeen stared at the woman. Could an aviator's daughter be this sheltered? What else could it mean when the captain of a vessel appeared on her doorstep? Every time that Yasmeen had knocked on a door belonging to one of her crew members' families, the understanding had been immediate. Sometimes it had been accompanied by denial, grief, or anger—but they all knew what it meant when she arrived.

Perhaps because Archimedes had been a passenger rather than her crew, Zenobia didn't expect it. But the woman should have made the connection by now.

"Shall we go inside?" Yasmeen suggested. "I'm afraid I have unfortunate news regarding your brother."

The "unfortunate news" must have clued her in. Zenobia blinked, her hand flying to her chest. "Archimedes?"

At a time like this, she called him Archimedes—not Wolfram, the name she'd have known him by for most of her life? Either they'd completely adopted their new identities, or this was an act.

If it was an act, this encounter was already turning out better than Yasmeen had anticipated. There was a small chance Archimedes Fox might be alive—which wouldn't displease Yasmeen at all. She didn't regret tossing him over the side of her ship, because he'd left her little choice. But when Yasmeen killed a man, she preferred to do it for reasons other than his stupidity.

If he had survived, perhaps he'd already contacted his sister. That might account for her strange behavior.

Yasmeen couldn't be certain, however, until Zenobia said more. "Perhaps we can speak inside, Miss Fox."

"Yes, of course."

Zenobia led the way into a parlor, her too-long skirts dragging on the wooden floor. A writing desk sat by the window, stacked with papers. No ink stained Zenobia's fingers. Obviously, she hadn't been busy writing the next Archimedes Fox adventure.

A shelf over the fireplace held several baubles, some worn by age, others encrusted with dirt—a silver snuffbox, a lady's miniature portrait, a gold tooth. All items that Archimedes had collected during his salvaging runs in Europe, Yasmeen realized. All items that he'd picked from the ruins, but hadn't sold. Why keep these?

Her gaze returned to the lady in the miniature. Soft brown hair, warm eyes, a plain dress. The description seemed familiar, though Yasmeen knew she hadn't seen this portrait before. No, it was a description from *Archimedes Fox and the Specter of Notre Dame*. In the story, Archimedes Fox had found a similar miniature clutched in a skeleton's fingers, and the mystery surrounding the woman's identity had led the adventurer to a treasure hidden beneath the ruined cathedral.

How odd that she'd never realized that fictional miniature had a real-life counterpart. That she'd never imagined him digging it out of the muck somewhere and bringing it to his sister. That he'd once held it, as she did now.

The stupid man. She hoped he wasn't dead.

Yasmeen lied often, and so she didn't care that he'd lied about his identity when he'd arranged for passage on her airship. Had she not discovered who he was, she'd have invited him to her bed—and he'd have come, would have submitted to her demands, because he'd wanted her.

But she could never offer an invitation after he'd made a fool of her in front of her crew.

It didn't matter that he'd lied. It *did* matter that she'd allowed Emmerich Gunther-Baptiste's son aboard her airship without knowing who he really was. It didn't matter that his son hadn't been seeking revenge.

But Archimedes *could* have been seeking revenge, and her crew knew it. A threat had sneaked onto *Lady Corsair* right beneath her nose.

She couldn't forgive him for that. Too often, she led her crew into dangerous territory, and they would only be loyal to a strong captain. A captain they could trust. She'd invested years making certain that her crew could trust her, and rewarded their loyalty with scads of money.

There wasn't enough money in the world to convince a crew to follow a fool, and Archimedes Fox had come close to turning her into one. She'd only been saved because he'd openly thanked her for killing his father, negating his potential threat. He'd become a joke, instead.

And later, when he *had* threatened her in front of the crew, she'd gotten rid of him . . . maybe.

Yasmeen turned to Zenobia, who stood quietly in the center of the parlor, tears trailing over her pink cheeks.

"So Archimedes . . . is dead?" she whispered.

Funny how that terrible accent came and went. "Dead," Yasmeen echoed. "Unfortunate, as I said. He was so very handsome."

"Oh, my brother!" Zenobia buried her face in her hands.

Yasmeen let her sob for a minute. "Do you want to know how he died?"

Zenobia lifted her head. She took a second to compose herself, sniffling into a lace handkerchief, her blue eyes bright with more tears. "Well, yes, I suppose—"

"I killed him. I dropped him from my airship into a pack of flesh-eating zombies."

The other woman had nothing to say to that. She stared at Yasmeen, her fingers twisting in the handkerchief.

"He tried to take control of my ship. You understand." Yasmeen flopped onto a sofa and hooked her leg over the arm. Zenobia's face reddened and she averted her gaze. Not accustomed to seeing a woman in trousers, apparently. "He hasn't come around for a visit, has he?"

"A visit?" Her head came back around, eyes wide. "But—"

"I tossed him into a canal. Venice is still full of them, did you know?"

Zenobia shook her head.

"Well, some are more swamp than canal, but they are still there—and zombies don't go into the water. We both know that Archimedes has escaped more dire situations than that, at least according to his adventures. You've read your brother's stories, Miss Fox, haven't you?"

"Of . . . course."

"He mentions the canals in *Archimedes Fox and the Mermaid of Venice*."

"Oh, yes. I'd forgotten."

There was no Mermaid of Venice adventure, yet the woman who'd supposedly written it didn't even realize she'd been caught in her lie. Pitiful.

But the question remained: Did that mean Zenobia wasn't the author after all, or was this not Zenobia?

Yasmeen suspected the latter.

"So he might be alive?" Zenobia ventured.

"He still had his equipment and plenty of weapons. But if he hasn't contacted you after a month now . . . he must be dead, I'm sorry to say." Yasmeen meant it, but she wasn't sorry for the next. "And so that's the second man in your family I've killed."

Surprise and dismay flashed across her expression. "Yes, of course. My . . ."

She trailed off into a sob. Oh, that was good cover.

"Father." Yasmeen helped her along.

"Yes, my father. After he . . . did something terrible, too."

That was good, too. Smart not to suggest that the armed woman sitting in the room had been at fault.

Obviously, this woman had no idea whom she'd targeted by taking Zenobia Fox's place. If asked, she'd probably say that her father's surname had been Fox, as well. She wouldn't know that Emmerich Gunther-Baptiste had once tried to roast a mutineer alive. Yasmeen hadn't had any love for the mutineer—but she'd shot him in the head anyway, to put him out of his misery. She'd shot Gunther-Baptiste when he'd ordered the other mercenaries to put her on the roasting spit in the mutineer's place. When Yasmeen realized that she'd attained a beauty of an airship in the process, she'd shot every other crew member who tried to take it from her.

After a while, they'd stopped trying.

"Was it terrible? I've killed so many people, I forget what my reasons were." A lie, but she wasn't the only one telling them. Now it was time to find out this woman's reasons. With a belabored sigh, Yasmeen climbed to her feet. "That's all I've come to tell you. A few of Archimedes's belongings are still in my ship. Would you like them, or should I distribute them among my crew?"

"Oh, yes. That's fine." For a moment, the blond seemed distracted and uncertain. Then her shoulders squared, and she said, "My brother hired you to take him to Venice, and was searching for a specific item. Did he find it . . . before he died?"

Ah, so that's what it was. Yasmeen had spoken to three art dealers about locating a buyer for the sketch Archimedes Fox had found in Venice. A flying machine drawn by the great Leonardo da Vinci, the sketch was valuable beyond measure.

She'd demanded that the dealers be discreet in their inquiries. Not even Yasmeen's crew knew what she'd locked away in her cabin. But obviously, someone had talked.

"It was a fake," Yasmeen lied.

No uncertainty weakened Zenobia's expression now. "I'd still like to have it. As a memento."

Yasmeen nodded. "If you'll show me out, I'll retrieve it for you now." She followed the woman out of the parlor and into the hallway. "Will you hold the rope ladder for me? It's so unsteady."

"Of course." All smiles, Zenobia reached the front door.

Yasmeen didn't give her a chance to open it. Slapping her gloved hand over the blond's mouth, she kicked the woman's knees out from beneath her. Yasmeen slammed her against the floor and shoved her knife against the woman's throat.

Quietly, she hissed, "Where is Zenobia Fox?"

The woman struggled for breath. "I am Zen—"

A press of the blade cut off the woman's lie. Yasmeen smiled, and the woman's skin paled.

Her smile frequently had that effect.

"Your hair smells of tobacco smoke but your clothes don't. The dress doesn't fit you. You've tried to take Zenobia's place but you've no idea who you're pretending to be. Where is she?" When the woman's lips pressed together in an unmistakable response, Yasmeen let her blade taste blood. The woman whimpered. "I imagine that you're working with someone. You didn't think of this yourself. Is he waiting upstairs?"

The woman's eyelids flickered. Answer enough.

"I can kill you now, and ask him instead," Yasmeen said.

That made her willing to talk. Her lips parted. Yasmeen didn't allow her enough air to make a sound.

"Is Zenobia in the house? Nod once if yes."

Nod.

"Is she alive?"

Nod.

Good. Yasmeen might not kill this woman, now. She eased back just enough to let the woman respond. "Where did you hear about the sketch?"

"Port Fallow," she whispered. "We also knew you were looking for Fox's sister. We realized he must have found the sketch on his last salvaging run."

Yasmeen had only spoken to one art dealer in Port Fallow: Franz Kessler. Damn his loose tongue. She'd make certain he wouldn't talk out of turn again—especially if this had been his idea. This woman certainly hadn't the wits to connect the sketch to Zenobia.

"You and the one upstairs. Was this his plan?"

Yasmeen interpreted her hesitation as a *no*—and that this woman was afraid of whoever *had* set it up.

She'd chosen the wrong person to fear.

"What airship did you fly in on?"

"*Windrunner*. Last night."

A passenger ship. "Who's upstairs?"

A different, deeper fear entered her eyes now, but she answered anyway. "My husband."

A man she genuinely cared for. A man who either didn't care as much in return, or was as stupid as his wife. "Did he create this plan to cheat me? Answer carefully. Whether he lives or dies depends on your response."

The woman finally used her brain, and gave up the name Yasmeen wanted. "No. It was Peter Mills. He's waiting for us at the Rose & Thorn Inn."

Miracle Mills, the weapons smuggler. A worthy occupation, in Yasmeen's opinion, but Miracle Mills sullied the profession. He always recruited partners to assist him with the job, but as soon as the cargo was secure, the partners conveniently disappeared. Mills usually claimed an attack by Horde forces or zombies had killed them, yet every time, he miraculously survived.

No doubt that if this couple had secured the sketch for him, they'd have disappeared soon, too.

"Did he hire you just for this job?"

"Yes. We're grateful. We've been out of work for almost a full season, and he promised us a share."

A full season of what? This woman's soft hands had never seen any kind of labor. Only one possibility occurred to her.

"Are you *actors*?"

The blond nodded. "And dancers. But they replaced us with automatons, and we lost our positions."

Yasmeen suspected that the automatons displayed more talent. "All right. Call your husband down."

"Why?"

"Because I'll make you a better deal than Mills will." Yasmeen wouldn't kill them, anyway. "And because if I go upstairs holding a knife to your throat, he might do something stupid to Miss Fox."

"Oh." Her eyes widened. "How do I call him?"

God save her from idiots. "I'll let you up. You'll open and close the door as if you've just come in from outside, and yell, 'I've got it! Come see!' You'll be very excited."

"And then?"

"I'll do the rest." She waited for the woman to nod, then backed away and hauled her up. "Now."

Yasmeen had to admit, she played the scene perfectly. Her husband rushed down the stairs so quickly, he didn't notice Yasmeen standing in the entry to the parlor until he was almost upon her. She smiled.

The man paled.

While two members of her crew escorted the husband and wife up to *Lady Corsair*, Yasmeen searched upstairs. She found Zenobia—still with brown hair, and just as handsome as her brother—tied and gagged in the first bedroom. Two maids lay next to her, bound hand to foot.

Yasmeen sliced through their ropes, and after accepting their thank-yous, returned downstairs to wait so that they could weep or rant in private. Her cabin girl, Ginger, brought Yasmeen's favorite tea down from *Lady Corsair*, and relayed that Peter Mills *was* in Fladstrand, and that Rousseau had sent messages to the passenger airship captains suggesting that they didn't allow Miracle Mills to board any of their vessels before Yasmeen had a chance to speak with him.

None of the captains had yet replied, but Yasmeen doubted that they'd risk *Lady Corsair* chasing them across the skies. So Mills couldn't leave town, even if he became aware that he should.

When Zenobia came downstairs, still moving stiffly after hours of being tied, Yasmeen relayed the same information to her. The other woman nodded and poured herself a cup before sitting on the chair opposite Yasmeen's.

"You've come to tell me that Wolfram is dead," she said.

"Yes." Yasmeen studied the other woman's expression. She saw resignation. Sadness. But no sudden grief. "You don't seem surprised."

"I was supposed to receive word from him six weeks ago. When I didn't, I gave him another week. And then another. By the third week, I had to accept that a letter wasn't coming. So I have had three weeks to adjust myself to the idea." She sipped from her tea before leveling a direct stare at Yasmeen. "Wolfram isn't part of your crew. So why have you really come?"

"He was on my ship. He wasn't my crew, but he was my responsibility," she said, marveling at the other woman's composure. How was it that Yasmeen didn't feel as steady as his sister looked? She slipped her fingers into her pocket, produced her cigarillo case and lighter. "Do you mind if I . . . ?"

"Yes," Zenobia said bluntly. "It reeks."

"If you smoke one, too, you won't notice it as much." Yasmeen smiled when the other woman only fixed a baleful look on the proffered cigarillo. She slid it back into the silver case. "I have his belongings and his purse—minus the five livre he owed to me for his passage."

Five livre was a large sum of money, but Zenobia didn't blink. "I'll take them. And the da Vinci sketch?"

"You'd be a fool to keep it in your possession."

"As aptly demonstrated today."

Though dryly stated, Yasmeen could see that the other woman knew it was the truth. "Mills will only be the first."

"Yes." Zenobia took another sip before coming to a decision. "Sell it, then."

Exultation burst through Yasmeen's veins. She contained it, and merely nodded. "I will."

A tiny smile flirted with the woman's mouth. "I understand that on dangerous flights, the airship captain receives twenty-five percent of the salvage."

Yasmeen met Zenobia's steady gaze. "For this job, I'll take fifty percent."

Her tone said there'd be no negotiation. Her face must have conveyed the same. Zenobia studied her, as if weighing the chances of coming to a different agreement.

Finally, she took another sip and said, "I suppose fifty percent of an absurd fortune is still a ridiculous amount of money."

Clever woman. *This* was the Zenobia that Yasmeen had expected to find. She wasn't disappointed. "I'll see that you receive your half when the sale is finalized."

"Thank you." She hesitated, and some of the hardness of negotiation dropped from her expression, revealing a hint of vulnerability. "I heard a little bit of what you said about the zombies, captain. Is it true that you deliberately threw him into a canal?"

So three weeks had given her time to adjust to the idea?

Obviously not completely. Yasmeen shook her head. "It was the middle of the night. I couldn't know where he landed."

Lies. Her eyes saw well enough in the dark. She'd watched him splash into the canal. She'd known that with luck and brains, he'd survive—and her crew wouldn't think she'd gone soft or weak.

But even for Archimedes Fox, his chances of survival were slim. She wouldn't give this woman any more false hope than she offered herself.

"I see." Zenobia's fingers tightened on her cup. "If, on your travels, you see him with the others . . ."

"I'll shoot him," Yasmeen promised.

"Thank you." The vulnerability left her face, replaced by sudden amusement. "Speaking of your travels, captain . . . you've tossed the source of my stories overboard."

Yasmeen looked pointedly at the ink staining her fingers. "You're writing."

"Only letters."

"You won't need the income when I've sold the sketch."

"You misunderstand me." Zenobia set her cup on the table and leaned forward. "I don't need the income now. I write because I enjoy it. Will you leave your airship when you've received your portion of the money?"

"No." When she left her lady for the last time, it would only be because her dead body had been dragged away.

"It is the same with me for writing. I won't stop, not voluntarily. But I do need inspiration for the stories. With the basis for Archimedes gone, I'll have to create another character. Perhaps a woman this time." She sat back, her gaze narrowed on Yasmeen's face. "What about . . . *The Adventures of Lady Lynx*?"

Yasmeen laughed. Zenobia didn't.

"You're not joking?"

The other woman shook her head. "You've killed my research source and taken an extra twenty-five percent from his spoils. You live a life of adventure."

"Yes, but—"

"I'll write them. You receive twenty-five percent of royalties."

The sudden need for a cigarillo almost overwhelmed her. A drink, a hit of opium. Anything to calm her jumping nerves. Was she going to agree to this?

Yes. Of course she was. Even without royalties, she would have.

But still, no need to be stupid about it.

"Fifty percent of royalties," Yasmeen countered.

"Twenty-five. You send me reports of where you go, who you see, what you eat. I need to know how long it takes you to fly to each location. I want your impressions of your crew, your passengers, and everyone you meet."

Impossible. "I won't share everything."

"I won't name them. I only seek authenticity, not a reproduction of the truth."

"I *won't* share everything," Yasmeen repeated.

For a moment, Zenobia looked as if she'd try to negotiate that, too. Then she shrugged. "Of course you can't. But let us begin with your background. Thirteen years ago, you joined my father's crew. After you killed him—well done, by the way—you sold *Lady Corsair*'s services as a mercenary in the French-Liberé war, where you worked both sides, depending upon who paid the most. You earned the reputation of being willing to do anything for money. But what happened before that? Where were you before my father's ship?"

In a very pretty cage. But did she want to share that? Yasmeen shook her head.

"As far as I'm concerned, my life started when I boarded *Lady Corsair*. Make up what you like about what came before."

"All right. A mysterious past will only make Lady Lynx more fascinating," she mused. "I could deliver the background in bits, like crumbs."

"Whatever you like." Yasmeen stood. "The other reports, I'll send to you regularly."

Zenobia's expression sharpened as she rose. "Where are you heading after you leave Fladstrand? Do you have a job now?"

"No. We'll spend the day traveling to Port Fallow. Mills is only here because another man talked about the sketch. I need to have a conversation with him."

Then she'd fly to England, and ask the Iron Duke to hold the sketch safe at his London fortress until she found a buyer. She couldn't risk carrying it with her any longer. *Lady Corsair* had become a moving target.

"And will you also have a conversation with Mills?"

A frown had furrowed the other woman's brow. Did she

think Yasmeen would leave without taking care of Mills, or did some other matter concern her?

"Yes," Yasmeen said. "Why?"

"Perhaps I should contact the town's magistrate, instead."

And let word spread that Yasmeen had run to the authorities after Miracle Mills had tried to cheat her, rather than taking care of him on her own? Not a chance.

"You can," she told Zenobia. "But I won't wait for you to arrive at the inn with him."

Indecision warred on the woman's face.

"Come with me," Yasmeen offered. "Call it research. I think you'll find that the magistrate will arrive sooner or later."

"To arrest you?"

That startled a laugh from her. "For what?"

"For whatever you do to Mills."

Ah. Zenobia assumed that Yasmeen would burst into the inn, guns firing. She wrote stories where characters did exactly that—but like most people, she balked when faced with the reality of that scenario.

Yasmeen tended to avoid such scenes herself. "I only intend to talk with him, and make certain that he knows—that *everyone* knows—you don't have the sketch, and that you'll never have access to it."

The woman visibly relaxed. "I see. Thank you."

"It's not personal. I simply want my twenty-five percent, and more stories." When Zenobia smiled in response, she gestured to the door. "Shall we go?"

She waited outside while the other woman retrieved her coat. The frigid air shivered through her. Lighting a cigarillo, she let the smoke warm her lungs and ease the tiny shakes.

A few neighbors had ventured outside, all of them watching Yasmeen without looking directly at her, or tilting their heads back to gape at *Lady Corsair*. Zenobia waved to them and called a good morning when she finally emerged, and Yasmeen couldn't decide whether surprise or relief added such volume to the *Good morning!*s they called to her in return. Feeling the cold down to her toes, she started for the rope ladder.

"Captain Corsair?" When Yasmeen turned, Zenobia avoided her gaze. She seemed to find the act of pulling on her gloves either fascinating, or extraordinarily difficult. "I thought we might walk rather than fly."

"I thought you might want to have a look at my lady. For authenticity." And because the steam engine kept the cabins heated and the deck beneath her feet warm.

"I've seen her." She shot a glance upward. "When she was my father's."

Damn it. Yasmeen wouldn't ask what had happened. She'd seen enough of Emmerich Gunther-Baptiste's cruelties to guess.

"We walk, then."

Zenobia's boot soles clipped across the cobblestones as she matched Yasmeen's long stride. So loud. Yasmeen's soft leather wasn't as warm, but at least it was quiet—and didn't announce her approach from hundreds of yards away.

"Perhaps I shouldn't have stopped you from boarding *Lady Corsair*." Zenobia's cheeks had already flushed with cold. "You only intend to talk, but who knows what Mills intends. You should have armed yourself first."

Funny. Yasmeen pulled open her coat, exposing the knives sheathed at her thighs. "I'm always armed."

"You're only taking daggers?"

No need to mention the pistols in her coat pockets. Yasmeen didn't intend to use them. "The only weapon I bring to a conversation is a knife. A gun means that the talking is over."

"Oh, I must make Lady Lynx say that." Without a break in her stride, she tore off her right glove with her teeth before digging out a paper and pencil from her pocket. She scribbled the line as she walked.

Inspiration was to be taken so directly? Yasmeen slowed to accommodate the other woman's preoccupation, wondering if she'd often done the same when walking with Archimedes . . . who was charming and fun, much like the character she'd written. Yasmeen had assumed it also reflected the sister, but she seemed far more sober and practical than her brother had been.

"How much of Archimedes came from him, and how much was you?"

Zenobia tucked her notes away. "All Wolfram. It was easy, though, because I know him well. Lady Lynx will likely have more of me in her."

Because she didn't know Yasmeen as well. Fair enough.

"If there is anything that you think she *shouldn't* be, Captain Corsair, I would appreciate your telling me now. I can't promise that you'll like what I write, but I prefer not to be . . . inaccurate."

Or to offend her, Yasmeen guessed. She appreciated that. "Don't let her be an idiot, always threatening someone with a gun. Only let her draw it if she intends to use it."

Zenobia's color deepened. "Unlike Archimedes Fox?"

In her stories. "Yes. He did it in every one, and I was always surprised that someone didn't shoot him while he was waving his gun around. You *have* to assume that someone will try to kill you while you're deciding whether or not to shoot them. And so by the time the gun comes out, that decision should have been made."

"I see." Her notes were in her hand again, but Zenobia didn't add to them. "Is that what Wolfram did—wave his gun around?"

"Yes."

Her eyes closed. "Idiot."

So Yasmeen had often said, but his sister should know the rest of it. "Stupid, yes. But also exhausted. He returned three weeks late, and Venice wouldn't have given him time to sleep or eat." Too many zombies, too few hiding places. "When he climbed up to the ship, he ordered my crew to set a heading for the Ivory Market. I refused and told him to sleep it off before making demands. That's when he drew his gun and—"

"You waited in Venice *three weeks* for him?"

Blissed on opium, and wondering why the hell she was still floating over a rotten city. But she'd known. She'd read through each damn story of his, each impossible escape, and she'd known he'd make it out of Venice, too. So she'd waited. And when he'd finally returned to her ship, she'd had to toss him back—believing he might still make it.

But after he'd tried to take her ship, she wouldn't wait for him again.

"I waited," she finally answered. "He still owed me half of his fee."

Zenobia studied her face before slowly nodding. "I see."

Yasmeen didn't know what the woman thought she saw—and didn't much care, either. Three weeks on an airship was nothing. Three weeks in Venice was a nightmare.

"He couldn't have known I'd wait, but he was late anyway. The sketch wouldn't be worth anything to him if he died there."

Zenobia's chin tilted up at an unmistakable angle, a combination of defiance and pride—as if she felt the need to defend her brother. "Perhaps he was late for the same reason you stayed: money."

Yes, Yasmeen believed that. If she had followed Archimedes's orders and flown directly to the Ivory Market, he could have quickly sold the sketch. Which meant that he'd risked his life those three weeks because if he'd left Venice without the sketch—or access to the money—he'd have been dead anyway.

He'd owed someone, and they intended to collect. Few debts would need a da Vinci sketch to cover them, though. Even small salvaged items like those Archimedes collected in Europe sold high at auction. Of the baubles in Zenobia's parlor, the miniature alone would purchase a luxury steamcoach.

"Does he really owe so much?"

"Yes."

"So you changed your names." Yasmeen had to laugh. "He said he was trying to escape your father's legacy."

"No. Just Wolfram's own."

Zenobia's sigh seemed to hang in the air. They'd almost reached the Rose & Thorn before she spoke again.

"Is there anything else? For Lady Lynx," she added, when Yasmeen raised a brow.

"Yes." The walk here had reminded her of one rule that she'd been fortunate to have learned before Archimedes Fox had ever boarded her ship. "Don't let her go soft for a man."

Zenobia stopped, looking dismayed. "A romance adds excitement."

"With a man who tries to take over everything? Who wants to be master of her ship, or wants the crew to acknowledge that she's his little woman." Yasmeen sneered. God, but she imagined it all too easily. "What man can tolerate *his* woman holding a position superior to him?"

Zenobia apparently couldn't name one. She grimaced and pulled out her notes. "Not even a mysterious man in the background? More interest from the readers means more money."

Yasmeen wasn't always for sale, and in this matter, the promise of extra royalties couldn't sway her. "Don't let her go soft. Give her a heart of steel."

"But . . . why?"

The woman had begun that morning tied up and gagged. Now Yasmeen was going to threaten a man's life to make certain it wouldn't happen again, and yet she had to ask why. Shaking her head, Yasmeen started for the inn.

"Because there's no other way to survive."

CHAPTER 2

Yasmeen flew into Port Fallow from the east, high enough that the Horde's combines were visible in the distance. After their war machines had driven the population away and the zombies had infected those remaining, the Horde had used the continent as their breadbasket. They'd dug mines and stripped the forests. Machines performed most of the work—and what the machines couldn't do was done by Horde workers living in enormous walled compounds scattered across Europe, while soldiers crushed any New Worlder's attempt to reclaim the land.

But thirty years ago, Port Fallow had been established as a small hideaway for pirates and smugglers on the ruins of Amsterdam, and had boomed into a small city when the Horde hadn't bothered to crush it. Either they hadn't considered the city a threat, or they hadn't been able to afford the effort. Yasmeen suspected it was the latter. Only fifty years ago, a plague had decimated the Horde population, including those living in the walled compounds. A rebellion within the Horde had been gaining in popularity for years and, after the plague, had increased in strength from one end of the empire to the other. Now, the Horde was simply holding on to what they still had, not reclaiming what they'd lost—whether that loss was a small piece of land like Port Fallow or the entire British Isles. No doubt that in the coming years, more pieces would come out from under Horde control.

Just as well. A five-hundred-year reign was long enough for any empire. Yasmeen would be glad to see them gone.

But then, she'd be glad to see a lot of people gone—and currently, Franz Kessler was at the top of her list.

It wouldn't be difficult to find him. Port Fallow contained three distinct sections between the harbor and the city wall, arranged in increasing semicircles and divided by old Amsterdam's canals: the docks and warehouses between the harbor and the first canal, with the necessary taverns, inns, and bawdyrooms; the large residences between the first and second canals, where the established "families" of Port Fallow made their homes; and beyond the second and third canals, the small flats and shacks where everyone else lived. Kessler's home lay in the second, wealthy ring of residences, and he sometimes ventured into the first ring—but he'd never run toward the shacks, and only an idiot would try to climb the wall. Few zombies stumbled up to Fladstrand, but not so here. The plains beyond the town teemed with the ravenous creatures, and gunmen continually monitored the city's high walls.

The harbor offered a better possibility for escape, but Yasmeen wasn't concerned. Though dozens of boats and airships were anchored at Port Fallow, not a single one could outrun *Lady Corsair.*

And though she could identify most of them, only one made her glad to see it: *Vesuvius.* Mad Machen's blackwood pirate ship had been anchored apart from the others, near the south dock. Yasmeen ordered *Lady Corsair* to be tethered at the same dock. She leaned over the airship's railing, hoping to see Mad Machen on his decks. A giant of a man, he was always easy to spot—but he wasn't in sight. She caught the attention of his quartermaster, instead, which suited her just as well. Yasmeen liked Barker almost as she much as his captain. With a few signals, she arranged to meet with him.

Quickly, she descended into the madness of Port Fallow's busy dockside. Men loaded lorries that waited with idling engines and rattling frames. Small carts puttered by, the drivers ceaselessly honking a warning to get out of their way, and rickshaws weaved between the foot traffic. A messenger on an autogyro landed lightly beside a stack of crates, huffing from the exertion of spinning the rotor pedals. Travelers waiting for their boarding calls huddled together around their baggage, while sailors and urchins watched them for a drop in their guard and an opportunity to snatch a purse or a trunk. Food peddlers rolled squeaky wagons, shouting their prices and wares.

In Port Fallow, Yasmeen's presence didn't make anyone run for their homes, but most recognized her and knew enough to be wary. She lit a cigarillo to combat the ever-present stink of fish and oil, and waited for Barker to row in from *Vesuvius*. His launch cut through the yellow scum that foamed on the water and clung to the dock posts.

Disgusting, but at least the scum kept the sharks away. In many harbors in the North Sea, a man couldn't risk manning such a small boat.

His black hair hidden beneath a woolen cap, Barker tied off the launch and leapt onto the dock, approaching her with a wide grin. "Captain Corsair! Just the woman I'd hoped to see. You owe me a drink."

Possibly. Yasmeen made so many bets with him, she couldn't keep track. "Why?"

"You said that if I ever lost a finger, I'd cry like a baby. But I didn't. I cried like a *man*."

Yasmeen frowned and glanced at his hands. Obligingly, he pulled off his left glove, revealing a shining, mechanical pinky finger. The brown skin around the prosthetic had a reddish hue to it. Still healing.

She met his eyes again. "How?"

"Slavers, two days out. I caught a bullet." He paused, and his quick smile appeared. "Literally."

"And the slavers?"

"Dead."

Of course they were. Mad Machen wouldn't have returned to port otherwise. He'd have chased them down.

She looked at the prosthetic again. Embedded in his flesh, the shape of it was all but indistinguishable from a real pinky, the knuckle joints smooth—and, as Barker demonstrated by wiggling his fingers—perfectly functional. Incredible work.

"Your ship's blacksmith is skilled." So skilled that Yasmeen would have lured her away from *Vesuvius* if the idiot girl hadn't gone soft on Mad Machen.

"She's brilliant," Barker said. He replaced the glove and glanced up at *Lady Corsair.* "None of your men have come down. Is this just a quick stopover?"

"Yes." Even if it hadn't been, she wouldn't leave the airship unmanned while the sketch was aboard. "I'm only here long enough to have a word with someone. We'll fly out in the morning."

"A word with someone?" Barker had known her long enough to guess exactly what that meant. "Would you like me to come along?"

She didn't need the help, but she wouldn't mind the company. "If you like."

"I would. Which circle? I'll fetch a cab."

His brows lifted when she told him their destination, but he didn't say anything until they'd climbed into the small steamcoach.

He had to raise his voice over the noise of the engine. "Why Kessler?"

"He talked when he wasn't supposed to."

"Is anyone dead?"

"Not yet. But he gave information to Miracle Mills."

Barker's frown said that he was having the same thought Yasmeen had: Men like Kessler and Mills didn't usually do business together. Though plenty of art was smuggled into the New World, it wasn't something Mills ever handled. If Kessler needed weapons, yes. Not a sketch.

The coach slowed over the bridge across the first canal, crowded with laborers passing from the third rings to the docks. Three well-dressed ladies stood at the other end, as if waiting for the bridge to clear of rabble before they crossed it. Yasmeen watched them, amused. Five years ago, the residents of the second circle had tried building bridges that were only for their use. That arrangement hadn't lasted beyond the first week.

By the time the bridge was out of Yasmeen's sight, the ladies still hadn't crossed it. She looked forward again. Kessler's home was just ahead.

"Do you want me to go in with you?" Barker asked.

"Just wait in the cab. I doubt I'll be long."

"What do you plan to do?"

"Find out why he talked—and make sure he won't talk again."

The cab rounded the corner and slowed. Yasmeen frowned, leaning forward for a better look. Wagons and carts blocked the street ahead, each one half loaded with furniture and clothes. Men and women worked in pairs and small teams, hauling items from Kessler's house.

Barker whistled between his teeth. "I don't think he's talking now."

Barker was right, damn it. The households in Port Fallow operated in the same way as a pirate ship. When the head of the household or business died, they voted in a new leader who took over the business. But Kessler's business was in knowing people, and keeping those names to himself. No one could carry on in his profession, and he had no family—and so everyone who worked for him, from his housekeeper to his scullery maid, would split his possessions and sell them for what they could.

Seething, Yasmeen leaned out of the coach and snagged the first person who passed by. "What happened to Kessler?"

The woman, staggering under the weight of a ceramic vase, kept it short. "Maid found him in bed. Throat slit. No one knows who."

He'd probably flapped his lips about someone else's business, too—someone who wasn't interested in just warning him not to do it again. Yasmeen let the woman go.

"So we turn around, then?" the driver called back.

If he could. She and Barker might have better luck getting out and walking. Carts, wagons, and people were in motion all around them, crowding the narrow street—several more had already parked at their rear. A steamcart in front of them honked, and earned a shouted curse in response. Beside them, a wagon piled high with mattresses lurched ahead, giving them more visibility but nowhere to move.

The short cart that took its place didn't block Yasmeen's view across the street. Her stomach tightened. A woman dressed in a simple black robe stood on the walkway opposite Kessler's house, watching the pandemonium. Unlike everyone else, she wasn't in hurried motion. She waited, her hands demurely folded at her stomach, her head slightly bowed. Gray threaded her long brown hair. She'd plaited two sections in the front, drawing them back . . . hiding the tips of her ears.

As if sensing Yasmeen's gaze, she looked away from Kessler's home. Her stillness didn't change; only her eyes moved.

Yasmeen had been taught to stand like that—to hold herself silent and watchful, her weight perfectly balanced, her hands clasped. She'd been taught duty and honor. She'd been taught to fight . . . but not like this woman did. Yasmeen knew that under the woman's robes was a body more metal than flesh. Designed to protect. Designed to kill.

It was difficult not to appreciate the deadly beauty of it—and hard not to pity her. Yasmeen couldn't see the chains of honor, loyalty, and duty that bound the woman, but she knew they were there.

And she knew with a single look that the woman pitied her in return. That she saw Yasmeen as a woman adrift and without purpose—a victim of those who'd failed to properly train and care for her.

Yasmeen lowered her gaze first; not out of cowardice, but a message that she wouldn't interfere with the woman's business here—and she certainly wasn't stupid enough to challenge the woman.

Releasing her held breath, Yasmeen caught Barker eyeing the woman with a different sort of appreciation. Of course he did. She'd been designed to provoke that response.

"Don't try," Yasmeen warned him.

"She's a little older, but I like the mature—"

"She's Horde. One of the elite guard who serves the royalty and the favored governors."

Barker didn't hide his surprise—or his doubt. He studied the woman again, as if trying to see beneath the demure posture and discover what had earned the elite guard their terrifying reputation.

He wouldn't see it. The elite guard earned that reputation when they dropped that modest posture, not when they wore it.

He shook his head. "She's not Horde."

"She's just not a Mongol," Yasmeen said. The Horde weren't a single race—only royalty and the Great Khan had pure blood, and they never ventured far from the Horde capital. In five hundred years, their seed and the empire had spread too far for every member of the Horde to be Mongols. "Just as not every man and woman of African descent born on the northern American continent is a Liberé spy . . . or a cart-puller."

His face tightened. "Cart-puller?"

"I am saying that you are *not*. You cannot even hear it without being ready to go to war again?"

"Because you haven't been called one," he said, before adding, "I wasn't a spy."

Yasmeen snorted her response.

He grinned and glanced over at the woman again. "Why is she here? No one in Port Fallow is Horde royalty."

"Then she's here to kill someone, or to take them back to her Khanate." Obviously not Yasmeen, or she'd already be dead—but instead, she was forgotten. She'd been pitied for a moment, but now the woman was watching the house again . . . waiting. "Whatever her purpose, don't get in her way."

"All right." Barker leaned forward and tapped on the cab driver's shoulder before dropping a few deniers into his palm. "Shall we walk? By the time we get back to the docks, I'll be ready for that drink."

Yasmeen would be ready for three.

Yasmeen drank three, but not quickly. Barker took his leave after finishing the one she owed him, but Yasmeen stayed on, nursing hers until they were warm. Some nights in a tavern were meant for drinking, and others were meant for listening. Fortunately, nothing she heard suggested that word of the sketch had gone beyond Mills and Kessler. She turned down one job—a run to the Ivory Market in central Africa. Lucrative, but he hadn't been willing to wait until she returned from England, and she wasn't inviting anyone onto her airship before the sketch was off of it.

She hadn't always been able to turn down jobs. Now, she had enough money that she could be choosy when she took on a new one. Even without the fortune that would come after selling the sketch, she could retire in luxury at any time—as could her entire crew.

She never would.

Midnight had gone when Yasmeen decided she'd heard enough. She emerged from the dim tavern into the dark and paused to light a cigarillo, studying the boardwalk along the docks. It was just as busy at night as during the day, but the crowd was comprised of more drunks. Some slumped against the buildings or slept beside crates. Groups of sailors laughed and preened and pounded their chests at the aviators—some of them women, Yasmeen noted, and not one of them alone. The shopgirls and lamplighters walked in pairs, and most of the whores did, too.

Yasmeen sighed. Undoubtedly, she'd soon be teaching some drunken buck a lesson about making assumptions when women walked alone.

She started toward the south dock, picking out *Lady Corsair*'s sleek silhouette over the harbor. Familiar pride filled her chest. God, her lady was such a beauty—one of the finest skyrunners ever made, and she'd been Yasmeen's for almost thirteen years now. She knew captains who didn't last a month—some who weren't generous toward their crew, or were not strict enough to control them. Some who were too careful to make any money, or too careless to live through a job.

She'd made money, and she'd lived through hundreds of jobs: scouting, privateering, moving weapons or personnel through enemy territory, destroying a specified target. Both the French and the Liberé officers sneered when she'd claimed that her only loyalties were to her crew and the gold, but they used her when they didn't have anyone good enough or fast enough to do what she could.

Then the war had ended—fizzled out. All of the same animosities still simmered, but there wasn't enough money left in the treasuries to pay for it. So Yasmeen had left the New World, returned back across the Atlantic, and carved out her niche by taking almost any job for the right money.

Lately, that meant carrying a lot of passengers over Horde territory in Europe and Africa—a route that most airships-for-hire would never take. Sometimes she acted as a courier, or she partnered with *Vesuvius* when that ship carried cargo that needed airship support, and then fought off any ships that tried to steal it from them.

A routine life, but still an exciting one—and the only kind of settling down that she would ever do.

Yasmeen flicked away her cigarillo, smiling at her own fancy. *Routines, excitement, and a particular version of settling down.* She'd have to record that thought and send it to Zenobia—along with an account of the little excitement that was about to take place.

Someone was following her.

A man had been trailing her since she'd left the tavern. Not some drunken idiot stumbling into a woman walking alone, but someone who'd deliberately picked her out—and if he'd seen her in the tavern, he must have known who she was.

But he must not have been interested in killing her. Anyone could have shot her from this distance. Instead he tried to move in closer, using the shadows for cover . . . but he was very bad at stalking. He paused when she did, and though he tried for stealth by tiptoeing, his attempts only made him more obvious. Of course, he couldn't know that Yasmeen was at her best during the night—and that she had more in common with the cats slinking through the alleys than the lumbering ape that had obviously birthed him.

She'd only taken a few more steps when he finally found his balls and called her name.

"Captain Corsair!"

The voice was young, and quivering with bravado. He'd either taken a bet at the tavern or was going to ask for a position on her ship. Amused, Yasmeen faced him. A ginger-haired boy stood quivering in the middle of the—

Something stabbed the back of her leg. Even as she whipped around, her thigh went numb, her leg rubbery. An opium dart. *Oh, fuck.* She ripped it out, too late. Pumped with this amount, her mind was already spinning. Hallucinating. A drunkard rose from a pile of rags, wearing the gaunt face of a dead man.

No, not a drunkard. A handsome liar.

Archimedes Fox.

Yasmeen fumbled for her guns. Her fingers were enormous. He moved fast—or she was slow. Within a blink, he caught her hands, restrained her with barely any effort.

She'd kill him for that.

"Again?" he asked, so smooth and amused. "You'll have to try harder."

The bastard. She hadn't tried at all. And though she tried now, she sagged against him, instead—and for a brief moment, she wondered if she'd fallen against a zombie. Each of his ribs felt distinct beneath her hands.

But zombies didn't swing women up into their arms. And they didn't talk.

"My sister sends her regards," he said against her cheek. "And I want my sketch."

"I'd have given it to you." She couldn't keep her eyes open. Her words slurred. "You just had to ask."

"Liar," he said softly.

Ah, well. He was right about that.

From the "dark, rich, and sexy"*
Guardian Series from

MELJEAN BROOK

DEMON BLOOD

In an effort to save his people, the vampire Deacon betrayed the demon-fighting Guardians. Now he lives only for revenge. But Rosalia is in love with him and willing to fight by his side—even if she has to stand against her fellow Guardians to save him.

**New York Times* bestselling author Gena Showalter